THE ZION
COVENANT
BOOK 5

Danzig Passage

THE ZION COVENANT • BOOK 5

BODIE & BROCK THOENE

TYNDALE HOUSE PUBLISHERS, INC. • WHEATON, ILLINOIS

Visit Tyndale's exciting Web site at www.tyndale.com

TYNDALE is a registered trademark of Tyndale House Publishers, Inc.

Tyndale's quill logo is a trademark of Tyndale House Publishers, Inc.

Edited by Ramona Cramer Tucker

Designed by Julie Chen

Published in 1991 as Danzig Passage by Bethany House Publishers under ISBN 1-55661-081-5.

First printing by Tyndale House Publishers, Inc. in 2005

Scripture quotations are taken from the Holy Bible, King James Version.

Library of Congress Cataloging-in-Publication Data

Thoene, Bodie, date.
   Danzig passage / Bodie & Brock Thoene.
     p. cm. — (The Zion covenant ; bk. 5)
   ISBN 1-4143-0111-1 (sc)
   1. Holocaust, Jewish (1939-1945)—Fiction. 2. World War, 1939-1945—Fiction.
I. Thoene, Brock, date. II. Title.
   PS3570.H46D27 2005
   813'.54—dc22   2004022002

Printed in the United States of America

11   10   09   08   07   06   05
7   6   5   4   3   2   1

This book is dedicated to you, dear friend and reader.
We have come far together, haven't we?
You have read enough to know our hearts by now,
and so we really are friends!
Your letters have cheered us and encouraged us.
Your prayers for this ministry have called
a mighty strength to help us and guide us as we work.
Your prayers and encouragement are as much
a part of the work as the writing of it.
Philippians 1:2-6 and 1:8-11 best say how we feel about you!
Baruch Hashem!
Bodie and Brock Thoene
May 1991
"In my Father's House"

SWEDEN

BALTIC SEA

EAST PRUSSIA

Danzig (Gdansk)

Berlin

Warsaw

GERMANY

POLAND

Sudentenland

Prague

CZECHOSLOVAKIA

Munich

Vienna

Budapest

(ONCE AUSTRIA)

HUNGARY

Prologue

Ten thousand candles flickered in feeble contrast to the floodlights that drenched the concrete wall with light. Television cameras panned, capturing a sea of hopeful faces. News anchors made their reports, while chanting throngs provided a united chorus in the background.

"Tor auf! Tor auf! Open the gate! Open the gate!" The shout resounded from the East and was echoed in the West. The words were no longer a plea but a demand. *"Tor auf!"*

The whole world watched this uprising of the human spirit. Men and women who had never known life without the Wall stood transfixed before their television sets to stare in wonder as the earth seemed to shift. Here was a miracle. Unthinkable, but real.

"Tor auf!"

"For twenty-eight years this wall has stood as the symbol of division for the world," a commentator said above the din. "A twenty-eight-mile-long scar through the heart of a once-proud capital city."

The camera view was crowded with bright, exuberant faces. Bottles of champagne popped open and bubbled in joyful celebration as thousands roared and rushed toward the barrier.

Young. So young, these faces. They had lived always in the gray shadow of this wall. It had ordered their existence; it had dictated the boundaries of freedom. It had held them captive by its very existence.

Now denim-clad men and women climbed onto it; trumpets rang out; hammers and chisels clanged down to break off chunks of concrete as horns honked and people danced along the Wall.

"Berlin is Berlin again!"

The camera caught an occasional glimpse of gray hair or a lined face streaked with tears. But few remained who remembered Berlin when it had been Berlin. Before Hitler. Before the war. Before the Communists.

Berlin had been beautiful, yes; and it had been proud. It had become too proud, and that pride had sown the seeds of violence and destruction. Few among the crowd this night could remember clearly when the Wall had first begun to appear. It was not a mere twenty-eight years before. The scar upon the heart of Germany was much older than that.

Elisa Lindheim Murphy wiped tears from her cheeks. She held tightly to the gloved hand of her husband as the crowd surged forward toward the Wall. At seventy-five, she was not a young woman anymore, but tonight she felt twenty again!

Fifty-one years exactly had passed since her father, Theo Lindheim, had witnessed the violence of Kristal Nacht in Berlin. Elisa wondered if these young people remembered that tonight was the fifty-first anniversary of that shame and sorrow, when the wound that had formed this concrete scar had been gouged deep and bloody across the heart of the nation.

She and Murphy had been young in those days, young like the people who danced and embraced on top of the Wall.

"They are kids." Murphy laughed.

"So were we." Elisa squeezed his hand.

"I didn't think we would live to see this." He raised his hand and whooped with the others. They moved slowly amid the crush.

"Hey, old grandfather!" shouted a young bearded man to Murphy. "What do you think? Berlin is Berlin again!"

Murphy nodded and raised his eyes toward Brandenburg Gate. Tears of joy brimmed over. "What does he know about Berlin?" Murphy said to Elisa. His thoughts were on the eastern side of the Wall, where the heart of Berlin had beat, where he had seen Elisa for the first time from a window at the Adlon Hotel.

Elisa forgave this youthful ignorance easily. "Perhaps it is good they can't remember, Murphy. Let them be. It is better they can't imagine the waste of it, the heartache of what might have been."

The passage of time had not managed to extinguish the brightness of Elisa's blue eyes. Her shoulders were as straight as the day she had given her first concert at the Prussian State Theatre. She knew what had been. She had been born there, had grown up and fallen in love and had her heart broken there. Her dreams had been shattered like the glass of Jewish shops along the Unter den Linden. She and her family had been hunted. They had fled, then returned to help those who remained. The full circle of love and tragedy had been enacted behind that wall. She could tell these young people a thing or two about Berlin!

Fifty-one years ago tonight Berlin had heard different shouts. Stones and hammers had smashed businesses and lives; prisoner lorries had rumbled through these streets, beneath the pillars of the Brandenburg Gate. Seventy thousand had been arrested and imprisoned on that night.

Lindheim's Department Store had been burned because it had once been owned by a Jew. Its smoke had mingled with that of the synagogues of the city and with the smoke of those who perished. New Church had opened its doors for refuge, and in so doing, had sealed its fate.

Theo Lindheim had seen it all from the window of the British Embassy in Berlin. He had heard the cry of the Jews who begged for refuge.

"Tor auf! Tor auf! Open the gate!"

On that terrible night the gate had remained closed, and Theo had seen the vision of what was to come.

Elisa fingered the yellow slip of stationery in her coat pocket. It bore the logo of the British Embassy, and beneath Theo's message was his signature and the date: *November 9, 1938.*

Suddenly, as they neared the gate, Murphy asked her, "Do you have it?"

She nodded, took the paper from her pocket, and held it up. "All these years I kept it," she said, "only half believing that this moment would come. Papa is here tonight, coming home with me at last."

"TOR AUF! OPEN THE GATE!"

Guards yielded at the stroke of midnight, and the crowds surged together in one vast embrace. At last the scar that Hitler had carved upon the heart of Germany was being erased!

Murphy pulled Elisa closer to him as they walked forward toward the East. Fifty-one years of marriage. Children, grandchildren, and soon a great-grandchild. Fifty-one years of joy and sorrow—the fullness of life and death. But this was the first time Elisa could look up at him and say, "I'm going home."

The opera. The university. New Church. Lindheim's Department Store—all were altered or gone forever. But tonight the Wall was coming down. Perhaps heaven offered another chance to the descendants of those who had destroyed the nation with hatred.

Elisa walked on with the knowledge that she and Murphy might not live to see what Germany made of that second chance. She prayed for the people of East and West together; prayed that true Light would shine here, lest a more terrible Darkness rush in!

"Tor auf," she prayed quietly for those around her. "Open the gate."

1

Martyr

The face of Big Ben's clock glowed like a full moon behind a veil of London fog. The chimes of the great bell tower rang out eight o'clock and were answered by the lonely bellow of a foghorn.

Below the crenelated spires of Parliament, the black waters of the Thames slid toward the sea. It was Thursday night, and most of the theatres and concert halls in London were dark and empty. The panic that had swept through the city with rumors of impending war had been replaced with tranquility. Nearly everyone believed Prime Minister Chamberlain. Peace was at hand. The Sudetenland of Czechoslovakia had purchased "peace in our time." The citizens of London had put away their gas masks and filled in the trenches that had crisscrossed Hyde Park. Flags and bunting were hung from public buildings and streetlamps in anticipation of the celebrations planned for the twentieth anniversary of the Armistice. It had been twenty years since the end of the war to end all wars. This year England had plenty to celebrate. The lions of war had been tossed a small bone and placated at last!

Tonight, London was safe. Safe beneath her fog.

The black bowl of the sky above Galilee was dusted with ten thousand bright stars. An arch of gold and silver glittered in the Milky Way, the constellations almost lost against such a backdrop.

Sharon Zalmon knew the constellations by name. She had learned them all in an astronomy class at the university in Warsaw two years before. The sky above Poland was not quite like the sky above Galilee, however. The lights of the city of Warsaw obscured the glory which the shepherd David had written about in the days when Israel had been a great nation.

Tonight, on duty in the tiny Jewish settlement of Hanita, Sharon only glanced at the stars. There was no time for contemplating their glory, no time for writing new psalms. On this night there was no nation of Israel. There was only a memory of what had been, the hope of what could be once again.

Little could she know that on this night, as in the times of David, enemies hid in the dark ravines of Galilee. They crept toward the outpost where Sharon stood guard with an old shotgun. Their single purpose was to destroy the memory of what Israel had been and to make certain that the nation would never exist again on the soil of Zion. *Kill the People of the Covenant! Kill the dream! Destroy forever the promise God made to the shepherd King, and to His people!*

At the cry of jihad, holy war, enemies came from Jordan and Syria and Egypt and Iraq. They banded together, united by hatred, beneath the banner of the prophet Mohammed and Allah. Their shouts in the city of Jerusalem grew silent; now they moved through the darkness of Galilee beneath the peaceful stars. They slipped toward the tiny mound of sandbags where Sharon Zalmon kept watch, planning to inflict the dreamless peace of death upon her and all the Jews of Hanita.

It was early yet. Sharon scanned the black rolling hills beyond the perimeter of the settlement. Shifting the aged shotgun in her hands, she rested the heavy barrel on top of the sandbags.

Three minutes before, Lazlo had left her here and gone to patrol the barbed barricade between this position and the next. The Arab gangs had cut through the wire before and had killed settlers. For this reason, the settlement posted stationary guards like Sharon and moving patrols like Lazlo, who would make his rounds and return in a few minutes.

Something terrible was coming to the Jews of the Yishuv; after the Jerusalem riots, everyone believed it, even the British High Command. They had sent Captain Samuel Orde to help the Jews of Hanita. Sharon had heard of this Englishman who was known as Hayedid, "the friend." Scheduled to arrive tonight, he would no doubt be out here to make the rounds of the patrol. This thought made the night seem not quite so dark, the unseen enemy not so terrifying. Hayedid, the friend, would help them.

Sharon looked up briefly at the constellation of Orion as it moved toward her from the horizon. She could just make out the stars where the ancients said his sword hung from his belt. *The stars remain unchanged since that time. Our dreams remain the same,* she thought.

In that moment she heard the sound of a stone as it slithered down an embankment twenty paces from the barricade beyond her post!

The sound jerked her back to the present earth, back to this small patch of ground that the dreamers had purchased and cultivated and made to blossom from desolation. They must now defend it as well. They must not look up at the stars and dream, or all their dreams would be destroyed!

"Who is it?" she demanded. Her heart pounded as she tried to fix the exact location of the falling stone. Was it there, behind the outline of a boulder? or to the left, where the ground dropped steeply away? Or maybe it was behind her. Perhaps it was only the footstep of Lazlo as he made his rounds.

She lifted the heavy barrel of the shotgun and pointed it out toward the boulder. If someone was there, he would not escape the blast of a shotgun. Lazlo had showed her. She did not have to take careful aim. The small pellets of this old British hunting gun would down a Holy Struggler like a pheasant rising from a bush. Still, the sound of movement left Sharon frightened. What might be beyond the reach of the shotgun's range? Her mouth went dry; she licked her lips and listened. What had she heard?

"Is someone out there?" she asked again. Her voice sounded small and vulnerable in the night. She wished Lazlo would hurry. She thought of calling an alarm, but what if it was nothing?

The silhouette of the land stretched out like an unmoving sea beneath the rolling star scape. Surely, Sharon thought, she would see movement if the stone had shifted outside the barbed-wire fence!

Why did Lazlo not return? Was it not time for him to call out the password and leap into the circle of sandbags?

At that instant another stone clattered down a few feet from her. She opened her mouth to call out the alarm just as a hand clamped down hard on her mouth.

Sharon Zalmon had no chance to scream.

Searing hot pain filled her. She felt terror and then a rush of warmth as she was pushed down onto the dirt floor of the outpost. She blinked twice in amazement at the brightness of the stars above Galilee and the realization that she was seeing them for the last time. Then the dreams died. Just that quickly, it was finished. The darkness of the land overwhelmed the brightness of the skies above Galilee, and the peace of death came once again for a child of the Covenant.

The German Führer promised weapons for the revolt of the Mufti's army against the Jews and the British. He made good on that promise.

On a dark field in Jordan, Haj Amin Husseini walked through the stacks of heavy crates containing rifles and ammunition from Germany. He felt the satisfaction of a man with great power behind him.

As Grand Mufti of Jerusalem, Haj Amin had also kept a promise to Hitler. He had issued the call for jihad, a holy war against the Jews and English infidels. Riots even now rolled across Palestine. These thousands of weapons would assure victory and an Islamic kingdom for Haj Amin.

For a time, to be sure, Haj Amin was forced to flee from the English law, which even now pursued him for inciting the riots in Jerusalem. But Haj Amin had no doubts about the ultimate outcome. He had Adolf Hitler behind him—an ally almost as powerful as the prophet Mohammed and the Koran! Both Hitler and the prophet proclaimed the destruction of the Jews. The Islamic religion provided passion to the people, while Hitler supplied crates of weapons and Nazi commandos to help accomplish that goal.

The three motors of the silver German airplane sputtered to life. Haj Amin extended his hand to each of his faithful commanders and the fair-skinned Germans among them. They would carry on while he was in exile. He had communications in place which assured that orders from Berlin and Baghdad would be followed with the same devotion as if he remained in Jerusalem.

"Allah is great." Ram Kadar bowed low before Haj Amin. "It will be a short time before you will return to us as king in Jerusalem."

These words made Haj Amin smile. "It has been two thousand years since any king has ruled over Jerusalem alone. I have seen the prophet in a dream, Kadar; the promise is given to *me*! Soon, indeed, I will sit on the throne, and you will sit at my right hand."

Others kissed his hand as he passed through the ranks. All vowed to finish what they had begun. There would be no more Zionist settlers. A new Arab kingdom would take the orchards and the fields the Jews had cultivated and distribute the bounty among the true believers. Thus it was written, and thus it would be accomplished.

The final words of the Mufti were almost drowned out by the hum of the engines. As he boarded the plane to flee from British justice, the Jihad Moquades repeated his words over and over to one another.

"This is only the beginning! The prophet has promised us victory in the Mother of All Battles against Jews and infidels! Only the start! The world and Paradise belong to those who believe this!"

The plane had barely lifted off the crudely constructed airfield before the Holy Strugglers cheered and cracked open the crates of new rifles and bullets—enough to kill every Englishman and Jew three times over. The Mother of All Battles against Jews had begun, even as it began throughout the Reich of the German Führer, Adolf Hitler.

It was early evening in Berlin. The headquarters of the Gestapo on Albrechtsrasse was lit up; each department prepared for the monumental task ahead tonight.

Teletypes clacked an urgent directive to every police headquarters across the Reich. What had begun in Munich and spread to Berlin must now be enacted in every city, large or small, with even one Jew as a resident.

It was a night unlike any other in the history of Germany—perhaps in the history of the world.

Lists of Jewish names and businesses, compiled over long and arduous months of work, were reproduced and transmitted to the appropriate authorities. Within an hour, the roads of Hitler's Third Reich were packed with truckloads of eager Storm Troopers dressed in civilian clothing and studying the names of Jews in the neighboring towns where they were assigned to duty. No man was allowed to participate in the demonstration in his own neighborhood, lest he come across a Jewish neighbor and take pity. Instead, the targeted victims would all be strangers to the troops. Thus the Jews became impersonal, generic vermin of the sort the Führer raved about in his speeches. *"Every Jew an enemy—man, woman, child—no better than bacilli, whose purpose is to infect the pure Aryan race!"*

Destinations were predetermined. Targets had been marked long before Herschel Grynspan ever contemplated the assassination of Ernst vom Rath in Paris. The orders came directly from the top, inviolate and explicit in their instruction.

To: All State Police Headquarters and Branch Offices:
All Secret Service Commands in the main and subdivisions . . .
Subject: Measures to be taken against Jews tonight
Urgent! Immediate delivery!

As a result of the death of Embassy Secretary Ernst vom Rath in Paris, anti-Jewish demonstrations are to be expected throughout the Reich tonight. The following instructions will be observed:

1. Demonstrations against the Jews and their synagogues will take place shortly. Measures will be taken to protect German lives and property (e.g., synagogues may be set on fire as long as there is no danger of spreading flames to neighboring buildings).

A. Jewish shops and homes may be destroyed but not looted.
B. The officers assigned this duty will proceed to arrest as many Jews in all districts as the available jail space will hold. Primarily well-to-do Jews will be chosen.

The German attention to detail had been honed to its sharpest cutting edge for just such a night. Those who had conceived the idea and brought the plan to reality smiled pleasantly at one another as they raised their wineglasses in congratulations.

Tonight was a night unlike any other in the history of Germany, after all. What nation had ever brought such discipline and organization to the goals of violence, destruction, and chaos?

A thick file filled with memos, letters, and photographs of the traitors lay open on the coffee table in front of Adolf Hitler. Others in the room, sitting across from the Führer, cocked their heads in an attempt to read the upside-down writing beneath the Gestapo insignia.

Hitler relaxed in his favorite overstuffed chair. He held up the photograph showing Thomas von Kleistmann crucified on a cross of ordinary planks taken from the scaffolding construction site on Albrechtstrasse. He leaned forward briefly and picked out the picture of Ernst vom Rath, dead on a hospital bed in Paris.

"Traitors, both of them," he commented.

In the background, a recording replayed the voices of Ernst vom Rath's father and another man who sounded near to tears.

"Herr vom Rath, every Jew in Germany deplores the murder of your dear son. . . ."

The Führer raised a finger to stop the recording. "And who is this again?"

"A neighbor of the vom Rath family. A Jew. He is the cantor of the neighborhood synagogue. Come to beg for pardon, I suppose."

"Play it over again," Hitler ordered calmly.

"Herr vom Rath, every Jew in Germany deplores the murder of your dear son by one of our own."

"It was not a Jew who killed Ernst." The elder vom Rath's voice cracked with grief. "Ernst was no Nazi, and it was the Nazis who have had him assassinated. I know who killed him. It was Hitler and his vipers."

Hitler's expression remained placid, unchanged, as he listened. Those in the room with him eyed their leader with alarm, expecting rage at such words from the mouth of Ernst vom Rath's father.

The recording continued uninterrupted. "But my friend," said the Jewish cantor, "it was not the Nazis, but a foolish young Jewish boy. We grieve with you—"

"No, Reverend," protested vom Rath. "I know what you think, but the Nazis are behind it. Ernst was too outspoken. Last time I saw him he seem troubled . . . as though he knew."

Once again Hitler raised his finger as though the recording bored him. It was stopped, and he shuffled through the thick folder again, laying photographs of the two dead men side by side.

"Both traitors," he muttered. "One is now ashes, sitting in an urn on his mother's mantel. The other—" he held up the photograph of Ernst. "We must spare no expense for the funeral."

Himmler dared to speak. "How should we silence his father? The old fool is telling Jews that we have killed his son."

Hitler smiled. "Then he is not such a fool."

A chittering of agreeable laughter followed, and the Führer held up notes posted in Paris and addressed to Elisa Murphy in London. Both were quite clearly the handwriting of Ernst vom Rath. These were proof that the German diplomat was a traitor to the Reich and that he deserved what he got. He would now be made into a martyr for the Reich to serve the convenience of the Nazi Party. What did vom Rath care? He was stone dead, anyway.

The Führer considered the photograph of Ernst's father—white-haired, dignified, aristocratic. It would not be good to kill the old man or arrest him for treason after making his murdered son a hero.

Hitler snapped his fingers impatiently. "This old man has Jews as friends, does he?"

"Yes. Quite a number."

"And he blames the death of his son on us, does he?"

"Entirely. We have showed him the picture of Herschel Grynspan, but he still believes we are behind it."

The Führer raised his chin in thought. "Then we shall pay off the old man with a position, some post where he might faithfully serve the Nazi Party. Perhaps he should be made head of Jewish affairs in some city. We will send him quotas for the arrests of so many Jews a week." He raised his hands as though this was merely a thought for consideration. "That should eliminate his Jewish friends."

Now the laughter was uproarious. Every man in the room agreed that no one could neutralize opposition with the finesse of Adolf Hitler.

"And what about the woman in London vom Rath send the messages to?" Himmler asked, tapping the address on the postcard.

"You are having her watched?" Hitler questioned Himmler carefully.

"We have an agent on duty now."

"Good." That seemed to satisfy Hitler. He snapped his fingers a few more times and then pushed the photographs across the table to Himmler. "I want this picture of Thomas von Kleistmann copied and circulated around the military. Send it to Admiral Canaris in the Abwehr. It will not hurt for these reluctant patriots to see what happens to a proven traitor. Crucifixion will have some effect. Not every traitor can be as lucky as Ernst vom Rath, eh? To die at the hand of a Jew and be made into an eternal martyr. No. It is good if they see the boards and the nails and the blood. It will make them think about it before they fall into something they may regret."

Hitler stretched and stood, moving slowly toward the curtained window. "The British Embassy in Berlin will hand over Theo Lindheim. And as for his family in London, we should plan something very discreet for them. Nothing flashy. We do not want to give the other side a host of their own martyrs to draw strength from, *ja*, Himmler?"

At that, Hitler pulled back the heavy drapery and stared out over the city. Vengeance for the death of martyr Ernst vom Rath had just begun.

2

The Mouth of Hell Has Opened

From his window at the British Embassy, Theo Lindheim could see them clearly—two Gestapo officers waiting outside the gates as the staff car from the German Foreign Ministry entered. The bright lights from the Brandenburg Gate lit the sidewalk where they stood watching truckloads of Storm Troopers drive past slowly. To the east a new and terrible light illuminated the underbelly of the clouds. Berlin's finest synagogue was on fire.

Mr. Kirkpatrick, first secretary of the embassy, entered quietly and stood at Theo's elbow, gazing out at the scene. Kirkpatrick had served for six years in Berlin. He knew everybody and everything, and up until this night he had been able to maintain his puckish Irish humor in even the most grim situations. But tonight an edge of fear crept into his voice as he took Theo by the elbow and urged him back from the window.

"One of our guards spotted three men on the roof of the Adlon Hotel," he warned, drawing the curtain. "All it would take is one bullet through the glass, and the Nazis could claim another assassination by the Jews, eh?"

Theo nodded. He sat down slowly on the bed. "I would not be mourned in Germany."

Kirkpatrick glanced at his watch. "Ambassador Henderson had a car waiting for you, but we cannot transport you as planned." He frowned. "The Nazis have sent a minor official from the foreign office to discuss your extradition and arrest. They claim you came here as the hub of some great Jewish plot to assassinate German leaders around the world. They have presented our ambassador with a sheaf of documents on your

criminal activities." He peeked out the curtain as the lights of another vehicle turned onto Embassy Drive. "We've contacted the American Embassy, and the ambassador is on his way. Your case should take most of
the night to discuss. By then you should be well on your way." He
looked again, then smiled. "And there he is. The American ambassador.
At the gate."

Theo resisted the urge to look out the window. Kirkpatrick hurried
from the room, leaving Theo alone to contemplate his fate. He was safe
for the moment inside the British Embassy. The Nazis would not take
him from here by force. There were other channels, legal methods of getting what they wanted. Clearly, Theo Lindheim was about to become another political issue for the Nazi Propaganda Ministry to use against
England. Theo found himself rethinking the British policy of appeasing
the Nazis. Since Prime Minister Chamberlain had barely noticed when
Germany swallowed Austria whole, and then had presented Hitler with
a massive piece of Czechoslovakia on demand, Theo Lindheim knew he
was not in safe hands. What was one man, after all?

And no doubt the Gestapo had compiled a convincing case with
forged documents and half-truths. "You can see, the father of Herschel
Grynspan once worked for Theo Lindheim. The connection is quite
clear."

Like a mouse drawn to a trap, Theo could see the iron rod poised
above his head, ready to break his neck. At this very moment the British
ambassador, Henderson, known for his weakness and vacillation in the
face of arrogant Nazi demands, discussed his case with the German Foreign Ministry representatives. The man had never held out against the
Germans on even one small point—except in his argument with Göring
about the proper way to hunt a stag, perhaps. Theo was grateful that the
American ambassador had called to request a meeting with Henderson
tonight.

Theo switched on a light and took paper and pen from the writing table. He closed his eyes and drew a deep breath as he tried to picture Anna
and Elisa in London. Tonight was the benefit concert for refugees in
Prague. It would just be finished. They would not have gotten word yet
about the riots here in Berlin. He would write Anna and tell her that he
was not afraid. Death had been very near to him before, and he was no
longer frightened of it. If he did not make it home to her, Theo wanted to
tell her that . . . and to include details of his meeting with Hermann
Göring. How he pitied the fat German field marshal and all of Hitler's
minions!

Even as they raged against the innocent in the streets of Germany, even as they bartered for the life of Theo downstairs, they had brought themselves into a judgment far greater than they could ever imagine.

Kirkpatrick had said it would take the entire night for the ambassador to consider his case. By then, Theo supposedly would be out of Germany. But if not, Theo wanted Anna to know that, although he trembled at the evil these men brought upon others, he no longer feared what they would do to him.

In that terrible hour he wrote:

A perfect peace has filled my heart. The mouth of hell has opened wide here, yet I believe in the coming justices of the Holy One. Even now I feel His perfect love, and all fear is cast away from my heart, cast into the fires and burned away. . . .

Lights shone brightly from the windows of the house in Red Lion Square. Automobiles crawled slowly around the corner and crowded against the curb outside the residence of John and Elisa Murphy. Taxi drivers who had picked up their passengers after the Refugee Relief Concert at Royal Albert Hall now grumbled about fares being the same in fair weather and foul. Unless the fog lifted, they warned, it might be difficult to find a cab later.

The night air resounded with rattling motors, laughter, and the music of a jazz band Murphy had hired to entertain the orchestra members after the concert. The music was more of a beacon than the lights of the house.

Little Charles Kronenberger rubbed a peephole through the steamy window to peer down at the arriving guests. The orchestra members, toting instruments of all sizes, were easy to spot. Men in overcoats and women in furs and high heels called to one another as they blended with arrivals from the press corps and members of England's clergy and a handful of politicians crowding up the stairs.

"They all came!" Charles called to Louis, who was looking for his missing right shoe beneath the bed.

With a gesture of triumph, Louis held up his wayward shoe and ran to join his brother at the window. His eyes widened at the sight of so many people carrying small paper-wrapped packages. Admission to tonight's party was new article of clothing or a pound note to be tied on the limb of a money tree. Charles and Louis were the gift takers and the tree tenders tonight.

"See, Charles," Louis chided as he tied his shoelaces. "I told you they would come. Even the journalists have come. They don't work all the time."

Charles nodded. Louis had been right after all. This afternoon, when Murphy had told Elisa and Anna about the German fellow who had died in Paris, both women had grown very pale and sad. Anna had looked away through the window, as if she could see something very terrible there. Charles had seen such an expression on the face of his mother in Hamburg when his father had been arrested. Hopeless. Despairing. It made him worry again. It made him wish that Theo was not away someplace in Europe. It had made him wonder if they would cancel the concert and the party to follow. He had taken Anna's hand and followed her gaze over the rooftops of the London twilight.

Louis nudged him hard on the arm, bringing him back to this happy moment. "You were wrong," Louis pronounced with finality.

Charles laughed out loud. How wonderful it was to be wrong about such a thing! In spite of bad news from far away, tonight would be a happy night after all!

He looked in the mirror at the thin pink scar that traced his upper lip to his left nostril. He smiled at himself, pleased that he and Louis looked so very much alike now. He still pronounced his words with difficulty, but he was learning to speak like other children. Seeing the six-year-old's toothless grin, Anna had winked at him and told him how handsome he was, and that he must be her escort since Theo was away on business and would miss the party. And when, for a moment, the sadness in her eyes had made him long for his own mother and father, Elisa had taken him on her lap and reminded him that his parents were both in heaven and could see him and Louis very clearly from there. "They will be watching, Charles," she whispered. "And they will be very proud that you are helping other people tonight. They will want you to be happy, *ja?*"

Now, as the music of the jazz trio vibrated up through the floor, the two boys ran for the door and clattered down the stairway to the light and noise of the great room.

Captain Samuel Orde looked rumpled and exhausted as he followed Zach Zabinski toward the small white building that served as the Hanita infirmary.

Moshe Sachar followed six paces behind the Englishman. His face reflected the exhaustion of renewed grief as he looked at the lights of the building and realized what lay within it.

Orde jerked a thumb back toward Moshe. "There is a rumor that there is also a price on Moshe's head. The Mufti himself has demanded that the second Sachar brother be executed for his role in the killing of Ismael Hassan. Totally fabricated nonsense, of course, but then, we have seen what the Muslim fanatics can do. Putting a price on the head of Moshe Sachar simply keeps the fires burning a little longer."

Zach turned toward Moshe. "You may not be any safer here than in Jerusalem." He motioned toward the infirmary to make his point. "But you are welcome, of course."

Moshe nodded in reply as Orde answered for him. "He will undergo the same training as your men." He reached for the door of the infirmary; the sound of sobbing filtered out. "We will begin training tonight." Zach opened his mouth to protest that training on such a tragic night was out of the question. Orde had already thrust open the door and entered the room, now a temporary morgue and place of mourning.

One bloody sheet covered two bodies lying side by side on the concrete floor. A dozen members of the settlement sat on cots or stood against the wall to weep or stare in silence at their fallen comrades.

Two women huddled together on the end of a cot. They wept loudly and did not look up as Orde entered with the others.

Zach's face instantly reflected his own pain as he looked down at the bodies. Bare feet protruded from the sheet, making it simple to identify which was the body of a woman and which a man.

Orde eyed the scene coolly, with the demeanor of a man who had seen such things many times before. He gestured toward the weeping women. "Get them out of here," he instructed.

The two clung more tightly to each other, as if to protest that they had the right to be here.

"This is Sharon Zalmon's sister," Zach started to explain.

"Then all the more reason for her to leave," Orde said. He glanced around the room to where a young man leaned in a corner beside a tray of surgical instruments. He stared silently, but his face was a mirror of intense suffering. "What about him?" Orde asked. "Husband?"

"Fiancé," Zach replied.

"All right," Orde said with authority. "Any of you who are family or close friends will have to leave now."

Hostile eyes regarded him. "We are all either one or the other," said a man who stood at the heads of the bodies. "There is no one in the entire settlement who is not a friend. And we are all like family."

Orde modified his command and searched each face for tears. He pointed to those who had been weeping and were now still sobbing. "Out, please. This is a battle, and we have work to do."

As if to back him up, Zach gently spoke to each one by name and requested that they leave the building. One by one they shuffled out past

Orde, whom they regarded as an intruder to their grief. Seven men, including Moshe and Zach, remained.

Orde slammed the door and then lifted the sheet from the faces of the fallen.

Zach's voice faltered as he named them. "Sharon . . . Zalmon. She is . . . was . . . twenty-one. From Poland."

Orde did not seem to notice that the ashen face below him was delicate and pretty. Blue eyes stared blankly up at the captain as he knelt to examine the wound. Flecks of blood were on her face, her short brown hair matted. A strangely peaceful smile rested on the still-pink lips.

Five minutes of silence passed as Orde lifted the chin slightly and learned everything he needed to know. Then he turned his attention to the man.

"Lazlo LaPierre." Zach muttered the name, but none of that mattered to Orde. The method of killing was identical. This was the only detail of significance.

"Quite professional," he remarked as he tossed the sheet back over the two. "You say there was no sound?" He searched the faces of the men in the room who had found them.

A small man with ruddy cheeks and a shock of black curly hair nodded once. "I was at the next post. I heard nothing. When Lazlo did not come on schedule, I sounded the alarm. Then some shots were fired."

"From our own men," Zach added. "Suddenly everyone seemed to hear things everywhere outside the perimeter." He gestured toward the bodies. "We found them. And the cut wire. It looks as if the alarm was given just at the moment Sharon fell. She was still . . . well, moving slightly when we found her."

Orde stared hard at the blood-soaked sheet. "And so the attackers fled." Pushing his cap back on his head, he considered what it all meant. "And you did not send a patrol out after them?"

Zach seemed startled by the question from an Englishman. After all, Captain Orde knew that the Jews within the British Mandate were not supposed to have weapons to fight with, let alone the means to pursue the enemy. "No. We brought our friends here. There are double guards at the perimeters now."

Orde seemed not to hear what Zach told him. He clasped his hands behind his back and paced up and down beside the bodies. "They were killed by the same fellow. I am certain of that. A professional. Not the sort of messy wound I've seen from the Muslim assassins. Not the same at all." He paused and raised a finger. "I would say we have an excellent chance of catching them."

"Catching?" Zach blinked at him in amazement. "But we are . . . self-defense. Defense of this place is all we are permitted by law—"

"Nonsense." Orde gestured first at the bodies and then at Zach. The men suddenly seemed awake.

Moshe Sachar stepped back and ran his fingers through his hair. He had dreamed of such a thing after his brother had been murdered. But he was not a real part of Hanita. He had never held a gun, and yet he wanted to go along. "I would like to help," Moshe said.

"Of course," Orde said with a smile. "You know the area. You've been on a number of archeological digs in Galilee. That is why I brought you."

"But I thought we would have some training." Zach looked concerned. He knew what lay in wait beyond Hanita at night. If a Jew left the settlement after dark, he did not come back.

"Right," Orde said briskly. "Training. We begin tonight."

The red silk-covered walls of Café Sacher glowed with soft candlelight. New patrons who had swept into Vienna from Germany on the first wave of the Anschluss crowded the tables. Most of the familiar faces of the old patrons had vanished from the opulent restaurant overnight as Austrians of power and influence had been arrested or forced into exile. Instead of the black dinner jackets and silk top hats of the after-concert crowd, these patrons wore uniforms adorned with medals of the Reich. Nonmilitary guests sported swastika lapel buttons and clicked their heels, giving the "Heil" in greeting.

The faces in Café Sacher had changed indeed, and few remained to notice or mourn the change. Here and there a few foreign newsmen managed to procure a table on slow nights, but they were last to be served and were often spoken to with a distinctly cold, unwelcoming tone by the help. Things were not the same at all.

But Café Sacher still had music, candlelight, and bright conversation. Still the very best food in the Greater Reich. Nazi soldiers and officers alike considered Vienna a most desirable city for duty.

Many times wives and children remained behind in Germany, while mistresses conveniently transferred to clerical positions in Vienna. This was particularly true among members of the elite SS Corps, who were expected to provide the Reich and the Führer with the bounty of their own Aryan offspring. Often promotion and rank depended on the ability of a man to reproduce sons for the Fatherland. With such high expectations, therefore, SS Commander and Gestapo Chief Heinrich Himmler made it possible for a man to have a wife pregnant at home as well as a mistress within easy access of his duty assignments.

For this reason Lucy Strasburg had been transferred from Munich to Vienna and was waiting anxiously at Café Sacher tonight.

SS Major Wolfgang von Fritschauer was already two hours late for their scheduled rendezvous. He had warned her impatiently that he might be late this evening, that something important was brewing. He had been angry with her tears and her telephone calls, but he agreed to meet her anyway. Lucy found this comforting. Wolf was an important and busy man, yet he would come to meet her, to hear her news. Although he never said the words, she was certain of his love for her. He was two hours late, yes, but he was coming. His secretary had phoned in the reservation for their usual table and had warned the Sacher head-waiter that Fräulein Strasburg might be waiting a while and must be treated with all courtesy.

Such a command from Wolfgang von Fritschauer was always taken seriously. Every few minutes an attentive waiter passed by and asked after her needs, warmed her coffee, and then went on as if it was not unusual for a beautiful young woman to be sitting alone in one of the finest cafés in Vienna. In the kitchen, of course, waiters exchanged looks and shook their heads in obvious disdain of Lucy and her arrogant SS officer. They had all seen her waiting for him dozens of times. He was a refined aristocrat. She was beautiful, yes, but definitely a country bumpkin from Bavaria. She did not even know which fork to use or what wine to drink with which course. No one doubted why the swaggering Nazi officer kept company with her. Only Lucy Strasburg seemed unaware.

Whispers filled the kitchen:

"Himmel! So this is the future of the Aryan race? Put two beautiful blond bodies together—one without a brain and the other without a soul! The Führer will have very pretty little idiots to run his Thousand-Year Reich!"

"Do they all have to bring their harlots here? Why not meet them at a café in the Seventh District where the red lights are always burning?"

"SS Major von Fritschauer does not meet her in a place like Sacher's for her sake. He comes here because it is he who likes it, and she is too dumb to know his motives are not the purest adoration!"

The whispers of truth may have been quiet, but the laughter that followed was uproarious.

Tonight the waiters had tossed a coin and vied for the pleasure of waiting on the mistress of Officer von Fritschauer. She was beautiful, after all, a delight to look at. Her dresses, selected by the major, were chosen to show off her perfect proportions; the waiters had overheard this bit of gossip from conversations that von Fritschauer had at dinners with fellow officers. He discussed her in the same way the aristocracy might discuss the attributes of a fine broodmare. He was envied by his com- rades, who often expressed the hope that when he was finished they might have a turn with her. To this request, von Fritschauer always chuckled with contentment and wagged a forbidding finger. For pure pleasure, there was nothing to compare with his "little cow" in Vienna. They would have to find their own concubines, he said.

Lucy was not only beautiful, she was also overly cordial to the waiters as Café Sacher. She called them by their first names and asked about families. She encouraged them to call her Fräulein Lucy until the major had overheard the offense and had demanded that the waiter be fired on the spot. She had intervened on the fellow's behalf, but he simply disap- peared one night after work. It was rumored that the major had accused him of being a Jew and of making improper advances to Fräulein Strasburg. From that moment on, the staff of Hotel Sacher treated Fräulein Strasburg as if she were a duchess. They overlooked her Bavar- ian peasant familiarity and answered her in single syllables.

"How are your children, Fritz?"

"Fine, Fräulein Strasburg."

"Are you staying in Vienna for the holidays, Johann?"

"No, Fräulein Strasburg."

Over the weeks she had grown accustomed to the aloofness of the at- tendants. Still, she smiled and asked the questions as though she were talking to an old friend in her village market.

Beautiful. Friendly. Ignorant. This was the final assessment of Lucy Strasburg by the all-seeing staff of Hotel Sacher. Tonight they might have added *hopeful* and *anxious* to their list.

The diners scarcely noticed when the string quartet finished playing and left their chairs for a few minutes' break. But Lucy noticed. This was the second break the musicians had taken since she arrived. Two and a half hours had passed, and Wolf had not come or even called.

She glanced at her watch, a fine Swiss watch Wolf had given to her for her birthday. He told her that when she looked at it she should remem- ber who she belonged to. It seemed that she spent a lot of time looking at the watch, waiting for Wolf. The doubts flooded over her in a wash of panic. Suppose he did not show up tonight? He had been very busy the last two weeks. He had not come to her apartment, and tonight he said he only had time for a quick meal. Suppose he had another girl? Sup- pose he would not be pleased with her news?

The thought made her tremble. Nervously she wound the watch and stared bleakly toward the door of the restaurant. She was not hungry.

Apprehension had driven away her appetite. She glanced down at the watch again and tried to remember whom she belonged to—*SS Major Wolfgang von Fritschauer, declared by the Führer himself to be a perfect example of German manhood. Devotion to the Fatherland kept him from her, not another woman!* These thoughts suppressed her anxiety once again.

The little Austrian waiter Johann paused and bowed at her elbow. "Would you like more coffee, perhaps?"

Lucy smiled nervously and nodded. She made yet another attempt at conversation. "The weather is getting very cold, isn't it, Johann?"

"Quite, Fräulein," Johann agreed without looking at her face. He started to go.

"Does it snow much this time of year in Vienna?" she asked, an edge of desperation in her voice. Could he hear it? Could he hear that she simply wanted to talk to someone? anyone?

"Sometimes, Fräulein," he answered. Then he bowed slightly and smiled that properly distant smile as he gazed at her hands. "Will that be all, Fräulein?"

She wanted to ask him to sit down, to talk a bit with her. But that was impossible, of course. Wolf had told her she must not speak to other men—waiters and grocers and such. They might get the wrong idea about her. And if they had the wrong idea about her, it was a reflection on his manhood. Wolf had been very angry with her when he explained these things. She was careful now about being too friendly.

"Thank you, Johann." She dismissed him and lifted her cup to her lips. The coffee was strong and very good, but Lucy only sipped it. Perhaps it was the coffee that made her hands shake. She should not drink so much coffee; it would not do for Wolf to see her hands tremble. Such a sign of weakness made him angry and sullen. He had been angry with her for crying, and this evening she would tell him how sorry she was, and that she would not cry again.

The string quartet returned and flipped through the music on their stands. They began to play a song that Lucy knew Wolf liked. She did not know the composer, but he did. This music always made him smile, and she wished he were here to hear it right now.

Just as she peered toward the arched entrance to the restaurant, Wolf strode in. His overcoat was unbuttoned, and drops of rain quivered on the visor of his peaked cap. He looked very handsome in his uniform, as always, but something smoldering in his eyes frightened her. His strong jaw was set, giving his face a hardness she had seen before. His ice-blue eyes seemed to look right through her relieved face as he spotted her and made his way through the tables to the corner where she waited.

She remained seated, although she wanted to jump to her feet and kiss his hand in gratitude that he had come. He loved her after all! It did not matter that his face was grim and irritated. He would look at her and want her again; she knew it!

She did not speak. He did not like it when she spoke first to him in public. Often he had things on his mind and did not want to be interrupted in his thoughts. She could tell by the look on his face that this was one of those nights.

He removed his gloves and tossed them on the table. Then he took off his coat and gave it to the waiting attendant. He doffed his hat, smoothed back his thick, close-cropped blond hair, and sat down. He did not acknowledge that she was there. Maybe he was waiting to see if she remembered the rule about not disturbing his thoughts. He lit a thin cheroot and inhaled deeply before he crossed his legs and sat back to appraise her. His eyes took in her royal blue knit dress and swept over on her softly curled golden hair, pausing at her throat, finally lingering on her breasts.

Then he smiled slightly and spoke. "Well, Lucy, I have neglected you."

Tears of relief welled up in her eyes, but she controlled herself as he required. "I have missed you, Wolf," she said softly. "I was hoping that tonight we could—"

He interrupted her with a wave of his hand. "Have you ordered?"

"No. I was waiting. Waiting for—"

The edge of hardness returned to his face. "You should not have waited. I told you I might be late. There are important things happening tonight in the Reich. I had a sandwich at headquarters."

She flushed. He was unhappy with her. "I thought—"

"It is best if you do not think," he said, flicking the ash of his cheroot.

She did not reply. Emotion was too close to the surface again. She should not have presumed. Wolf always told her not to presume anything.

He continued as though speaking to a junior officer. "You said you had news for me?"

This was not the way she had imagined telling him. She bit her lip and looked at the flame of the candle for an instant. The music he liked was playing. Did he notice it?

"Well? Really, Lucy. I am busy. You cannot imagine how difficult it was to get away. Tonight of all nights, you have to talk to me or die!"

Her hands began trembling again. She put them on her lap so he would not see. She wished she could tell him how much she loved him, how much his harshness hurt her, especially now. She had hoped that she might give him the news while she was in his arms.

He sighed impatiently and looked over his shoulder at the exit, as though he would stand up and leave.

"Wolf," she said in a cracking voice, "I have good news. Well, I hope you will think so."

"I could use good news."

"I am . . . we are . . . going to have a baby, Wolf." She smiled hopefully. Had he not told her that more than anything he wanted to give her a child? His child? Had he not spoken of fulfilling her highest purpose as a woman?

Wolf smiled at her, then let out a short laugh of satisfaction. He reached across the table and pulled her hand into his own strong grip, then touched her cheek with as much tenderness as he ever displayed. "A child?"

She laughed too, but not too loud. The tension melted. "Yes! You are pleased, Wolf? I can tell you are pleased."

"Pleased! It will mean a promotion. I told you. A raise in my salary. I was afraid something was wrong with you, but you really are my good little cow, aren't you?"

Lucy did not hear his words, only the tone of his voice. Wolf was happy with her. He was happy with the thought that she would bear him a child. She had nothing at all to worry about. They would be married in a civil ceremony at the Rathaus, and no one would even think twice about the fact that she was pregnant beforehand. Such things were common in the Reich these days. Her parents would not know until the matter was all settled. And then they would be glad that their daughter had married an aristocrat and an officer. The reason would not bother them once she and Wolf were married. And if her family insisted, she would ask Wolf if they might also find a priest to marry them a second time!

She began to babble as she held his hand. All about the wedding. Her family. A priest. Marriage, so that the child would have a father and mother and a name. . . .

"I would like my parents to meet you, Wolf," she said. And then she looked into his face. None of her emotion reflected in his eyes. There was only a sort of cold derision for her. She drew back, horrified. She had been talking too much, making plans. He did not like that in her. "Oh, Wolf. I did not mean to—"

He shook his head and pulled his hand away. "You have thought all this out, have you, Lucy?"

"I thought . . . I mean—"

"What have I told you about thinking too much, Lucy? It is for me to think, *ja*?"

"Of course, Wolf. I did not mean . . ."

He was cool and businesslike again. "So I will tell you what we will do. Just outside Vienna the SS has a very nice place for young women like you and SS officers like me who make little babies for the Führer. It is called a Lebensborn. A very nice place where you will have all your needs met. You will be pampered and well fed, and you will have the baby. An SS baby. SS babies are considered worthy of such special treatment. As are mothers of SS babies."

"You will be with me, Wolf?"

"Fathers are forbidden to visit. Such visits often cause difficulties."

"But if we are married—"

"We did not speak of marriage."

"But the baby—"

He jutted his chin up in an impatient gesture to silence her. "We did not speak of marriage," he said firmly.

"But—"

"I told you. No commitments, eh?"

"But the child must have a . . . father. A name."

He smiled patronizingly. "Of course. I am the father. He will have my name."

She frowned. "Then we will . . . marry?"

He eyed her with incredulous amusement. "Lucy, little cow." He tapped her on the forehead with his finger. "I *am* married. I have a wife in Prussia. And three children. All girls. We will hope this one is a son."

She blinked at him in horror. *Married!* How could it be? All this time, and he had not told her! All this time, and he had led her to believe . . .

"So," he continued matter-of-factly, "you will have a lovely pampered stay at the Lebensborn. It is a resort, really."

She could barely speak. "Our . . . baby."

"And when you deliver the child, I will adopt him if it is a boy. He will be raised in Prussia with my other children. A very nice home, I assure you."

"But, Wolf—" Tears came in spite of her vow. "I thought . . . I *hoped* you loved me." She bit her lip and stared hard at his hands. Such beautiful hands. She loved his hands because they were the most gentle part of him. Would those hands now take her baby away and never touch her again?

His tone became conciliatory and patronizing. "You will be cared for afterward as well, of course. And if the child is as fine as I expect, then we will continue our relationship. Really, Lucy. I should think you would be relieved. You receive all the pleasure and benefits of being an SS mother and none of the responsibility of raising a child."

She did not reply. She thought of all the things he had said to her over the last few months. Everything made sense now. All of it was suddenly clear. Words about the nobility of motherhood for the sake of the Reich. His praise of beauty and perfection. None of that had meant that he loved her! He intended to give her baby to his wife, and all the things she had dreamed of would belong to another woman. How would her family react to such news—her father and the priest at home?

"We will raise him in the State Church," Wolf added. "It does not bother me that you are Catholic. The child will never know the difference." He checked his watch. "I cannot stay any longer." He held himself aloof, as though they were speaking of business. He tossed some money on the table for her. "Have something nourishing to eat," he instructed. "And take a cab home, will you? Tonight I do not want you out walking. There are important demonstrations planned for tonight. You are carrying a baby for our Führer, and so you must be especially careful."

He stood and then bent to kiss her cheek. "Heil Hitler," he said in farewell, and then he left her sitting alone and stunned at Café Sacher.

3

Inferno

Neither the acrid smell of smoke nor the crash of breaking glass could drag the sixteen-year-old boy into reluctant consciousness.

"Peter!" The voice of his mother came as a hoarse whisper. "Wake up! Peter!" She shook him gently in spite of the terrified urgency of her tone. "Wake up! Get up! *Quickly!*"

Peter Wallich opened his eyes to see his mother's shadow against the wall, backlit by an eerie orange light.

Was he still dreaming? His gangly body remained tangled in the blankets, binding him like the ropes of his dream. He blinked and then closed his eyes, certain he was dreaming.

He had been fighting *them* again, even in his sleep. His arms and legs had lashed out against the skull-faced phantoms dressed in the black uniforms of the Hitler Youth Brigade. They had tied him up and beaten him as they shrieked through wide, grinning mouths, *"You cannot hurt us, Jew-pig! We are dead already! Already dead!"*

"Peter!" The voice of his mother penetrated the dark image once again. "Wake up!" The hand on his shoulder was less gentle, the voice impatient. *Frightened!*

He opened his eyes to the strange light, fully awake at last. He smelled the smoke. The exploding of glass and the harsh voices in the street below pierced his confusion with a terrible clarity. *"Judenschweine! Verrecken!* Die, Jew-pigs!"

Peter bolted upright. He kicked himself free from the blankets as he grabbed his knickers and pulled them on in one quick movement. Then, his nightshirt half tucked into the waistband, he stood transfixed beside his mother. His eyes stared at the yellow fire that seemed to dance and sway in midair beyond the lacy web of curtains.

Vienna was burning!

He looked at his mother. She stared in unblinking horror toward the window. Her long red hair, always neatly pinned up, tumbled down around the shoulders of her dressing gown. At five feet, eight inches, Karin Wallich was as tall as her son. But tonight she seemed very small next to him.

A woman's scream echoed up from the street. Peter's mother winced and clutched his arm. More crashing glass. Now she looked back through the darkened doorway of the bedroom as if she expected the shouts of Nazi voices and the pounding of fists against the front door at any moment. Her wide brown eyes brimmed with tears. In spite of the terrifying sounds emanating up from the streets of Vienna, Peter could think only of how weary his mother looked. Weary and very, very sad.

She took his hand. "Come to the window, Peter," she whispered softly, as if she had wakened him to watch the first snow fall.

He obeyed without speaking. The floor felt cold beneath his bare feet. He reached to pull back the curtain.

She stopped his hand with her arm and warned him with a look. She parted the lace a mere inch to reveal a slice of the inferno that raged beyond the thin pane of glass.

Putting his eye to the slit, Peter gasped. "The synagogue!"

Ashes swirled up. Tongues of fire leaped from the broken windows of the synagogue at the end of the block. The great cupola of the building resisted the ring of flames that danced around it. For an instant Peter hoped the city fire department might come and save the shell of the imposing edifice. His mother directed his eyes to the west and then to the east. The horizons of Vienna glowed with a false and horrible dawn.

"There," she said. "Do you see? Not just our synagogue, but all over Vienna." Her voice faltered. She stepped back and sat down heavily on the edge of the bed as Peter continued to watch the fire. So beautiful. So terrible. The burning of the Torah scrolls. The defying of God Himself, it seemed.

As Peter watched, orange sparks showered the cupola, glowing bright as stars. Then the orange pinpoints deepened in color and spread in broad, hot patches on the surface of the roof. Suddenly a blade of flame pierced through the dome. Another stretched upward. Within moments the roof collapsed with a tremendous roar, and the fire blazed skyward through the skeletal frame of the building.

Hearing someone in the room whispering, "Why? Why?" Peter realized with a start that it was his own voice. He turned briefly from the scene to peer with questioning eyes at his mother. Light and shadow played on her pale face. Gold reflected in her hair until it seemed to him that she was also being consumed with flame. He looked down at his own hand. Yes. The inferno touched him as well.

And then he saw *them* moving slowly up the narrow street from the synagogue—a dozen of them in the back of an open truck. They were not phantoms, these arrogant Nazi gangsters; they were the stuff his nightmare was made of. They gestured wildly and shouted as the truck approached a Jewish shop. By law, each Jewish business was required to identify itself by displaying the name of the owner painted in large white letters across the window. Not even the most illiterate Nazi could miss such a sign. And so, as they rounded the corner to turn on the street, they saw the name *J. SINGER* stenciled across the window of the lingerie shop.

The truck squealed to a halt. A clamor of shouts echoed up, ricocheting off the facades of the surrounding buildings. Men tumbled out of the truck, directing curses and obscenities toward the Jewess who owned the once-fashionable shop.

Peter thought he saw a movement of the curtain in the window above the store. "Frau Singer," Peter said softly.

The gracious old lady was a legend in the neighborhood, a legend of kindness. A widow for twenty-eight years, Frau Singer had supported herself with the lingerie business. When times had become desperate in Vienna, she had held classes in corset making for the young women who hoped somehow to leave Austria. *"Surely such a trade will be useful in the world beyond the Reich,"* she reasoned. But as for herself, she chose to remain in Vienna. *"Bad times cannot last forever. I will wait it out. Even Aryan women are in need of excellent corsets. Good times will return for my little shop."*

But good times had not returned.

Peter's mother joined him at the window. She held her hand over her mouth as she watched a large stone being handed down from the truck and passed from man to man like a bucket brigade. Then the last fellow hoisted the stone to his shoulder and hefted it through the air into the shopwindow.

The name of *J. SINGER* shattered into a million shards of jagged glass. More obscenities rang out as yet another huge stone was hurled to smash what remained of the shop name. A ragged guillotine of glass hung above the display. Glass fragments slithered down to cover the sidewalk with shimmering crystal.

Peter glanced back along the route the men had taken to come this far. In their wake it looked as if the dome of the sky had shattered and fallen to earth. The street, the sidewalk, caught the reflection of the raging fire until even the ground seemed to be burning.

"What did we . . . do . . . to them?" Peter's mother croaked.

Peter did not reply. The Nazi answer to that question was that a Jewish boy named Grynspan had mortally wounded a German in Paris. That answer was enough to unleash a wave of fury that swept across all of Hitler's Reich.

From the other direction a second group of Storm Troopers moved inexorably toward the first group. Behind them lay the rubble of their hatred. Everywhere along the route, Peter saw men pounding against doors with ax handles and crowbars. Although the lights inside Jewish apartments remained off, the Nazis knew the location of each Jewish residence as well as they seemed to know the stores and businesses.

From the high angle of the third-story window, the scene took on a surrealistic appearance, as if Peter and his mother had awakened to a vision of judgment and hell. Peter shuddered and looked back through the doorway toward the front door. It was locked and bolted. But Peter knew, as did his mother, that locks and bolts meant nothing at all tonight. Nothing if you were Jewish.

Now the terror began in earnest. More screams. Shouts and demands reverberated through the street.

"Filthy Jew-pig!" A middle-aged man in his nightclothes was pushed onto a pile of broken glass. "We Germans have had enough of your treachery!" The toe of a jackboot swung up to catch the man in his face, throwing him back against the wall.

Three doors down and across the street, the plate glass of a window burst outward. A human body flew screaming through daggers of glass and fell in a bloody heap on the sidewalk.

Others, pulled from bed, were herded into the street and beaten. More Storm Troopers came. A fire truck moved slowly past; the fire brigade made no move to put out the fire that consumed the synagogue. Firemen sat languidly on the fenders of their truck and watched to make certain the fire did not spread to Aryan buildings. German-owned shops must be protected, after all.

A distant explosion rattled the windowpanes. Peter's eyes widened with horror. Flames and smoke billowed over the rooftops. "It is the Hietzinger Synagogue! They have blown up the Hietzinger!"

His mother crowded next to him, as if she could not believe it. Her head moved slowly from side to side in disbelief. The most beautiful synagogue in all of Vienna! A series of explosions followed in quick succession, as each of twenty-one synagogues was demolished in turn.

The Aryan citizens gaped from their windows, some smug and satisfied, others grim. Still others seemed numbed by what they saw.

It all made perfect sense. The destruction was so organized, the violence so methodical, it had to have been planned long before. Peter stared at the fragments of lettering that identified the corset shop as a Jewish enterprise. The edict ordering labeling of Jewish-owned shops had been carried out just the week before:

> Letters to be stencilied in both Hebrew and German must be clearly visible from the street.

Frau Singer had smiled and shrugged as the sign painter carefully painted the Hebrew letters she ordered. *NO NAZIS NEED APPLY*, the sign read in Yiddish.

"Those hoodlums will not know the difference," she had chuckled when it was finished.

Such small displays of defiance and humor had lifted the spirits of the Jewish community in Vienna. Frau Singer's business had improved the past week.

But tonight the civilian Nazis of Vienna came like vultures after the front line of destroyers was finished.

A portly couple from two doors down appeared outside the shattered window of Frau Singer's shop. Good people. Moral, upright citizens. They reached in through the shattered glass to pull out lingerie from the debris. Underwear. Nightgowns. Stockings. These things they stuffed inside their coats until they looked fatter than ever.

Peter's mother gasped indignantly and rapped on the window to admonish them.

They glanced up furtively, wondering who had seen them looting. Everyone had seen them—everyone who was not being beaten and dragged away. And others were coming to join the plunder.

"What am I doing?" Peter's mother cried as she stepped back from the window and pulled Peter away as well. "Those thieves! What is to stop them from coming up here next? Stay away from the window! They might see us and come up here!"

She put her hand to her forehead in a gesture Peter had seen made by the heroine of a movie before she swooned. He guided his mother to the edge of the bed.

"We are safe here, Mother." He tried to reassure her, even though he was uncertain as well. "They would not dare to break into Herr Ruger's apartment. He is not Jewish. Why would they think to come here?"

She nodded, glanced at the front door again and then back toward the eerie light. "Do not go near the window," she managed to whisper. "They must not see us here. Herr Ruger would also be punished."

Herr Ruger was away on a business trip. He had left the key with Peter along with strict instructions on the care and feeding of his two cats, Mozart and Gert. Tonight, when news of the death of Ernst vom Rath had been broadcast on the radio, Peter had insisted that he and his family come here to sleep, just in case there might be a demonstration. Another mass arrest, perhaps, like the one in which Peter's father had been taken.

Mozart, one of Herr Ruger's cats, rubbed against Peter's leg, then jumped onto the windowsill to stare out peacefully upon the carnage below.

Peter moved to the window again and peered around the golden tabby to their own neighborhood. No smoke; nothing happening there—*yet!*

"I should have known," Mother moaned. "Why didn't we bring the Fischers here with us?"

"The Storm Troopers are not there yet, Mother," Peter reported. "I can sneak out the back, through the alley. I know a short cut. The Nazis are staying on the main streets. I'll bring the Fischers back."

She shook her head in stern disagreement even though she knew he was not asking permission. Since her husband's arrest two months before, Peter was the man of the house. He was telling her what he was going to do. "Peter, do not go!" she cried as he pulled on his socks and shoes.

Reaching for his coat and cap, he said confidently, "I know this neighborhood better than anyone. I tell you, they won't even see me, these Nazis!"

He was not afraid. A strange sense of adventure filled him, first with excitement and then with guilt. *Such a terrible night*, he thought. How could he feel anything but anger and sadness? He was grateful, at least, that he was unafraid.

Peter took one last look at his mother on the edge of the bed. She would be safe here. He did not doubt that.

"Just keep away from the window," he warned. "And if Marlene wakes up, don't let her know what's going on out there." He gestured toward the second bedroom where his nine-year-old sister and baby brother were sleeping. Marlene should stay asleep; otherwise she would be gawking out the window before they knew it!

"Be careful," his mother managed to say before she turned away, as if trying to hide the emotion. But he had already seen in her eyes that she felt everything he did not yet feel. Fury. Grief. Fear.

He buttoned his coat and slipped out the door quietly. Hanging back in the dark hallway, he listened as the bolt slid into place on the other side of the door. Satisfied, he ran down the stairs, then through the long corridor that led to the back door of the building. He reached for the knob, then froze as a gruff voice penetrated the door from the outside: "Stand here. If there are any Jews hiding in the building, they will try to sneak out the back way. Heil . . ."

Peter stared at the knob. He had almost touched it, almost betrayed himself. What could he do now? They were guarding his escape route, looking for Jews in the shadows! He had better rethink his plans.

Turning on his heel, he walked back toward the front of the building. It was more sensible to hide in plain sight. Smarter to walk through the demolished street just like the other Germans who now roamed to watch the assault against the Jews. No one would question that. If challenged, he would pick up a stone and prove that he was not a Jew. That would work. Tonight no one would dare deny a good little Nazi boy the right of tossing a stone through a plate-glass window.

He drew a deep breath and stepped out into the smoke-filled street. The mob had grown. The violence became more fierce. Men and teenage boys held clubs aloft. Some carried cans of kerosene. All of them, though dressed in civilian clothes, wore the jackboots of their Storm Trooper uniforms. Screams and explosions and breaking glass filled the air of Vienna with a long, continuous roll of destruction.

Called to Berlin to report on Secret Police progress in Vienna, Otto Wattenbarger was on hand when the first directive was sent out from headquarters. Seldom had anyone seen this sullen Austrian smile, but tonight he smiled.

"There," he said. "This will solve a lot of problems in Vienna."

"In all the Reich," agreed Heinrich Himmler, rolling his stamp of office across an official document. "This is long overdue."

"The directive comes from the Führer, then?" Otto clasped his hands behind him and watched as the second wave of trucks rolled ominously up Albrechtstrasse.

"We have all had a hand in it," Himmler replied icily. He disliked not getting credit for the coming raids. After all, no matter who conceived the action, it was ultimately Himmler's elite corps who would begin it and carry it through to its violent end. "It is this sort of thing that demonstrates the strength of our race; don't you think?"

Otto's mouth twitched as he agreed with the head of the SS and the Gestapo. He must show no sight of wavering or disapproval for what was to happen tonight. "*Ja*. The Führer seals us to him with blood. It is true."

Himmler seemed to approve of the answer. He silently considered the red-bearded Austrian before him. Questions about his loyalty had arisen over the last several months. After tonight, Himmler could reply easily one way or the other to the superiors in Vienna who had suspected the true fidelity of this sullen and solitary man.

The eyes of Heinrich Himmler narrowed as he considered the case that had been presented to him. "You are suspected, Officer Wattenbarger."

The unsmiling face looked amused at the news. "Everyone is suspected, Reichsführer Himmler. I myself trust no one."

"A wise policy. But what do you trust in?"

"My own loyalty to a just cause. Our party. Our people. Our Führer."

Himmler raised his chin slightly. This was a stock answer. Memorized and repeated by rote by those who even now awaited execution. "Which cause? Which people?" Himmler queried. "I myself requested to review your case. It would be a pity to mistakenly lose even one loyal officer who is Austrian by birth—or so you seem to be."

"I am what I have always been."

"We have had to replace many native Austrians with those more agreeable to our methods. And our goals." Himmler clasped his hands on the desk and tapped his thumbs together thoughtfully. "Tonight our goals and methods are made public for all to see. No hypocrisy in the Reich. Not like Western nations. We do not want our Jews, and so we get rid of them. We are partners with the West in this enterprise. Only we are not hypocrites about the matter."

Otto inclined his head slightly as if this discussion of well-established doctrine was not really necessary. "All of this is true."

"I knew you would agree." Himmler paused. The reflection of Otto's face glinted in his glasses. "But the question has been raised whether you are hypocritical also. Do you agree with the Reich policies to save your own skin? Or . . . perhaps the skin of others who do not agree with us?"

From the beginning, Otto had felt eyes watching him. His private thoughts and motives were concealed beneath a veneer of coldness and cruelty. He did not blink or turn away from torture, even the torture of those whose hearts had been knit to his by the shared goal of the end of Hitler. He had pulled the trigger and blown the heads off his own compatriots when they could not stand Gestapo torture any longer and so became a threat to the resistance. He no longer considered his actions murder, but rather an act of mercy and self-preservation. In this way, he had been able to remain in a position to help men of great stature escape to freedom. He had made decisions about life and death: which man must be sacrificed so another might be saved. Otto felt his own soul condemned to a hell in which his fellow Austrians hated him, even as he did what he must for Austria. He had come too far to lose it all now.

It was important that no fear show on his face. He knew what the message of fear told these men. Fear was weakness. Fear was guilt of some violation of their twisted code. "Someone is wasting your time, Reichsführer Himmler," Otto replied coolly. "If I were the investigating officer, I would address a case like this by looking first at those who accuse me of disloyalty. What is their motive? Jealousy because I do a job without flinching? Or perhaps it is they who are disloyal. Eliminating me would make their job easier." Otto raised his eyebrows with a sigh of resignation. "Me? Like I said, I suspect everyone. Everyone but myself."

"An interesting defense."

"A better defense is the performance of my duty. Which—" he raised his hands and then let them fall to his sides in a gesture of frustration— "I am kept from tonight."

Himmler scratched his chin as he scanned the papers in front of him. He did not respond for a time; at last he jerked his head up as if satisfied. "Our Reich gives splendid opportunity for young men," he remarked, as though Otto had applied for a bank. "Forgive me. I, too, trust no one. I question and reevaluate everyone. It is the job. We have considered you for promotion, you see, and so had to make certain that you are not involved with . . . hypocrisy." The corner of Himmler's mouth turned up in a tight-lipped smile. "You are promoted." He scribbled his signature on a slip of paper that had been prepared ahead of time. Laying it aside, Himmler then handed the photograph of Thomas von Kleistmann to Otto, who looked at it without emotion.

"A messy job." Otto managed to tinge the words with a hint of amusement.

"It is impossible to recognize the man, of course, but he was linked to traitorous operations in Vienna."

"He failed miserably at his task, then."

The humor in Otto's voice must have satisfied Himmler.

"The Führer has asked that the photograph be circulated in Intelligence departments as an example of what happens to a hypocrite," Himmler stated.

"A unique sort of death. Will the Führer have him bronzed and hang him in St. Stephan's?"

Himmler laughed, a short burst of laughter. He would have to remember to tell the Führer about the comment. "Well, I am certain you can carry out this order then." He handed the signed slip of paper to Otto, who read it as though it were a grocery list.

Here was the final test of his hardness and loyalty. It was everything he had dreaded over the last two months. Quietly, Otto had been searching for some way to save the life of Michael Wallich, a well-respected attorney in the government of the Austrian Republic before the Anschluss. Otto had supplied information about the well-being of Wallich and encouraged that negotiations be stepped up for a ransom. Now Otto was commanded to execute Michael Wallich upon returning to Vienna next week.

Otto's hand did not tremble as he read the order for Michael Wallich's execution. In a gesture of unconcern, he folded the slip in half and slid it into his pocket. "Is that all?"

The murder of this good and innocent man had been first on Himmler's mind. Now there were other matters to address. "Next week we begin meetings in Vienna to establish the final borders of Czechoslovakia. The Hungarians, who did not cook this stew, want to eat at our table. It is important that you organize unrest among the Hungarians in Vienna. We will need some demonstrations." He waved his hand as the sound of an explosion rattled the windows of the office. "But, never mind. We will discuss details later. There is enough going on tonight."

4

Auf Wiedersehen

Once the place had been called Sisters of Mercy Hospital for the Infirmed. But sisters no longer glided through the antiseptic halls; mercy had long since vanished. Only wards of patients, now called inmates, remained. Soon even they would be gone. In the interests of the State, they would be eliminated to make room for yet another fine hospital for the citizens of the Reich.

The smell of antiseptic did not completely mask the strong smell of urine in the boys' ward for the hopelessly defective. Twenty beds lined each side of the room. In those beds lay boys from ten years old to fourteen, many of whom had come here as tiny children to be cared for by the sisters. Cerebral palsy robbed some bright children of their ability to speak or care for themselves. Polio or accidents had paralyzed others, but left their minds quick and active. Others, like Alfie Halder, were judged to be mentally incompetent.

Alfie lay awake on his bed. A strange bright light came through the barred window and flickered on the empty beds. Some of the boys had gone away today and were not coming back: the boys who could not walk or speak. The orderlies had taken them out one at a time this afternoon and this evening. Werner, Alfie's friend, had cried tonight. Werner was ten. He had contracted polio last year; Alfie, fourteen and very big for his age, carried him places. Alfie liked it when Werner talked about the American president who had polio and yet was still president. Werner wanted desperately to go to America and told Alfie all about it. "The Promised Land," Werner called it.

But tonight the orderlies had come to take Werner away, and Werner had cried and looked at Alfie with sad eyes.

"Where are you taking him?" Alfie asked the orderlies.

"To the Promised Land," the ugly-mouthed orderly said, and then he had opened his big lips and laughed as Werner cried and cried. Werner did not seem happy about going away, even though he had always wanted to go to America.

Others had gone, too—Michael and Heinrich and Fredrich. But they did not know they were leaving, and so they did not cry like Werner.

Alfie thought about Werner's dream of America and felt sure his friends would be happy there. But Alfie felt lonely tonight without them. The orange light from outside the window made moving shadows on their made-up beds. Something inside Alfie felt bad, and he did not like it. He felt like he used to when they first made him come here. He missed Werner already, just like he missed Mama.

Now that Werner had left, who would call Alfie by his real name? The orderlies called him Dummkopf. They did not know his real name. Only Werner knew that Mama used to call him Alfie before she died and they put her in the stone shed at the New Church graveyard. After that, Pastor had come to visit sometimes. He knew Alfie's name and promised that soon he would be out of this place. Then there were no more visitors for anybody. "Verboten," Werner had told him. Now, nobody was left to call him Alfie.

He sat up and hugged his knees and closed his eyes to say his prayers. "Ich bin klein . . . I am small; my heart is pure; nobody lives in it but Jesus alone."

The door banged open, and a light caught him sitting up. It was forbidden to sit up after the lights were out.

"What are you doing, Dummkopf?" shouted Ugly Mouth.

Alfie lay down and did not answer. Sometimes they beat him, but maybe tonight they had other things to do.

"Leave the poor idiot alone," said Skinny Man as they wheeled the gurney in and to the side of Dieter's bed. Dieter had been hurt in a car accident. He could not speak. They lifted him onto the gurney.

"Let the Dummkopf sit up if he wants. Poor monster. By tomorrow he'll be dead, and where's the harm?"

Dead. Alfie knew the word well.

He lay very still, wishing they had not noticed him. He felt the nearness of the empty beds. Soon his bed also would be empty. He remembered Mama, beautiful in her best dress as she lay unmoving in the coffin. He wanted her to open her eyes and speak to him, but they closed the lid, and that was death. When someone was dead it did not matter if they closed the lid and never opened it again.

"Hey, Dummkopf!" said Ugly Mouth as they wheeled Dieter past. "Sit up and say *Auf Wiedersehen*!"

Alfie did not sit up. He held his breath until they closed the door behind them. Then he let his breath out in a slow groan. He bit his lip and dug his fingers into his palms. *All his friends!* He got up and tiptoed quickly to the window. Through the bars he could see a great fire in Berlin. The clouds were lit up. Smoke poured out of a building. This also meant death.

He wished he had asked Werner what to do. He did not want anyone closing the lid on him. He turned to look at the ward. Half the beds were empty. Only Wilhelm and Daniel were next before his bed. *What would Werner do?*

Alfie closed his eyes tight, hoping the answer would come. Then he saw it. He knew what Werner would do. Werner had told him about the pillows and sneaking out the window.

Alfie took Werner's pillow and stuffed it under the sheets of his bed. He stepped back and looked. Yes. It looked as though someone were sleeping in Alfie's bed. The orderlies would think he was still there.

Out the window would be harder. There was a storage room two doors down the hall that had a window with no bars. But the window was very high. Above the shelves. Alfie could climb up, maybe even crawl out, but it was a long way to jump.

The Promised Land. Death!

Alfie glanced back at those who remained sleeping in the ward. He could not take them with him. He stared at the barred window and the fire beyond. With a shudder, he went to the door and opened it a crack. The hall was empty. Lights reflected in the green tile floor. He could see the door to the storeroom.

"Hurry, Alfie," he said aloud to himself. "They will come!"

He nodded in agreement and slipped out, running to the storeroom and jumping into it. He closed the door behind him and looked to where the same orange light shone close to the high ceiling. He grasped the shelves and climbed up easily, just as he had climbed the trees at home.

A flimsy chain lock held the transom window. Alfie broke it easily and pulled down the frame. A blast of cold air hit his face as he lay along the top shelf. He laughed. The air smelled clean, not like the ward. It smelled like the Promised Land!

He did not care that it was a long way down to the ground or that it was cold and he was still in his pajamas. Alfie looked toward the row of trees that bordered the high wall of the hospital. He could climb those, too!

With that, he swung his legs around and eased himself through the window. He hung there for a moment, then smiled and let himself drop.

The ground of the flower bed was soft and muddy. He was not even hurt. For an instant he stared up at the brick wall to the little window. Then he let his gaze drift to the window of his ward. *"Auf Wiedersehen,"* he said and ran toward the linden trees and the wall.

He did not feel frightened, yet the hands of Berlin's Pastor Karl Ibsen trembled as he fumbled to insert the long key into the lock of the churchyard gate.

"Hurry, Karl," his wife, Helen, urged as she looked over her shoulder. *"Tor auf!* Open the gate!" Fear filled her voice, a fear echoed in the hearts of the dozen Jewish members of the congregation who had come to Berlin's New Church for sanctuary.

Karl fixed his eyes on the leaping flames of the great synagogue that burned only a block away. By the light of the fire, he found the keyhole. The latch clicked, and the gate swung back on its hinges, moaning in chorus with the groaning timbers of the synagogue.

The inferno illuminated marble headstones in an unearthly dance of shadow and light. Karl stepped aside as the trembling members of his flock filed hurriedly into the cemetery. Their huddled forms reflected the shimmering colors of the fires. Faces grim with terror looked up to watch the Star of David twist in the blaze that consumed the cupola. Molten metal shrieked and folded inward, collapsing to the cheers of a thousand Germans who watched in the street beyond.

"The church key, Papa." Lori, Karl's sixteen-year-old daughter, tugged the iron key loop from his hand and rushed ahead to open the rear door of the church building. Karl slammed the gate and bolted it securely from the inside. For an instant Karl stood transfixed as Nazi cheers rose in volume and the fires soared to singe the belly of a cloud of billowing smoke.

A small hand tapped urgently on his arm. "Papa, *please!*" Karl looked down to see the pleading eyes of ten-year-old James. His blond hair fell over his forehead and moved slightly in the unnatural wind that swirled from the fire. The air filled with a terrible roar as the entire dome collapsed. More cheers. The triumphant cry of Aryan voices almost drowned out the rumble of destruction.

"Papa!" James pulled his father's arm hard, straining to move toward the safety of the open church door, where Lori waited for them. She raised her hand to beckon as a shower of ash rained down, momentarily obscuring the light.

Karl let himself be pulled along by James. He covered his nose and mouth and squinted against the sting of the smoke. His lungs ached. His mind reeled with the unreality of what was taking place tonight in Berlin.

James and Lori were coughing hard as the four tumbled into the church and slammed the door, bolting it securely. For an instant total darkness overwhelmed them. He heard the sound of a woman weeping softly, the hacking cough of a man, the sniffle of a child—hollow echoes in the vast church.

The light of the fires penetrated the thick smoke and filtered through the high arches of the stained-glass windows. Karl wiped his eyes with the back of his hand. Through the soft hues of red and blue glass, he could see the group sitting in the front pews. Men and women clung to one another, their heads raised as they listened to the last triumphant cheers of the mobs.

Still holding tightly to James' hand, Karl walked toward them. Their world burned tonight, these Jews of his own congregation. These People of the Covenant, believers in Messiah, had become the hated victims of Hitler's Storm Troopers. On such heads fell all the blame of one foolish boy's actions in Paris. And Pastor Karl Ibsen felt powerless to help them in the face of such vengeance.

He looked toward the plain wooden cross suspended above the altar of the church he had pastored for ten years. He had watched as other Protestant pastors had been arrested, led away, and replaced by state-appointed clergymen. He had privately anguished while he publicly distanced himself from the politics that ravaged the church in Germany. He had been successful in walking the tightrope. He had managed to shield the Jews of New Church. But tonight the tightrope had been cut. A yawning abyss opened beneath him. For the sake of his eternal soul, he must plunge over the edge.

"What should we do?" croaked the voice of Henry Reingolt as he put his arm gently around the shoulders of his wife. Their three-year-old son lay sleeping in his mother's arms, oblivious to the terror of the night.

Karl sat down slowly. James sat beside him, while Lori stood gazing solemnly at the rose window that seemed alive with light and movement.

"What shall we do, Pastor?" Reingolt asked again. Did Pastor Karl have no answer for them? He had not failed them before now. When the racial laws had begun to destroy their lives, Pastor Karl had found ways to help. The church had eased some of the pain for them. But what was to happen now? They had not thought it could come to this.

"All of you stay here," Karl answered in a low voice.

"Will they kill us?" asked Reingolt's wife in a terrified voice.

"For tonight you will stay here," Karl said. "This will pass. They cannot keep on with it forever. Tomorrow we will decide what we must do. Perhaps we can find a temporary place for the children with the Protestant charity in Prague, just until things return to sanity. But you are all safe here tonight." More cheers from the mob penetrated the windows and shook the confidence in his statement. No one spoke until the cheering died away. "You will stay here," Karl said firmly. "I will be back by morning."

"Back?" Helen sat forward and took her husband's hand, as if to prevent him from leaving. He caught her gaze and held it in his steady brown eyes until her fear and resistance melted into understanding. Of course he could not stay here in safety when others of the congregation remained in grave danger. He must go to them, help them—if he could.

James clung to his father's arm. "Let me go with you, Papa," the child pleaded.

"You must help your mother, James," Karl said gently.

Only Lori was silent. She stood with her head raised slightly as she listened to the sounds of vengeance outside in the streets. Karl had not noticed how his daughter had grown into a young woman. Tonight he looked at her as if he had not seen her at all since she was a little girl. Her thick blond hair, braided, framed an oval face much like her mother's. Such a night, such a crisis, demanded that children suddenly become adults. Perhaps that had happened to Lori. Her blue eyes mirrored concern, but it was clear from her glance she knew why he must go. She nodded almost imperceptibly, as if to give him her blessing.

"The Kalners, Father," she said. "I telephoned. There was no answer. Please see if they are all right."

Karl stood. Suddenly he understood his daughter's unwavering agreement with his decision to go out in the midst of the riots. The Kalner family—Richard and Leona Kalner, members of the church, were Jewish by birth. Their son Mark, like James, was ten years old. Jacob, three days younger than Lori, was handsome, athletic. *Is he also interested in Lori's safety?* Karl wondered.

Helen reached up and took her husband's hand. She whispered the names of other members of the congregation who had not made it to the church. "We will pray, Karl."

He nodded, brushed her cheek with his lips, then hurried out the side door of the church into the unnatural night.

Leona Kalner had long since removed the family name from the tiny window above the mail slot. These days it was better not to display a Jewish name in any neighborhood in Berlin.

There had been other apartments before this one when Leona had been careless; she had placed their name above the mail slot. As flies swarmed toward death, members of the neighborhood Hitler Youth converged to beat her sons as they walked home from school.

Perhaps tonight she imagined some safety in anonymity. But there was none. The Gestapo kept a complete file on the Kalner family, as it did on every Jew in the Reich. The fact that they were members of New Church made no difference. Days before, the yellow card bearing the name *Kalner, Richard: Juden* had been plucked easily from a file containing five hundred thousand records of potential enemies of the State.

Being a convicted criminal as well as a Jew, Dr. Richard Kalner's name and most recent address appeared on the list. The vacant window above the mail slot made no difference at all.

From the first broadcast of Ernst vom Rath's death, Richard had resigned himself to what the long night must bring. Had Hitler not spoken of reprisals that would take place against every Jew in the Reich in such an event? *"The entire Jewish race will be held responsible for the rash act of even one Jew,"* Hitler's voice had growled for all the world to hear. No nation had challenged such a policy. Therefore no one could be surprised at the ferocity of Nazi vengeance for the murder of one of their own by a young Jew in Paris.

The apartment was lit by the fires that raged through all Berlin. Jacob was banished to the attic to hide with Mark. The two boys had protested, saying that they should stay downstairs and fight the Nazis, to defend their few remaining possessions.

"You are the only possessions we have that matter," Richard Kalner had explained. "Do not be so brave, Jacob, or they will succeed in destroying everything."

Leona, who maintained faith in the nameless mail slot, held out hope. "Maybe they will not come here. It is just a precaution. Do as your father says."

Fully clothed, dressed for the cold November night, Jacob and Mark crouched in the narrow crawl space that led to the roof. If the Gestapo came, they were instructed to flee to New Church for refuge.

A small skylight above them provided ventilation for the attic and access to the steep roof. The dirty panes of glass reflected the blaze of Berlin's great synagogue, illuminating the boys' hiding place.

For hours they had listened in silence as the orgy of violence rolled over the city. A dozen times the phone rang. Richard did not answer, fearing the Gestapo might be checking.

Mark studied the shadowed features of his brother. In the strange light, Jacob looked much older than sixteen. His nose, broken in a fight with a gang of Hitler Youth, gave his face the look of a prizefighter. This distinction, along with his athletic build and large, thick hands, had earned him the nickname Max, after the German boxer Max Schmeling. Even after Schmeling had been soundly beaten by the American Negro, Joe Louis, Jacob still enjoyed being called Max. He bore the title proudly, as if it signified knighthood.

Mark deferred to his brother's wishes. "Max," the younger boy whispered at last, "you think the Gestapo has forgotten?"

As if the mention of the Gestapo might draw them to the Kalner residence, Jacob silenced Mark with a frown and a finger to his lips. It did not matter that Father and Mother were just below them; Jacob was in charge.

"But they have passed us by," Mark began again. He was tired of this cramped position. His back hurt, and he wanted to go to bed.

Jacob nudged him hard. "Shut up, I said." Then with a jerk of his head he indicated the soot-covered skylight that led to the steep shale roof. His gesture seemed to say that the Nazi Storm Troopers and the Gestapo were everywhere tonight, maybe even prowling over the rooftops, perhaps hiding outside the skylight, where they could listen for the whispers of concealed Jews.

The younger brother's jaw jutted slightly forward in resentment. His eyes stung from the smoke that drifted into the attic. Mark wanted to believe that the Nazis were not coming tonight. Maybe they had forgotten to add the Kalner family to their list of Jews.

But Jacob did not believe in miracles. The long night was far from over.

Mark closed his eyes and leaned against a rafter. He listened to the voices of his father and mother below. He could not understand what they were saying, but the fear in their voices was unmistakable. Outside, a truck rumbled past the building. Far away, men were shouting. *Why do Nazis always shout?* Mark wondered. *Everyone can hear them easily enough without the shouting.*

For a time, Mark listened to the rustle of an unseen mouse in the corner of the attic. They had disturbed its sleep, invaded its home—just like the Nazis. Opening one eye, he could see that Jacob also leaned against a rafter. His eyes were closed. Not even fear had kept him awake. Mark followed his brother's example and finally let himself drift into an uneasy sleep.

5

Retribution

From his position at the punch bowl, Murphy conceded that Elisa had been right all along about the perfect acoustics of the main room in the Red Lion House. Of course, tonight's musicians were a world away from the classical longhair types she originally had in mind to play for the party. Famous and much loved by the radio fans in the States, the trio had begun to make its mark in Europe.

In front of the bay windows of the crowded room, D' Fat Lady Jazz Trio belted out the raucous melody of a Fats Waller song. A massive, large-mouthed black woman in a shiny red dress rocked and swayed and tapped her feet until the oak plank floors vibrated. Her eyes widened coyly as she sang, "Yo' feet's too big!"

Charles sat cross-legged on the floor, just an arm's length from the tapping red-patent-leather shoes. Half a dozen other children who had come with their parents squealed with delight as the ebony songstress reached down to pluck off the tiny shoes of an eight-year-old girl. The woman held them up with the musical explanation, "Oh, ba-by! Yo' feet's too big!"

Party hats askew, faces full of laughter, the children howled and held up their feet, waving them in the air. The laughter of Charles, clear and bell-like, made Murphy laugh too. He had never seen the child so joyful and without care, never seen his bright blue eyes so free of pain.

Murphy was glad they had gone on as if nothing had happened in Paris. International crises seemed a small matter compared to the happy face of Charles. Elisa and Anna had both squared their shoulders and shaken off the news. Elisa had not mentioned it again. Whatever fore-boding she felt was well concealed.

Elisa, radiant, wore a royal blue satin evening dress with a trim waist that had made her grimace when he helped her with the buttons. "There's not enough room in here for two." She had smiled over her shoulder as Murphy kissed her back and slipped his arms around her. In another week or so Elisa would have to hang up this particular dress un-til after the baby was born. For the moment, however, she was still a knockout—smooth cream poured into a slender blue mold.

Murphy eyed her approvingly as she chatted with several members of the press corps. He was glad she was his wife; otherwise just seeing her would be an agony of longing. He caught her eye and touched his hand to an imaginary hat in salute.

She raised her glass slightly in acknowledgment of his admiring glance.

He pointed up toward the bedroom with his thumb and raised his eyebrows questioningly.

She rolled her eyes in disapproval and turned to chat with the round-faced Betty Boop wife of Harvey Terrill.

Ah, well, Murphy thought, *I'll try again later. After all, Elisa can't unbut-ton the dress without my help*. He grinned and handed a cup of punch to the vicar of the little stone church across the square.

"Lovely party." Vicar Hight raised the cup as if to smell the punch. "Interesting music." He blinked toward the gyrating trio who pounded out a rhythm the likes of which had never been heard before in Red Lion Square. "Wherever did you find such an unusual group?"

The fame of D' Fat Lady in America had obviously not reached the ears of the astonished vicar yet. In Paris, crowds stood in line for hours to hear the group. But this *was* London, after all.

Murphy was glad they had included the neighborhood cleric on the guest list; otherwise the noise might have been a subject for his next ser-mon. He seemed quite taken with the energetic performance of D' Fat Lady.

"They were playing at a little club in Soho. Trying to earn enough money to get back to New York on a cattle boat," Murphy joked.

The vicar's eyebrows raised a row of furrows on his high forehead. "Most unusual! Most, *most*, unusual!" He sipped his punch and nodded his long, thin head in time to the music.

"Glad you approve." Murphy refilled the clergyman's cup and looked around the room at the faces of the other guests. Nothing like a pastor or two to add respectability to a get-together.

Elisa's orchestra friends listened with a sort of stunned astonishment. The music seemed totally improvised and, after all, members of the London Philharmonic did not often visit the kind of places D' Fat Lady Trio performed. This was a novel experience. Perhaps some quietly wondered how a fellow like John Murphy had ended up with a musician like Elisa, and how such a mismatched union could last. But for the most part, cellists and horn players and violinists thumped him on the back and told him what a *smashing* couple they made, and that they were certain to liven things up in London.

Murphy's friends put a different emphasis on the situation. "How'd he ever end up with such a classy dame? You think she's got sisters?"

Elisa had no sisters, but her mother still turned heads. Anna moved among the guests, speaking first in English and then in German, French, Czech, or Polish. Whatever nationality was represented here tonight, Anna always had a warm comment on the tip of her tongue. The only people she could not understand were the members of the jazz trio. This brand of English, she confessed to Murphy, was quite beyond her reach. Even the language of their keyboard was totally unfamiliar to her.

Anna stood to one side of the piano and shook her head in awe. Louis sat beside Philbert Washington, the piano player, watching his ebony fingers fly over the ivory keys while he tap-danced at the same time.

"I will ask Nana to teach me to play piano like this," Louis said gravely in German. "This kind of piano I like."

At that, Anna rolled her eyes in mock dismay and retreated to the kitchen to check on the supply of hors d'oeuvres.

Charles, on the other hand, was fascinated by Hiram Jupiter, the trumpet player. He held the shiny silver instrument to his lips and bent back and back until the trumpet pointed at the ceiling. Notes wailed out like a human voice, surpassed in volume only by the voice of D' Fat Lady herself.

It was only a matter of time before the less stodgy of the orchestra members had American jazz pounding in their blood. One by one, instruments were unsheathed—trumpets, trombones, clarinets. And D' Fat Lady Trio grew in numbers as well as in volume.

In the center of all this was Dr. Patrick Grogan, Charles' American speech therapist. To the amazement of everyone, the normally serious scholar borrowed a fiddle and joined in with what he termed "Irish-American jazz." Red hair flying and face flushed, he danced a jig and whooped as loud as anyone! Charles decided that he would never be intimidated by Doc Grogan again after such a lively show. Strange how this music cracked the reserve of the most sedate personalities!

This evening was a wonder, a miracle. The London *Times* society correspondent promised a stunning write-up. "Who would have imagined that

a benefit for refugees could turn out to be the party of the season?" he babbled ecstatically. "Surely you could not have found this group penniless in
a club in Soho? A cattle boat to New York, you say? Good heavens!"

Murphy confessed that the group was second only to Glenn Miller in
U.S. popularity. The correspondent seemed unclear about the identity of
Glenn Miller, so Murphy let the Soho story stand.

When D' Fat Lady finished her song, the applause was deafening.
Charles and Louis cheered the stiffly bowing orchestra members who
now flanked the trio. Rowdy pressmen and the less expressive guests
joined together in a shout of approval and a cry for more. The trio had
grown to a band of twenty-two.

D' Fat Lady leaned down and cupped her big pink palms around the
chins of Charles and Louis. "Oh, babies, so you likes D' Fat Lady's singin'?"

The twins nodded vigorously, their bright eyes filled with the wonder of warm chocolate skin, hair black and curly like a lamb's, and lips
that split the happy face in a dazzling smile.

"Would you babies like fo' Fat Lady t' sing somepin' jes' fo' you?"

Murphy thought the blond heads might bob off the shoulders of
Charles and Louis as the boys nodded enthusiastically.

D' Fat Lady had so many teeth! She laughed and showed them all.
She dedicated the next song to "Charlie" and "Louie," who both blushed
with pride at the attention. Although the vast majority of those at the
party were still unclear as to who D' Fat Lady was and where the group
had come from, Charles and Louis had become fans listening to the radio in New York. Finally meeting D' Fat Lady in person was more than
either had expected, it seemed.

"Well now, babies, then D' Fat Lady gonna sing you what my mama
use to sing me 'fo I went to bed." She winked at Elisa, who nodded with
approval. It was nine o'clock—bedtime. Perhaps this moment had been
prearranged between the two women.

D' Fat Lady stood up straight and tall in her glittery red dress. She
filled her lungs and opened her mouth to sing:

"Hush! Lit-tle baaaaby! Don' you cry! . . .
Mama's gon' sing you a lul-la-by!"

The first bar was sung without accompaniment—very slowly, almost
like a love song, Murphy thought. But it did not take D' Fat Lady long to
get wound up. The trumpeter joined in, and then the piano as the lul-
laby turned into a full-fledged attack of Cotton Club jazz. Heads
bobbed. Sweat flew. Feet tapped.

D' Fat Lady pulled Charles and Louis up and began to dance with them while the trumpet player wailed. Never had there been a moment to equal this one in the boys' lives. To dance! They had never danced. To laugh! They had never been anywhere where the very air was bursting with laughter! They danced and mimicked the movements of the tap-dancing piano man. And when the trumpet wailed its last, D' Fat Lady took their hands in hers and made them bow with her and bow again while everyone applauded wildly.

"But I want to go!" insisted Artur Bader, the fiancé of Sharon Zalmon. "I will kill them with my bare hands!" His face was contorted with rage. Tears streamed from his eyes as he spoke.

"You will get us all killed." Orde roughly brushed away the man's tears. "Go and sit shivah. Cry for her for seven days. Cry until you have no more tears, because if you wish to beat the Arab gangs, you must not cry again." Orde turned slowly, looking over the group of determined faces who stared back at him. "Those who come with me tonight—or any night—must not sniffle or cough or slip on a stone."

"I will avenge her!" cried Artur. Others joined in angry agreement. "They will find the bodies of their women and children when they return from here!"

Without thinking, Orde slapped the man across the face. The room grew suddenly silent, as though he had slapped them all. He stared back at each one with a withering look. His eyes demanded that they listen and learn from him.

At last Orde spoke. "We are not making war on the Arab nation, but on Arab gangs. Toward the ordinary Arabs, we will refrain from cruelty and brutality. A coarse and savage man motivated by revenge makes a bad soldier. And after you are through with your grief"—he looked at Artur Bader—"then you will behave with respect toward Arab wives and children and innocent individuals." He gave a slow, knowing smile. "But you will not let a single culprit escape." He addressed the others. "Do not imitate the British Tommy. Learn his calmness and his discipline, but not his stupidity, brutality, and vengefulness."

This was lesson one, words spoken to the grieving men of Hanita over the still-warm bodies of their loved ones. To Moshe, this Captain Samuel Orde seemed a strange man, yet a man to be admired as well. Weariness seemed to vanish when he spoke. The meaning of *Haganah*, or "self-defense," took on a thousand nuances.

In the end Orde chose six who showed no sign that they had mourned. The others—the ones with runny noses or coughs or tears in their eyes—simply listened to the instructions Orde issued to the six who would leave the compound tonight. They would bring back a few checked keffiyehs, the Englishman promised. Tonight they would see what could be done with the help of Almighty God!

Then the English Zionist insisted they stop and pray, the strangest instruction of all. Orde would not take them unless they knew how to pray, and pray silently.

As Orde made his entreaty to the Almighty for the safety and success of tonight's mission, he kept his eyes open and watched the men, noting those who did not bow their heads. From this group, two more men were eliminated from the patrol. They, like men with sniffles, were placed on the sideline. The mission was too dangerous for atheists, Orde insisted, and this eliminated Moshe from the group.

Moshe was about to argue when a knock sounded at the door of the infirmary. Zach opened it, revealing a middle-aged Arab in traditional dress. Bowing in salaam, he looked first at Zach and then at the bloody sheet. His eyes were wide as he explained the purpose for his visit.

"My friends," he said in a voice thick with sympathy, "our village heard that you were raided tonight. That some had been killed. May Allah the great and merciful have compassion on you, our neighbors."

"And have you come to tell your neighbors this only?" Orde interrupted, looking sternly at the man.

"No. We heard that an English officer came through the gates and now will go after the criminals who have done this thing." He waved a hand toward the bodies. "Our village knows where these wicked members of the Mufti's gang are hiding tonight, and I will lead you there."

"For a price?" Orde asked, staring hard at the man's head covering.

"For friendship." The Arab spread his arms wide and smiled broadly. His glance involuntarily flicked to the bloody sheet, then back again to Orde.

Orde did not return the smile. His eyes were hard and cold, dissolving the overly eager smile of the Arab. A muscle in the man's cheek twitched as he struggled to maintain the illusion of grinning friendship. Orde stepped closer and, pushing the Arab with one finger, backed him out the door.

"How do you know these details?" Orde queried.

The dozen members of the settlement followed Orde and the Arab out into the darkness.

"We have spies who have seen them. A shepherd. The vile enemies of peace are hiding in a wadi not far from our village."

Again, Orde pushed the man back until they stood in a circle of light that came from the window of the little morgue. "How many raiders?" Orde asked in a flat tone.

The Arab shrugged. He was nervous; he did not like the finger of the Englishman pointing at him. "Fifty, maybe."

Orde reached up and took the edge of the man's head covering between his fingers. Then as beads of visible sweat formed on the Arab's brow, Orde poked two fingers through a tear in the fabric. "How many men came through the barbed wire, friend?"

At this question the Arab grew dark and sullen. His mouth turned down, and his eyes were black with hatred of this Englishman. "How could I know that?"

"Because you were there." Orde jerked the keffiyeh from the Arab's head and tossed it to Zach. "Take this to the cut in the wire. You will find the patch missing from this keffiyeh is still there."

Zach stared at the hole in the fabric and then, as an angry realization filled his face, he tossed it to a young man who ran into the darkness toward the fence.

"No. Me? I was not there!" protested the Arab, backing out of the light.

Orde jerked him back. "You are a liar." He smiled coldly. "And a murderer of women."

"No!" Sweat poured from the accused. "Not me, Englishman! I did not . . . not my dagger!"

"Were they killed with a dagger, then?" Orde pretended surprise. "How would you know that? Did you see the wounds?"

The Arab laughed nervously. He looked from one angry face to another. Friends. Neighbors. They had lived side by side a long time. "I did nothing wrong!" he protested. "Let me go. I see I am not welcome here among you anymore!" Once again he tried to back out of the light. This time hands from the circle pushed him inward.

"You are the spy," Orde said coolly, certain of the truth. "You have not come here to help but to lead us into a trap."

"No! It is not so! I am a friend! They know me!"

"They do not know you well enough." Orde raised his head to the sound of footsteps running toward the group. The circle parted and the young man with the keffiyeh came into the light. He held up the head covering in one hand and then presented a small square of cloth to Orde.

"It is not mine!" cried the Arab. "I borrowed—"

Orde held up the torn keffiyeh and fit the fragment of fabric into the hole for all to see. The match was perfect. An angry murmur circled the group. The Arab trembled as he stared at the evidence of his treachery.

"You led them here to the weakest position in the line. You brought them to kill the woman."

"Not my dagger!" the Arab screamed.

"You knew she was on duty tonight, didn't you?"

"I know nothing!" he begged.

Orde slapped him hard on the cheek, sending him whirling to the ground. He lay there for a moment on his belly as Orde stood over him; then, in a voice dark with rage, the man muttered, "*Allah Ahkbar.* You are all dead men."

In one swift movement he rolled over and pulled the trigger of a revolver pointed at Orde. The shot missed the side of Orde's head by an inch, and he slammed his foot down on the wrist of the terrorist. In that same moment he drew his own gun and fired once, killing the man instantly.

The circle leaned back in shocked disbelief. As the report of the second gunshot echoed in the distant wadis, they looked at the Arab, at one another, and then at the Englishman in astonishment.

Orde did not speak for a moment. He did not lift his foot from the wrist of the dead man. Great sadness marked his face as he leaned down to pry the revolver from the fingers of the assassin. He held the weapon up for all to see, and his eyes met those of Artur Bader.

"Tonight we prayed that we might bring to justice the enemies who murdered our brother and our sister." The Jews were no longer surprised that the Englishman identified himself with their besieged community. In that moment he had become brother to Sharon and Lazlo. The grief of the family was his own. "We did not have to go out to find the enemy. He came here to us. And this is what will come of all who seek to destroy the chosen people of the Lord God of Israel!"

He stepped away from the dead man and presented the weapon to Artur. "Believe it. This is your first lesson tonight. They are many and well armed. They would murder our women and drive us into the sea. They would trap us and lead us to destruction. But the Lord has not forgotten His Covenant. He will bring all deception into the light. Learn this tonight, and remember it in the long struggle for survival that is ahead." Orde searched each face and won each heart to loyalty to his leadership. "We will do what is in our power, and the Lord will do the rest."

Members of the press corps seemed drawn to Elisa, while Murphy was equally plagued by musicians from the Philharmonic.

As D' Fat Lady began to belt out another tune, a dozen latecomers pushed into the packed room. Murphy was uncertain who they were. He certainly did not know any of them, and they did not look like classical musicians.

Three British members of the woodwind section had cornered

Murphy and were simultaneously expressing their support for the appeasement policies of Prime Minister Chamberlain.

"Saved us from another war, he did."

"A brave man to stand up to Hitler."

"I know what war is about. Toured the front in France during the Great War. Clarinet in one hand and gas mask in the other."

Murphy simply listened with steely silence. These were colleagues of Elisa's, after all. There was no use arguing with such ignorance. They would find out soon enough what Chamberlain had traded for the illusion of "peace in our time." For the moment, at least, Murphy would let them believe that things would go on as they always had. He might have said much after a day like today. Reports poured in that new waves of violence were heating up to a rolling boil, but he had not shared the news with Elisa. This was a joyful night after all, and he would not let one shadow cross the light in her eyes.

For this reason he interrupted the clarinet player and stepped away when Harvey Terrill appeared in the room. Harvey had been left at the offices of Trump European News to man the clacking wire machines during the party.

Harvey's face showed lines of concern. His thinning hair was disheveled, and his suit was wrinkled, as if he had fallen asleep in it. But then Harvey always appeared as if he had been on a bender, even though he never touched a drop of liquor. Now he stood swaying beneath the arched doorway into the room as he scanned the smiling faces. He seemed not to notice the song of D' Fat Lady. He was looking for Murphy. Something was up.

Murphy inched through the crowd. Reaching through a dancing couple, he tapped Harvey Terrill on the arm.

Harvey's face showed relief, then worry. "Something's up, Boss," he said over the din.

Murphy motioned toward the study. He had kept the door locked in anticipation of the overflow crowd tonight. With Harvey at his heels, he unlocked the door and slipped in, warding off a journalist from the INS who assumed the door led to the men's room.

Harvey fought past the man and slammed the door. Murphy locked it behind them as the shunned newsman continued to knock.

The music, laughter, and the pounding fist on the door followed them into the study, but at least they were protected from the eyes of rival newsmen. Harvey had managed to slip in unseen by his wife, who attended the gathering without him.

"Some party," Harvey said glumly, then went to business.

"Let me have it."

"Nazis are rioting in Germany. Timmons wired in from Berlin. But it's not just Berlin. Everywhere, from Austria to the Sudentenland, the Gestapo has rounded up thousands of Jews. They're arresting thousands, he said." Harvey shrugged. "He was calling from a public phone booth near the Friedrichstrasse train depot. I could hear them shouting in the background. The phone went dead. They got Timmons."

Murphy crossed his arms and sat back against his rolltop desk. He would put in a call to the German Embassy. He had connections there. But first, there was something else Harvey wanted to tell him. "Is there more?" Murphy leveled his gaze at the little man.

Harvey worked his mouth nervously. "And there was this guy—" He started his sentence in midthought, as if someone suddenly turned up the volume on a recording. "He came into the office tonight and brought this." He produced a crumpled envelope. "Said it was something . . . about your father-in-law. Theo Lindheim." Sweating, Harvey thrust the envelope into Murphy's hand. "So here it is."

The envelope, addressed to Murphy, bore lettering in German script. Murphy did not open it, but instead thanked Harvey, who seemed frightened. "A German?" Murphy probed.

Harvey nodded.

"Tall and dark-haired?" Murphy considered his source at the German Embassy.

"No. Short. Thinning gray hair. About fifty. Overweight, with thick spectacles."

It did not sound like anyone Murphy knew. "No name?"

"The guy came in the back way. Through the alley door. Wouldn't come clear inside. He just said you gotta have this tonight." Harvey glanced toward the fireplace and then toward the window as if he sensed some danger. "He seemed so secretive. Scared, even. I didn't know. I locked up and came right down here."

Murphy nodded and bit his lip. He was anxious to read the letter, but not with Harvey looking on. "Go on back to the office now, Harv. I'll make a couple of phone calls, tell the German Embassy that a TENS Berlin reporter has apparently been illegally arrested. Where was he?"

"Friedrichstrasse Bahnof."

"They won't hold him. Don't worry. I'll wrap things up here and grab a couple of copywriters. With everything breaking this fast, it sounds like we'll have the wires jammed with stories before long."

Harvey edged toward the door. "There was stuff coming in from Vienna when I left."

"Grab a sandwich on your way out." Murphy pocketed the letter as if it were of little interest. In fact, it burned in his hand. The messenger must have been terrified to pass the letter along through the hands of an ordinary reporter like Harvey. Most likely he had been tailed by Gestapo in London.

Murphy put an arm around Harvey's shoulders. "Just don't mention this to anybody, will you, Harvey? Especially not Elisa."

Harvey placed his hand over his heart in solemn oath.

As Murphy unlocked and opened the door, his eyes caught Anna holding a tray of hors d'oeuvres and smiling. Instantly, her smile faded. *Something to do with Theo,* the look said as she stared at Murphy framed in the doorway.

Murphy looked away and closed the door against her knowing glance. Beyond the heavy door, D' Fat Lady crooned, "I'd rather be bluuuue!"

Murphy tore open the letter and began to read. The message was written in English in all capital letters:

THEO LINDHEIM TARGETED FOR ARREST BY GESTAPO IN BERLIN. YOU ARE ALL WATCHED VERY CLOSELY. BE WARNED. IT IS NOT FINISHED YET.

No other word, no signature. Murphy felt the blood drain from his face as he read and reread the message. *Theo in Berlin? He told us he was going on a business trip to Switzerland. Geneva. He would not go to Berlin! Somebody is way off on their information—unless . . .*

He jammed the letter into his pocket and burst out of the study to see Elisa. Just to see her! His heart was pounding as the implications of the warning raced through his mind. Suddenly the illusion of personal peace vanished for him. The towering form of Freddie Frutschy stood in the corner smiling over the assembly like an enormous bear. Then Freddie noticed the look on Murphy's face. He moved toward him. With a jerk of his head Murphy indicated that the big man should keep a close watch on Elisa. There were so many people here tonight, people Murphy did not know.

Anna worked her way through the crowd toward him. Her smile blinked on and off as she politely acknowledged those she passed. Her eyes betrayed her concern. Murphy could not shut her out again.

"What is it?" she asked quietly, imploring him to speak the truth.

"Anna . . ." He drew a deep breath and stepped back into the study, pulling her after him and locking the door. "Where is Theo?" he asked bluntly.

Anna looked at the floor and then up into Murphy's eyes. "How much do you know?"

"Anna, is Theo in Geneva?"

She hesitated, then shook her head slowly. So, the warning was true. They had sent Theo to Berlin to present the economic trade plan in hopes of securing the release of Jewish assets in Germany.

He answered his own question. "So. They asked him to go."

"How do you know this?" Anna pleaded. Tears brimmed in her eyes. "Has something happened to him? What news have you heard?"

"There are riots in Germany. Retaliation against the murder of vom Rath. We expected as much."

"But what of Theo? How could you know about this? I only knew because I guessed. We decided Elisa must not know. He left under a false name and a British diplomatic passport. 'Top secret,' they said. How can you know this?"

Murphy did not take the note from his pocket. His fingers closed around it as he considered what he should say. "Somebody recognized him in Berlin," he replied, trying to sound calm, although his insides were churning. "You know, the newsmen always hear rumors. I wanted to check this one out with the boss."

Anna sat down heavily in the chair before the fire. She looked terribly weary, much older than even a few minutes ago. "And what rumor have you heard? You must tell me. Is my Theo dead, John?"

He laughed—a short, incredulous burst. "Anna! I told you all I know. Someone recognized him in Berlin. I heard about it."

"And there are riots in Berlin. Against the Jewish people. Ah. Göring never intended to negotiate with Theo for the release of even one, did he?" She looked up, suddenly angry. "I am going home with our sons. My little sister is in Berlin with her family. I sent her our phone number with Theo. Perhaps there will be a phone call." She stood. "I must go home." She trembled as Murphy took her by the shoulders.

"I did not mean to worry you." He was mentally kicking himself for the tactless way he had handled the matter.

Anna patted his cheek affectionately. "Say nothing to Elisa. I am . . . I have learned that Theo and my sister are in God's hands. I know it here." She tapped her temple. "It has not yet sunk in here, however." She pointed to her heart.

She drew herself erect, and with a smile, she left the study and made her way through the crowd to hug Elisa good night. Murphy watched her with admiration and then instructed Freddie to escort her safely home.

Murphy tried to smile as Elisa slipped her hand in his. "You sure do know how to pick a band, Mr. Murphy!" She tucked her arm through his and leaned her head against his shoulder.

"You didn't realize I knew so much about music." He attempted to sound light, relaxed. It worked; she did not seem to notice that he was searching every face, looking for some unseen threat.

"Even Horace Bently, the publicity man at the Opera House, is impressed. He says that D' Fat Lady could have been the finest contralto in the world with such a voice!"

"She would have added an interesting aspect to Wagner's operas. Dress her up in a Viking helmet and . . ." He was babbling, noticing all the faces he did not recognize.

"Well, the success of the party is due to you. Charles and Louis are going to remember this night forever. Tap dancing with D' Fat Lady— much more exciting than an evening of Bach!"

Murphy wanted the party to end. He looked at his watch. *Nine-thirty!* This could go on indefinitely. Who were all these people, anyway?

The piano player began a slow jazz piece. Sandwiches and hors d'oeuvres were disappearing at an astonishing rate. The offices of American News Agencies on Fleet Street were abandoned for the most part. This party could, indeed, last until morning.

But it did not.

Murphy glanced up as someone began shouting from the arched doorway. The music died down.

"They've done it! The Nazis have . . ." The voice rose and fell, struggling to be heard above the din. "I just got it over the wire! Where is Ted Richter? Richter? INS! Come on! I tell you, the Nazis are tearing up the place!"

Murphy never got a clear view of the face of the man who was calling for Richter. The members of the press suddenly stampeded for the exit, pocketing sandwiches, grabbing coats in a mad scramble. Within moments the room had emptied by half.

Murphy watched the mass exodus with a sense of relief. He did not move from Elisa's side. He would not.

"Well, now we know who all the guests were," Elisa said. "Your friends, darling."

"My competition," he said.

"You're not going to the office?"

"I sent Harvey back. The staff will manage without me."

"What is it?" Her brow puckered with concern.

"Riots in Germany. Nazi retribution."

"Jews?" she asked.

He nodded a reply. He would not give her more details. She had been through enough. Unless she asked, he would not tell her. And even then, he would not tell her everything he knew.

6
A Tour of Hell

Peter Wallich found himself among a crowd of thousands in Vienna. He did not recognize the faces of those who ran past him. He peered back toward Herr Ruger's apartment, where his mother waited.

The smoke stung his eyes. A shout sounded from above, and he turned his face upward as two Nazis gleefully tossed a small dog out of a fourth-story window. The creature landed with a yelp and managed to drag itself a few feet before it collapsed. Furniture rained down from the apartments above the shops on the north side of the street. Clothing floated like tormented spirits in the turbulent air.

Peter forced himself to keep walking. He tried not to look up as a crowd gathered on the sidewalk below an apartment.

"Throw him down!" jeered the mob. "We'll catch him!"

There was nothing left to throw out of the window except an old Jew and his wife. Screams and pleas for mercy blended with Nazi curses and laughter.

"Tell us where it is, old man!" shouted two big Storm Troopers as they dangled the old man over the pavement by his bare feet, four floors above the sidewalk.

"There is nothing more! Nothing I tell you!"

"Tell us where you've hidden your gold, or—"

Peter looked up for a fraction of an instant. His breathing grew shallow with fear as he recognized the old watchmaker's wife tearing at the men who held her husband.

Peter looked away. He jogged toward the corner; a few more steps and he was safely out of sight. But he heard the final agonizing cry as the man hurtled to his death.

After a moment of total silence, a mighty cheer rose up. Peter felt suddenly ill. Leaning against a lamppost, he fought for breath as the crowd surged around him. His sense of adventure vanished as the scream echoed in his mind. *Now* he was afraid! Fear made him want to run. And if he ran, they would recognize him for what he was and chase him down as certainly as hounds chase a rabbit.

He had forgotten his purpose. For a moment he could not think why he had come out or where he was going. He saw the flames of Turnergasse Synagogue. Another explosion sounded, far away. Peter shook himself away from the terror that rooted him to the sidewalk. He pushed himself away from the streetlamp and staggered numbly toward his own neighborhood. Remembering the Fischer family, he quickened his pace and moved in and out of the throngs who had come out for the show. The street widened and the crowd thinned. Peter hoped they had not reached his apartment building. Perhaps there was still time to lead the Fischers back to the safety of Herr Ruger's apartment.

He jammed his hands down in his pockets and leaned forward as he walked, as if struggling to move against a great wind. He no longer looked to the right or left. Shopwindows were broken everywhere. Men and women, even small children, reached through the showcase windows to gather what they could.

On the corner, two policemen watched the looting. They talked with each other as if nothing unusual were happening. Peter pressed past them. They did not challenge him.

He felt the crunch of glass beneath his feet as he turned onto his own street. He stopped and gasped. The scene was the same. The destruction was complete.

A large open truck was parked outside his apartment building. Uniformed Nazi troopers and Gestapo men in trench coats supervised the loading of Jewish prisoners into the back.

Peter stepped back into a shadow to watch. He looked up at the window of the Fischers' apartment. The window was open; lace curtains wafted out.

He followed the facade of the building to the window of his own apartment. The light was on; shadows of men moved inside, searching, tearing the place apart.

Peter clenched his fists. His nails dug into his palms as he battled the urge to run screaming at the Nazis who now shoved Herr Fischer out the door of their building. The man was hatless. His overcoat was open, revealing his nightshirt tucked into his trousers.

The butt of a rifle urged him, stumbling, toward the back of the truck. In the dim light, Peter could see blood on his face. His nightshirt was splattered with blood. He wore a bewildered, frightened expression. His captors looked confident and righteous, amused by their own cruelty.

Peter was too late. With horror, he recognized the faces of a dozen boys his own age peering out from the back of the truck. Adam Siebenson was only fourteen, and yet there he was, jammed against the wooden slats of the vehicle.

Peter could do nothing. Blood drumming in his ears, he turned away to walk back to Herr Ruger's apartment. He tucked his head down in the collar of his coat, fearing that he might be recognized as a Jew by someone in the district. It would take only one hostile neighbor and Peter would find himself in the back of a prison truck headed for a concentration camp!

He stared at his shoes and the shards of glass beneath his feet. He no longer raised his eyes to gape when men shouted and women cried out. In the center of the street a pile of furniture, doused with kerosene and set ablaze, illuminated the area like daylight. The carnage and looting proceeded with ease by the light.

Peter fearfully tugged the brim of his cap down low over his eyes. He grimaced as the fumes of kerosene and smoke stung his throat. Such bitter smells did not seem to bother the rioters. They laughed and jeered at their victims as if the air were untainted. Only Jews seemed to cough. Only the tormented wiped their eyes and covered their noses against the smoke of Vienna. Trying not to cough, Peter plunged on through the crowds. He did not think of the Fischers any longer, only of himself. Of Herr Ruger's apartment. He wished his mother had not awakened him tonight. His nightmares had been much less frightening than reality.

He glanced ahead toward Frau Singer's shopwindow, nearly picked clean. The mob moved away from him, farther up the block where new targets were being hit.

Only half a block to safety! Peter looked up toward the window of Ruger's apartment. Still dark—a good sign. They had not come there. The hounds had not sniffed them out!

Against his own will, Peter quickened his pace to a jog. The glass cracked beneath his feet. People darted in and out of the demolished shops at the far end of the block. For them, the night was a celebration.

The flames of the Turnergasse flared and then dimmed, leaving the afterimage of terror etched on Peter's mind. He lunged toward the door and tumbled, panting, into the dark foyer of the apartment building. Kicking the door shut, he groped toward the stairway and clambered up on his hands and knees. Too weak from fear to stand, he clutched at the banister and pulled himself up step by step. The howling of the mob penetrated the heart of the building. Visions of darkness pursued him and seemed to pull him back.

Until now Peter had not noticed that his face was wet with tears. Had he wept openly in the street? The thought brought a new wave of fear over him. They beat anyone who wept, Peter knew. And then they arrested them.

He wiped his cheeks with the back of his hand. On the landing, he pulled himself upright and managed to climb the remaining stairs. Leaning heavily against the doorjamb of the apartment, he knocked softly, fearful that a neighbor might hear and peer out at him.

"Who is there?" His mother's voice trembled.

"Mother?"

The door swung wide, and he fell into her arms.

She closed the door and locked it, then guided him to the sofa. "You are safe! Safe!"

"They took Herr Fischer, Mother! And some of the boys in my class! I am too late! Too late!" He was filled with remorse. Why had he not brought someone else along to Herr Ruger's apartment tonight? Why had he not known what would happen?

His mother cradled him but said nothing. She stroked his back and stared through the window at the dying glow of the Turnergasse Synagogue.

The murky waters of the Danube slid silently beneath Stephanie Bridge. The fires around the city reflected orange against the moving blackness of the river.

Lucy Strasburg leaned heavily against the stone railing of the bridge and stared into the current. Beyond her, on either side of the banks, Vienna was rocked by violence and torment. She did not think of those she saw being beaten in the streets on her long walk here. It simply seemed a suitable backdrop to the chaos of her own life.

On the Stubenring she had watched an old Jew leap to his death as Storm Troopers broke into his apartment. Vienna was filled with the presence of death tonight.

This was the important demonstration Wolf had told her about, the Reich business that made him late to see her! This was a reflection of the glory of the Reich he served! For the fulfillment of fire and destruction Lucy carried the child of Wolfgang von Fritschauer.

She disobeyed him. She had not eaten as he instructed her, and yet now she vomited into the Danube. She had not taken a cab to her apartment, but had wandered aimlessly through the streets for hours, hoping that somehow a stray bullet might find her, or a trooper might mistake her for a Jewess and kill her.

Foolish hope. She looked so Aryan that the club-wielding Nazi patriots nodded in respect as they passed her. One policeman had asked her why she was out tonight. *"Is it to see the Jews get what they have coming?"*

And so Lucy had come here, where others had come to end their lives. She longed for the cold water to silence her problems. She watched it move away and imagined it carrying her into a long, untroubled sleep.

Her eyes were dry. She was past crying. She had been a fool. She had thought that Wolf loved her as she loved him. *Married!* She had interpreted everything he said through her own twisted idea of imagined love. She had left the church, her home, her job in Munich for the sake of being near him.

Dying would be easy compared to facing her family with the truth. It was bad enough that she was forced to admit the truth to herself.

She looked across the rooftops toward the Seventh District, where the men of Vienna took their pleasures at the brothels and cabarets of the city. She had scorned the women who lived and worked in such places. But was she any different? Lucy let her eyes move from one fire to another on the horizon, where synagogues and Jewish businesses were being destroyed by a man-made hell. She was consumed by a hell of her own making. The smoke made her eyes burn as she turned her gaze again toward the water and wondered. . . .

As a child she had heard that there was another hell that burned beyond this world. What if the waters of the Danube did not carry her to a peaceful sleep but into that raging inferno beyond life?

Lucy feared the possibility, and fear alone kept her from throwing herself over the rail and into the water. She feared God and feared hell and feared her own terrible sin. She might escape Wolf and this unwanted baby, but what if the frescos of Judgment Day in the church were true? Even the Danube could not let her escape all that! Perhaps death was only a door to something worse than this.

An open truck rumbled across the bridge. Haunted-looking men peered out at her from between the slats. Where were they being taken? What sort of hell awaited them at the end of the Nazi road?

Lucy stared down at her own hands. Her nails were perfectly manicured, painted red, as Wolf liked them. The watch on her wrist reminded her that even her soul now belonged to him. She had sold herself, and there was no way to buy back what she had lost.

"I am a whore," she said aloud. "I belong to SS Major Wolfgang von Fritschauer, and I am his whore."

Lucy did not need to jump off Stephanie Bridge to die that night. The hopelessness of this terrible truth killed something in her heart as certainly as the dark currents of the Danube could have stolen her breath forever.

Lucy stepped away from the cold stone and wiped mist and ashes from her cheek. Hell had come to earth tonight. Lucy could not think about any torment more terrible than her own.

She walked slowly back toward Franz Josef's Kai, where elegant hotels and shops lay untouched by the violence of the demonstrations. People milled around everywhere, enjoying the spectacle. She moved among them, not noticing or caring that tonight was a night unlike any other in the history of the world.

Something horrible had happened downstairs. Charles could tell because the music stopped and people were shouting. The party was over.

Louis rubbed the sleep from his eyes and joined Charles at the window. Members of the press corps and their ladies piled into a long line of taxis, and still there were not enough taxis for everyone.

"Ten bucks! Come on, Phipps! I'll pay the fare and give you ten bucks! Lemme sit on your lap!"

It was strange to see grown men fighting over how many bodies could be crammed into one vehicle. Charles would have laughed at them—except he knew down deep that something bad had happened.

"What do you think?" Louis frowned, pressing his forehead against the cool pane.

Charles shrugged. He did not know. Maybe they should call Elisa. There were still some guests at the party. The members of the orchestra were not pushing and shoving on the curb. Either they had gone out the back way or whatever was happening did not affect them. He could hear the low murmur of voices through the floor. The voices did not sound happy anymore. Nobody was laughing.

He looked at his pajamas and bare feet. Maybe they should get dressed. He was scared. Maybe the Nazis had come into London the way Hitler had come into Vienna without anybody knowing it. The newsmen had run around and looked unhappy on that day, too.

"S-something . . . bad," Charles stammered. His mouth did not want to talk. "Hitler, maybe."

Louis' eyes got big. He nodded, remembering the way the grown-ups had acted in Vienna. He looked out the window and then hugged Charles. He was crying now, and he needed Charles to comfort him

again. It was always that way when things were bad. Charles was stronger than Louis.

Horns hooted angrily outside. And then, as Charles held his trembling brother, the voice of D' Fat Lady began to sing again. There was no
trumpet or piano behind her. The song was slow and sad. Her voice,
deep and rich, pierced the walls until it sounded as if she were right there
in the room with them. Charles had never heard her sing so beautifully,
not in all the times he heard her on the radio.

> "Go down, Moses . . .
> Waaaaay down, way down in Egypt La-and!
> Tell ol' Pha-raoh! Tell 'im!
> Let. My. People. Go!"

She sang songs like this for a long time. Instruments from the orchestra joined in. Charles sat still with his eyes shining in the dark as he listened. He could hear the sweet cry of Elisa's violin playing. He knew the
voice of her instrument as easily as he would recognize the voice of his
mother. Tonight it was sad, crying music like Charles had never heard
before. Louis fell asleep with his head still cradled in Charles' arms.
Charles stroked his brother's hair the way Mama used to do, and eventually he fell asleep as well.

"Tor auf! Tor auf! Bitte! Please! Open the gate!" Desperate voices of hundreds rang in the air outside the British Embassy. Theo wondered if his
friends were among those begging to enter. He frowned and thought of
Anna's only sister. Little Helen. She and her family were not Jewish, but
here in Berlin, they might be brought under suspicion because of their
relationship to Theo.

Embassy Secretary Kirkpatrick was no longer filled with the assur-
ance that Theo would be out of the Reich by morning. He glanced nervously at Theo's packed luggage as he explained the negotiations taking
place downstairs in the office of the ambassador.

"The Nazis have stated that since you are an escaped criminal of the
Reich, you will be arrested the moment you leave the compound. Of
course you are safe as long as you remain here within the walls of the
embassy." He cleared his throat nervously, as if he did not believe what
he had just said. "They have told the ambassador that the Führer would
much rather this matter be settled through proper political channels.
That in light of what happened in Paris, it would be a gesture of goodwill
by His Majesty's government if—"

"If I were handed over immediately," Theo finished.

Kirkpatrick nodded once, then pointed toward the shuttered window. "There are hundreds of Jews outside the gate, begging to get in, begging for refuge. It is the same at the American Embassy." He gestured toward Theo's valise. "You must leave your luggage. Come with me. Hurry."

Theo picked up two sealed envelopes. The first contained his letter to Anna. He held it out to Kirkpatrick. "A letter to my wife—she is in London. The other is to my sister-in-law. She lives here. Please see that they get delivered, will you?"

Kirkpatrick took the notes and pocketed them with a preoccupied nod. "Please, Mr. Lindheim. We must hurry."

Newly waxed hardwood floors squeaked beneath their shoes as Theo followed Kirkpatrick down the broad hallway of the old mansion to the servants' back stairs. Theo could not help but wonder if the Nazis downstairs could hear them, if even now his eyes turned upward with the knowledge that his prey was attempting to leave by the back door.

"*Tor auf! Tor auf!*" The pleading penetrated even here.

Kirkpatrick glanced over his shoulder at Theo and held a finger to his lips as if he, too, felt the eyes of the hunter.

The corridor was dimly lit by electric lights that had been converted from gas lamps at the turn of the century. The electric wires ran exposed along the baseboard of the wall, evidence that embassy renovation had been halted since the discovery of listening devices installed by German electricians in remodeled rooms downstairs. Were others planted elsewhere in the embassy? Neither Theo nor Kirkpatrick spoke. Theo did not ask where he was being led, nor did Kirkpatrick offer explanation.

Somewhere in the building a telephone rang insistently. Theo counted ten rings before it fell silent.

Kirkpatrick led the way down a steep stairway. The scent of baking bread drifted up, a strange contrast to the distinct odor of smoke that blanketed Berlin. Kirkpatrick did not switch on the lights. With a touch on Theo's arm, he guided him across a tiled floor.

In the kitchen, a tall, cadaverous man in a chauffeur's uniform waited silently beside a much shorter, stocky man dressed in a business suit and a raincoat. Both looked up when Theo and Kirkpatrick entered the room.

Wordlessly the short man took Theo's hand; then Kirkpatrick offered a silent farewell. Theo's eyes had adjusted to the darkness, and he followed the short man toward the servants' entrance to the embassy.

The chauffeur preceded Theo out and opened the door of a black limousine that bore the insignia of the American ambassador. With a nod he motioned for Theo to get in, and be quick about it.

Sliding into the backseat of the car, Theo looked up to see that Kirkpatrick had already closed the embassy door. In a moment the chauffeur started the engine and pulled slowly around to the front entrance of the building. Theo did not look out the curtained windows of the vehicle, but he could clearly hear the cries of Berlin's Jews who had gathered outside the embassy gates to beg for asylum. *"Tor auf!"* Then other cries arose—shouts of the men who had pursued them there.

"It will only be a moment, sir." The chauffeur turned his long face to look at Theo. He heard the people too, and his eyes reflected anger and frustration that there was nothing to be done. "We'll have you out of here in no time." Perhaps there was some comfort in the fact that Theo, at least, could be helped. The chauffeur sprang from the car and circled around. A moment later he opened the door and stepped aside as the short man in the raincoat slipped in beside Theo. The door shut quickly behind him.

Once again the short man took Theo's hand. "Ambassador Hopewell." The man smiled. "We'll give you a lift to the airfield." His handshake was as warm as his eyes. "They're quite intimidated by us Americans, these Nazis are." He seemed pleased. "I'll be flying with you to London tonight."

Theo barely managed to repress a shudder. He felt the nearness of those who would not be leaving Berlin by their own free will tonight.

"Tor auf!"

If he looked out the window, would he see the faces of friends and family pleading to go with him? Such a thought robbed him of any relief he might have felt.

The climb over the wall was easy. Alfie wondered why he had not done it before. Perhaps it was because Mama had always told him to be a good boy; and good boys, she said, obeyed.

Alfie jogged along the wooded lane that wound through the park outside the hospital compound. It was dark, but he could see the bright light of Berlin and the big fire. Home was there somewhere.

The cold stung his bare feet. Sometimes he stumbled and almost fell, but he did not slow down as he ran. Mama had said that he was a good runner. A deer in the forest. A fine strong boy. Here he was not a Dummkopf.

The air cleared his lungs and he was not afraid anymore. The city was ahead. He would go home and get some clothes, and—

Suddenly it came to him that he could not go home. Mama would not be there. She was at New Church. Dead. Alfie stopped running now. He braced himself against a tree and struggled against the confusion that filled his head. "Dummkopf!" he said aloud. What had he been thinking of? He had been so happy that he had forgotten Mama was gone.

But there was still Pastor Ibsen! Pastor would be at New Church. He would be glad that Alfie had come back!

The other children at New Church would be glad to see him, too. Lori had always been nice to him. She did not let other children make fun of him. And Jamie had been his partner in hide-and-seek. Together they had found a dozen places to hide that no one knew about. And Pastor's wife, Frau Helen, had loved Mama. He could still remember the comfort of her hug when Mama had died.

Such thoughts led to a decision as easy as climbing the tree. Alfie would go home to New Church! They would be glad to see him come home.

The American ambassador seemed in no hurry to leave Berlin.

"Turn here!" he ordered the chauffeur, who turned toward the brightest glow on the Berlin horizon. Then he looked sternly at Theo. "The president will ask me what I have seen. I intend to have something to tell him."

And so, like tourists cruising through hell, they viewed the carnage. Theo followed the example of the American and rolled his window down slightly so that he might hear as well as see what was happening.

The largest fire in the city consumed the wealthy Fasanenstrasse Synagogue near the zoo railway station. Clouds of dense smoke rolled up from the three domes of the stone building. The interior of the synagogue was a white-hot furnace; tiles of the roof glowed from the heat that devoured the rafters. Theo did not doubt that passengers arriving by train from the West could clearly see the conflagration. He watched without comment. After all, what could he say at such a sight? Did it matter that he held memories of this place and this city in better times?

The embassy vehicle inched along, hindered by the thousands who gathered in central Berlin. Dozens of men and women rushed into a smashed toy shop in the arcade on Friedrichstrasse to scoop up merchandise.

"Come on! Free Christmas presents!" they shouted.

Theo knew the owner of the elegant little shop. Anna had purchased Elisa's dolls there. Theo wiped a hand over his eyes. *Am I dreaming?* he thought. *Can this be happening?*

Gangs of youths followed the looters, smashing plate-glass windows, glass display cases and counters, partitions, and even leftover toys.

The American car watched the destruction from a discreet distance with the engine still running. Five other shops in the arcade were plundered within minutes of the first.

A short distance away, on the corner of Jaegerstrasse, a second-story pawnshop became the focus of violence. Nazi youths with lead pipes broke the windows and threw fur coats down on the heads of the waiting crowds. Around the corner a tailor's shop was looted. In the doorway the tailor's dummy, with a hat on its head, was hung from the neck. *Gynspan the Tailor* read a sign pinned to the chest.

In front of one magic shop, children lined up, holding broomsticks with string and safety pins tied onto the ends. A policeman laughed as they fished through the broken window for boxes of tricks.

While older boys and young men threw typewriters and furniture out onto the street, another gang wheeled a piano out of a music store and began to play the latest Berlin tunes for the onlookers.

The ambassador sighed heavily, glanced at his watch, and tapped the chauffeur on his shoulder. "I have seen enough," he said. The limousine slid by a shoe store, where myriad laughing men and women sat on the curb and tried on stolen shoes.

These were the scavengers, Theo noted. They came in after the Rollkommandos, the wrecking crews who proceeded from shop to shop under the command of a leader. This was not the spontaneous outbreak the Nazi propaganda machine had been speaking of. From start to finish, it seemed highly organized and well thought out.

"He owns the young people," Theo whispered, heartsick as he gazed at the evil light in their young faces. How thankful he was that his own sons had been forbidden to belong to the Hitler Youth because of their heritage! How grateful he was that they would soon be leaving for American schools, thanks to the help of Murphy's boss, Mr. Trump! Once, Theo had imagined Wilhelm and Dieter as part of Berlin. He had thought they might become businessmen, or maybe belong to the German Reichstag. But now, on this night, he saw the destruction that Hitler had brought to the souls of Germany's young people, and he rejoiced that his sons were not considered worthy to be part of German culture.

Everywhere they passed beatings and arrests; every streetlamp provided a spotlight for a tiny human drama. The audience cheered as Jewish men were kicked and stripped and beaten.

The ambassador hastily scribbled notes, writing down the names of ransacked shops he knew to be owned by Americans. Some official protest could be made based on the destruction of American-owned enterprises—three small businesses among hundreds now in ruins.

Ambassador Hopewell rolled up his window as a shout of "Hang the Jew in his shopwindow" was called by a jeering young man in a Storm Trooper uniform.

"And now we take our leave, eh, Mr. Lindheim?"

Theo nodded curtly. He also raised his window but could not take his eyes from the spectacle.

"You lived here your entire life?" the ambassador asked, many questions summarized in the one. *Has it always been this way with the German people? How did you survive their hatred?*

"Nearly all my life," Theo said in a barely audible voice. "And life was nearly always good here."

The eyes of the ambassador narrowed with doubt. "But how—" He swept his hand toward the flames of a newly lit bonfire of furniture and clothing on the sidewalk. A Jewish couple in their nightclothes wept and begged for mercy in this tableau of horror beyond the window of the limousine. Theo wanted to jump from the car, to drag the couple into the vehicle and speed away. He could do nothing. Nothing but watch and wonder how. . . .

Finally the vehicle turned onto a dark street, an obviously Aryan street. There was no destruction here, only silence and unlit windows.

Finally Theo found an answer for the American. "It is happening because we thought it could never happen here." He looked away at the slumbering houses. "We were naïve. We were asleep. The Christian church was also asleep, Mr. Hopewell. And now we have lost our children and our nation to the darkness of that terrible sleep."

Theo did not look back toward the glowing skyline during the short trip to Tempelhof. The ambassador did not ask him any other questions, but did provide him with an answer as they turned through the gate of Tempelhof Airfield.

"They will not question you," Hopewell said. "We are blackmailing the Nazi thug who will examine your papers." He shrugged. "Sometimes we have to play the game by their rules."

7

The Death of All Hope

Pastor Karl looked in the rearview mirror of his automobile. New Church shone bright in the reflected light of the dying synagogue. He turned onto Friedrichstrasse and glimpsed the torch-bearing gangs in the shopping district eight blocks ahead.

For the first time he regretted his decision to drive the old Damlier-Benz to the Kalner apartment. Even from this distance he could see the shimmer of broken glass on the cobbled street. Crowds of spectators ringed the Storm Troopers as they hefted stones through plate-glass windows and doused heaping piles of furniture and merchandise with kerosene. Suddenly bonfires blazed on the boulevards of Berlin's finest shopping district. Ten thousand voices raised in triumphant cheers against the Jews.

Karl slowed and pulled to the curbside. He gripped the steering wheel in astonished horror at the sight unfolding before him.

A fire truck lumbered indolently around the corner of Wilhelmstrasse. It blocked the intersection, helping to hold back the human tide from the government section of the city.

Hundreds of people swarmed the truck, climbing onto the idle equipment to sit beside firemen and watch the planned conflagration.

A group of two dozen rowdies emerged from a side street half a block from Karl's car. They seemed intoxicated with the pleasure of their task, their young faces wild with excitement as they called out to yet another group on the opposite side of the wide street. "Are we too late here?"

"Never too late until every Jew is dead!" came the reply. "Heil Hitler!"

"The next block over!" shouted another young man.

Karl tugged the brim of his hat low over his forehead and walked toward them. They appeared no older than Lori, no older than Jacob Kalner, whom they would kill with little provocation tonight. The thought made Karl shudder. He wondered if he was too late. *The next side street. The street where the Kalner family lives. The pogrom is just beginning there.*

Karl felt the gaze of a thousand spectators from the apartments above him. Some members of his congregation lived on this street, including two families who left the church when Karl had refused to allow Lori and James to join the Hitler Youth. When he did not expel the non-Aryan members of the congregation from the church, still another spate of defections had occurred.

Karl looked up at the darkened windows of one such home and saw the fires reflected in the glass. He wondered if that man and woman, who had denounced his pro-Jewish policies so loudly, now recognized him and watched. Perhaps they stood just beyond his view and made cynical bets about his purpose for going out on such a night as this: *"There is Pastor Jew-lover. Probably going to the Kalners'."*

Karl quickened his pace. He stepped off the sidewalk to pass around the gang of laughing young men.

The cans of kerosene they carried were all the same: government issued. These young Storm Troopers, dressed in civilian clothes, still sported their military boots. They stood languidly on the street corners, exchanging stories about the old Jewish cloth merchant they had beaten, the daughter they had raped after locking her mother in the closet.

"Teach those pigs a lesson."

A wave of fury washed over Karl. He wanted to shake them, to shout at them. Nazi law made it illegal for Aryans to have physical relations with Jews, but the rape of a Jewish woman was permitted, condoned, even admired.

Karl felt his face flush with shame and anger. He ducked his head and walked even faster, turning down the side street where the Kalner family lived.

He moved into the shadow of a shop entrance and looked for the white Hebrew lettering required by all Jewish shops. He had managed to duck into the doorway of an Aryan shop. Breathing a sigh of relief, he took a moment to think, to study the window shades of Dr. Richard Kalner's apartment. No movement. No light. The place looked vacant from the street. Karl wondered if they were there. Had they sat in the dark and let the telephone ring in their fear that the Gestapo would be calling to check on Richard's whereabouts? Karl frowned at the thought. He wished they had foreseen this. That they had devised some sort of telephone signal in the event of just such a night. But then, who could have imagined this?

The shrieks of Jewish victims echoed up the dark street. There was not much time. Karl stepped from the shadows and half jogged across the street to the three-story apartment building. He looked to the right and the left. The Nazis, preoccupied with the beating and arresting of a father and son, did not notice him. Haberdashers. Karl knew them. He had purchased his hat at their store. He touched his fingers to the hat brim in a gesture of futility and frustration. Another ten minutes and the Nazis would be here, breaking down this front door, beating Richard and Jacob, and doing whatever they pleased to Leona Kalner.

Karl charged through the door. He considered the elevator but did not want to wait. Taking the stairs two at a time, he reached the third-floor apartment in a matter of seconds. He stood panting for a moment, then knocked softly. He waited. There was no light under the door. Two newspapers lay outside the threshold. Perhaps the Kalners really had left town.

"Richard," he whispered hoarsely. "Richard. Leona. It is Pastor Karl. Are you there?"

Ten seconds passed. There was no response. He raised his hand to knock again. Then the door opened, and the dark silhouette of Richard Kalner appeared, half concealed by the door. His long arm reached out and grasped Karl by the lapel of his heavy coat, pulling him in and quickly shutting the door behind him.

"Pastor Karl!" Leona was weeping softly.

"What are you doing here?" Richard sounded angry.

Karl rubbed a hand over his face. Relief and fear flooded him. He had hoped there would be nothing more to do than return to the church and report that they had slipped away.

"Get your things. N-no—" he stammered—"no. Best you don't bring anything more than a toothbrush. Thank God you are all right. They're coming. We have a few minutes at most. Come on!"

"We decided not to go to the church," Leona said in the dark. She did not get up from the couch.

"You are in enough trouble already." Richard's voice sounded near to tears. He had not let go of Karl's coat. "Now get out of here, Karl!"

"Not without you. No time to discuss it. Where are the boys?"

"We aren't going," Richard said firmly. "Get out of here. If they are coming and they find you here—" He did not finish the thought.

"A dozen are already at the church. I cannot be in any more trouble than I am already—unless I let you face this alone. Then I will have the Lord to answer to."

"He is more merciful than the Nazis," Richard said. "Now go back."

"You have five minutes," Karl insisted, breaking free of Richard's grip. "Get the boys. I am not going back without you."

They stood in the dark surrounded by silence, except for the approaching sounds of breaking glass and screams and shouts of exultation.

Leona stood. "Richard?" she pleaded.

"I am not like the others at the church," Richard said. "I am a political. Once a member of the Reichstag. Already I have been arrested. This time they will not let me off so easy, Karl. You do not want me at the church."

Karl turned to Leona. She seemed fragile in the half light. "Get the boys, Leona," Karl ordered. "There is no more time for discussion."

She obeyed him, as if she had been waiting and praying for someone to come for them.

Richard also appeared relieved. "Take them, then. But I must stay here. I am a danger to whoever helps me." He shrugged. "I had already instructed Jacob and Mark to go to you if the Gestapo came."

"I can hide you, Richard." Karl ran a list of places through his mind as Leona called to her sleeping sons in the attic. "For Leona's sake, Richard. For my sake. We need to try until we can find some way to get you out of this."

The violence in the street grew more insistent; there could be no question that the men were coming here. Yes. Dr. Richard Kalner was on their list.

Sleepy voices echoed from the attic crawl space.

"What?"

"What is it, Mama?"

"Is it over?"

"Come down," Leona instructed calmly. "We are going to New Church. Pastor Karl has come for us."

"Papa too?" Mark asked.

"Papa too," said Leona.

Richard moaned softly at that, then nodded. "All right." He ran his hand through his hair and gathered up their coats. "Dear God . . . Karl."

At that moment there came the explosion of shattering glass directly below. Then a stone smashed through the window.

Leona gave a little cry. "No! Oh, no!" And then, "Jacob! Mark! The Gestapo!"

Karl grabbed Richard's hand and checked the bolt on the door.

Wordlessly the two men moved into the bedroom to stand beside Leona. She wept and trembled silently. Richard put his arms around her.

She buried her face against him as shouts and obscenities followed still more stones through the window.

"We know you are in there! Hey, Jew-pig! Richard Kalner! We know you are there!"

The thump of jackboots sounded against the stairs. They were taking the steps two at a time, just as Karl had. An instant later Nazi fists and crowbars hammered against the thin wood of the apartment door.

Shouts and curses resounded from below. Jacob slammed his hand against the latch and thrust back the skylight. A shower of ash and soot descended through the opening as he hefted Mark up and then pulled himself out onto the slick slate roof.

Carefully he lowered the window back into place, shutting off the sound of blows and the cries of his mother. Mark was crying. Tears streaked the dust on his face. Again and again he called, first for his mother and then for his father as Jacob dragged him away along the ridgeline of the steep roof.

In the streets the voices of a thousand tormentors and victims covered the boy's cries. His small agony was lost beneath the howling of the night. Jacob did not try to quiet his little brother. He simply held tightly to his arm and propelled him away. From one building to the next, jumping over the narrow gaps, sliding down one roof and creeping up another. Always he moved toward the dark streets, the quiet streets, where *they* had not yet come.

In the distance he could see the illuminated stone figures atop the Brandenburg Gate. A block from there he could make out the Storm Troopers beating people outside the gates of the British Embassy. Tiny human figures in the streets below cringed beneath the blows and fell onto the glass-strewn sidewalks.

"Why don't they fight back?" Jacob cried in rage and frustration. He dragged Mark into the shadow of a chimney. Holding tightly to his brother, Jacob leaned against the warm brick and tried to think what they must do next. He peered cautiously around the corner of their hiding place. No one had followed them. For the moment they were safe, but how would they get down? Which would be the safest route to New Church? Throughout the city he could see the orange glow of fires. Yet some streets were still dark, sleeping on as if nothing were happening, as if hell itself had not come to earth.

Smoke lay thick across the rooftops. Jacob's eyes burned and watered.

"They were hurting Mama, Max!" Mark sobbed. "They hurt her!

I want to go back! I want to . . ." His breath came in short spasms of anguish as he replayed the scene.

"I have to think!" Jacob shouted, feeling the crushing weight of responsibility and fear. He had not imagined that it would come to this. Now he was truly in charge. His brother's safety depended on him. He stared, transfixed, at the leaping flames of the dying synagogue. He had never been in the building before, and yet those flames singed his heart. He clenched his fists, again wishing that he could stand and fight them. But he could not. He must run and hide for Mark's sake, for the sake of the promise he had made to Papa.

"What will we do?" Mark cried. "Oh, Max! What will we do?"

In reply Jacob removed his belt and made a loop that he fastened around Mark's wrist. He then tied the other end around his own wrist, cuffing them to each other.

He put his big hand on Mark's shoulder. "First you must stop crying," he said firmly. "We must go down to the street."

"No!" Mark shook his head in terror.

"Listen to me!" Jacob cuffed him impatiently. "We *must* go down. If we stay here they will see us and know that we are Jews. They will shoot at us."

"In the streets they will catch us! Please, Max!" Mark crouched lower against the bricks as if he wanted to disappear into the chimney.

"We are going down. Going to New Church. If you cry, they will see your tears and they will know. You must not cry, Mark! Do you hear me?"

This did not stop the flow of tears. "But they have got Mama and Papa, and they will come for us at New Church, too!"

"Then we will fight them at New Church! But we must go down. We *must* get to the street and walk through them. You cannot cry! They will beat you if they see you are frightened. They will know what we are!" He removed his handkerchief and gruffly wiped the tears and soot from the cheeks of his brother. "We cannot be babies," Jacob warned. "Tonight we must be brave!" He said the words convincingly, although he did not feel very brave.

Mark wiped his nose on his sleeve. He tried to smile, but his eyes betrayed his misery. He nodded. He would not cry in front of the Nazis. *He must not!*

Jacob patted him gently and pointed toward the dormer window leading to the attic of the Thieste office building. Perhaps the window was unlocked. They could get off the roof and sneak down the stairs.

The drone of an airplane engine passed overhead as the boys crept along the ridge of the roof. Jacob looked up, resenting and envying the freedom of flight. For an instant he wondered what it would be like to

launch himself and Mark from the steep roof, to fly free for a few seconds and then be free forever! The thought made him pause and peer
out over the edge.

"What is it?" Mark cried in alarm, as if he could see the terrible
thought pass through Jacob's mind.

Jacob observed the blinking lights of the plane that passed far above
the smoke and the terror of the German revenge. He watched the plane
as it circled and passed over the city once again. Then Jacob shook himself free of the force that urged him to fly away forever.

Without answering Mark, he crept forward again, straddling the roof,
bracing himself on the slick shingles lest he slip and take his brother
over the edge with him.

Great plumes of illuminated smoke rose in the night sky over the city of
Berlin. The British transport plane circled back over the city for one last
astonished look after takeoff.

Theo Lindheim rubbed a hand across the stubble of his unshaven
face as he gazed wearily down on the city that had once been his home,
the nation he had loved.

In some quarters shone the even lines of streetlamps—the calm of a
city asleep. But in other neighborhoods, different, brighter lights
glowed. A group of small sparks rushed together in the center of one
street before dispersing again. On another corner the sparks merged to
transform a building, a shop, a synagogue, into a brilliant orange and
yellow flower that grew upward into the night sky.

The facades of Protestant churches and Catholic cathedrals were illuminated by the raging infernos that consumed the great synagogues of
Berlin.

Theo pressed his forehead against the glass of the windowpane and
watched the blossoming fires. There were far too many to count. The
meaning of Hermann Göring's warning became clear: *"That is you, burning out there, Theo Lindheim. All your thoughts. Everything you are. See how
the flames of our fury consume you. And you are dying there."*

Surely this night was the death of all hope that reason might prevail
in Germany. The words shrieked by Hitler now took human form:
"Juden! Verrecken! Jews perish!"

Theo Lindheim was the messenger Göring had chosen to tell the
Jews of the world: *"You blacken and shrivel and perish! Take word of your
death back to England! Tell them you have witnessed the death of your God
and yourself tonight!"*

Was he to carry the message that there was no hope, no justice? Was he to cry to an unhearing world, to live his last days in the knowledge that the nations had turned silently away while millions died?

The sorrow of such a task was almost more than Theo could bear. A physical pain clutched his heart, and silently he cried out to God for some other answer.

Berlin dropped to the horizon behind the retreating airplane. Other glowing cities appeared out of the darkness. Another and another and still more.

What do you see, Theo?

Theo turned to answer, startled to find that the others on the plane were sleeping soundly.

What do you see? The voice was clear, nearly audible above the drone of the engines. Theo knew the voice well; he had heard it speak before in other dark hours.

Theo studied the chaos below and answered in a whisper, "Destruction, fire, division—the death of justice and mercy."

They have turned from My truth and from My people. All the things they do to others will come upon them and their children. The voice was not angry, but filled with sadness and certainty of what was to come to the people of Germany.

Grief struck deep in Theo's heart. Germany had, after all, been his home. "But not forever, Lord," he pleaded.

Tell Me the date, Theo. The voice spoke gently.

For a moment Theo could not remember times or dates, as though years meant nothing and time did not exist. Was he sleeping like the others on the plane? Was this a dream? "November," he replied haltingly. "November 9, 1938."

Remember the date. From this night there will be fifty years of judgment; then they will remember this night and all their sins. For one year they will pray and repent, and after that will come a Day of Jubilee when I will break down the walls. Many will call upon My name, and I will answer. I will forgive.

Theo leaned his cheek against the cool windowpane and looked down over Germany. The entire horizon seemed to be in flames, hours before the light of dawn.

Fifty years? For Theo that meant an entire lifetime. He would not live to see the fulfillment of that hope. And how many others would vanish between this terrible night and the promised night in a far-distant future?

"But what should we do now?" Theo asked imploringly.

No answer came—only the monotonous drone of the engines as the plane slid toward the borders of the Third Reich.

8

No Quiet Place

Armed only with a child's crayon and a piece of paper, Captain Samuel Orde made his frontal attack on the terrorists hiding in the Arab villages beyond Hanita.

> PLEASE IDENTIFY ATTACHED CORPSE KILLED DURING
> TERRORIST ACTIVITIES AGAINST HANITA.
> SIGNED, SAMUEL ORDE, CAPTAIN
> BRITISH COMMAND, HANITA

He pinned the note onto the coat of the dead Arab and glared at the men of Hanita who gathered around him.

"This"—he pointed to the body—"is the reason I will not take the atheists along on any sortie against the enemy. Look at him!" He seemed angry. "This could be you. His body is dust. His immortal soul now regrets the wickedness of his life!" He glared at Moshe and then at each observer in turn. "Think about it."

The men exchanged astonished looks. Samuel Orde preached with the zeal of a prophet in the wilderness. Some were angered by his boldness, but most were simply surprised.

Orde opened the trunk of his staff car and spread out a canvas tarp. With a jerk of his thumb, he instructed the four men chosen for tonight's action to load the body into the car. He bowed his head and prayed for the family of the fallen enemy and for the safety of the coming mission, but not for the dead Arab. It was too late to pray for him.

With a resounding *amen*, echoed by a handful of the uneasy men,

Orde issued a Webley revolver to each of the four troopers. This astounded those who watched and envied the lucky few who were privileged to carry such a weapon. Orde presented one bullet per gun to his troops and ordered them into the car. Without explanation, he sped off down the road toward the village.

Moshe watched and waited at the gate with the others as the red taillights grew small and then disappeared behind a cloud of dust.

No one spoke. They stood with arms crossed over their chests and stared off into the darkness, listening and hoping, and considering the eccentric English soldier who thumped his Bible with one hand and his enemies with the other. Definitely odd.

Fifteen minutes passed. Zach consulted his watch. "They should be near the village now."

"The question is not where, but why," another remarked.

"Four bullets," added another puzzled voice.

Moshe started to remark that it was not so very far from this place that Gideon had routed the enemy using only clay pots and trumpets, but at that moment, a distant shot rang out. Then another and another echoed from the hills and wadis until it sounded like a hundred guns firing at once.

The men of Hanita stepped forward in alarm. The last echoes died away, and still these men stood transfixed and frightened by what they heard.

"They must have been ambushed," said Artur glumly, his face again streaked with tears.

"Fifty Arab Moquades." Zach frowned and shook his head sadly. "I knew the Englishman was a fool. Now he has gotten more of us killed."

Moshe did not speak. He was glad he had not mentioned Gideon in the face of such a massacre by Arab gangs along the road.

"Should we go after them?" Artur held up his gun.

"Do you want to die as well?" Zach demanded.

Artur did not answer; Moshe thought that perhaps this fellow did indeed want to die.

"What else can we do?" Artur said. "We asked for help from the English, and they send us this reject from a Gentile Yeshiva school!" He was raging now, pacing back and forth in front of the gate. "Shall we call the British army and tell them that their preacher has just been killed by fifty Arab raiders? Tell us what to do?"

"He's right," agreed two grim-faced settlers who still had blood on their shirts from carrying Sharon and Lazlo in from the fields. "What did those British think they were doing? They send us a crazy fanatic! He preaches the Bible to the People of the Book, and then he gets more of us killed!"

An angry murmur filled the night air. "What did they expect one lousy man to do? What use is one English soldier to us anyway?"

They debated further about whether to call in the British to retrieve the bodies from the road. It would have to be done in daylight. That much was agreed to.

Then a small double light swept up over a distant hill and down again. Was that an English vehicle? a truck? Had the British soldiers come upon the ambush?

Moshe stepped out of the crowd and walked toward the end of the dirt road that led from Hanita to the highway. Again the lights rose up and then disappeared behind a hill.

Zach stood at his elbow. "What do you think?"

Moshe managed a smile. "Captain Orde's staff car," he said in a low voice.

"You are certain?"

"The right headlight is off a bit. He bumped it going around a narrow corner in Jerusalem. It is Orde, all right."

The others rushed forward with a cheer as the vehicle turned onto the lane. Hands reached out to thump the battered vehicle as it passed through them and entered the compound.

Orde set the brake, turned off the engine, and stepped out of the car to face the same thumping as his battered car.

"You're back!"

"Of course." He frowned. "What did you think?"

"You made it!"

"Were there many of them?"

Orde shrugged off the queries and scratched his head languidly. "You'll have a briefing in the morning," he said gruffly. "But for now, I am in need of sleep. My quarters?"

Enthusiasm waned as Orde stalked off to a tent set up especially for him. The others, including Orde's four troopers, retired to the camp kitchen, where a briefing took place in spite of the commander's absence.

Over cups of coffee, they considered the events of the evening and this strange English soldier.

"What happened?" Zach demanded that Larry Havas, an American from Cleveland, give the details of the sortie.

"Like I said, he dumped the body at the entrance to the village. Arranged it like he was laying a stiff out in a coffin. Hands folded over the note. Pointed the index finger at the writing. It looked like the guy was pointing at the note, you know? They won't miss it."

"And then?"

Larry shrugged. "Orde said, 'Gideon routed the Philistines not far from here. Great acoustics.' And then he sort of spread us out along the road. One on each hill. He fired first. We fired at five-second intervals." He grinned sheepishly. "Guess we woke up the neighbors."

Moshe considered Zach Zabinski for a moment. With his receding hairline and countenance of a scholar, thin and fine-boned, Zach did not have the look of a man in charge of a settlement of three hundred. His sunburned face displayed the sensitivity of one better suited to working in a library than plowing the hard fields of Palestine. Moshe guessed that such a face seldom smiled, but tonight Zach smiled slowly and raised his eyebrows in appreciation.

"We asked ourselves what one man can do," Zach said with a shake of his head. "They will think we have an army here. And the Muslims are not so eager to go to Paradise . . . or hell . . . quickly. Our Englishman has bought himself some time, I would say."

"Do you trust him?" asked Dori Samuels.

Zach nodded. "When he looks us in the eye and talks about Zionism and God, I believe him. When he walks away or drives down the road, I wonder about his motives. We asked for a troop of British men to defend us. We got one man. Maybe he is as good as a troop. We will see."

Larry Havas laughed again. "All the way out there the guy quoted to us from Isaiah—he's more Zionist than Ben-Gurion!"

"But effective," Moshe interjected, conscious that he was an outsider, but more aware of Samuel Orde's methods than the others were. "I saw him in action against the Mufti in Jerusalem. He is all he seems to be, and more. I am sure of his sincerity." Moshe's eyelids sagged, heavy from the long trip and the unending tension since their arrival here.

"Some say he is responsible for the death of your brother," Zach said, testing Moshe's defense of the Englishman.

"My brother was responsible for his own death," Moshe said flatly. "Captain Orde brought me here for protection, and I will not be so foolish as my brother was to leave him."

"You believe in him, trust him, this Christian fanatic?" Larry sipped his coffee and waited for Moshe's careful reply.

"Entirely."

Zach nodded with resignation. "When you have been plowing all day and repelling snipers and infiltrators all night, and when you have gone out to relieve a sentry post only to find the girl who guarded it dead and mutilated, you are not particularly glad to see strangers. Particularly not British officers; I admit it. I was . . . maybe still am . . . suspicious."

Larry added, "He has the smell of a soldier about him. Maybe he can help. But what we need from the English are real guns with more than one bullet, and the legal right to use them when we are attacked. Tonight he has made the death of an Arab terrorist legal because he signed his name to it. But if I had killed him—or you, or any of us—we would be arrested by the same people Captain Orde works for."

"I will wait and see." Zach sighed. "What else can we do but wait and see?"

As she wandered through Vienna, a flash of emotion ripped through Lucy's dull senses. She had wanted to belong to him forever. Every waking moment had been spent imagining life as the wife of Wolfgang von Fritschauer—little Lucy Strasburg, from a village in Bavaria, wife of a wealthy Prussian aristocrat! But she meant no more to him than the cattle on his estate. She must not let herself love him, even if she longed for him to hold her again.

Her thoughts returned to Wolf. *"Remember who you belong to."* He would not ever let her forget that she belonged to him—body and soul. Lucy was at the mercy of Wolf. He would never let her leave him willingly. If she tried, he would simply have her taken to the Lebensborn, where she would be locked away until the baby was born. *His baby, not mine. The child I carry for him and for the Reich. Pure Aryan sons for the future of the Thousand-Year Reich.*

Shouts and cries of anguish drifted on wisps of smoke, but Lucy did not hear them. The cries of her own heart were too loud to hear anything else.

She had no place to run, no safe haven where she might hide, no refuge where Wolfgang von Fritschauer would not find her. *"Remember who you belong to!"*

Lucy regretted that she had told Wolf the news. Maybe there was still time. Perhaps she could tell him that she had been mistaken, that she was not pregnant. For the first time she considered the possibility of having an abortion. Such a thing would have been simple for her a few years ago. And if she were Jewish, the government would not only encourage it, but pay for the procedure and sterilize her without charge. But she was Aryan. Her family pedigree had been researched before Wolf had even dared to take her into his bed. For an Aryan woman, abortion was forbidden by law and punishable by prison, even death. Beyond that was the higher law of faith—the killing of the unborn was counted as murder by the church. Lucy feared that law and judgment as much as she feared the Nazi racial edicts.

Killing the baby was not an option for her. Lying about the pregnancy to Wolf would be foolish. He wanted everything verified by an SS doctor; to attempt to deceive him would mean that she would be locked inside the SS maternity home immediately. And after the child was born, who could say what would happen to Lucy?

She frowned and stepped back to make room for a gang of young Nazis who pushed a dozen Jews down the sidewalk.

"What are you looking at?" a young Austrian shrieked. He pounded a prisoner across his shoulders. "Pig! It is *verboten* to look at an Aryan woman!"

"I only . . . she is out alone . . . and I . . . this night . . ." The prisoner attempted to explain but was silenced by kicks and blows to the stomach.

Lucy looked up sharply, realizing that she was the reason the man was being beaten. He fell to the ground and lay in his own blood.

In this way the Nazis of Vienna honored her, the perfect Aryan woman. Fair-haired, blue-eyed, striking in beauty, she inspired men to violence and hatred . . . *for a look*!

The terrible irony of it made her suddenly feel ill again. She averted her eyes in shame and hurried on, looking for a quiet place to rest. In all of Vienna, it seemed, there was no quiet place left for anyone.

The beams and timbers of the Red Lion House creaked and groaned in the darkness as if the noise of tonight's party had made the walls ache. Elisa lay awake in the darkness, staring at the ceiling and wondering if she should wake Murphy.

The dream had come to her again tonight. Fresh and terrifying in its detail, she had seen the trains filled with children as they headed into the blackness of the East. On the battered cattle cars, uniformed skeletons had stood guard and laughed when the little ones stretched their arms through the slats and begged for water. Elisa, with one tin cup, had tried to reach them all. She had run beside the train and cried out for help as the water splashed out and fell to the bloodred ground. Only then, when the last drop had spilled, did she wake up.

The grandfather clock in the foyer chimed two o'clock. Elisa reached out and touched Murphy's back, finding comfort in his nearness and warmth. This nightmare had not returned since they moved into the peaceful old house. She had begun to think of herself as free from all that, free from the sense of helplessness she had felt over the suffering of so many. After all, here in London they were doing what they could to ease the suffering. Concerts and benefits and parties like tonight's had netted several thousand dollars in aid for the homeless refugees who still flocked to Prague. Schools for refugee children had formed in southern France. Things were being done that did not require Elisa to risk her own safety or that of the baby she carried.

But in the small quiet hours of this morning, none of it seemed sufficient. She sat up and cradled her head in her hands as images of Berlin and Vienna paraded before her. Timmons had wired that the synagogues were being burned, shops and homes destroyed, men arrested. Berlin. Vienna. Cities she had once called home. The children of her dreams came from those cities.

Elisa heard a stirring in the front room—the sound of feet against the oak plank floor, then padding across the thick Persian carpet in the center of the room. A small knock sounded on the door. Without waiting for a reply, Charles nudged it open and stood silhouetted in the doorframe.

"'Lisa?" he said in a small voice. He was too tired to care how well he formed the words. "I dreamed."

"A bad dream?" She put out her arms to him, drawing him to the bedside and under the covers.

"Uh-huh. Real bad. Lots and lots of men chasing. 'Lisa, can I stay?"

His little toes were ice-cold against her legs. She cuddled him close, holding his feet in her hands. "Yes, you can stay. Don't be afraid," she whispered in German. "You are safe."

"No," he replied in English, "not me and Louis. The men was chasing other kids. I saw them."

So, they had the same dream—similar, anyway. The realization was sobering. "Were you in the dream?" she asked.

"*Ja.* I told them kids to come here. To Red Lion, and we will take care of them."

She smiled in the dark at his answer. At least he felt unthreatened here. "That was a good thing to tell them."

"But, 'Lisa, they couldn't hear me. I was talking in English, and they was German-talking kids, and they can't hear me." He sounded so sad that Elisa wondered if he was still half dreaming.

"Go back to sleep, Charles," she urged gently.

"But I couldn't talk German. Because, you know, my mouth was all—"

"You are safe now, Charles."

"But *they* are not!"

"Then I will tell them myself to come," she whispered, feeling his little body relax. "I will tell them in German so they will hear me . . . *Kommen Sie hier, bitte. Kommen Sie, Kinder . . . ist das gut,* Charles?"

Charles sighed with renewed contentment. "*Sehr gut,* 'Lisa."

Soon his breathing regulated, growing deep and even with sleep. Elisa laid her cheek against the softness of his hair and closed her eyes to pray that he would never again be touched by the darkness that raged through the streets of Germany even now.

There are so many like him, Lord. So many little ones. If there is more that I can do, show me. Show us. Help us.

Jacob and Mark straddled the ridge of the steep roof. A strong breeze whipped them with ash, still warm from the Berlin fires. Fragments of voices blew past them; the curses of Nazis and the cries of their victims blended into an unintelligible chorus.

Jacob halted when the dormer window was ten feet directly below them. A metal rain gutter sloped down the slippery shale roof to provide a handhold.

"Listen," Jacob said as he examined the rusty bolts that held the pipe in place. "We will keep the pipe between us. We must slide down feet-first on our bellies to the roof of the dormer."

Mark swallowed hard and then obeyed, positioning himself with his feet dangling over the steep angle of the roof.

Jacob held up his hand, displaying the belt that linked them. "Don't be afraid. If you slip, I have you."

This was true. Jacob could hold him, Mark knew, but could the pipe support their weight? And what if Jacob slipped? Mark could not hold him. "But what will I do if you slip?"

Jacob laughed as if such a thought was impossible. "Then we will both slide off the roof. Just be sure to aim for the head of a Nazi, *ja?*"

Mark managed a weak smile. Jacob lay down on his stomach and grasped the rain pipe. Carefully he eased himself off the ridge. Mark followed, clinging desperately to the groaning metal of their lifeline.

The leather soles of their shoes slipped against the shingles as they scrambled for footing. A strong hand seemed to grab their ankles, trying to pull them over the edge to fall three stories to the sidewalk.

"Hold tight!" Jacob urged as they inched lower, hand over hand.

The edge of the roof seemed all too near; the fall to the cobblestones seemed too possible. Metal cut into Mark's fingers. The shingles tore at his knees and stomach. He kept his eyes riveted to Jacob's grim face. Their breath rose in a steamy vapor to mingle with the smoke.

"Just a few more feet," Jacob whispered tensely.

Mark looked over his shoulder at the roof of the dormer. Only four feet to its safety. Beyond that was empty space; below he could see men sloshing kerosene into a shop while a crowd watched.

Mark's hands ached from the cold metal. He could not find bracing for his feet. Only hands and arms kept them from sliding off into the abyss.

Jacob did not seem frightened. He slid down another few inches and then waited until Mark followed. "Just a little farther . . ." The words were accompanied by a groaning as the pipe pulled free from its rusted anchors.

"Max!" Mark gasped as his section of the rain pipe bowed and broke free beneath him. He clung tighter to the useless metal as he began to skitter down past Jacob, who struggled to grasp a fragment of still-connected pipe.

"Hold on!" Jacob cried hoarsely as the length of the leather belt snapped taut. Mark dangled crazily at the end, just out of reach of the dormer. Jacob strained to hold him up with one arm while his other hand grasped at the end of the rain pipe.

"Let go of the pipe!" Jacob ordered, his face full of pain and fear as he struggled above Mark. If he could swing his brother to the right, the boy could touch the dormer roof with his feet, slide onto the perch, and . . .

Mark released the metal, which clanged and sparked as it rolled and launched from the roof, tumbling down and down. He reached up and grasped the tether with both hands. He kept his eyes on Jacob's face and on the big hand that clung tightly to the end of the belt while his other hand gripped one remaining anchor in the roof.

"I'm going to . . . swing you over." Jacob's words were halting, pained with exertion. "Get your . . . feet on the roof."

Mark kicked his legs, swimming toward the little island of safety. The toe of his shoe brushed it; then he swung away again, causing Jacob to cry out as if his strength threatened to give out.

"Again!" Jacob urged. "Come on!"

One more swing of his arm to the left and Mark found himself with his feet straddling the peak of the dormer. Still he dangled like a fish on a line below Jacob, but there was at least hope beneath him now.

"I can feel it!" Mark said. His hand was numb from the tight loop around his wrist. "How do I get down?"

"Untie the belt. Drop down."

Untie the belt? Their one link? Mark balked. Although Jacob was in a worse position than he was now, Mark was too frightened to think of letting go. "Max!"

"Untie the belt or you will kill us both!" Jacob whispered back angrily. *"I can't . . . hold . . . on!"* Blood oozed from his fingers where the metal bracket cut into them.

Mark gasped and reached up to fumble with the loop of leather around his wrist. His full weight pulled it tight. The fingers of his free hand could not pry the leather loose. He moaned with fear as he looked up at the exhausted face of his brother. Blood dripped from Jacob's hand onto Mark's cheek.

"Come on!" Jacob cried through gritted teeth.

"I'm trying!" Mark stood on his tiptoes on the dormer, trying to relieve the pressure and ease the weight. His arm felt as if it would break loose from its socket. His fingers dug at the leather, found the barest fraction of give, then finally pulled it loose.

Suddenly free, he fell down hard against the dormer. His feet slipped to the right, and he dangled by one arm just like his brother above him. Mark's throat constricted with fear, but he didn't dare shout.

With a loud thump, Jacob slid down and hit the dormer. Then, without hesitation, he scrambled to pull Mark up beside him. They were safe!

They sat panting atop the little roof. Burning cinders blew past them, and one landed on Jacob's coat sleeve. He did not have the strength to brush it off. Mark slapped it for him and then hung his head and closed his eyes, refusing to look over the edge where they had nearly fallen.

Five minutes passed, then ten. Wrapping his bloody hand in a handkerchief, Jacob spoke at last. "We will break the window and swing in over the top." His eyes were calm, his voice even.

"Break the window?"

Jacob mocked him. "Yes. Break the window. You think anyone will wonder about one more broken window tonight? Look out there—" He swept his injured hand toward the panorama of the city: bonfires in the streets, broken glass shimmering on the boulevards like sunlight on the water.

Without further explanation, Jacob scooted forward until his legs dangled in front of the window. With a hard kick backward, he shattered the panes with the heel of his shoe. Then he looked back at Mark with a smile of smug satisfaction. "Well, then. It seems we have smashed the window of an Aryan-owned business. See, no Star of David?" He raised a finger. "That makes the score Jews, one; Nazis, ten thousand." He grasped the edge of the roof and slid down through the window. "Follow me," he called. "Mind the glass." Jacob reached a hand up to help his brother, who was still almost too frightened to move. "Hurry up!" he coaxed impatiently from inside. "Or I'm leaving without you!"

Mark began to cry again as he lowered himself off the little roof. Jacob clasped him hard by the legs and hefted him into the dark storage attic of the Thieste Building. Then both boys collapsed onto the floor.

9

To Pray and to Fight

The city of Berlin was not like Alfie remembered it. Everywhere there were people. Hitler men were smashing shopwindows and hitting other men. Women reached through the broken windows and took things out! There was shouting and screaming, and Alfie could not think where he was.

His flimsy pajamas were soaked with sweat and covered with mud. He stopped on a street corner. He could not walk any farther because of the glass that sparkled on the sidewalks.

A group of laughing women walked toward him. Their shopping bags were full of clothes and they talked about what they had gotten, like Mama used to chatter about sales and bargains at the stores.

"Look!" shouted a fat lady who pointed at Alfie. "I'll bet he's a Jew!"

"Hey you! Are you a Jew?"

Alfie frowned and stared back at their faces. They had the same mean look as Ugly Mouth when he called Alfie Dummkopf.

"Are you a Jew, boy?" called another woman. "Or only sleepwalking?"

Alfie was much taller than all of them. They made a circle around him and sneered up at him. He thought about breaking through them and running, but there was the glass.

"Answer me!" said the fat woman. "Are you a Jew? Should we call the police to arrest you?"

"I am going to church. But the glass," he said slowly. "I have no shoes."

Peals of laughter rose up. "Well, there's a shoe store with free shoes right across the street. The Jews are having a sale! A giveaway!"

Alfie could see the broken window of the shoe store. Men were sitting on the curb trying on shoes. Maybe if he was careful he could walk around the glass and get a pair of shoes.

"I am not a Jew," Alfie said earnestly. "But I need shoes. *Danke.*" He was polite even though they were not polite. He pushed through them and jumped from one tiny glass-free cobblestone to the next, reaching the curb where the men sat passing shoes from one to another.

"I need shoes, too," Alfie said. "I don't have money."

"These are free, boy!" A jolly man in leather pants reached up and pulled him down to the curb. "A gift from the Jews to the German people."

"That is nice of them," Alfie said. Smoke was stinging his eyes. Someone passed him a nice pair of shoes that were only a little too big, then gray woolen socks. He put them on. The shoes did not have laces, but it did not matter. With the socks they fit just fine.

"Where are the Jews?" Alfie smiled broadly as he stood. He wanted to thank them for the gift. The shoes made him feel as if he could run fast. It had been a long time since he had new shoes.

In answer to his question the men at the curb roared with laughter. "Where are the Jews, he says?" They did not answer Alfie and he was ashamed that he asked. They all knew the answers. Why was he so dumb?

Shirts and trousers and coats came flying out of the broken windows along the broad avenue. Other people were out in their pajamas, too. A big crowd of men and women wandered about with the cuffs of pajamas and nightgowns showing out the bottom of their coats. Some people dressed in the street—right on the sidewalk they pulled trousers over their nightclothes and then walked on and put on another layer.

Alfie found trousers, too big at the waist. He picked up a heavy coat, too short in the sleeves. "Where are the Jews?" he asked. "Why are those men hurting those people there?"

No one took the questions of this big teenage boy seriously. Everyone knew where the Jews were, after all! Alfie was the only one in Germany who wanted to thank them for the clothes.

Explosions continued at regular intervals throughout the long night. Even as the gray Vienna dawn seeped in around the window shade, two more charges roared in quick succession to demolish the last of Vienna's synagogues.

Peter had fallen asleep with his head on his mother's lap. He opened his eyes only when his baby brother cried and Marlene wandered out in her nightgown. She rubbed her eyes and stood blinking at Peter and her mother, who were fully dressed.

"What is going on?" She made a face at the smell of smoke. The steady drone of a truck passed on the street below. Three rapid pops of rifle fire sounded from somewhere in the distance. "Mama?" Marlene asked again. "Why are you dressed?"

Peter sat up and eyed the rumpled form of his sister with sibling contempt. "Leave it to Marlene. The Nazis are blowing apart our world and she can only ask why we are dressed."

Marlene's expression changed from sleepy confusion to fear. "Mama? What does he mean?" She stared at the window, afraid to look beyond the backlit shade.

Karin Wallich chose her words carefully. "A pogrom, Marlene. But we are safe here. They will not think to look for us here." She glanced at the clock. Not yet six o'clock. The riots had been in progress only a few hours, yet it seemed like days since she had awakened Peter. "Go back to bed, Marlene," she instructed as if the event was not at all unusual.

Marlene walked numbly toward the window shade. Peter sprang up and blocked her. She tried to go around him, suddenly desperate to see what was outside. Peter grabbed her by the arms and she cried out, although he had not hurt her.

"I want to see!" Her screeching whine set Peter's teeth on edge.

"Marlene!" Karin was up, wide-awake and filled with fresh fear as she pushed her daughter away. "You must not—*must not*—go near the window until they are finished!"

"They can smell a little Jewish girl," Peter snarled. "You want these Aryans to catch a whiff of you and—"

Karin turned on him now, angered by the cruelty in his voice. She raised her chin, ordering him with a look to be silent. Marlene whimpered, rubbing her arm where Peter had grabbed her.

"He hurt me," she sniffed. "I only wanted to—"

"You can let her go out there as far as I'm concerned!" Peter scowled at her. Marlene could not take anything. Mother shielded her, protected her, pampered her, even though their peaceful world was irrevocably shattered.

Peter sat down heavily on the sofa and stared at the photograph of Adolf Hitler that hung on the wall above the radio. Herr Ruger had apologized for the picture, explaining that it was only for show in case the Gestapo should ever come with their list of questions. For this same reason, Herr Ruger wore the Nazi armband and said "Heil Hitler" as naturally as he had once said *"Grüss Gott."* After Peter's father had been taken,

Herr Ruger had given Peter an armband as well in case he had to travel outside his own neighborhood. He was a strange man, this Otto Ruger.

Karin Wallich was still uncertain of Herr Ruger. He seemed to move altogether too naturally among those who now set explosive charges around the support pillars of the synagogues and doused the floors with kerosene and laughed as they lit their pipes and tossed their matches into the buildings. She did not trust his paternal interest in Peter; she deplored the swastika armband slipped into her son's pocket. And yet, last night, she had no choice but to obey the instructions he had left with Peter.

"If there is even a whiff of trouble in the air, you must bring your mother and sister and brother to my apartment. It is the season for violence again. The season of martyrs."

Herr Ruger had proved to be right. His knowing disturbed Karin Wallich most. She had expressed her doubts to Peter, but they had come to Ruger's apartment anyway.

"There now, Marlene," Karin soothed her daughter. "You are just tired. The noise awakened you. Go back to sleep and when you wake, we can go home again."

Peter leaned back against the sofa and closed his eyes as his mother led Marlene back into the bedroom. How he longed for sleep—sleep without dreams, without warnings that played in his own mind. He really despised his little sister, yet she was now his responsibility. Father had told him it might come to this—Peter in charge of protecting Mother, Marlene, and baby. Such responsibility had come too soon. Eight months ago, before the Nazis marched into Austria, Peter would have welcomed being a man. Now, with the arrest of his father, Peter wished only for his lost childhood to return. But the scene beyond the window shade convinced him—that dream was gone forever.

Of course Wolfgang von Fritschauer had an extra key to Lucy's apartment. He had found the apartment for her, after all, and in the beginning he had spent as much time here as he had in his own quarters. But Lucy had not expected to see him this morning. Not after the things he had said to her last night. Somehow she had not expected to see him ever again—except perhaps to place her baby in his arms and watch him walk away.

He stood over her bed, swaying slightly as if he had been drinking. His hat and overcoat were already off when Lucy realized that she was not dreaming.

"Wolf?" she asked sleepily.

He did not reply but sat down on the edge of the bed. His uniform was impeccable, but there were flecks of blood on his face. *Is it his own blood?* she wondered briefly.

He began to unbutton his tunic as if he had the right. He motioned for her to move over. "I have been working all night near here. Too tired to go home." He did not ask permission, simply pulled off his boots and lay down beside her. She did not protest when he reached out for her. After all, what did it matter now? What was done was impossible to undo. Was that hell beyond the Danube any fiercer because he had come to her as he always did, and she did not send him away?

Only the hell of this moment mattered to her now. Somehow the nearness of Wolf made her existence seem less terrible. She was grateful that he wanted her, even if he did not love her. Now she would not wonder or hope. *"No expectations,"* he had said. *"No commitments."*

Within her remained only despair and physical hunger for him. With her hopes and dreams for the future reduced to ashes, no illusions were left. And so she yielded to his desire just like any other woman who worked the back streets of the Seventh District.

Later, Lucy felt awake for the first time since she had met the handsome SS officer over a year ago in Munich. She lay beside him, studying his features as he slept. Always she had interpreted his cold expression as the smile of an aristocrat, the look of a man who was better than other men. And also better than her. Now she watched his thin lips and pictured the smile again. *Cruel and distant. Charming only when he had something to gain.* She had feared the aloofness of his smile. She had melted in its charm. But now that she knew the truth of it, she would never again cringe beneath it or be wooed by it.

Yes, Wolf was the picture of Aryan physical perfection. But then, so was she, wasn't she? Wasn't that why he had chosen her? In this way they were equals. The realization gave her confidence; she would not be afraid of his disapproval any longer.

For the first time she wondered what his wife looked like. Maybe she would ask him, wonder out loud to him about the woman who would take her baby from her.

Lucy's heart felt cold and distant as she watched the sleeping form of the man she had loved so deeply. She did not hate him; she simply viewed him as he must view her. He was someone she would use, as she had been used. She would make her smile into a reflection of his smile. And her hands would no longer tremble in his presence.

At all costs, she knew she must not go to the SS maternity home. She must somehow remain free in Vienna until she could win her freedom in another place.

The gate of Lebensborn was locked on both sides—on the inside to keep lovers out, and on the outside to keep the women in.

She studied Wolf's profile in the semidarkness. This man demanded instant gratification of his desires. She must make him see that the lock on Lebensborn would deny him access to that satisfaction. She must sell herself to buy precious time.

Early morning found the violence in Berlin undiminished. Thousands of shops to be wrecked, after all. What was sleep compared to the thrill of destroying in one night what it had taken generations to build in Germany?

Jacob and Mark woke to the sound of a fire truck clanging wildly past the Thieste Building. Fire had spread from a Jewish-owned shop to an Aryan building, and several trucks rushed to the scene.

"Where are we?" Mark raised his head to blink in confusion at the strange surroundings. File cabinets, stacks of boxes, and unused office furniture were piled everywhere. Mark and Jacob had fallen asleep near a large wooden desk with chairs stacked on it. There was no light except for the ever-present illumination of the fires.

"The Thieste Building." Jacob sat up slowly and crawled over to peer out the window they had come through hours before.

"Ah." Mark remembered; the memory brought a renewed stab of worry for their parents. "Can we go back home?" he asked miserably.

Jacob did not reply. He simply stared down at the wreckage beneath them. The street had not yet been touched when the boys had slid in to the attic. Now it was smashed as if a bomb had exploded. People walked through it, picking over the merchandise that had been thrown into the street. On the corner, men with guns surrounded a group of two hundred Jewish men. A truck was waiting to carry them away. *Away to where?*

Jacob scanned the tiny figures for some sign of his father and Pastor Karl. Were they down there? And what had happened to Mother?

"We're going to New Church. Father told us to go there; if Mother is free, she will look for us at New Church."

The thought of seeing his mother renewed Mark's energy. He jumped to his feet and picked his way through the cluttered attic to the stairs. He reached for the light switch, but Jacob stopped him.

"The building may have a watchman," Jacob warned.

"He will be out stealing with the rest of them," Mark said, but they made their way through the office building without light all the same.

In the lobby, a single lamp burned at the vacant desk of the night watchman. Jacob nudged Mark hard, and they ducked behind the banister at the foot of the stairs.

He jerked his thumb toward the glass doors leading from the building. Outside, the watchman leaned against a pillar and smoked a pipe as he placidly watched the looting of a shoe store across the street.

"How will we get out?" Mark asked.

In reply, Jacob took his hand and simply walked across the lobby and through the doors. The watchman did not see where they had come from, but he turned and raised his pipe in acknowledgment. His eyes swept over the two boys in amusement.

"*Guten Morgen,*" he greeted them. "It looks as though you two have been in the thick of the fray." His glance lingered on the blood-soaked handkerchief wrapped around Jacob's hand.

Jacob nodded curtly and raised the hand with an air of nonchalance. "Plenty of glass broken last night. I got careless." He kept walking, pulling wide-eyed Mark after him.

"A battle scar." The old watchman laughed. "You can tell your grandchildren you got it the night we taught the Jews in Germany a lesson, eh?"

Jacob managed a laugh and stepped off the curb to hurry away through the ruins toward New Church. This time Mark did not cry. Terror and exhaustion had left him numb, and he followed Jacob like a sleepwalker.

The entire city crawled with looters. No one attempted to stop the thieves. In the frantic scramble of Aryan citizens to snatch useful items from the bonfires, no one paid any attention to two soot-covered boys walking briskly toward New Church.

Jacob prayed that they would not come face-to-face with anyone who knew them, who knew they were Jewish. In the past two years hardly a day had passed without some arrogant Hitler Youth gang confronting Jacob. Lately they had been careful not to challenge him without several members on hand to help out. He had beaten every boy his age in an eight-block radius. Tonight those familiar faces were nowhere to be seen. Jacob guessed, correctly, that they were busy in another neighborhood of Berlin.

The people they passed on Friedrichstrasse were strangers to them. Jacob looked at the eager faces of these noble members of the super race. Many of them, with their dark eyes and hair, fit the Nazi caricature of a Jew much better than either Mark or Jacob. Both boys were fair skinned and fair haired. Mark had curly hair, which was a sign of Jewish origin according to propaganda, but other than that, their faces were just faces. Jacob unconsciously touched his crooked nose, the nose of a street brawler. Together with his fierce green eyes, it marked him as a young man to be careful of.

This dirt-caked, angry face cut a swath through the Aryan populace this morning. The defiance in his eyes made even grown men step around him. If anyone had looked down into the younger boy's eyes, they would have seen a different story. Confusion, shock, fear for his parents filled Mark's face, marking him as a victim. But Jacob met every glance with an angry glare. Such a look could only exist in the eyes of a leader of the Hitler Youth. And so no one stopped them. No one asked why they were roaming the streets of Berlin at four in the morning. Their purpose was clear enough.

"Be there!" Jacob slammed his fist on the locked door of New Church. "Be there!" he growled again impatiently.

From the other side of the door he could just hear Lori Ibsen's muffled voice. "Who is there?"

"It's me, Jacob Kalner. Me and Mark. Let us in!" He looked back nervously, hoping that no one had seen them scale the stone fence of the churchyard.

He leaned heavily against the door, as if he could melt through the thick wood. Lori fumbled with the latch until it clicked open and the two boys fell into the church. Instantly a crowd gathered around them, firing questions from every side.

"Where is Papa?"

"Pastor Karl?"

"Why did Richard and Leona not come with you?"

"Are they following after?"

Mark began to weep again. He shook with sobs, unable to speak, but giving the terrible answer by his tears.

Frau Helen enfolded the little boy in her arms and gazed steadily into the sooty face of Jacob. "Where is my husband? Where is Pastor Karl? Did he make it to your flat?"

Jacob nodded. Overcome with exhaustion, he groped for a place to sit down. "He came," Jacob said dully. "He was going to bring us all back here."

"Then the Gestapo . . ." Mark sniffed and buried his face against Frau Helen's sleeve. "They banged on the door and broke it. They hurt Mama. I heard them."

"There was no chance for them to get away," Jacob explained. "They arrested Mama and Papa and Pastor Karl. Mark and I went out through the skylight. Over the rooftops."

Lori stepped forward. Even in the dim light of the church Jacob could see an angry glint in her eyes. Her fists were clenched as if she wanted to hit someone. This was one of the things Jacob admired about Lori Ibsen.

If she had been born a boy, no doubt they would have fought each other. Or perhaps they would have fought side by side against the Hitler Youth. This morning Lori looked strong in spite of her slender figure. "Where have they taken them?" she demanded. "We will go after them. Tell the Gestapo they have made a mistake. Your parents are Christians. My father is a pastor. They have made a mistake."

From a dark pew a woman snorted in ridicule at the words. "The Nazis do not make mistakes. It does not matter, Lori, who is a Christian. What matters is who is not a Nazi."

Frau Helen stared up at the rose window above the altar as though there might be an answer written there for her. "What to do, Lord?" she whispered.

Jacob said sternly, "You cannot go out there, Frau Helen. You must not think of it."

"But if I can find where they have taken them—"

Mark clung tighter to her. Jacob shook his head in disagreement. "We have seen what they are doing. Sooner or later the Nazis will grow tired, but right now they are still wrecking everything in sight, arresting everyone who questions them—not only Jews; do you understand? We should stay here. If they release my mother, she will come here and tell us. If Pastor Karl is set free, he will come home. We should stay here."

Jacob had not mentioned the possibility of his father being released. That would not happen—not without payment of a big fine, like the last time. But the Kalner family had no money left to pay the Nazi jailers; Richard Kalner might never be released. For Mark's sake Jacob did not say these things, but all night long the terrible reality of the situation had played over and over in his mind.

Frau Helen let her breath out slowly. She put her hand on Lori's arm, then touched her face. Lori's cheeks were wet with tears of frustration.

"Jacob is right, Lori," she said softly. "Your father will come here. We must be here to meet him when he comes."

Two cots stood in the newest tent in Hanita—one for Captain Orde, the other for Moshe Sachar. Moshe crept quietly to his cot. He was certain that the English captain heard him and was aware of his presence. Nothing, it seemed, slipped past Orde. And yet Orde pretended not to hear Moshe until he slipped beneath his blankets.

Then, as Moshe stared up at the black canvas, Orde spoke. "Well?"

Moshe frowned. "Well what?"

"What did they think of tonight's mission?"

"They are somewhat impressed. Somewhat suspicious. They definitely think you are a real . . . what is the American word?"

"Nut."

"That's it. A religious fanatic."

Orde laughed for the first time in days. "Good. Let them be a bit intimidated."

Moshe snorted his disapproval. "And what is all this about not taking an atheist out on patrol? You cannot treat these men like students in Shabbat school! You sound more . . . fanatic than my brother. And that says a lot."

"I feel strongly about it."

"Ridiculous."

"I would hate for my Jewish brothers to be killed and end up in the same unpleasant fix as the Muslims we must fight. I pity even the Holy Strugglers of the Mufti. They will wake up dead, and then it will be too late for them."

"You should have been a preacher, not a soldier," Moshe scoffed. "Such nonsense will not go down well with the Jews of Hanita. Or anywhere else in the settlements. If you pity that dead assassin who killed the girl tonight, keep such misplaced pity to yourself!"

"If men's hearts were turned toward God, there would be no need for soldiers. Then I *would* be a preacher. As it is, the world is a rotten place. And I am speeding men to hell against my will."

Moshe let out an angry laugh. He did not like this conversation. It was too much like the talks he had once had with Eli. Love or duty. How to reconcile the two? "Then why are you here?"

"Because forces exist that will push you Jews into the sea. A Darkness much bigger than the Arab Mufti or even Hitler would destroy every last living son of the Covenant."

"That is our problem, Christian!" Moshe propped himself up on his elbows. He was genuinely angry now—maybe not at Orde but at the governments who looked away while the Darkness pressed nearer to the Jewish people.

"No. It is my problem. Because I am a Christian and a Zionist who believes you will have your nation. God has promised it, and that is why Satan fights so hard against it. And so I must fight against those who seek to discredit God's promises."

This perspective made very good sense from Orde's point of view, but still it left Moshe feeling frustrated and bitter. After all, had Eli not believed in the same promises and died at the hands of an Arab mob anyway? Where was the justice? Where was this great God of Israel? Moshe thought all these things but did not say them.

"Don't push us. Don't push these men. If they are killed and go to hell fighting Arab gangs, that is not your business. This world is hell enough for us. We have no homeland. No peace. No safety. What could be worse? Leave your God out of it, I say! Teach us to fight, and we will make our own heaven here in our homeland!"

Orde did not reply for a long time. Moshe wondered if he had drifted off to sleep in the middle of the conversation. Then he said, "Without the Lord, Moshe, all the training I give you will not make a difference. With God you will defeat them with clay pots and trumpets; the sea will open before you, and you will walk on dry land."

"Then we won't need you." Moshe lay down hard on his pillow.

"Yes. You will need me. Until you believe what I tell you is true, you do need me to teach you to pray and to fight."

10

A Day of Mourning

Ambassador Hopewell slept soundly in his seat as the plane passed over the border of the Reich into Holland.

Theo glanced at him as the drone of the engines changed to a different tone during the descent. *From G to C*, Theo thought as he recalled the way Anna interpreted all engine noise into a musical scale. The thought made him smile for the first time in days. He checked his watch and wondered if Anna had heard of the riots in Germany. If word of the pogrom reached England before he did, Anna would be frantic with worry.

The landing on the grass airfield was rough and bumpy. Hopewell still did not awaken. Nor did he stir when Theo got off the plane and limped toward the small terminal.

"Only thirty minutes," the pilot called after him.

Theo waved in acknowledgment, then hurried to make the telephone connection with London. Twenty minutes passed before the operator came on the line to announce that the call to London was through. Anna's voice followed, surprisingly clear, clear enough for Theo to know that she had heard what was happening in Germany.

"Oh! Theo, darling! Where are you? Berlin?" She sounded frightened. "Are you all right? Are you with Helen and Karl?"

Theo dreaded telling her that he had not dared to even go see her sister and brother-in-law. A visit from him might have put them in jeopardy. "I am coming home," he replied, trying very hard to sound light. "Just refueling in Holland. We'll be in London by morning." He paused, uncertain if she was still on the line.

He did not need to tell her about Helen. "You could not see my sister," she said, disappointed but understanding.

"It would not have been safe for them to have me as a visitor, Anna. But I left your letter with the British Embassy. They are clear about the situation and will see she gets it."

"Did you see what they are doing in Berlin? Is it true?"

"I saw enough, Anna. It's true—whatever you have heard in England, and more besides." His voices sounded hollow and very tired.

"They have gone mad!" she cried. "Oh, Theo! Thank God you are safe! But the others . . . our friends. My family! What will come to them?"

The pilot rapped loudly on the glass of the phone booth. "She's all fueled, Mr. Lindheim. Two minutes." He held up two fingers and then hurried back to the aircraft.

Theo cradled the telephone, suddenly desperate to talk to her, to comfort her and be comforted. Only Anna would know what he was feeling tonight. Only she could soothe away his sense of hopeless frustration and personal failure. "So much to tell you, Anna. Meet me at the airfield in London. Call Murphy and Elisa. We can breakfast together."

At those words the tension left her voice. Theo was all right. He was coming home. *Breakfast together!* Never had such an ordinary thing sounded so wonderful.

The buzz of the telephone awakened Charles from his restless sleep. He snuggled closer to Elisa and lay very still to listen to Murphy's raspy whisper.

"From Amsterdam? Amsterdam? How did he sound? Good. Yes. Of course. I'll run by the office and then we can go together. Right. Thanks for calling."

Murphy replaced the receiver, picked up the alarm clock, and peered at it for a moment before Elisa spoke.

"That was Mother?" she asked, her voice foggy.

"Uh-huh. Go back to sleep."

"It's about Papa, isn't it?"

"Yes. He's on his way back to England."

"From where?" she asked, sounding very awake.

There was a long pause as Murphy considered how much to tell her. What would it hurt for her to know about Theo's trip now that he was safe? "He has been in Berlin. Negotiating for economic relief for the refugees."

Elisa raised up on her elbow and considered the news. Then she lay back down and stared up at the dark ceiling. "I thought so. I could see it on Mother's face. You really don't need to keep everything from me, you know. I am not that fragile."

"I didn't know about it either, not until last night." His voice cracked. "A note was brought to the office. Harvey Terrill brought it along with the news of the riots."

"A note?" She put an arm protectively over Charles, who still pretended to be sleeping.

"From a German. His description didn't sound familiar, but I don't doubt his message."

"Which is?"

"We're being watched. I've asked Freddie if he can move into the studio downstairs just to keep an eye on you when I'm gone. And . . . I want you to carry the gun." He cleared his throat nervously, as though he expected her to argue.

"Okay. If you think it is necessary, Murphy."

"You know how to use it?"

She gave a short, sarcastic laugh. "Well, I can load it and pull the trigger. At least I could make a little noise with it if I had to."

Murphy sat up and swung his legs over the side of the bed. "Elisa . . . those other notes . . . the ones from Paris?"

She listened in silence, considering the unsigned message from Paris that had told her about the death of Thomas von Kleistmann. "What about them?"

"Have you put them . . . *away* somewhere?"

"No. I thought you had them."

"Yes. On my desk. They're gone now. Do you think the boys could have maybe . . . I don't know. Maybe they took a scrap of paper to write or draw on?"

Charles' eyes opened wide as he heard Murphy's question. He had never taken anything from Murphy's big desk. Louis would not take anything either. They remembered their father's desk in Hamburg. It was fun to play under, but *verboten* to touch anything on it or in it!

"No!" Charles sat up beside Elisa and shook his head in horror at the thought that Murphy could imagine the brothers would take even a scrap of paper without permission. "Me an' Lou . . . we don' take nothing!"

Charles' response broke up the discussion. Murphy switched on the lamp and blinked at the rumpled little boy in their bed. "What are you doing here?" he asked gruffly.

"He had a dream," Elisa explained. "I thought he was sleeping."

"Go get in your own bed, Charles," Murphy ordered, an unusually harsh command. He was angry that Charles had heard about the gun and about tonight's communication from the German and the missing notes. Murphy looked sternly at Elisa as Charles slipped from the covers and padded quickly out of their room. The boy closed the door behind him as Murphy demanded. Still, Murphy's unhappy voice drifted after him. "Why didn't you tell me the kid was . . ."

The rest of the night Charles lay awake, considering what it all meant.

The first soft light penetrated the stained-glass windows of New Church. A patchwork of colors and images spread over the sleeping fugitives like a quilt. Unbroken windows meant safety, Lori thought as she looked out over the pews where men and women lay stretched out, head to head, foot to foot.

From the choir loft beside the huge pipe organ, Lori could see them all. Her mother slept with James at the opposite end of the front pew. Jacob Kalner and Mark had climbed into the choir loft to tell Lori everything they had seen out there, but now they, too, had dropped off into the deep, dreamless sleep of exhaustion. Only Lori remained awake to watch, to stand vigil and pray until her father came. She did not doubt that he would come. In her mind she could imagine an angel loosening his chains and setting him free just like the story in the book of Acts. She did not want to be like the doubters who questioned such a miracle. When he came home, she would run to the door and throw it open and tell him she had believed all along.

But she had not expected the Gestapo to come to New Church. No one who had taken asylum here expected the crash of fists and gun butts against the door that suddenly awakened them.

From her perch, Lorie could see the faces of the fugitives as they rose in sleepy confusion. Fear flooded their eyes as realization struck them. The same fear rooted Lori to her seat.

Jacob Kalner was on his feet in a moment. At first Lori thought he would leap over the rail and fight the intruders, but instead he grabbed Mark by the arm and took Lori by her hand. Dragging them up the steps toward the pipe organ, he warned them to be quiet. No one must know where they hid!

The outer doors splintered and split open. Clear light washed in, dulling the colors of the windows with harsh reality. It did not matter if the windows were broken or intact. No one was safe, not even here in New Church.

The giant organ bellows smelled of dust and moldy leather. Lori, Mark, and Jacob crouched close together inside its dark interior.

They could hear everything clearly as the threats of the Gestapo officer ricocheted off the vaulted ceiling of the church and permeated every corner with arrogance and anger. "Why have you sheltered enemies of the Reich? Why have you not allowed your children to join the Hitler Youth? Are you also an enemy of the Reich, Frau Ibsen?"

Each answer Helen Ibsen attempted to make was cut short by the stamp of a boot against the stone floor and a tirade about ungrateful citizens who wanted all the benefits of the Fascist government but were unwilling to make the necessary sacrifices.

The sacrifices, Lori thought grimly, *are human.*

The officer turned his attention from cursing the Jewish members of New Church to the little blond Aryan son of Pastor Ibsen. "Now, here is a handsome child." Lori was sickened by the sound of a smile in the evil man's voice. "What is your name?"

"James." The reply was sullen.

"Do not talk to him, Jamie," Lori whispered. Jacob nudged her to silence.

"James. *Ja.* A good name. From the *Holy Bible.*" There was the popping sound of a riding crop slapping against a boot top. Hitler also carried a whip, and such props had become the fashion of the Nazi Party members. "So, James. You are blond. Obviously Aryan. And yet your mother and father keep you here in this dark place, away from others who are your equal in race. You cannot go camping or hiking with boys your own age, *ja?*"

James was expected to reply, but he did not. Inwardly, Lori cheered her little brother.

The officer continued. "Instead you are forced to stay here in the company of Jews and enemies of the Fatherland. How do you feel about that, James? Being here with these Untermenschen? Look at them! Can you not see a difference in the way they look and carry themselves? Look at the big nose of that woman. And her eyes set close to each other. You see she is a Jew. Very different from you. How do you feel about being made to stay in the same room with these pigs?"

"Papa says the Lord was a Jew. I guess I like it fine."

The officer snorted in derision. The crop slapped harder against his boot. He was growing impatient with the game. He turned on Frau Helen. "I see how you teach him! How you fill his mind with nonsense!" He snapped his finger and suddenly the church was filled with the boy's screams as James was grabbed up and carried out. Helen Ibsen cried after her son but was held back. No one else spoke.

"We will see to it that James is properly educated, Frau Ibsen. You may weep if you will, but I tell you this. Your son will forget about you soon enough. In one month color will return to his cheeks, and he will become strong and disciplined and will not think about you except to marvel at your backwardness." His boot heels clicked against the slate floor as he circled the group of new captives. "You have another child, Frau Ibsen. You have also refused to allow her into the party organizations. It may go easier for you and your husband at the trial if you will voluntarily tell us where she is."

Helen spoke through clenched teeth. Her words were full of pain. "She is with friends. You cannot . . . take our children from us."

"But they are of minor age. With their parents in prison they naturally become wards of the state. Now, where is your daughter?"

"You think we would ever allow her—"

"You have no choice!" A clap of the hand and the shouted order followed. "Search the place! Find the girl!"

Lori trembled all over. Her teeth chattered with fear and grief. Jacob put a hand on her shoulder to steady her as jackboots slapped against the floor of New Church. Lori held tightly to Mark's hand as footsteps clambered up the stairs to the organ loft. Would they think to look in the bellows? This had always been a wonderful place to hide in a game of hide-and-seek. She prayed that some soldier would not know of a similar hiding place and look here.

Lori could feel Mark's heart pounding wildly as the soldier entered the loft. The man's breath was clearly audible as he stopped to search under the seats and around the pipe organ. Only the thin leather of the bellows separated them from capture. She bit her finger to stop the chattering of her teeth.

"Any luck, Dietz?" a voice called up the stairs.

The reply of the hunter was like a shout in her ear. "Just a minute, Paul, there was something . . . I thought I heard . . ."

Lori held her breath and prayed that the man would not hear her heart pounding in unison with Mark's. And then, for a wild moment, she considered turning herself in, walking out of the bellows and going to prison with Mama. The Nazis would send her to prison if she refused to join their organization. And then she would be with her mother. What other future did she have?

Jacob's fingers tightened on her shoulder, holding her back. With a shake of her head she realized that if she gave herself up, it would also mean the end for Mark and Jacob. She closed her eyes and leaned back against him. His heart beat in a calm rhythm, as if he were not afraid. Somehow it soothed Lori.

The soldier cleared his throat and spit on the floor before he turned to call down, "Nothing up here but dust and hymnbooks."

Lori let her breath out slowly, quietly, as the soldier retreated down the steps.

Moments later other men shouted the results of their search. "No one else in the building!" They had searched from bell tower to basement and found nothing.

"Come on, then." The Gestapo leader did not sound disappointed. After all, he had made quite a catch. "Put a chain and padlock on the church doors, Sergeant. If anyone is in here, they will starve soon enough."

Within moments the shuffling of feet and the crash of doors marked the exit of the prisoners and their guards. But even after the building grew silent and empty, the three remained in the hiding place to listen and wait in case someone remained behind.

Someone had thrown them into the street, and Alfie picked them up—rings with diamonds and rubies in them and two jeweled necklaces. In the deep pockets of Alfie's new coat the jewelry jingled softly. One for Frau Helen Ibsen and one for Lori. Papa had always brought him a present when he came home from a long trip; it seemed like a good idea to bring something home to Lori and Frau Helen. He had picked up a toy truck for Jamie, but a Hitler man had knocked him down and kicked him hard and taken it from him. That explained why so many people were getting beat up. They had things other people wanted. Like the truck.

At dawn Alfie finally spotted the steeple of New Church. Across from it lay the smoking ruins of the church where the Jews went on Saturday. It was all burned to pieces. Four blocks away, Alfie stopped and stared at the sight. "Where are the Jews?" he muttered aloud again. He looked at his shoes and his trousers and coat. His fingers closed around the jewels in his pockets, and suddenly he knew where the Jews were and why everyone had laughed when he said he wanted to thank them.

The face of Ugly Mouth flashed in his mind, and he remembered the empty beds in the ward and why he had run away! In the streets he had heard people cry like Werner. He had seen them loaded into big trucks. "Where are they going?" he had asked.

"East."

"To a better place."

"The Promised Land."

Now Alfie realized that they were going to the same place Werner was going. The lid of the box was closing. Probably all the beds in the ward were empty this morning, empty like the smashed shops. Alfie shuddered. The clothes he wore were stolen. Everything was stolen from the Jews! Alfie would tell Pastor Ibsen that he had taken the things and they needed to be given back!

He frowned and stared hard at the smoldering ruins of the synagogue. "But who is left to give the things back to?"

Alfie stepped off the curb and walked slowly to New Church. He felt ashamed that he had been so dumb, ashamed that he had stood and watched while men like Ugly Mouth beat up people and hauled them away. He had felt only confusion when he had seen it. Only confusion. But now he was ashamed that he did not know when everyone else did. He would not have stolen the shoes or the trousers or the coat. He would have walked barefoot all the way here to New Church and let the good pastor find him old shoes and clothes to wear. Frau Helen and Lori would not want his presents because they were stolen. Mama had told him about stealing, and he had never once taken anything that was not his. Now, one night out of the hospital, he had suddenly become a thief!

Three police cars drove slowly past him toward New Church. A cold lump of fear made him forget that he was hungry. Had the police come to arrest him? to take him back and close the lid on him, too?

Alfie's eyes widened as the police cars slid to a stop in front of New Church. He halted in his tracks and stared as men piled out and ran to each door and began to shout and pound! Had they heard that Alfie was coming to New Church? "No," he said dully. He watched as the doors collapsed inward and men charged in. "Pastor did not take anything. It was me!"

Alfie did not walk forward to confess his guilt. He simply stood weeping on the corner and watching as familiar families were dragged out and loaded into the cars and vans. "Frau Helen!" he cried weakly. And then he saw the blond hair of little Jamie! Poor Jamie! His eyes were scared, like Werner's eyes when they took him away.

"I'm sorry," he cried softly. "I'm sorry!" Alfie sank down on the curb to wait, certain that they would come for him as well.

Sleep was a muddle of dreams for Moshe, and he lay restless in the tent at Hanita. Through a mist he saw the face of his brother, Eli, pale and lifeless on the stone of the Temple Mount. He heard the screams of the rioters in Jerusalem as Haj Amin Husseini stirred them with the passion of his own hatred against the English and the Jews. Far away his mother and father looked on and wept over the body of Eli. Then his mother raised her eyes toward heaven and cried out that Moshe, as well, had been killed.

Through the jumble of bloody images, Moshe knew he was in a tent, knew he was only dreaming. Yet he could not remember where he was or why he had come here. *The archaeological dig at Gilboa? The secret training camp for student members of the Haganah?* Then the image of Captain Orde came to him.

"We'll have to hide you for a bit, Moshe, until we can get you to England. The Mufti, it seems, thinks you had something to do with the death of Victoria and Ismael Hassan. There is a price on your head. The Hassan family is keen on wiping out both brothers of the Sachar family."

Straight from Eli's muddy grave Moshe had left Jerusalem. He and Orde had driven to Hanita, only to find still more bodies beneath blood-soaked sheets.

The memory awakened Moshe with a start. He was tangled in the blanket of his cot. Light filtered through the tan canvas of the tent, creating a dusky gloom inside. He could hear the crunch of footsteps on the gravel, the sound of shovels slapping against the ground as two fresh graves were prepared for the fallen of Hanita settlement.

He turned his head toward Captain Orde's bed. The blankets were smoothed and made up in military fashion. Orde had managed to straighten up his side of the tent and slip out without awakening Moshe.

Moshe sat up, feeling chagrined. Not even the sound of breathing escaped the attention of Samuel Orde. Moshe had slept through a complete tent cleaning, and the captain was gone. Well, there was the difference of a true soldier and a fellow like Moshe who would rather have been out on a solitary dig or sitting in a classroom at Hebrew University.

The tent flap opened, revealing the librarian face of Zach Zabinski.

"Shalom," Zach said, taking in the tousled appearance of the newest fugitive. "Where is Captain Orde?"

Moshe rubbed a hand across his face in confusion. "I barely know where I am myself. Orde? I don't know. He isn't here."

That was obvious. Zach frowned and stared at the empty cot and the perfectly arranged belongings of the Englishman. "Well, did he say where he was going?" Zach demanded.

Moshe shrugged. "I didn't hear him say anything except his prayers just before I fell asleep."

"Get up!" Zach ordered. "He's gone, then. Just gone."

"Gone?"

"Nowhere in the compound. Not in the settlement, and no one saw him leave."

Entirely awake at such news, Moshe swung himself off the cot and pulled the cold trousers over his bare legs.

"Is his auto still here?"

"Yes." Zach was angry with Moshe. "You said you trusted him. We asked you to keep an eye on him—"

"My eyes were closed," Moshe said defensively. He did not admit that his mind had been hearing other voices and seeing dark images while he slept.

"Well, he is not here. And for a man to leave the settlement alone . . . especially today. The whole world has gone crazy, Moshe. Word just came in over the BBC that the Nazis have decimated the Jewish communities in Germany. At the same time, we were being hit last night— twenty-seven attacks throughout the Yishuv. The Jihad Moquades of the Mufti have been slitting Jewish throats in Palestine from north to south. That crazy Englishman is going to get himself killed if he is out of the settlement, and the British High Command will blame us for it!"

Moshe finished dressing but did not make up his cot. Pulling on his heavy blue cable-knit sweater, he followed Zach out into the misty morning air.

Larry Havas, an empty revolver tucked in his belt, strode purposefully toward the two from the mess hall.

"Where is he?" he demanded of Moshe.

The conversation in the tent was replayed, ranging from concern to blame. Why had Moshe trusted Orde? And why had Moshe not kept an eye on him? Reports came from other men and women as every foot of the settlement was searched again. Orde was not in the latrines. Not in the kitchen. Not at any sentry post. Not in the machine sheds or the barns. No one had seen him leave. He was definitely on foot, and probably well into enemy territory.

Larry Havas, who was American in every sense of the word, peered off over the rolling hillsides scarred by ravines and stubborn brush. "Crazy Englishman," he said. "Hanita is like a little wagon train circled against the Indians—only the moquades are a lot meaner than any Indians I ever heard about. He's had it out there." Larry grimaced and patted the revolver in his belt. "I sure hope he didn't take all the ammunition with him."

The settlers had other things to tend to in Hanita. The graves were dug; the dead awaited burial. While the sentries kept watch, Moshe again found himself among mourners, and again he let himself weep for his brother Eli and for all who had fallen here and in the Reich throughout the night. The fate of the fanatic British captain seemed a small thing compared to the news of what had happened in Germany and the reality of two dead people lowered into the damp clay of the settlement. If Orde had gotten himself killed by being foolish, that was his own fault. Sharon Zalmon's only fault was being Jewish. It was enough to earn her and a thousand others their own plot of ground this morning.

11

No Right to Hope

It was a morning unlike any other in the history of Germany. A gray pall of smoke hovered over every city in the Reich. When the last synagogue had been incinerated and the last shard of glass had fallen to the street, the people came out to tour the devastated Jewish districts to see for themselves just what had happened. By the thousands and tens of thousands, Germans wandered speechless through the wreckage. And by their coming, they removed forever the excuse that they did not know what was being done to their Jewish neighbors.

On that cold day in November, no one in Germany could say, "I did not know. I did not see."

Blackened fragments of Jewish lives filtered down in a gritty film that clung to the majestic new buildings erected in Berlin and Nuremberg and Hamburg. Ash coated the Nazi monuments and statues, a black-and-white relief like a photographic negative. But there were no actual negatives. Men and women alike were arrested for taking pictures; the Ministry of Propaganda did not fancy the idea of photos of destroyed Jewish shops and synagogues shouting accusations from the front pages of foreign newspapers. Even one photograph was worth a thousand self-righteous news stories. Without pictures, however, the destruction remained a private matter. As the Führer said, no other nation had offered to help Germany solve her Jewish problem. So what right did any nation have, therefore, to interfere in a purely German solution?

Everyone understood that there were bound to be a few sanctimonious proclamations in the Western press, but all that would soon be forgotten. Other news would occupy the world tomorrow.

But on this morning, good German housewives brought their children to see what had been done to the Jewish vermin. Some regret arose among the stunned, silent crowds. In the ashes of one bonfire lay the remains of a perfectly good chair. Might that chair not have been used by an Aryan family? A half-charred bolt of cloth lay amid the rubble in a street, cloth that might have been made into pretty dresses for Aryan children. Such excess shocked the frugal Germans—such waste. Everything that had been destroyed would have belonged to the great Aryan race in time. Why had it not simply been confiscated and given to the German population?

This whispered question lay on many complaining lips this morning, but few other questions were voiced. Of all those tens of thousands of good German people touring the wreckage, few dared utter a single moral objection to the violence. A few fools interfered with the beating or arrest of a Jew; their interference, in turn, led to their own arrests. It seemed much wiser, then, to limit one's disapproval to the smashing of good, usable material goods. Never mind the smashing of lives. Never mind that seventy thousand men were being loaded into cattle cars and shipped to any one of a hundred concentration camps. Never mind that women were left without sons and husbands, children without fathers. The Nazi Reich was evenhanded in its justice, after all. Soon all Jewish families would be in the same place.

On November 10, the Berlin headquarters of the Secret State Police sent out a wire at the instruction of Gestapo Chief Himmler.

To All State Headquarters and Branch Offices:

Buchenwald Concentration Camp is filled to capacity with current deliveries Stop Further transfers to Buchenwald are to be canceled, with exception of transports already underway Stop To prevent errors, this HQ will be informed well in advance of transfers to Dachau and Sachsenhausen camps Stop

Pastor Karl Ibsen stood in line with three thousand other newly arrested prisoners outside the warmth of the railway terminal, Bahnhof Friedrichstrasse. Damp mist from the Spree River clung to his face and hair and soaked through his coat. Like the others, he had not slept in over twenty-four hours. The stubble of a reddish gold beard frosted his face; his eyes stung with the stench of Berlin's burned-out buildings.

On the platform, two dozen SS strutted above the prisoners. At the opposite side of the miserable group, soldiers patrolled with dogs. Prisoners were not allowed to sit down or speak or relieve themselves. Respected men who had once taught at German universities or practiced medicine or led a congregation in worship were forced to defecate or urinate in their clothing. They had learned in the early hours of their captivity not to question, not to ask for favors from their guards.

Karl spotted Nathan Thalmann, a faithful member of his congregation. Their eyes met. In a look, Karl hoped to give Nathan encouragement and hope. Nathan simply shook his head and looked away. *What was the use?* A Christian of Jewish heritage, Nathan had been singled out when he went to the aid of an old shopkeeper who was being beaten to death. His concern, like that of Karl, had brought him here to the gates of hell.

An SS officer, resplendent in his tall boots and black uniform, walked out onto the platform. He spoke briefly to one of the guards who nodded, saluted, and then fired his machine gun into the air with a burst that sent the prisoners to the pavement in their fear.

Screams pierced the morning, then silence followed by the laughter of the guards and the officer.

The officer stepped forward and looked over the faces of his prisoners. He was still smirking. "Well, Jews!" he boomed, and his voice carried well in the still, cold air. "How do you like the sound of guns, eh? The last sound Embassy Secretary vom Rath heard before a Jew shot him full of holes. How do you like the sound of death?" He raised his hand in signal, and half a dozen weapons sputtered an ominous warning.

Although the guns shot over them, prisoners ducked, shielding their heads, covering their ears. Once again there was total silence. No one dared breathe as the echo of machine-gun fire died away.

Karl glanced across the street toward the Winter Garden Theatre. Only three weeks before, he and Helen had gone there. They had eaten at the Aschinger Restaurant on the next block. Karl focused on those places, reminders of a saner world. How far away!—a gulf separated by guards and dogs and strutting Nazi officers.

The officer assessed the grim faces of the three thousand captives before him, reveling in their fear. "You do not enjoy our humor, I see." He shrugged. "Wait until you experience the jokes of the concentration camp commandant, eh?" He seemed pleased with himself, keeping his men amused with his great wit. "Well, Jews, we have gotten the news that Buchenwald is filled. Sachsenhausen is also filled. There is still room enough in Dachau for most of you, however. How do you fancy a little train ride to Bavaria?" He raised his chin as if waiting for an answer. The breath of the silent captives rose into the air like steam from a stewpot, giving the illusion of heat. "What? Not anxious to see Bavaria? Ah, well, it is very cold. I hope you have all brought your warm ski clothes."

In fact, some men among the group were dressed only in nightshirts and stocking feet. Karl had given his sweater to one older fellow at the police station. Karl's overcoat was warm enough for now, but he regretted not having the foresight to put on woolen socks and heavy boots instead of street shoes. Perhaps Helen would be allowed to send him a package. She would think of such things without being told. She would feel the ache of the cold in his limbs as if it were her own.

The officer smiled as he spoke. Then his tone changed to a patronizing whine, as if reprimanding naughty children. "What? You forgot your gloves and cap? You do not have shoes? Well, without your shoes you will no doubt lose your feet."

A cry rose up from a small group of women clustered beyond the outer perimeter of the guards. At his words, they covered their mouths in horror and wiped angry tears from their cheeks.

These were the wives—Aryan wives of arrested Jews, Karl guessed. He admired their courage to follow their husbands and face the ridicule of the Nazi guards. The women stood on tiptoe and strained to see their husbands as they peeled off their own coats and sweaters and held up bundles that were forbidden to be passed to the prisoners.

Karl searched the group of women for some sign of his wife, but Helen was not among them. No doubt she had heard of his arrest. Karl hoped that the Gestapo had released Leona Kalner, who would have carried the news to New Church. He thought of Jacob and Mark escaping over the rooftops. If they managed to make their way through the riots, surely they had alerted Helen to his fate.

He had not seen Richard Kalner after their arrest. The two men had been separated immediately. Karl had not been beaten badly, but Richard was almost unconscious when they threw him onto the truck.

Karl shuddered at the thought of what would happen to Richard Kalner. At that same instant, the press of prisoners surrounding him parted slightly, and he caught sight of Richard's bloodied face. Right eye swollen shut. Cheek blue. Lips cut and puffy. Brown hair caked with his own blood.

Richard saw Karl, too. He raised his hand and let it drop. He did not look away even when the shrill wail of the train whistle announced the beginning of their journey. The two men moved toward each other in hopes that they might be loaded into the same freight car. Then they could talk. After the doors slid shut, they would be free to talk.

The airplane passed over the industrial center of London. Smoke from hundreds of factory chimneys mingled with fog to blacken endless blocks of identical houses with soot.

Theo watched as thousands of workmen made their way in the gray morning light toward the huge barnlike factories that cluttered the docks along the Thames River. With the eye of an experienced Luftwaffe pilot, he could easily see what perfect targets the English factories would make from the air. He scanned the riverbanks for possible antiaircraft guns. Although Parliament had been discussing the need for defense from air attacks, nothing was being done. That fact, coupled with the brutality he had witnessed last night, frightened Theo. What would it take to awaken England? Life seemed to flow on peacefully, monotonously, as though nothing at all had happened in Germany.

He looked across the aisle at the sleeping American diplomat who had helped him pass so easily through German customs. Hopewell's mouth hung open, his head flung back. He had not uttered a word since five minutes after their takeoff from Tempelhof. Had he seen all the fires across the landscape of the Reich? Had he witnessed enough to sound the alarm for his own countrymen to hear? And, wrapped in their own apathetic dreams, would the Americans want to hear?

Theo frowned and looked down across the city of London. In Germany, they battled the Nazis, a tangible enemy. Here, the enemy was less obvious—the apathy of people who would simply rather not have their personal comfort disturbed. As the plane dipped lower toward the airfield, Theo prayed that the sleepwalking world might awaken before the darkness also crossed their threshold.

As if startled by an inward alarm clock, Hopewell sat up suddenly, yawned, and wriggled a finger in his ear. "Is it London yet?" he asked as the drone of the engines slowed and deepened.

Theo nodded and pointed down. "You've been sleeping since Berlin."

"The only way a diplomat can sleep at all." Hopewell smoothed his rumpled suit and straightened his bow tie. "En route somewhere. That's the best sleep I get these days. And I can tell you, after what I saw last night, it may be a while before any of us is able to sleep through an entire night." He checked his pocket watch and squinted in thought. "I called Joseph Kennedy last night before we left. You know Kennedy, American ambassador to England? Blasted pacifist thinks Hitler is a swell fellow, and we ought to mind our own business. That sort of rot. Anyway, we'll be having breakfast together this morning. I'd appreciate it if you could join us. Maybe open the eyes of the blind ambassador, if you know what

I mean. We can go over the dispatches from our consulates in Germany as they come in this morning. Seems to me that might be of help to you as well, eh?"

Moshe felt out of place among the mourners of Hanita who gathered in the mess hall after the brief services. He left them there and retreated with his own grief to the privacy of his tent.

The strong smell of onion greeted him as he entered. Before his eyes adjusted to the gloom, he knew he was not alone. Samuel Orde lay on his cot. He took a bite of a raw onion as though it were an apple and then answered Moshe's astonished expression.

"If you are going to bunk in my tent, you cannot live like a pig." The captain gestured toward Moshe's unmade bed. "I am not your mother or your maid to clean up after you. Keep it neat, or I will throw you out on your ear."

The words slapped Moshe in the face. He exploded with anger. "Where have you been? The whole camp was looking for you, and believe me, these people have more important matters to think about this morning than the whereabouts of some arrogant Englishman!" He tossed his coat onto the unmade cot. "And I will make up my cot when I'm ready! At least I do not stink like an Arab onion field!"

"Exactly." Orde took another bite. "That is because you have not walked through an Arab onion field recently." He held the onion up. His meaning was clear. Samuel Orde had been deep in hostile territory, and he had come back safely.

"So what? Am I supposed to be impressed? You made me look like a fool this morning. I stood up for you. No one trusts you, but I stood up for you."

"You are a fool. You all are. Fools and infants facing something you cannot possibly imagine or fight against because you haven't the slightest idea how to do it." He threw the onion at Moshe, who tried unsuccessfully to dodge it. "That is why I am here."

He stood and pushed past Moshe. Moshe followed angrily after him. In the daylight he could see that Orde was filthy and scratched. Even without the onion the Englishman smelled of sweat. Orde walked toward the mess hall. It did not matter to him if Moshe tagged along.

The murmur of conversation fell silent as he entered the building with Moshe at his heels. Eyes widened. The missing-and-presumed-dead Englishman was alive. How had he reentered the compound? Where had he been? Hostility showed on the faces of many who looked at him. After all, how could anyone slip out of Hanita and return alive on today of all days? *He must be a spy,* some thought. The accusation was not on their lips but in their eyes.

"Where have you been?" Zach demanded. "We were looking."

"He has been to an Arab onion field," Moshe blurted out harshly.

Orde's strong aroma confirmed his words.

Zach was not amused. "And what did you find there?"

Orde lifted his chin slightly, exuding the authority of his rank and addressing the men of Hanita as through they were his soldiers. "Come with me," he commanded, pointing to the same four men who had driven out to deposit the dead Arab on the threshold of his village. Then he also pointed at Moshe and Zach. "You come as well." He smiled coolly at Moshe. "And if you wake up in hell tomorrow, you have only yourself to blame."

"Where are we going?" Zach was defiant, suspicious.

Orde turned back the others who followed them curiously across the compound toward the gates. Only the six he had chosen were allowed to hear what he had to say next. He passed out bullets enough to fill each Webley revolver completely. Only then did he explain where he had been and where they were going.

"I tracked the trail of the men who raided you last night. I found where they keep their weapons stashed."

"So. This is news?" Larry said. "The Arabs have weapons, and we are left with guns for shooting clay pigeons and target practice."

Orde ignored the complaint. "You Jews of the settlements have been fighting a defensive war against the Muslims for too long. Such tactics will not save your lives or your settlements. You will never put down the enemy that way." He looked out beyond the barricades. "We will wage a new kind of war."

"We?" repeated Zach skeptically.

Orde turned on him fiercely. "Yes, *we!* You must stop thinking of me as an Englishman and consider me as one of you—fighting the same fight as you, with the same idea in mind and the same goal! I am with you with every beat of my heart. So let's have no more of these suspicions." He shifted his gaze and abruptly took charge. "Henceforth, we will not wait for the men of the Mufti to come to us and murder us in the settlements. We shall go out and meet the enemy in the open, near their villages. We shall carry the battle to them."

The law of the British Mandate declared such actions by Jews were punishable by prison and death. Orde wore the uniform of the British government.

"But that is illegal," Larry Havas protested.

Orde waved his hand in dismissal of such puny matters. "Leave such little details to me. But first we will need weapons. The Holy Strugglers have kindly provided fine German-made rifles for us just a short hike from here. The seven of us will fetch them and carry them back to Hanita under cover of night."

By the time the plane had bumped down on English soil, the London presses were running hot with the news of Kristal Nacht, the "Night of Broken Glass." From all indications, the violent night rolled over into a violent morning. The breaking of glass and lives continued after the breaking of a new day.

Murphy had been up since Anna had telephoned with news that Theo was en route across the Channel from Holland. He had not stopped to eat breakfast, but instead went immediately to the TENS office for three hours of work. As he walked quickly beside Anna toward the tarmac, his stomach rumbled. It was only 7:00 AM, but it felt like the middle of the day.

Word had somehow leaked that an American bigwig diplomat was flying in straight from Berlin. Dozens of reporters from various news agencies jostled for position at the gate. Anna held Murphy back from the hubbub. She did not want to have to fight her way to Theo.

The hum of conversation rose to a shout as the grim American ambassador emerged from the plane. The man looked surprisingly rested and unruffled after last night's ordeal. He fielded questions easily, replying that he had a report to make to President Roosevelt before he went into much detail, but that he had been witness to the blackest night in history since the Dark Ages. Pens flew at this reference to darkness and ignorance. Bulbs popped frantically, stinging Ambassador Hopewell's eyes, but missing the exhausted and disheveled figure of Theo Lindheim as he stepped from the plane and searched the crowd for Anna.

"Theo!" she cried, standing on her tiptoes and waving. "Theo! Over here!" For the first time, she let her heart admit that she had spent every moment of his absence wondering if she would ever see him again.

She wept happily as she pushed through the reporters and ran to Theo. It didn't matter that he was unshaven and rumpled; she wrapped her arms around him and said his name again and again as he stroked her hair. But when she looked up into his face she saw only sadness there. She had seen this look when he spoke softly about the men in the Herrgottseck, "the prayer corner," at Dachau, and when he spoke about the Covenant—grief coupled with helplessness. She reached up and touched his cheek.

The reporters did not notice him. Murphy hung back for a few minutes while Anna and Theo had their silent reunion.

"One look at you and it all recedes," Theo said at last. "Like a bad dream, Anna."

She searched his eyes. "But it is not a bad dream, is it, Theo? And it will not go away like we all hoped, will it?"

"We are past hoping now, Anna," he answered. "Unless we fight, we have no right to hope."

12

Through a Wall of Fire

Hours passed slowly inside the stuffy organ bellows. Lori slept standing, leaning against Jacob, who held her up. A wooden brace pressed painfully into his back. He imagined them all dying in here, being found by some organ repairman sent to find out why the bellows did not work.

"I have to use the toilet," Mark croaked. His voice shattered their miserable silence, and Lori woke up as Jacob knocked Mark on the side of the head. Mark began to cry. "I have to . . . I need to use the toilet," he wailed.

"Shut up!" Jacob hissed, kicking him in the leg.

"Leave him alone," Lori demanded, suddenly too uncomfortable to care anymore. All she wanted was to get out. Out of the dust and the darkness. To breathe real air again. "We can't stay in here forever. Leave him alone!"

Jacob groaned as his endurance faded. He was hungry. They had not eaten or had a drink since last night. He needed a toilet, too. Lori was right. They could not stay in here forever. *Die standing up in the bellows of a pipe organ? Even the Nazis could not think of a worse prison.* "Come on, then," he said through parched lips.

The trio tumbled out of the bellows, each stumbling in a different direction, away from the enforced closeness.

A cloud of dust followed them. Cobwebs streamed from their hair and hands and clung to their clothing as though they had been entombed for a hundred years.

Like a bird trying to fly, Lori raised her grimy hands toward the high window where a shaft of light beamed down into the little room behind the organ.

Mark stumbled toward the door. A helmet of cobwebs coated his curly blond hair and hung from his chin. He pushed hard against the door, then kicked it when it did not yield. His face was desperate.

Jacob grabbed him by his jacket and pulled him back. "You want them to hear us?"

Mark began crying again. "I don't care. I want to go to the toilet. I can't get out. It's locked."

Lori shook her head at the two warring brothers. With an air of aloofness, she reached over and grasped the handle of the door. "Pull," she said, opening the door.

Mark broke free and charged out the door, clattering down the stairs as quietly as an army on the march.

Jacob stared angrily after him, then brushed the dust from his clothes and followed.

Lori came last, closing the door behind her. She stood at the head of the stairs and listened to the hollow echo of their retreating footsteps. A knot of apprehension formed in her stomach. Her eyes brimmed with tears. She did not want to go down into the emptiness of the church. Mama was not there. James had been taken away. Papa was arrested. And Lori was alone. It did not matter that Mark and Jacob were downstairs; she was still alone.

A wave of dizziness hit her as the reality of it all sank in. She would walk down the steps into the auditorium where Papa preached and Mama played the piano and Jamie fidgeted in the pew with his friends . . . but they would not be there.

Lori sat down on the top step and stared at her shoes. It occurred to her that she had not had her shoes off since yesterday morning, just before breakfast, when they had all eaten together and talked about ordinary things. Papa had gone off to his study to work on his sermon. Mama and Lori had done the dishes. Jamie had prowled around outside through the fallen autumn leaves in search of a pocketknife he had lost. *Only yesterday?*

"Lori?" Jacob stood at the bottom of the stairs. His hand was on the banister as if he wanted to come up. His face reflected concern. "They have all gone." Then, "Are you all right?"

She bit her lip and shook her head slowly. "No . . . I . . . I am not all right."

He climbed the stairs and sat down below her. "We are safe here for now."

"I was hoping this was all a terrible dream. While we were inside the

bellows, I could not quite believe they came and took Mama and Jamie
. . . and the rest."

He reached up and patted her awkwardly on the arm, as though con-
soling a teammate after losing a game of soccer. "All last night I kept
thinking I would wake up. I wanted to wake up." He gestured toward the
light. "And now it is morning."

"Oh, Jacob, what will we do?" She rested her head in her hands and
closed her eyes against the light.

He exhaled loudly and cleared his throat, trying to force away the
sadness in his own voice. "First, we should eat something. I'm hungry."

Lori looked up at him in disbelief. Everyone was taken away. Only
the three of them were left in this place, and all Jacob Kalner could think
about was his stomach. "Eat?"

"Breakfast."

"But where—"

"I sent Mark to look for the Communion bread. Do they keep the
wine in the same place?"

Alfie's stomach rumbled. It was long past time for lunch. He was hungry,
and he thought about mealtimes in the ward. He remembered the way
he had fed Werner with a spoon and Werner had told him funny stories
between bites. Werner was gone now, and that fact made Alfie more sad
than hungry. Maybe even if he had food he would not be able to eat it.
He decided not to pay attention to the pain in his stomach. The hurting
in his heart was much worse.

People still milled about everywhere in the streets of Berlin. Some
came to look and not steal. Their faces were sad, too, Alfie noticed. Some
of them would look and shake their heads and then look away. Maybe
some of those sad-eyed people had friends like Werner who had been
taken away in the night.

Alfie walked slowly along with the crowds. Glass crunched beneath
his shoes, and he was worried the glass might cut his new shoes. He followed a man in a business suit who wore a hat like Papa used to wear.
The man exclaimed over and over, "We are animals! *Animals!*"

A lady in a brown coat stood beside him. She shook her head and
said, "Not even animals would do such a thing."

Alfie thought she was probably right. He liked animals. He had a dog
once, and she was nicer to Alfie than anyone. Her name was Sally, and
she thought Alfie was smart and wonderful. But that was a long time
ago, before Mama died and they took him to the hospital.

If the lady in the brown coat had asked him, he would have told her

that dogs were very much nicer than people. But she did not ask, and so
Alfie followed the man and the lady for a long time through the wrecked
parts of Berlin. After a while they came to an apartment building and
went in through the front door.

Alfie was alone again. He peered through the glass of the door and
watched them get into a lift. He wished he could have told them about
his dog and Mama and Werner.

The rumble of a car engine pulled him around. A green police car
drove by him with men in a cage in the backseat. "They are Jews," Alfie
said aloud. He said what he knew was true so he would not forget it.
"Jews they are taking. And boys who cannot walk, like Werner. And boys
who cannot talk, like Heinrich and Dieter. And boys who are
dumbheads, like me. Just like Jews." He frowned. "And nice people like
Frau Helen and Jamie. People who love Jesus. They are taking them with
the Jews."

Pastor Ibsen had once promised that he would help Alfie get out of
the ward. He had not been able to help. Alfie had been sad, but he did
not blame the pastor. Now Alfie wondered who would help Pastor and
Frau Ibsen? Where were the police taking Jamie and the others? It was a
sad day in Berlin.

Alfie began to walk again, past houses and apartments he did not recognize. Alfie was not sure where he was. Mostly the street was quiet.
Everyone must be tired from smashing things all night, he thought.

Alfie's stomach began to hurt too bad to ignore. Up ahead was a wide
street. A traffic policeman was directing cars to turn because the street
was blocked. The man wore a uniform and white gloves. His eyes were
stern and sad. He blew the whistle in his mouth and waved for some
taxis and cars to stop and others to go. Alfie watched him for a while and
then made his decision. Everyone was arrested. Everyone Alfie wanted to
see was gone. It was best, he reasoned, if maybe he got arrested, too.
What was the use of anything, after all, if there was no one to be with?

Alfie waited until the policeman signaled for people to walk across
the street. He hurried to reach the policeman first.

"*Bitte,*" Alfie said, showing manners as Mama said he must.

"*Ja?*" The policeman did not look as if he wanted to talk.

"I need to be arrested."

The policeman stared at him with the whistle hanging on his lip. "Arrested?"

Alfie nodded. "I stole these clothes last night."

The policeman blinked at him as if he did not hear. Horns began to
honk. The policeman waved cars through while Alfie stood quietly be-

side him. Then the policeman whistled and more people crossed the street.

"Nobody will miss those clothes, boy," the policeman said. "Most of Germany would be in prison if it mattered."

"But everyone is arrested."

Crowds brushed past them as they talked.

"Are you a Jew, then? I've got nothing against Jews. I was standing on this corner before Hitler, and I have nothing to do with that. Go home, boy; go home to Mama until this thing passes. Don't speak to another police officer. That's my advice. Now get going!"

Alfie did not argue. It was not polite to argue with a police officer. He nodded his head with a jerk and hurried to the opposite sidewalk.

"Home to Mama," he repeated. The policeman did not understand anything at all. Alfie raised his eyes for some sign of the smoke from the Jewish synagogue beside New Church. A thin black smudge floated overhead and then to the east. Alfie followed it back a different way than he had come. Some streets were not damaged; in others, everything was ruined. In front of a smashed grocery store, broken tins of crackers were scattered everywhere. Alfie kicked a tin with his toe and a wrapped packet of crackers fell out. Alfie picked it up and put it in his pocket. He would eat it later, when he was home with Mama.

Wolf seemed lost in thought as he sipped his coffee at the breakfast table. This was the sort of mood that always before had commanded silence from Lucy. But she was no longer afraid of him, and so she spoke anyway.

"I did not take a cab home last night." She announced her disobedience confidently.

His blue eyes flashed anger, "I told you—"

"I wanted to see." She shrugged. "And so I walked. No one would hurt me, anyway." She reached up and pulled back the curtain, revealing the smoke that tarnished the sky above Vienna. "So you spent the night Jew bashing. Was it fun?"

He answered her with a black look. "A waste. Not that I care for the life of one Jew, but the destruction of property—"

"I saw for myself. Better to hand it over intact."

Wolf appraised her with surprise. He did not imagine that she had a brain in her head to form any opinions at all.

"Orders came from the top," he said with dissatisfaction.

She buttered her toast with real butter. "All this over one German diplomat?" she asked, enjoying the freedom to question him.

He answered truthfully, suddenly opening up in a way he never had before. "It was all arranged ahead of time. This was Hitler's answer to the Armistice Day celebrations of the democracies. France and Britain have their big parades to celebrate the defeat of Germany, and Germany smashes the Jews who, according to Hitler, caused us to lose the war. It is a game with him. A way to let the little men wield power against those who are more helpless than they." He stopped and eyed her quizzically. "Do you understand?"

She nodded and smiled. She understood perfectly about people wielding their power against the weak. She had not understood before last night, but now it was very clear. "And this place?" She swept a hand around the kitchen. "Where did it come from?"

She had never asked before. In all these months she had simply accepted the apartment and furnishings as though Wolf had handpicked it all just for her.

"Where do you think?"

"A Jew? Or a political prisoner?" Genuinely curious, she had spent hours considering the tasteful decorating of the flat. The delicate furnishings and petit-point chair seats indicated a woman's touch.

"A Jewess. A musician, I hear. A friend of mine at the Gestapo knew it was vacant and managed to hold it. I owe him a favor now." He seemed amused that he was only now telling her this.

"What is his name?" she asked boldly.

He frowned. This frank questioning was unlike Lucy. She had always been so timid with him before. "What does it matter?"

"I would like to send him a note of appreciation, Wolf. Tell him what magnificent taste he has. And how we have enjoyed this place." She poured coffee into his cup. "It is always a good idea to cultivate the Gestapo, *ja?*"

He laughed in amazement at the new Lucy. "Pregnancy is good for you, my little cow. It sharpens your wits."

"Then maybe you should call me your little fox instead."

At this Wolf laughed again. "The English would call us a pair—Wolf and vixen, eh?"

"I like this place. I would like to stay here as long as possible, until I have to go to Lebensborn. I would rather be free to walk about Vienna and go to work. Peasant stock, you know, unlike your soft-handed aristocratic women. I enjoy work. I cannot imagine sitting around a resort with a clique of fat, gossiping mistresses doing needlepoint until the baby comes."

Wolf found himself enjoying this side of Lucy. He eyed her for a moment and then agreed to her request with a shrug. "If you prefer. But I insist you see the doctor there regularly. The Lebensborn obstetrician is the best, of course. The clinic was taken over from two Jewish doctors after the Anschluss. You may change your mind about staying there after you see it."

"It is not just Vienna I would miss, Wolf." She touched his hand and smiled the reflection of his most charming smile.

His gaze swept over her and then back to her face. "I stayed away too long," he said, his interest renewed. "I was bored. Now I see it was wrong of me."

Lucy, no longer the beggar she had been, intrigued Wolf. He had taught her the game, and she intended to play it without conscience.

"I'll stay here then." She decided the matter without further discussion. "You have a key to this place. It would be quite unpleasant for you if I was locked away behind the gates of your little SS farm and you could not visit when you liked."

He considered that inconvenience and agreed. "Then you should stay here as long as you like." He was not really thinking of her, but of his own appetites. Yesterday Lucy would have seen it differently, but overnight she had become a realist.

"It is cold," she said. "I will need another coat. Something to keep me warm this winter. Fox fur would be appropriate. After last night there should be some very nice ones without owners, I would think."

He shrugged in acquiescence. She was right. "For the baby," he said.

"No. For me. The fox will keep me warm, and I will keep the baby warm. But first you must bring the fox."

He frowned slightly. As if he had heard another whisper from her heart, he said, "Remember who you belong to."

"Why, to you, of course, my Wolf. You do not want me to look inferior to the women of other officers."

He grunted and continued to stare thoughtfully at her. "And remember who the child belongs to."

She did not lower her eyes from his, but looked at him with amusement, as though she could not understand what he was getting at. "The Führer?" she asked coyly.

He clouded at her joke. "It would not be wise for you to make plans—"

She looked at him with scorn. "You know me better than that, Wolf."

He shrugged again, content with her answer. She had silenced his doubts. A woman like Lucy could not see past the next hour, he reasoned, let alone leave him.

"Well, then. We will enjoy ourselves for now, my little fox."

Reichsmarschall Hermann Göring's angry face flushed with emotion beneath the rouge he had carelessly applied before this morning's meeting.

"I wish you had just killed Jews instead of destroying so many valuables!" he said bitterly to Reinhard Heydrich, who had come to the meeting as a representative of Gestapo Chief Himmler.

Heydrich raised his long, narrow head defensively. "Plenty of Jews were killed. And there will be more!"

The stenographer took notes furiously, hardly glancing up at Heydrich. The large beaked nose of the iron-willed Aryan was still raised proudly, his blond hair slicked back, every hair in place. The SS uniform remained impeccable in spite of a long night's work directing the attacks against Jews and the arrest of over seventy thousand men. His thin lips turned slightly downward as Minister of Propaganda Goebbels spoke up in defense of the violence.

"The attack on Ernst vom Rath is perceived as an attack on the entire German nation. Therefore every Jew must pay."

Göring's eyes bulged. He slammed his fist on the table and shouted, "The synagogues demolished, yes! Jews arrested and held for fines, yes! But don't you see? If a Jewish shop is totally destroyed and its goods thrown out into the street and burned, it is not the Jews who suffer the damage; it is the German insurance companies! Furthermore, the goods that are being destroyed are consumer goods, belonging to the people! In the future, when demonstrations against the Jews are held, they must be directed so they do not hurt *us, us, us!*" Göring emphasized each word by pounding his meaty fist on the conference table to the new German Air Ministry.

Silence descended as the dozen men before him sat in deep thought. Insurance companies. No one had thought of that as they destroyed millions of marks' worth of plate glass.

Göring sat back and focused on his thumbs. The entire episode had not turned out as he had expected. Theo Lindheim had slipped away through the tumult of the riots without even being stopped or questioned. Someone would pay for that oversight. Apprehending Lindheim had been the responsibility of the Gestapo. Theo might have been worth millions to the Reich treasury in ransom. Now that opportunity had been lost, and Jewish goods, which should have simply been confiscated as the owners were hauled away, smoldered in the ashes.

He looked sharply at Heydrich and Goebbels, who seemed pleased with the excesses of Kristal Nacht. After all, it had given the Jews a certain vision of their future.

Hermann Göring rested his hands on his fat paunch and eyed the committee that the Führer had appointed to settle the Jewish problem once and for all. "It was insane to clear out a whole warehouse of Jewish goods and burn the lot. German insurance companies will have to pay, and all those goods were things I need desperately for the economic plan. Whole bales of clothing." Again he smashed his fist against the black tabletop.

Goebbels, as thin and emaciated as Göring was fat, rubbed his hands together and grimaced slightly in thought. "Why not simply make a law?" Making laws always seemed to provide solutions to such matters as who would pay for what. "Why not simply exempt the insurance companies from having to pay?"

Göring considered the suggestion. A murmur of approval rippled around the table. "I am going to issue a decree," he said, his anger finally giving way to practicality and the power he had to remove all obstacles. "And I am going to expect the support of all government agents in channeling the claims so that the German insurance companies will not suffer."

From the far end of the table a small, timid-looking fellow raised his hand at that suggestion. He smiled nervously, his left eye twitching behind thick spectacles.

Göring waved a hand expansively at the little man. "For those of you who have not met him, this is the representative of the insurance industry, Herr Hildegard." He sniffed impatiently as Hildegard opened his briefcase and removed a file folder, laboriously laying it out before him.

"This is a delicate situation," Hildegard said sadly. "You see, many of the German companies have reinsured in foreign countries."

"Explain this, please," Göring said. "Most are soldiers and politicians. Explain the term to *reinsure.*"

The little man drew himself up, suddenly confident in his role as advisor to this august body of Nazi leaders. "Simply this: German companies did not wish to carry all the risk themselves. So part of the risk is also borne by foreign insurers in countries like France and Belgium and Switzerland, you see?"

Heads nodded in unison.

Hildegard continued his explanation. "We would like to make a point, Herr Field Marshall, that we must not be hindered in fulfilling the obligations the contracts call for. Even to Jews. We must make certain that there is no loss of confidence in the German insurance companies, or our foreign companies will pull out. It would be a black spot on the honor of German insurance companies."

A few moments passed in thought. Göring sucked his cheek and toyed with a pencil. "It would not blacken your honor if I issued a decree, a law sanctioned by the state, forbidding you to pay."

Heydrich leaned forward, a spark of amusement in his cold, pale eyes. "Why not this? The insurance may be granted, but as soon as it is paid to the Jews, it will be confiscated. That way we will have saved face."

The spidery insurance executive clasped his hands together and nodded vigorously. "I am inclined to agree with General Heydrich."

At last Göring grinned, then laughed. "You'll have to pay, then. But since it is the Aryan people who really suffered the damage, there will be a lawful decree forbidding you to make payment to the Jews. After all, it is the Jews who incited the demonstration, is it not?" Göring pointed his meaty finger at the little man. "By my decree, you will not make payment to the Jews, but to the Ministry of Finance."

"Aha!" cried Hildegard with relief. The solution was so simple.

Göring continued with a sharp warning. "As minister of finance, I will tell you that what is done with the money is my business."

Others rushed to join in the economic reprisals against the Jewish victims of Kristal Nacht. Schmer, a junior member of the Finance Ministry, spoke up for the first time. "Your Excellency, I should like to make a proposal. I understand that this morning the Führer decreed also that a fine of one billion marks is to be levied against the Jews for provoking the German people into demonstrating against them. Perhaps with that fine, the insurance companies could be refunded?"

Göring balked at the very thought that any money extracted from the Jews might be given to any entity but the Reich Ministry of Finance, which he headed. "I would not dream of refunding the insurance companies," he blustered. He turned to Hildegard. "That money belongs to the state. You will fulfill your obligations; you may count on that!"

Göring looked pleased; suddenly all the destruction of property had turned to advantage for the four-year economic plan he had struggled with. Suddenly, through the insurance payoff and the fine of one billion marks against the Jews, the coffers of his Ministry of Finance were filled. No longer did he need to consider economic plans like the one proposed by Theo Lindheim. No, the Reich was free to discard outright the scheme that would have allowed Jews to emigrate with a portion of their wealth in return for trade agreements between Germany and the Western nations.

Göring muttered under his breath. "If those bleeding hearts in England and America wish to have the Jews, they must take them as paupers." He raised his eyes to the group. "Not one penny will be taken out of the Reich. We have shown the Jews their way out, eh? They will leave this country through a wall of fire."

13

Night Squad

From across the street, Alfie watched as men worked to nail boards across the doors and low windows on New Church. Signs with the crooked cross on them were nailed up also. Alfie could not read very well, but Mama had taught him some words like *stop* and *go* and *no* and *danger* and *verboten! Forbidden!* It was the biggest word Alfie knew, and he had been very proud when he learned it. It kept him from walking on the grass in the parks and going in the wrong door.

When the Hitler men made laws about the Jews, another word went up with *verboten*—the word *Juden*. Signs everywhere said *Jews Forbidden!* Alfie had learned the word *Juden*, too, because Mama said that otherwise he might only see the word *forbidden* and think he could not enter into a place. He was not a Jew, and so he could go in even though the word *forbidden* was written on a sign.

The sky was getting darker, and Alfie looked at the Nazi signs all over New Church—the word *verboten* painted with a lot of other words. He waited as two men hammered up the last sign. On the top was the crooked cross, then letters and words:

> *CLOSED BY ORDER OF THE REICH GOVERNMENT FOR VIOLATION OF RACE LAW AND STATUTES CONCERNING ILLEGAL PROTECTION OF CRIMINAL JEWS. TRESPASSING FORBIDDEN.*

Among all the letters, Alfie could make out those two words that Mama said he could ignore: *Jews . . . forbidden.*

The sign was not for Alfie because he was not a Jew. The church was boarded up, but the cemetery where Mama lay in the stone shed was not closed. For the first time since last night, Alfie felt good again. He had crackers in his pocket, and over the fence he could see the top of the white stone building where all the Halder family was dead together under the same roof.

The men loaded their ladders and tools into the back of a truck and drove away. They did not see Alfie looking at the graveyard and the place where Mama lay. Other cars drove past, but they did not notice him as he walked across the street and into the little park beside New Church. He followed the wall along the side of the church. Stopping at the metal gate, he shook it hard, but it was locked. It did not matter; Alfie knew another way into the churchyard—a secret he and Jamie kept because of hide-and-seek. No one could find them when they played around the church because they were the only ones who knew.

At the rear of New Church stood the shed where the gardener kept his tools, built almost against the wall that enclosed the churchyard. Between the shed and the wall was a space where Jamie could scoot through easily. It was harder for Alfie because he was big, but just like old times, he dropped to his hands and knees and crawled into the space. A plank covered a hole that went right through the wall and into the cemetery. Grown-ups did not know about it because the slab of an old tombstone leaned back and covered the opening.

Alfie laughed when he crawled through into the churchyard. He felt the same kind of happy feeling that always came to him when he and Jamie ran to hide, and nobody could ever find them! Alfie hadn't played with Jamie in a long time, and now Jamie was gone, but Alfie remembered how to do it and where to go.

Alfie knew where to hide. It was not really a game anymore, but he decided that maybe he did not want to be found or arrested after all. This felt good! He felt smart!

He picked his way carefully through the headstones and the other square stone sheds where families liked to be dead together. He had one more secret that he had shared with Jamie, a secret better than the hole in the wall behind the tombstone.

The place where Mama was buried stood just a little ways in back of the church. It was square like a big stone box. *HALDER* was carved in the stone above an iron gate that opened into a room where the Halders were stored in the walls behind stone partitions.

Alfie touched the gate and looked in. Mama had told him not to be afraid of this place. Six generations of Halders slept here, waiting until Jesus would come wake them up. She explained that generations were grandmothers and grandfathers who lived a long time before Alfie, and that one day they would be alive again and very pleased to meet Alfie. He looked forward to that and thought how fine it would be if Jesus came and everyone woke up while he was here.

"Hello, Mama," he whispered, leaning his head against the bars.

Mama's place was the very top space against the back wall, right above Papa's space. Her name was carved in the stone covering that hid the coffin: *Irene Halder.* Papa's name was also carved on the stone that covered his space: *Alfred Halder.*

But here was the secret Alfie had shared with Jamie: Papa's space was empty. He had disappeared in a shipwreck, and so they could not put him in his place to wait for Jesus. Mama just had the name carved there so it would look as if Papa was there. A memorial, she told Alfie. A way to remember Papa.

Alfie clung to the bars and looked at their names. He was glad he had come back here. He cried a little bit, but not because he was sad. He cried because he was happy that someday for sure they would all wake up and they could hug and laugh and talk about good things.

It was almost dark when Alfie reached his hand up on the stone ledge above the gate. He knew just where the key was. It was long and heavy and rust red, just like the last time Alfie and Jamie had used it.

Alfie unlocked the gate. The hinges groaned inward, and he stepped into the echoing little room. Then he closed the gate behind him and locked it tight. Now Alfie was safe. He had come home to Mama, just like the policeman said, and he wouldn't tell anyone where he was. This was his place. There were lots of empty chambers where he could hide if someone came. And in the back, in an alcove, a square stone trapdoor opened to a chamber below. There were much older Halders down there, and it was damp and musty. Mama never went down there, but Jamie and Alfie had explored it all with a tickle of fear and excitement in their stomachs.

This chamber held the most wonderful secret of all. Alfie had brought food and candles and blankets and had hidden them all in an empty space so that they could keep warm and have lots to eat and could see in the dark while everyone else looked and looked for them in hide-and-seek. He had intended to surprise Jamie next time they played the game, but then Mama had died and the men had come. . . .

Alfie suddenly grew very tired. He touched Mama's name and remembered to say his prayers as she had taught him. And then, without bothering to eat his crackers, he climbed into Papa's empty place and went to sleep.

◯

A tall neon sign announced the appearance of an old comedian at the Winter Garden Theatre in Berlin. Otto Wattenbarger parked the car across the street and sat for a while to study the smiling faces of uniformed officers of the Reich and their women. Furs and diamonds glittered in the harsh light. Complexions seemed lifeless in the unnatural glow.

This was the one theatre in Berlin where people could still come with some measure of freedom. The resident comic had been arrested and released a dozen times for insulting the state and the party. He was always back to his old routine within a matter of days. Goebbels came here sometimes; Hermann Göring was a regular customer. They came because this was the only way they could face the truth and face themselves—through laughter. Strip away the joke, and the truth was a hideous monster. Laugh, and it was almost bearable, like releasing steam from a pressure cooker.

Otto had intended to go in tonight, but if he heard even one fragment of truth covered by a joke, he knew he would go mad. He should mingle among these people, hear their music, know their faces. But he could not. Not now. Tomorrow he would return to Vienna and pass a cyanide tablet through the bars to Michael Wallich. Tomorrow he would be merciful and let the man die an easy death before he was forced to die a difficult one. Ease of death was the mercy of the Third Reich, the justification of murder. Like the truth, it was cloaked with laughter. Cyanide and gas, killing the helpless. Otto had heard the stories. Today they had shown him the photographs.

"God!" He gripped the steering wheel in anguish; he wanted to tear it apart with his bare hands. He had seen the neatly stacked bodies in a row and heard how painless it had been, how merciful.

Otto knew he was going back to whisper to Michael Wallich that he brought him a more merciful end than the death the Gestapo had planned for him! *No torture. Just a little pill, and Michael Wallich would be laid out for a photograph. Not so gruesome as the picture of Thomas von Kleistmann. Not crucifixion. Just this pill . . .*

Otto could not think clearly enough to walk inside the theatre and grin among the other living dead men. They would turn their hollow eyes on him and know that he was a traitor to their conspiracy of death.

He had seen too much; he had walked among these specters and reported their intentions. And no one had believed his report. All this had been useless. Useless! In England they said they were listening, but their listening had not saved Thomas. Or Austria. Or Czechoslovakia. It would not save Michael Wallich from dying or save Otto from helping him into his grave!

The thin veneer of cold control finally cracked and fell away from Otto Wattenbarger. He had done what he needed to do, but today he had seen the photographs, and he could no longer pretend to smile or listen to the music.

He started the car and drove slowly past the neon sign. He would have to regain his sanity again somehow, or he could not return to Vienna. Whatever cause he lived for would be gone unless he could find his mind again tonight. If not, he would be better off to swallow the pill he carried in his pocket for Michael Wallich. Indeed, that seemed the most merciful solution right now for Otto.

But if he died an easy death, would they also crucify Michael?

Would Michael talk, and others die? From their tortured mouths would the rest also be condemned?

Perhaps another time Otto would listen to the music. But not tonight.

Whole streets throughout Berlin seemed deserted, buildings shuttered and dark. As Otto drove from place to place, he measured the destruction and felt small and useless in the face of it.

"What can one man do?" he muttered aloud as he passed the boarded facade of New Church and the burned-out hulk of the great synagogue.

From there he drove into the wide parks that lined the rivers. A bed of dead leaves carpeted the ground beneath trees that seemed lifeless and barren. Like those trees, the freshness of illusion and hope had fallen from Otto. He knew too much to believe in the goodness of men's intentions. He had seen too much darkness to believe that God's light was not in danger of being snuffed out forever in the soul of mankind.

Many who believed in the goodness of humanity had already given in to evil. Beyond Germany, people spoke out against this barbarity but did not fight it with their hands as well as their mouths. They, too, had given up righteousness for the sake of ease. Their consciences were satisfied with moral outrage, but nothing further was accomplished.

"I am too evil, my Lord." Otto wept as he passed the high walls of a hospital where the state had murdered the weak and given beds to the strong. "I am dark!" he cried. "But I long to be light!"

The headlights of his car swept over the dull face of the river Spree. He had seen the sunlight sparkle on its water. He could remember when he had sparkled in his own goodness. Now even kindness in his life seemed tarnished. The sunlight on the water had only been superficial. Night had come to Germany and to the world and to Otto Wattenbarger.

And in seeing what Germany had become, he saw himself.

◯

Orde formed his small troop into a single file with about five yards between them. As he placed them in position he gazed steadily into each
man's eyes. Satisfied that he saw no lingering doubts, he laid a clenched
fist on his mouth in a renewed demand for silence, then clapped each
shoulder as he received a nod of agreement.

Moshe wondered how Orde had picked up the trail of the raiders. He
himself could see no sign of their passing. But Orde walked unerringly
across a rubble-strewn hillside, turned up another canyon, and followed
an ancient watercourse to where it opened out onto a broad plain. Still
without making a sound, he pointed to the marks on the ground that
plainly showed the assembly point of another group.

A few hundred feet along the trail it became obvious that their present path would carry them very close to two Arab villages lying on the
sweep of the plain below them. Zabinski started to point this out but
changed his mind at a sharp look from Orde, so he merely waved his
hand in the direction of the villages. Orde nodded curtly and indicated
by a motion of his hand that they would avoid the trail.

Several hours later, Moshe recognized that this was no stroll in the
countryside. They had tramped miles from the compound and its relative safety and deep into Arab territory. If apprehended here, they would
not live long enough to worry about being handed over to the British authorities. What remained of their corpses would be dumped in some ra-
vine, and no one would ever know of their fate.

Passing the outskirts of a village, they heard approaching voices and
jumped into a culvert at the edge of a field of onions. Only a thin screen
of brush sheltered them. Arab farmers bantered back and forth, exchanging coarse jests.

Moshe drew the British-made pistol from his belt and started to raise
his head from the dirt of the culvert. In the next instant a viselike grip
closed over his wrist, and Captain Orde's other hand firmly pushed
Moshe's head down. With a start, Moshe realized that Orde was paying
more attention to his patrol to see that they did not do anything foolish
than he was to the passing Arabs.

Moving out when it was safe, they continued. It was dusk, and the
glow of firelights in the Arab villages was beginning to show against the
gathering shadows of the Galilean evening. Orde turned abruptly away
from the plain and into the fringe of hills. At the base of a dusty cone-
shaped mound, he held up his hand to call a halt, then waved toward a
rocky outcropping about halfway up the slops. In the lee of a cliff,

Moshe saw the outline of a crude structure, only barely distinguishable from the rock pile.

With a sweeping motion, Captain Orde indicated that his commandos were to spread out on the hillside, with himself near the center of the line. At another gesture they drew their pistols and then began moving forward cautiously. The little arc of men crept slowly up toward the shepherd's hut. Moshe listened keenly for any sounds from the shelter. His eyes darted back and forth to catch any hint of movement. There was no sign of human presence. Orde signaled the all clear and they approached the deserted structure. Through clenched teeth, Zach spoke for the first time. "This is what you brought us all this way for? To attack an empty shepherd's hovel?"

"Empty?"

Zach snorted once, then comprehension crossed his face. He plunged inside, followed by Larry Havas. A moment later the two men dragged long, heavy crates out of the hut. Moshe stooped to enter and retrieved leather bandoliers of cartridges that he swung over his shoulders. Emerging from the structure, he heard a cracking sound as Zach pried open the lid of his crate.

An unmistakable note of shocked triumph echoed in Zach's voice. "Rifles! Real weapons! Still in oilcloth, and German, I think."

"Of course German," Orde replied softly. "What else? You can manage to carry six apiece, plus ammunition. Put the rest back inside and take cover."

Exultation filled every face, a heady excitement at the prospect of being able to defend their settlement with real weapons. Then the full import of Orde's words sank in.

"You mean we're not ready to leave now?" asked Larry nervously. "If we stay very long, we're gonna get caught. I mean, the Arabs won't leave stuff like this alone."

"Precisely."

"What do you mean, precisely?" demanded Zach.

"I mean," Orde said, "we're waiting for them to return."

The little band wasted no time in dividing up the weapons. They examined the barrels to see that the rifles were not plugged with grease. They distributed cartridges and loaded each rifle. Orde inspected each soldier and issued last-minute instructions. Then he glanced at his watch and gathered them in a tight circle like a coach on the sidelines with his soccer team.

"The horse is prepared for battle—" He thumped Larry Havas on the back. "But tonight you will see that victory is from the Lord." Without further introduction, he turned his attention to the Almighty. "We thank

You, Lord, for the victory You have given us. We ask Your mercy for the men who are about to die because of their own foolish actions against Your people Israel. Amen."

The six troopers barely had time to bow their heads before the prayer was finished. Their nervous expressions reflected surprise. Orde held up a finger and in a sudden gentle voice said, "Remember, this is your land, promised to you by the Eternal. You must do your part, just as the Israelites did, and the Lord will be with you. Think of Gideon. Do not be afraid of them, although there will be many."

It was apparent that Orde himself was thinking of Gideon. He stationed his men in a ragged semicircle among the rocks that overlooked the trail and the hut. Once again he demanded silence. A distant night bird sounded a lonely call above Moshe.

In spite of Orde's encouragement, Moshe's unsettled conscience nagged him as the long minutes passed. From his perch above the trail, he had a clear view of the door to the hut. Anyone entering would be within his sights. He had practiced firing an old rifle in Haganah training, but for the first time he realized that the targets would be real and human. Minutes dragged into hours, and the night deepened. Moshe told himself that the Arabs who came—if they came tonight—were coming in preparation for attacking another Jewish settlement. He thought of Eli. He remembered the body of the pretty young woman at Hanita. With these vivid memories he managed to strengthen his resolve. But waiting like this, with a weapon in his hands, still felt cold-blooded.

A half-moon was pushing against the blackness of the eastern sky. The hills seemed to light up with its strange fire. Then suddenly the silence was broken.

Far down the narrow canyon the sound of happy voices drifted up through the stillness. Startled, the bird fluttered away from the nest above Moshe. The Jihad Moquades tramped up the trail noisily, without fear.

Whatever doubts Moshe had were quickly replaced by a sense of panic. This was not a mere handful of men approaching, but a large troop of fighters. A long line of lights moved and swayed upward. Moshe tried to count them, but when he reached seventy-five, his mind went blank. He checked the steep embankment above him. Would he be able to escape up it? Too steep, impassable. He envied the night bird and suddenly felt angry at the English captain for making them stay here and fight when they should have taken their weapons and made a dash back to Hanita!

Moshe blinked hard; at least three times more lights gathered now than when he had stopped counting. He could make out the features of the Holy Strugglers by the glow of ancient lanterns and modern flashlights. Moshe suddenly realized that Captain Orde was not surprised by the numbers of Arabs coming boldly to this place. He had expected it. Like Gideon, he had known his men would be vastly outnumbered.

Voices and laughter grew clearer. Unlike the farmers of this afternoon, these men did not jest among themselves; instead, their conversation was full of boasting about last night's attacks against a dozen settlements, how the Jews and English were quaking with fear in their holes! Another added how easily the Jewish throats had bled, and how he regretted that these new weapons would replace the pleasure of the old ways of fighting.

It was the last thing he ever regretted. Two dozen Arabs moved into the clearing and toward the door of the hut. Orde shouted, "In the name of the British government—" The startled faces of the jihad warriors raised to the rocks. Their hands reached for their weapons, and a shout of rage and alarm swept through the line.

Orde did not need to issue the command to fire. Each of the Hanita fighters picked out a lighted figure and claimed it as his own. Their fingers tightened automatically around the triggers, and the air thundered with what sounded like a thousand Englishmen tucked among the rocks. The blast of rifle volleys resounded amid screams filled with terror.

The Arabs attempted to fight back. Those in the clearing shot wildly up into the rocks as they fled back down the path. Lights and lanterns tumbled down the dusty slopes at the side of the trail.

Moshe kept his sights on the door of the hut as Orde had instructed. Two men charged for its shelter and tumbled back to the ground. A third dropped in midair and fell like a stone on his dying comrades. One Arab pushed forward, shouting for his men to have courage for the sake of the Mufti and Allah and the prophet! His flashlight went spinning out of his shattered hand, and he fled away after his troops. Moshe continued to fire after them. Larry and Zach and the others continued to pump bullets into the blackness.

Three times Orde called for a cease-fire. One at a time his six soldiers heard him, and the night became silent once again.

Orde scrambled down from his position. "Now we need to hurry," he said as the breathless men gathered around him.

Twelve bodies littered the clearing. Orde removed a folded slip of paper from his jacket and pinned a note on the robe of one of the fallen enemy.

PLEASE IDENTIFY ATTACHED CORPSE KILLED WHILE
PROCURING SMUGGLED WEAPONS FOR USE AGAINST
BRITISH FORCES.
SIGNED, SAMUEL ORDE, CAPTAIN

"Will they come back?" Zach asked.

"Yes," Orde said calmly. "Gather what you can carry. Wait for me at the head of the trail."

Each man shouldered six rifles plus leather bandoliers of bullets. No one questioned Orde any longer. They had managed to face at least three hundred Arabs and lived to tell about it! For the moment they still lived, anyway!

Moshe trailed after the others as Samuel Orde dashed into the hut. The minute he remained inside seemed longer than the hours they had waited for the moquades. At last he sauntered out easily, a grenade in his hand. He tossed it into the hut and made a run for a heap of boulders just as the whole structure lifted from the ground in one giant explosion.

The rumble of a rockslide was still audible fifteen minutes later as the seven men scrambled over an obscure goat path by the light of the moon. Carrying forty-two new rifles and four thousand rounds of ammunition for the protection of the Jewish settlements of Galilee, the new trainees of Orde's Special Night Squad melted undetected into the labyrinth of the rugged hills.

14

Nameless Prison

Hitler made a bad attempt at tossing the blame for Kristal Nacht to Winston Churchill and Anthony Eden in England. "It is no accident," he proclaimed, "that this vile little Jew in Paris holds the same views about our Reich as Winston Churchill and his Jew-loving cronies!"

For seven days the world cried out in mourning and in outrage against the Nazis. Churchmen and diplomats and politicians had one voice: "We must find a place of refuge for these poor, downtrodden people! Somewhere in the wide world we must find a haven for them!"

Men and women fleeing Germany spent the nights in cold, wet irrigation ditches on the borders of France and Holland and what remained of Czechoslovakia. Turned away at the crossings, they returned by cattle truck to German concentration camps.

Those who managed to escape into other countries bordering Germany also went into camps for aliens, with the promise that they would stay for two weeks, no longer, and then they would be returned.

In the United States, the cry for mercy rang out so loud that President Roosevelt appointed another commission to decide how the refugees might best be taken into the country. America seemed to be having a change of heart. Perhaps the torch of freedom might burn brightly again.

The wilderness of Alaska was chosen as a likely place for the settlement of unwanted Jews. A very good place. They could not possibly cause trouble there.

American church leaders sounded the warning that Christian concern must not be allowed to wither and die. America had traditionally been a land of refuge for those who were persecuted, and so a hand must be extended. Homes must be provided.

Inundated by telegrams, President Roosevelt announced that he had every intention of taking in as many refugees as possible.

Here was hope! In England, Elisa and Anna and Theo read Murphy's news wires with joy, praying that they would prove true.

Spurred on by this show of support, the British prime minster finally admitted publicly, "It seems all the reports from Germany are indeed true!" Although further settlement of Jews in Palestine was out of the question due to the daily violence, perhaps there was a colony somewhere in the British Empire that could allow the Jews to settle.

By the seventh day, however, Kristal Nacht had become old news. Leaders in England and the United States as well as France seemed irritated that the Jews had gotten in the way of Nazi clubs. The Germans claimed that Jews had gotten what they deserved, that they had provoked the outburst.

By the 20th of November, the head of St. Paul's Cathedral in London had written an article that declared: *The Jews are using their not inconsiderable influence in the press and Parliament to embroil us with Germany!*

At almost the same moment, the president of the Council of Churches in America announced: "Though we as Christians are sympathetic to the plight of the Jews, we do not in any way support a political Zionism or the settlement of Jews in the British Mandate of Palestine."

From that moment, mercy became tempered with practicality. Settling thousands of homeless people would take money. Whose money? Whose land?

Murphy brought the bad news home to dinner that night. It had all come in at once—the smashing of hope, the final revelation of the utter hypocrisy of the democracies.

He tossed a sheaf of paper down on the dinner table in front of Theo.

Theo looked up at him. He did not pick up the dispatches but waited instead for Murphy to recite the news out loud.

It took a moment for Murphy to find his voice. The roast grew cold on the platter as appetites waned.

"Alaska is out. The honorable Representative Dies from Texas and Senator Borah from Idaho have said that America will not take one more refugee than it has to. That Congress will vote down anything that comes through that even hints of enlarging the immigration quota." He paused as Theo's face reflected acceptance, but not surprise. "The Alaskans—" Murphy faltered in disbelief at what he had to say—"well, they say that European Jews are not suited for settlement in Alaska. They would interfere."

At this, Elisa burst out angrily, "So what *are* we suited for? To die? Wasn't this enough? How can they—"

Murphy sighed and took his seat. "Now President Roosevelt is back-pedaling as if his life depended on it. He says he didn't mean to imply that the United States would actually take in more refugees. No sir. What he *meant* was that those twelve thousand German Jews who are in the States on visitors' visas as tourists can have their visas renewed for another six months if they want."

"Visas renewed." Anna and Theo exchanged looks. Dieter and Wilhelm had just left for New York on visitors' visas as guests of Mr. Trump. They hoped to go to school there, out of reach of the turmoil of Europe. "Six months?" Anna said, her voice thick with emotion.

"Of course, that could change overnight." Elisa's eyes brimmed with tears of frustration. "After all, it has only been a little more than a week since Kristal Nacht. They have made themselves feel better by talking about compassion and mercy! They condemn the Nazis and then give Hitler the right to do what he wants. These people will not remember our suffering at all a month from now!"

"No homeland in Palestine," Theo repeated. "No support from the churches for Zionism. Then where shall we turn? Who will help us?"

Every news publication of the Western democracies was analyzed by specialists within the massive Reich Ministry of Propaganda. The experts assessed public sentiment based on what the democratic press published every day. They discussed demonstrations of outrage against the policies of the Reich and took propaganda measures to counter any disfavor.

Of course the Reich minister of propaganda, Joseph Goebbels, showed no surprise at the outcry against the pogroms of Kristal Nacht. What did startle him, however, was the speed with which that outcry subsided. Hitler was not at all taken aback. He recognized that the free press moved from one sensational story to the next, tiring of "yesterday's news" before the blood congealed on the sidewalks.

Goebbels brought several articles to the Chancellory to review with the Führer after the evening film screening of *The Big Broadcast of 1938*. Somehow it seemed fitting that they should gauge the effect of the press and radio broadcasts after watching the antics of Hollywood entertainers.

The Führer, in an excellent mood, sent his mistress, Eva Braun, up to bed and promised he would be along shortly. He was particularly jovial and uncharacteristically ordered a glass of beer.

Minister Goebbels felt that the clippings would not upset Hitler's charming mood in any way—with the possible exception of one small detail that could easily be remedied.

He threw open the leather portfolio containing the various newspapers. Hitler tossed several German magazines onto the floor and cleared the coffee table for action. His translator, Dr. Schmidt, read aloud the various condemnations in the articles, emphasizing the fact that the democracies were quick to add they could do little to help.

The last newspaper was from the TENS London office. A predictably critical article by Winston Churchill on the back page of the first section was none too alarming. But as the pages turned, photographs displayed various Christian pastors who had been arrested in Berlin—not just their photographs alone, but pictures of their families as well. Articles explained in detail why these men had been in disfavor within the Reich. Descriptions were given of their families. The question about their fate was raised. The implication was clear: These men were not Jews; they simply disapproved of the Reich. Was the Nazi Party frightened of small voices of individual disapproval? Was the Führer so insecure that he could not tolerate dissension even from the pulpits of the churches?

Hitler frowned as Dr. Schmidt translated the lengthy articles. He leaned closer to stare at the smiling face of Pastor Karl Ibsen, his wife, and two children as they sat on the garden wall of New Church. This fellow had been nothing but trouble for the party. Since 1933, he had spoken out against every Reich policy designed to rid the state of beggars, cripples, and imbeciles. He championed the cause of hopeless causes! He proclaimed that every human life was of value. He decried the evils of euthanasia and forced sterilization.

Hitler tapped his finger on Ibsen's picture. "He is in custody?"

"Arrested for violation of the Nuremberg racial laws. Hiding Jews," Goebbels said in a positive tone.

"His family?" The Führer looked thoughtful. Too thoughtful. Perhaps he was disturbed by this display of German churchmen.

"Also in custody." Goebbels did not tell Hitler that the daughter still remained at large. He chose to overlook that small detail. Besides, he and Himmler had the best agent in the Gestapo working on that matter.

"Good." Hitler seemed satisfied. He sat back and sighed deeply. "You can see how it is, Goebbels. These sniveling democracies are not really worried about Jews, either. Ah! But the Zionists will find a way to stir up the pot over these Christian pastors. No one in the West will care if we eliminate every Jew between here and Moscow. But arrest a handful of preachers, and they scream like it is their own family. Immense hypocrisy."

Goebbels started to close the paper. The Führer put a hand on his arm to stop him. He wanted to look a moment at the photograph of the man who had caused him so much trouble.

"We handled the father of Ernst vom Rath quite well." Hitler yawned.

"Head of a racial office. Yes. He does not oppose us any longer." Goebbels could not see the connection.

"You see, Joseph, handling men is an art. Some you bribe with positions. Others you break with an iron rod. Some you simply persuade. Or torture." He smiled. "And then there are men like our pastors here—paragons of German manhood. God and family come first. Honor, loyalty, and other admirable qualities fit in there somewhere." He motioned toward the photograph. "Do you understand me?"

Goebbels was not certain he did. It was late, after all. Past midnight. But he nodded.

Hitler tapped on Ibsen's photo again. "The Western press dotes on men like these. They make men like Karl Ibsen their martyrs."

"What can we do about it?"

"We get them on our side. Every man has his price. Money, prestige, position. Torture. A quiet word to the wise. These methods will work with nearly every man on this page. Pressure applied wisely will have them speaking out in public and proclaiming the greatness of the Third Reich. They will extol my rule and loudly denounce the West." He frowned. "Every one of them but this fellow, I think."

"Shall we simply kill him, mein Führer?"

"And make him an eternal martyr? No." Hitler laughed. "I know something about making martyrs. I would rather have Karl Ibsen on our side. One hundred percent."

"But you said yourself—"

Hitler raised a chin to silence Goebbels. "We will try all these other methods first with Pastor Ibsen. It will be best if we break him for reasons less noble than his love for his family. Save that threat as a last resort. If such a man succumbs for the sake of freedom, or perhaps good food, or a bribe, his own hypocrisy will forever make him say to himself that he really had not understood the justice of the Nazi cause. His self-hatred will make him ours entirely."

Goebbels nodded. It was better to use methods that appealed to a man's own selfish nature. The question was, of course, whether Karl Ibsen had such a nature. "And if such things fail to get results?"

"Keep his family on hand. We will use them as our weapon. If we must. A man like Karl Ibsen will say or do anything if his loved ones are threatened. We will own his soul one way or another. First, make it a goal to reeducate him. Eventually, I promise you, Minister Goebbels, we will have Pastor Karl Ibsen on the Reich state radio to broadcast the justice of the Aryan cause right back into the teeth of Churchill. Our own *Big Broadcast of 1938."*

A blast of cold air hit Jacob's face as he opened the door leading up to the bell tower. He pulled his stocking cap down over his ears and ascended the stone spiral steps to the top.

The wind blew strong from the north. Flags on top of ministry buildings stood out stiff on their poles. Jacob ducked low and remained out of sight. He did not care if he could not see the traffic rolling by as long as he could glimpse the sky for a few minutes.

He sat on the floor of the round tower and watched a gray pigeon hop along the ledge above him. The great green bells were covered with pigeon droppings; the birds of Berlin had already lost their fear of the thundering bells of New Church. Like the voices of Pastor Ibsen and Jacob's father, the bells were silent now—no reminder to the consciences of the Berliners who had so easily resumed their daily life.

Jacob closed his eyes and tried to pray. In the end he could only tell God that he was afraid, that he was not ready to assume the responsibilities of manhood. How could he properly take care of Lori? He thought of her too much; he felt things for her that made being near her painful. He must steel himself, be brother and father to her, distance himself from those feelings. If he really was her brother, maybe he could fight with her and be angry with her the way he always seemed to be angry with Mark. She seemed so sad and alone. Jacob wanted only to comfort her, but to do so would be disastrous. It was difficult enough to sleep without the thought of reaching out to touch her.

He inhaled deeply, then let his breath out slowly. Cold air and the bell tower seemed to help him breathe easier.

He closed his eyes and listened to the hum of traffic on the street, the cooing of the pigeons and the hooting of horns. . . . Then suddenly he heard the sound of voices in the yard below—people in the churchyard! Two men!

"I check it every night. No need to worry. Nobody will break in!" It was the old watchman.

"I just want to have a look around," said a pleasant-sounding voice. "Perhaps there is some clue about the girl's whereabouts. We have checked as many of the former church members as possible. No sign of her. No hint as to where she is."

Jacob's breath grew shallow with fear. He slid down the stairs, praying that Lori and Mark would be close enough to hide! Through the door and into the corridor he could hear the rattle of chains and locks stirring on the entrance door of New Church. They were coming in!

He wanted to yell for Mark and Lori, but of course they would be caught if he made a sound. His shoes sounded like gun blasts to his ears as he attempted to move silently. He pulled them off and ran in his stocking feet. The chains still rattled behind him! He dashed up to the choir loft and met Lori, pale and trembling, at the top of the steps. Mark held open the door to the bellows room. His eyes blinked with his heartbeat.

A finger to his lips, Jacob pulled Lori into their hideout. They crammed into the bellows just as the laughter of the two men echoed into the foyer and permeated the walls of the entire church building.

"They went over this place with a microscope, Agent Hess," said the watchman.

"There may be things they missed that I would see," the second man replied without arrogance. He was not vaunting his ability; he was simply stating a fact. "Certain leaders feel it is important that this girl be found. I have specialized in rooting out difficult cases."

Enclosed in the leather cocoon of the organ bellows, the words sounded distant and muffled, but the threat seemed more terrible than even the first day. *They have come back! Gestapo! They have not simply forgotten about Lori Ibsen!*

Lori wrapped her arms around Jacob's middle. He held her close against him, and suddenly felt the obligation of father and brother to protect her. Mark squatted down in a little ball. Footsteps ascended into the choir loft. *Only one set of footsteps*, Jacob thought. The agent was alone.

He smelled the bitter odor of cigarette tobacco. The agent stopped at the door of the dusty room and peered in. Lori, Jacob, and Mark held their breaths. They could hear the man mumbling as he stared in. Jacob prayed his lungs would not explode. He eased his breath out slowly as the man turned away and shouted down from the choir loft to the watchman below.

"Keep a sharp eye out for any light or movement, will you? If the girl comes back, no doubt she will look here first for her family. You will get a reward if we find them here, provided you are in on it."

The garbled reply of the old man was lost beneath the pounding of Jacob's heart. He prayed that Gestapo Agent Hess would find no sign. After all, they had been so careful; everything was left exactly as it had been the first time the Gestapo ransacked the church. The floor was littered with torn hymnals. Paper was strewn everywhere. The cross, which had been ripped down from above the baptistery, lay where it had fallen across the altar. The pinwheel of a Nazi swastika was painted on the pulpit. Jacob had prevented Lori from cleaning it off.

It seemed a very long time before the voices moved toward the door. Chains clanged against the heavy wood doors, sealing the church again. Only then did the trio relax a bit. Even so, Jacob insisted that they remain in the bellows until long after the sun went down.

Many of the prisoners arrested with Pastor Karl Ibsen and Richard Kalner were shipped by train or truck to the overcrowded prison camp of Dachau. The younger, stronger men like Karl and Richard were sent to a new place several hours to the east of Berlin.

Vast and still uncompleted, the nameless compound was being hewn from the forest that bordered Poland.

From behind the layers of barbed-wire fence, Pastor Karl could clearly see the Polish guards who patrolled their side of the fences in search of any desperate refugees who might have attempted escape from Germany.

Since Kristal Nacht, many such people cut through the wire in the night and carried children across the open field, only to be sniffed out by dogs or trapped in the long serpentine ditch just at the top of the rise. Most were caught and promptly returned to the German side of the line and handed over to the authorities. Men, women, and children were then brought by truck through the fortified gates of Nameless camp. Surrounded by gun towers and smirking guards, they were put to work building their own prison.

Only a dozen prison barracks had been completed on the day Karl and Richard stepped stiffly onto the frozen ground. Those dozen were crammed to bursting with thousands of prisoners judged fit enough to construct the remainder of the facility.

Heat and blankets were promised after the job was done. In the meantime, men in ragged street clothes, torn nightshirts, and sagging trousers worked urgently beneath the watchful eyes of gray-uniformed men in heavy winter coats and boots. Gloved fingers curled around the triggers of machine guns and pointed at the bare-handed prisoners who strung the barbed wire that surrounded them.

The whack of hammers echoed in the dark green forest from early morning until it was too dark to see the head of a nail. When the first snow fell, silent and beautiful against the evergreens, one hundred men died of exposure in a single day. A grave-digging detail was appointed the task of carting off frozen bodies and digging shallow graves for them in the frozen earth.

Even so, those who had come from other prisons said that this was a virtual resort compared to Dachau. There was food here, at least—if a man could choke down rancid bacon and rotting potatoes. Most managed to eat. Those who did not were the next to die.

Although it was forbidden to call out another man's name during work hours, Richard managed to let every prisoner nearby know that Karl Ibsen was pastor of an evangelical church in Berlin—a man with a good position who really did not have to be here if he had only followed the Nazi doctrine against his Jewish parishioners. These facts caused others in the camp to look at Karl with an attitude of respect, even admiration.

Most were here because they had no choice. They were Jewish; they were anti-Nazi; they had said the wrong thing to the wrong person. Few at Nameless camp would not have gladly forsaken everything to get out of this place. They would have kissed the boot of a Storm Trooper and called Adolf Hitler blessed if only the gate of Nameless would swing open for them and the border guards in Poland would look the other way. And then they would have run hard and fast and never looked back at those they were leaving behind.

This was sensible thinking, logical for any man who loved life and longed to live past tomorrow. But this Pastor Karl Ibsen—now here was an unusual man, arrested while trying to convince Richard Kalner to come along and be hidden away from the Nazis!

Some said that Pastor Karl was a fool. A few encouraged him to claim that a mistake had been made, that he had only gone to the Kalners' apartment to collect on a debt when along came the Gestapo.

But Pastor Karl would not deny what he had done. It was a small thing. Small and pitiful and much too late.

"They will ask him to make a confession of his error," said a fellow who had been behind the wire for months. "And he will say he was a fool for helping lousy Jews, and then they will let him go back to Berlin. Maybe even back to his church if he is a good boy and promises to proclaim the wisdom of *Mein Kampf* from the pulpit."

"Pastor Karl will not deny us," Richard defended. "You will see. He is one with us."

Jacob strode from the charity room holding cans of tuna high in the air. He had found a treasure of foodstuffs in there, he declared—everything that had been collected since the beginning of the food drive in October.

"Tuna and canned meat. Flour in barrels! Salt and beans!"

There was even more than that, as it turned out—everything three people would need to survive for a long time. They could live here for months like three castaways on a desert island. The Nazis had sealed them in, but if they were careful, they could survive, and no one would ever know.

Mark looked less gleeful than his brother, Lori noticed. Maybe he was homesick and heartsick, as she was. At least Jacob and Mark had each other. *Family!*

She could not make herself care about the food. The prospect of being shut up inside New Church without Mama or Papa or Jamie seemed like prison. Jacob had already begun making rules:

Thou shalt not listen to the radio until the watchman is gone.

Thou shalt not take baths in the baptistery lest someone hear the noisy water pipes and sound the alarm.

Thou shalt sleep in the organ bellows room for quick escape.

The list went on and on.

"Well, what do you think?" Jacob balanced the canned tuna on his head and turned slowly as if he were modeling a hat.

Lori did not smile. Not that he was not funny—at least he had always been able to make her laugh before. But not now. She shook her head and tried to tell him she was not in the mood for games.

"We're rich!" Mark crowed, producing a bag of hard candy. "I thought they looked everywhere, took everything not nailed down."

"You think these thugs will look in a room marked *Charity* when they just looted every fancy shop in Berlin?" Jacob still smiled, but not so broadly. He let the cans slip off his head into his hands. "Practically a miracle, eh, Lori?" He was trying to cheer her up, but it was no use.

She bit her lip and tried to keep from telling them both that none of this mattered, that she wished she had been arrested and taken away with Mama and Jamie. "It's just food," she said. "It doesn't matter unless Mama and Papa come back here. What's the use of any of it?" With that she fled the room, leaving them staring after her and wondering what more she could ask for in such conditions.

Down the darkened hall she heard Mark's voice: "Girls! I wish the Nazis had taken her instead of Jamie! We might have had a better time of it then."

Lori muttered through her tears, "I wish so too, you little brat!" But she was too far away for him to hear.

15
Prophetic Voices

The woman clerk at the Foreign Ministry office removed the envelope from a scuffed brown leather letter case and placed it on the desk in front of Anna and Theo Lindheim.

"I am sorry," she said. "This was returned from Germany by diplomatic courier. The attaché in Berlin attempted to contact your sister, Mrs. Lindheim, but apparently the family has . . . left town."

Left town. The very words carried the suggestion of doom.

"But surely there is some explanation," Theo began. "They have just left Berlin? their home? work? How can this be?"

"Really, that is the only message I have for you." The clerk directed her gaze to Anna. "We are not in the business of delivering personal messages, you see. And your sister is a German citizen." She nudged the letter across to Anna. "There is really nothing more our embassy in Berlin or this ministry can do."

Anna took the letter and held it in her hands as though its return to her conveyed a message too ominous to contemplate. "Certainly there must be a way for me to contact my sister."

"Perhaps through the German Embassy?" The woman knew, of course, that this was impossible. How could the Lindheims approach the German Embassy and expect help?

"You will not assist us, then?" Theo took the letter from Anna. "What about their children? Surely you understand the danger they could be in because of our own efforts to aid German refugees."

The woman shrugged and looked to other work. "They are not refugees, are they? They are full German citizens. Not Jews. Not involved in the pogrom, certainly. Mr. Lindheim, are you aware of the caseload we are dealing with? Requests for visas from truly desperate people. My heavens, our fellow in Berlin went beyond his duty in this instance. He is not a mail carrier." She offered no sympathy. She was busy, and she let them know it as she thumbed through a stack of papers.

"If there is any word of my sister's whereabouts—" Anna tried again to find some spark of hope.

"There will be nothing from *this* department," said the clerk abruptly. "Perhaps you should put in a request with the Red Cross. And certainly you must have connections still in Germany that might assist you in locating your sister and her family."

Anna told herself that Helen and Karl and the children must be safe. Perhaps they had simply taken a holiday from the terror of Berlin. Maybe even now they were in some quiet refuge in the Harz Mountains. A thousand times Anna had begged them to leave the new Germany. They had refused, citing their duty to remain and work even as the world seemed to crumble around them.

Anna had not written them for fear of jeopardizing their safety through contact with her. She and Theo were labeled as criminals by the Nazi government. A phone call or a letter from her to her sister might have cast suspicion on them as well.

Somehow Anna had continued to picture Helen shopping on Unter den Linden or playing the organ at church. As Anna and Theo descended the broad staircase of the government office, Anna wondered if she would ever again play a duet with her sister. Suddenly nagging doubts transformed into full-blown fears—for Helen, for Karl, for the children. Anna knew well enough how caring Christian people had managed to fall through the cracks and then totally disappear from the face of the Third Reich.

Within the refuge of King Faisal's palace in Baghdad, Haj Amin maintained his own staff of bodyguards and servants as well as a late-model shortwave radio to keep in touch with his fighters in the British Mandate. Although reports from the majority of Jerusalem and the southern area of Palestine had been excellent, news from Galilee had been dismal. Holy Strugglers owned the roads after dark everywhere—except around Hanita. The pace of terrorist attacks against the English and the Jews was increasing everywhere—except near Hanita. German SS commandos were training Arab mercenaries; their success was undeniable throughout the Mandate—except near Hanita. And now its neighboring Jewish kibbutzim seemed to be gaining strength as well!

At last Haj Amin held the explanation of that success in his hands. A dozen notes, all written in the same English scrawl in green crayon, were signed by one man: Samuel Orde, Captain.

Some notes were stained with the blood of those who had fallen in the fighting against this dangerous English officer. All of them served up the same message to the guerrilla fighters in northern Palestine. The resistance of the Jews in that area had suddenly become fierce and deadly! Where twenty thousand British troops had failed, this one English captain and his secret army succeeded.

And his success made Haj Amin extremely angry.

"This Samuel Orde—" he drummed his long, effeminate fingers against the notes—"you call him the most dangerous man in the British Mandate, Herr Vargen." He narrowed his eyes and glared at the German commander chosen by Hitler to assist with the Muslim rebellion.

"Dangerous," Vargen repeated, his face betraying no emotion, "because he is not afraid to fight."

"We are not afraid to fight."

"You pay these men of yours ten pounds a month and promise them Paradise if they die fighting Jews and killing Englishmen. But they are still not half the fighters this Orde has managed to bring in. Professional British commandos, I believe, dressed as Jewish settlers. Your peasants are no match for them."

Haj Amin flushed with anger at the insult. "Then perhaps if the British are bringing in more special troops, we shall put the question to the Führer as well. Is that what you are suggesting?"

"For a start. I have sent my recommendations to Berlin. But most of all, I believe it is essential that we eliminate the Englishman, Captain Orde. Perhaps we might issue a bounty for his head. And then, politically, we must have the Arab leadership remaining in Jerusalem file an official complaint. The Führer agrees. This is not a matter of self-defense any longer, but attacks." He passed a memo from Berlin to the Mufti. It had just arrived at the German Embassy in Baghdad and bore the official seal of the Reich. It was signed with the name of Adolf Hitler, and addressed to the Mufti of Jerusalem in exile.

One cannot forget, my friend, that the British are basically political beasts, swayed by all political criticism, very conscious of public demonstrations and disapproval, and eager to please whoever is the most vocally unhappy. I would recommend a two-pronged attack on this one English captain in Palestine who is effective against us. Eliminate him physically, if possible. The Reich will transfer ten thousand pounds into your account for this purpose. Failing that, make certain that the Arab Higher Committee of Jerusalem in your absence files protests of outrage against Captain Orde's obviously pro-Zionist leadership.

We work together in a common cause. Stand firm in your resolve and we will live to see the world rid of the troublesome Jews without fail.

Warm greetings,
A. Hitler

Along with the personal note of encouragement from the Führer, plans were included that duplicated the concentration camps already built throughout the Reich. Written neatly in Arabic script at the bottom of the blueprint were these words: *For the elimination of the Jewish problem in Palestine.*

This brought a smile to the lips of Haj Amin for the first time in days.

The study in the Red Lion House seemed uncomfortably warm to Theo. He tugged his collar and mopped his brow.

Murphy tossed another scoop of coal onto the fire. He was not perspiring. Elisa sat wrapped in a blanket. Anna wore a sweater. Perhaps the open threats in Hitler's speech made Theo sweat.

He looked up at the clock: half past eight. The voice of the Führer, like a razor, cut away the self-righteous illusions of the nations.

> *"Nor can I see a reason why the members of this Jewish race should be imposed on the German nation, while in the nations so enthusiastic about these 'splendid people' their immigration is refused with every imaginable excuse. I think the sooner this problem is resolved the better, for Europe cannot settle down until the Jewish question is cleared up! It may well be possible that sooner or later an agreement on this problem may be reached in Europe, even between those nations that otherwise do not so easily come together. The Jewish race will have to adapt itself to sound constructive activity as other nations do, or sooner or later it will succumb to a crisis of an inconceivable magnitude."*

Elisa raised her head, daring to interrupt for the first time. "What can he mean by that? Wasn't Kristal Nacht enough? Can there be more?"

At the time, the violence of Kristal Nacht had seemed inconceivable to Theo. Now Hitler declared something more terrible, something that the human mind could not imagine. And he was stating his intention over the airways of the British Broadcasting Corporation.

*"One thing I should like to say on this day, which may be memorable
for others as well as for us Germans: In the course of my life I have
often been a prophet and have usually been ridiculed for it. During the
time of my struggle for power, the Jewish race received my prophecies
with laughter when I said that one day I would take over the leadership
of the state and the nation and that I would settle the Jewish problem.
Their laughter was uproarious. But now they are laughing out of the
other side of their face! Today I will once more be a prophet!"*

Here Hitler paused as the world waited to hear the prophecy he
would utter to the Jews of Europe. Anna took Theo's hand and glanced
fearfully at him as Hitler boomed:

*"If the international Jewish financiers in and outside Europe should
succeed in plunging the nations into a world war, then the result will
not be the bolshevization of the earth and the victory of Jewry but the
annihilation of the Jewish race in Europe!"*

Annihilation. The word was simple enough. It was, indeed, inconceivable, and yet no longer did Theo doubt what the Führer of Germany was
saying.

"He means to kill them all," Theo said quietly.

Eyes raised to look at him, to study his face, to see if Theo truly believed such a thing was possible.

Theo cleared his throat. "He means it. And he has made the German
people ready." He wiped beads of perspiration from his forehead. "In
1933, the year he came to power, one million babies were aborted in Germany. Then came permissible euthanasia, mercy killing of the old. That
led to *selective* euthanasia, the murder of those who were mentally unworthy, racially unworthy. And then there were the children like Charles—the
killing of babies who were considered imperfect." He stared at each member of his family. "Annihilation of the Jews of Europe. His excuse for that
will be war. The inconceivable is not only possible; he means to do it."

Murphy no longer needed convincing. The Kristal Nacht reports had
eliminated all pretense that Germany was still a basically civilized country. "What do we do now, Theo?" Murphy asked. "What will it take before people believe this?"

"They believe it already." Theo rose and walked slowly toward the
window. He swept his arm across the sleepy little square. "They have
heard it. Who can doubt that the threat is real? Most do not care to think
about it. But those who do hear and think and have a conscience must
also have a plan."

"We can't wait for the British government," Murphy said, leaning heavily against the mantel. "And no one in America is any better as far as the government is concerned."

"Then I say we go back to doing things the old way." Elisa raised her chin defiantly. "Passports smuggled in. Forged papers. Why do we need to play their game? Hitler is right. The democracies are barrels of hypocrisy. The churches will not help. Why don't we go back to doing it the way it was done before?"

Anna answered. "Because we are being watched. Your father has been warned that if he works outside the immigration laws and quotas, he will be deported back to Germany."

She did not need to explain further. The group fell silent once again under that ominous reality.

Minutes passed. The speech of the Führer continued. Crowds roared their approval of his policies. *Yes, he is a prophet,* they seemed to say. And they were all quite willing to fulfill his prophecies.

The telephone call from Sir Thomas Beecham, conductor of the London Philharmonic Orchestra, issued a call to arms for every musician.

"Yes, yes!" he said to Elisa. "It is already arranged with the BBC. We begin rehearsal in an hour. Bring your fiddle and be ready to work!"

And so the musicians who had fled Germany for the safe haven of Covent Garden prepared for their first battle cry against the horrors of the Night of Broken Glass. Every face was grim; many eyes were red with tears of anger and fear for loved ones who remained behind in Germany. But their hands did not tremble as they held their instruments and listened to Sir Thomas as he explained the message he intended to send straight to the Chancellory in Berlin.

Standing tall and bull-necked on the conductor's hand, Sir Thomas directed his steely gaze to those musicians he knew had suffered the most under Nazi policies. He had heard Elisa's story of the fall of Vienna. He knew well the part her Guarnerius violin had played in that struggle to save the lives of Jewish children. He also suspected that the darkest days were yet to come.

"In Germany, those of you who are Jewish are forbidden to play the works of Beethoven. But we shall throw this music back in the teeth of Adolf Hitler!" He paused and thumbed through his music folder. "We had planned to open our season with Mendelssohn tonight, but since this is to be broadcast also in Germany, it occurred to me that Beethoven's Fifth might be a better message to send, eh?"

No one smiled. Elisa looked from face to face and pictured where old friends might have been sitting on the stage of the Musikverein. She felt homesick for them and angry.

Sir Thomas Beecham continued. "For those of you who are not familiar with Morse code, I will tell you that the letter *V* is three dots and a dash. The opening notes of Beethoven's Fifth are . . ."

One at a time, faces broke into smiles as the musicians remembered the score, and Sir Thomas held up his fingers in the V-for-victory sign. Simple. Three dots and a dash put to music. The letter for victory had been written by Beethoven long before Morse had invented his code.

"We must speak to the persecuted who remain trapped in the Reich, my children!" Sir Thomas held his fingers higher and answering hands rose among the orchestra. "Hitler thinks he has refused you victory, but we here in England will send the message back to Germany. Your friends and family will hear it on the BBC and have hope tonight!"

Peter tuned Herr Ruger's radio with the delicacy of a safecracker. Suddenly the static gave way to clear, elegant tones of Sir Thomas Beecham's voice.

"Among the musicians of the London Philharmonic are men and women driven from the orchestras of Germany by policies of racial madness that transcend any since the Dark Ages. Intolerance by Germany has blessed the democracies with great talent; for this we may thank the German leaders with all our hearts! These talented people belong with us now, and through their instruments we send a message of victory yet to come to those who still cringe beneath the lash of the tyrant!"

It was a good speech. Peter and his mother took turns translating the best of it to Marlene, who was not really interested.

England! For Peter, the voice of the BBC was like water in the desert of last night's destruction. Through forbidden music, a sermon of hope was preached, and for an hour tonight, he did not think of the smoldering ruins of the Turnergasse Synagogue or the prisoner lorries that had taken his friends away. He found himself looking at Herr Ruger's photograph of Hitler and feeling strangely triumphant, as if a prophecy rang out in the notes, as if victory lay nearly within his reach.

The Nazis had searched New Church from top to bottom, and a miracle had occurred. Not only had they passed by the organ bellows, they had also overlooked the cupboard in Pastor Ibsen's office where the radio was kept. God had somehow blinded the eyes of their pursuers to keep them from finding the radio.

For Lori, food did not seem half so important as that link with the outside world. Tonight, in the nearly total blackness of the church, she led Jacob and Mark to the windowless study and ordered them to sit. She did not need to switch on the light.

She groped along the wall of cabinets to the one containing the radio. Jacob closed the door of the study as she turned the knob and a low whistle announced the first words from the outside.

"Papa kept it tuned to the BBC," she said in a hushed voice. "The only real news."

The voice of Sir Thomas Beecham crackled over the radio. Lori, a shadow by the light of the dials, turned down the volume.

Jacob spoke impatiently. "How will we know the news if this fellow is talking in English only?"

Lori translated the little speech given by the British conductor about Beethoven and victory. The words made them all feel better. *Someone in England knows what happened in Berlin! And now they tell us to have hope!*

Jacob had never cared much for classical music, but he sat spellbound as the forbidden music of Beethoven signaled that the sound of smashing glass had been heard beyond the borders of the Third Reich.

Lucy lay in the dark on her bed and listened to the faraway music of London's BBC. It was forbidden, of course, but everyone with a radio listened to England all the same—for this reason the authorities had demanded that all Jews turn in their radios. Hitler did not like the thought of Jews taking comfort from the self-righteous pronouncements of the British against the Reich.

Tonight Lucy felt especially sorry for the Jews of Germany who could not hear this musical condemnation of the riots against them.

Beethoven's Fifth. Music and victory. Only an Englishman would make such a connection and have the audacity to announce it over the radio. Three dots and a dash, indeed! According to rumor, Hitler himself listened to the BBC to hear what the British were thinking. Maybe tonight he had heard the English conductor thank the Führer for sending England the finest musicians in the world. Perhaps Hitler paced and raged while the London Philharmonic Orchestra gave his nasty racial laws a good stiff slap in the face! Lucy hoped so. She hoped that Sir Thomas Beecham had ruined Beethoven's Fifth Symphony forever and always for the Führer! From this night on, Beethoven's Fifth would be Lucy's secret theme song.

16

Death by Politics

The wind blew high above Jerusalem, pushing the clouds across the sky like sailing ships. The British Union Jack strained against the flagpole; metal clips on the flag clanged like a warning bell as Samuel Orde strode up the steps of the British High Command.

Soldiers on either side of the door saluted, their neatly pressed uniforms and spit-shined shoes a distinct contrast to Orde's rumpled khakis. He returned their salute. *I haven't missed all this,* he thought as he caught some hint of foreboding in their manner toward him. *So. Here I am again. Up to my neck in hot water.*

"General Wavell will see you, Captain Orde." The adjutant led him into the small office that overlooked the Old City panorama across the Valley of Hinnom.

Wavell barely acknowledged Orde's salute. He motioned to a chair and studied his reports before he cleared his throat in an embarrassed way. "Well, so you have been cleaning out the rats' nests in Galilee."

"Been quite successful. Night raids. Catching them off guard. Striking first."

Wavell slapped a hand down on his desk and leaned back, glaring at Orde. "And who are you using for soldiers, Orde?"

The general did not need to ask. He knew. Everyone knew what was happening in the north. A collection of ragtag Jewish settlers, trained and armed by this English officer, were beating the socks off a combination of Arab mercenaries from all over the Middle East, who were armed with German- and Turkish-made rifles. It was a stunning success. Orde had written about it himself and sent the stories to Murphy's TENS office in London under a pseudonym.

Orde considered the red face of the commander opposite him. "I am using anyone who is available and not afraid to die."

"You are training Jews! Everyone knows it, Orde. Strictly against the policy of the Mandate! You are putting weapons into the hands of the Zionists, making them potentially capable of turning those weapons on us."

"Their weapons are captured German ordnance." He did not back away from the challenge. He had broken every rule in the book and yet had been right in doing so. "German-made. You know what that means." He leaned forward with urgency. "The Nazis have come here, just as they are fighting with the Fascists in Spain and calling the Loyalists who oppose them all Communists—"

"We are trying to keep a lid on this thing."

"The lid was off long ago. The Zionists are the only friends we have, General Wavell. And we have tied their hands and put them in front of a firing squad where Hitler is the judge and Haj Amin is the executioner!"

"We are protecting the settlements as well as possible. That was your assignment as an English officer!"

"And I have fulfilled my duty!" Orde replied angrily. "While Arab gangs have closed down the roads to British vehicles every night since the rebellion began, I have kept our roads open in Galilee. There have been murders all over the rest of the Mandate, but only two since I arrived in Galilee."

"You know most of the staff officers favor Arabs."

"A sentimental hangover from the days when Lawrence led the Bedouins against the Turks."

"And you fancy yourself another Lawrence of Arabia, eh? Orde of Palestine?" His eyes burned with the challenge. "Savior of the Zionist cause?" He held up a sheaf of articles Orde had written about his own exploits in Galilee against the gangs. "You are your own press agent—exploitation and egotism in the highest!"

Orde managed a slight smile. He never expected to fool anyone with his pseudonym. He had only wanted to shame the British High Command into training and equipping the Jewish settlers to fight a mutual enemy.

"We are defeating the enemy on the field of battle. There is nothing written in the articles that is not absolute truth."

"I will tell you the truth, Captain Orde, and the truth comes to me straight from Whitehall in London! The truth is that our government does not consider the Arab gangs of Haj Amin to be our enemies. They are simply discontented with the way things stand. They may well be future allies, and the Arab Higher Committee does not consider it in the interest of future peace in this region for us to allow the Jews to fight at our sides. Arabs do not fight at our sides in this conflict, after all."

Orde managed to stifle his sarcasm at this remark. "No, sir. I do not expect them to."

"Well, then?"

Orde smoothed his mustache and took his time. "Well, then, I propose inducting the Jewish night squads into our military. It is not required that we state they are Jewish, simply that the men I command are effective in stopping ambushes on the roads and the blowing of pipelines from Lebanon." He inhaled with an air of satisfaction. "Regardless of what truth Whitehall sends us from London, we know that a bit of sensible muscle applied correctly here in Palestine is much more effective in keeping the peace than all the politics in the world."

"Jewish soldiers?" General Wavell shook his head as though he could not believe his ears.

"With proper training we could clean out a lot more nests than just Galilee."

Wavell looked out the window. The weary expression on his face indicated that he agreed. But there was something else. "The Arabs and our own colonial secretary are discussing the idea of a peace conference. Talking."

"Ah. And they cannot talk if we fight."

"They say you must stop fighting before they will even talk about talking," he said evenly. Regret filled his voice. "You have done too well, Orde." His eyes met Orde's. "I must order you now to defend your perimeters and nothing else." He frowned. "Is that clear?"

"Clear. Politics—and dirty politics at that," Orde said angrily. "You and I both know the intentions of Haj Amin. He would be king here and take over every good thing the Jews have done for this rock. Great Britain is the biggest loser in this political game. We may well be handing over Palestine—first to Haj Amin, and then to Hitler."

"We are soldiers, Orde. Bound to obey." The general seemed to sink down in his chair. "Even when we cannot agree." Tapping his pipe against the ashtray, he considered just how much he could say. "You have been tagged the most dangerous man in Palestine by the Mufti's henchmen. Watch your back, Orde. You're a fine soldier. I would hate to lose you to a dagger through the ribs."

"That might be preferable to this slow death by politics."

The story would rate only a couple of columns on the back page of American newspapers, but in London, it was front-page news.

LONDON: AT LEAST 12 PERSONS WERE KILLED IN THE
WINTER'S FIRST GALE, WHICH AT ONE TIME TODAY REACHED
A VELOCITY OF 108 MPH.

For some U.S. publications, that one line would be all the news
printed on the subject. *So who cares about a little storm in England?*

For those who lived through it, however, every other news in the
world seemed to recede into the background. Winds howled down the
English Channel, tossing the huge battleship *Royal Oak* like a champagne cork on the waters. Waves eighty feet high smashed seawalls and
tore steeples from cathedrals. Twice Murphy looked out the window and
thought he saw the spires of Parliament bending like trees.

The *Queen Mary* was unable to reach Southampton and was forced to
spend a long night bobbing at anchor off the Isle of Wight. Bridges and
homes were swept into the sea. The funeral procession of Queen Maud
of Norway, who had died on a visit to England, was abandoned as royal
mourners were threatened by the force of the storm.

A flock of fifty sheep were blown off a cliff into the sea. Murphy wondered if this last incident might be some sort of divine warning to the
political sheep of England that a much more terrible storm was brewing.

Just as he mentioned this idea to Elisa, the electricity winked off for
the rest of the night, leaving the entire nation in a total blackout. Another portent of things to come?

The storm created quite a bit of inconvenience around London. Only
total fools and taxi drivers dared to brave the roads. Business was virtually
locked up tight—every business but that of gathering the news, that is.

Ordering doors at home locked and windows taped, Murphy cast his
lot among the fools and went to the office hoping, like Prime Minster
Chamberlain, that peace was at hand.

But there was no peace. It began to snow, and word came in from
Southampton that the TENS Paris correspondent was stranded on the
English side of the Channel. This was especially bad news; the English
prime minister was in Paris with the French appeasers attempting to get
in on the latest diplomatic maneuvers by the Germans.

Every reporter was safe at home. As Murphy prepared to close up
shop, the telephone rang. He stared at the receiver for a moment, astonished that the telephone was still working. Then he picked it up. "TENS
head office."

A nasty crackle hissed into his ear, telling him that the phones did
not have long before they would be gone as well.

"Operator . . . Jerusalem . . . Palestine . . . personal to . . . John
Murphy."

Jerusalem! It was a miracle; while the water of the English Channel sent British battleships running for cover, the cable beneath eighty-foot waves was still intact!

"Right! Murphy here!"

Another long vibration ran through the line as words pulsed through Paris and Budapest and Istanbul and then on to Jerusalem. The faraway voice of a Britisher broke through. "Hallo? Are you there, Mr. Murphy? This is your Jerusalem correspondent on the line! Hallo? Are you there?"

Captain Samuel Orde! TENS' anonymous correspondent in Jerusalem! Lately, he had filled the wire with glowing reports of battles against the Arab gangs in Galilee. He mentioned his own name in every article as the daring British captain who led the troops to victory. Not a modest man, this unnamed correspondent. He managed to get credit for the skirmishes even if he did not get his name on the byline.

"Orde! A lucky break! We just got word about the Arab-Zionist conference! What's the reaction there? Any hopes for peace?"

Silence seemed louder than the crackle on the line. "Word is that the plan comes straight from Berlin. Rerouted rather like this phone call through the Mufti in Baghdad."

"What's the point?"

"They are hoping to tie the hands of that dashing Captain Orde who is smashing them in Galilee," Orde said with a laugh, the words suddenly as clear as if he were in the next room. "The Arabs coached in every word. I'm afraid the Zionists are about to be sold out. Another Munich." His voice faded. "A hefty price on his head . . . wanted you to have the straight story in case . . . tell Winston that—"

"Tell Winston what?"

The crackle turned into a roar, and the phone went dead. So much for a modern miracle.

Murphy scribbled notes from what little he had gathered from Orde. There was a price on Orde's head. There was a plan behind this offer of peace from the Arabs. The British High Command in Palestine was also in the mood for appeasement. Sam Orde might have been winning battles, but they were all in danger of losing the war.

Murphy stared thoughtfully at the downpour and then picked up the telephone to call Churchill. No luck. The lines across London were down.

Otto smelled the woodsmoke of his mother's kitchen stove before he topped the rise. The air was still, broken only by the jingle of harness bells and the rush of the runners across the snow. On either side of the road, fences and pastures were concealed by a thick carpet of snow that banked the edge of deep green forest. Above the trees, the rocky peaks of the Tyrol were lost from view behind the clouds.

He slapped the reins down hard on the back of the mare. In spite of the cold, she was sweating after an hour's hard pull over the snow. Still, at his urging, she picked up her pace, giving the harness bells a ring of urgency.

At the sight of the farmhouse, Otto swallowed hard and brushed his eyes with the sleeve of his coat. The tears were only from the wind, he told himself as he resisted the temptation to cry like a homesick child.

Snow was almost to the eaves on the right side of the chalet. A thin ribbon of smoke rose from the chimney, carrying the scent of baking bread into the crisp afternoon air. "Home," Otto whispered, suddenly certain that he would not go mad after all!

Papa stepped out of the front door. Tall boots topped his baggy trousers. His heavy coat was buttoned crooked and his hat was off. He lifted his chin to gaze with alarm at the distant sleigh. Who would be coming up to the farm after such a storm? Maybe a lost tourist? Maybe Gestapo? Karl Wattenbarger's posture conveyed suspicion and then, after a long moment, the stiff back relaxed with delight as he recognized his son!

Otto could hear the call back into the house: "Mama! It is our boy! Otto is home! Marta! You hear me? It is Otto!"

The Wattenbarger farmhouse was full of guests. Nineteen in all, none of them tourists.

Children hung on the banister and peered down at Otto like stone carvings that had come to life in the care of the Austrian family. Those same faces had been gray and unhappy when Otto had brought them here. There had been so many over the months that he could not remember every name or the exact circumstances of their desperation.

"We cannot take in any more," Karl said sadly to his son.

"But, Karl—" Marta started to argue as she poured hot cider for Otto.

"No." Karl silenced her. "When there were nine and the first snows closed the passes through the mountains, we said, 'Well, we have nine guests for the winter.' *Ja.* And then there were eleven, and then fifteen. Now nineteen. We have food enough if we eat twice a day. Porridge in the morning and milk for a snack. But nothing to spare. We must pray that the snows melt early and the pass opens before the Nazis come up here to steal our pantry clean."

"They have taken seven cows," Marta added, sitting down beside Otto. "Gert and Ilse and Buttercup, who gave the most milk, as you know. Yes, I think the Nazis will let us alone now. They will let us feed the livestock through the winter, but in the spring they may take everything into their own pastures."

"Do the neighbors have any room?" Otto asked, not willing to let go after what he had seen in the cities throughout the Reich.

Karl shook his head sadly. "Most are as crowded as we. At least those we could trust to ask. Here in Kitzbühel alone there are over two hundred children hidden." Karl's brow furrowed with concern for the thousands of children outside the tiny circle of safety. "Maybe the American troopers and the English will come through now, after what the Storm Troopers did."

"It wasn't just troopers, Papa," Otto said. "It was everyone. Friends. Neighbors. Everyone turned out, as though hell had taken over and turned men inside out." As he stared at his cider, he wondered if he should tell them about the empty hospitals. He could not make himself say it out loud. The brutality of the world outside was measured only in missing cows and homeless children. The reality of it had not yet penetrated, and Otto would not speak of the darkness as long as some light remained here.

"Surely there are people in Vienna who will help, *ja*? Just until spring when the snow melts and we can take them out." Karl was torn by his inability to offer a solution. "And maybe by then the English government will have a plan."

Otto nodded. Some families would never be allowed to leave the Reich no matter how wide any nation opened the gates. Children of political prisoners were as despised as their parents. These were the people Otto would face when he returned to Vienna. He would be forced to look into the eyes of Michael Wallich's children and tell them there was no room for them. No escape.

Karl seemed to read the unspoken pain in his son's eyes. He put a leathery hand on Otto's arm. "You must think of the Holy Family, *ja*?" He gestured toward the crucifix above the table. "Only they escaped from Bethlehem when Herod's soldiers killed the little ones. Even the angels of Almighty God could not warn every mother to flee."

Marta nodded. "We do what we can, Son. And God does not judge for what we cannot do."

Emotion crowded Otto's throat again. "There is so much I must do that I hate. And so much I want to do that is impossible." He listened to the clatter of young footsteps above them. "There will be a terrible slaughter . . . " He did not finish. What was left to say? *"Save a few while multitudes perish, and pray you made the right choices."*

"You are not judged, Otto," Karl replied quietly. "Do what you can and know the angels wept also in Bethlehem."

The Jews of Vienna, forced to clear away the debris of their own broken lives, swept the streets and sidewalks clean. Shopwindows were boarded over, never to open again.

But Lucy Strasburg's life remained littered with the shards of her shattered illusions. They cut into her heart, then sealed into tough, impenetrable scars. She saw no one's misery but her own. She grieved for no one but herself.

Sometimes she felt drawn to walk again on Stephanie Bridge, to look longingly down at the brown waters. But in those moments, certain of hell, she glimpsed her own judgment. To die now would mean that she would take a second life, the life of her unborn child. Could she add murder to her roster of sins?

Twice she wandered into the great cathedral of St. Stephan's. Wolf did not like her to go there; the Catholic church labored under the heavy scrutiny and disapproval of the party. But she was a woman and so he overlooked her weakness for religion.

She did not tell him that she came here like a starving child going to a bakery to smell the baking bread. Like a pauper who looks at a grocer's stand and longs for what he cannot buy, Lucy sat in the back of the great cathedral and wished that she had whatever was for sale in such a place. But she had nothing with which to buy her salvation. She had given everything good in her for the sake of Wolf's passion.

Priests and nuns with worried faces moved about St. Stephan's. The Nazis had stoned the residence of Bishop Innitzer, declaring war on Catholics as well as Jews in Austria. Maybe the priests had no comfort left to offer Lucy. With that thought in mind she left the cathedral without asking for help. There was, it seemed, no help left for anyone. *Look out for yourself*, her heart whispered. *You are the only one you can count on.*

Lucy walked a precarious high wire with the ravenous Wolf waiting below for her to slip. She teased him and she baited him. She made demands on him and then scorned him when he failed to meet them.

When he brought her the fox coat, she pretended that it was not good enough quality. "The sort of thing a junior officer would give his spinster sister," she mocked.

He had responded with anger, perhaps even with disappointment. She remained unmoved, and so the fur had been returned and replaced by one of richer color than the first. She rewarded him with her passion and left him happy that he had pleased her.

Only a few weeks before, she would have been ecstatic about the first coat, of course, but she did not let him know that. It was a game. Sometimes she rewarded him with her approval, but not always. And so he began to work at pleasing her without ever knowing that she did not still love him. Power filled the void love had left in Lucy's heart.

Secretly she called Wolf her little hound, uttered with the same disregard with which he had once called her his cow. She made him beg for her and try to please her. He never knew that all she wanted was to escape from him, to carry this baby far from the beautiful hands of Wolfgang von Fritschauer and his dutiful little Nazi wife. She determined that the thing he wanted most from her would never be his. How to accomplish that, however, was still a problem she grappled with. Even in their most tender moments that thought occupied her mind. As she smiled and whispered his name, she thought of trains and obscure places beyond the borders of the Nazi Reich.

One single beam of sunlight broke through the overcast sky and filtered through the window of Lucy's apartment. Somehow that shaft of light lifted her spirits.

She sat alone in the elegant little parlor of the apartment. From left to right, according to value, she laid her assets out on the cushions of the pale yellow Queen Anne sofa.

The Swiss watch Wolf had given her came first, then a small gold and amethyst ring she had received from an aunt who had purchased it in Paris years before. An assortment of gold and silver bangle bracelets and a necklace lay next to the ring. On the far right she placed the large solid silver crucifix that she had inherited from her grandmother.

It seemed a pitiful little pile against the expensive furniture of the parlor. She had saved only a few marks from work; the rest she had squandered on clothing and handbags and shoes and treats that she had sent home to her younger brothers and sisters.

"I have been a fool," she said aloud to the empty room.

Few of these possessions could she sell. To sell the watch would incur Wolf's wrath and suspicion. To present the little ring to the appraisers might cause them to smile and toss her a handful of change. Bracelets and the necklace would bring nothing but outright laughter. "Gold plated, my dear! Not real silver, only polished nickel!"

Only the silver crucifix offered any hope. Lucy suspected that it was very valuable. She had placed it on the end of the row because it was the one thing she had that she dreaded selling. Still, it seemed that she had nothing else.

The cross itself was a full twelve inches from top to bottom and quite heavy. The metal was a work of art. Patterned to mimic the grain of wood, Lucy could almost see the rough splinters tearing into the flesh of the mourning Christ who hung on it. And silver spikes ran through hands and feet; a crown of perfect little thorns jammed down into the forehead. There was no wound yet in the side of Christ. Lucy's grandmother had explained to her many years before, *"He is not finished dying yet, you see, Lucy. The soldier thrust the spear into His side after He was dead. But this shows that our Lord still suffers for our sakes."*

Indeed, this was a different picture of Christ than the one Lucy had always seen above the altar of every church. Limp and pierced, those Christs were dead, indeed. Ah, but this one—His eyes looked right at Lucy, His mouth open as if He tried to make her hear His words. Every tiny detail was flawless. A picture of horrible suffering and grief.

Lucy had often contemplated that image as a child. It had hung above the dining table in the Herrgottseck of Grandmother's little house. Grandmother had often raised her eyes and spoken to the suffering Christ, as if He were an old familiar friend.

The sunlight inched across the cushions, finally resting on the gleaming silver crucifix and glinting back into Lucy's eyes. She looked away, unwilling to admit that there was nothing else of value that might provide funds enough for her to escape Wolf.

She shook her head. How could she sell the cross her grandmother had cherished? With an audible sigh, she stood and studied the delicate petit point on the chairs that flanked the sofa. Her eyes swept around the walls at the paintings that hung there. The paintings were ordinary, of the type sold by itinerant artists in the alleyways along the Danube. She looked back at the chairs. They were far from ordinary. Although Lucy had no knowledge of their style or maker, Wolf often touched their hand-carved gilded frames with an odd sort of reverence, just as her grandmother had touched the crucifix.

These chairs were of great value, as were the Persian rugs she stood on. But how could she sell such things? They did not belong to her, and Wolf would certainly notice their absence the instant he came through the door.

The bronze clock on the mantel struck four. The sunbeam that had raised her spirits for a moment slipped away as Lucy heard the clank of the elevator arriving on her floor.

Quickly she scooped up her treasures and carried them into the bedroom to dump them in the bureau drawer. In a moment, the sound of Wolf's latch key scratched in the lock, announcing his arrival.

He did not speak, but with a heavy sigh, pitched his hat at the bronze cherubs on the clock and then sat down on the sofa. He propped his feet on the coffee table, never noticing that she had entered the room. She hurried toward the kitchen to brew a pot of coffee. Removing a bottle of brandy, she splashed a bit into his cup as he always liked.

Only then did he speak. "No brandy." His words were clipped like commands. "The Führer is here, and it would not do for him to smell a whiff of it on my breath. He disapproves of strong drink."

With a broad smile, Lucy looked out from the doorway. "Well, Göring drinks, as does every other German general, I hear."

"I am only a major," Wolf replied. "When I am a general, then I will not fear the Führer smelling brandy on my breath."

She was disappointed. Wolf was always less harsh when he had a little to drink. She carefully poured it back into the bottle. She did not ask him how the meetings were going. "You will be a general soon enough," she said brightly.

"You are right," Wolf called to her. "If this matter deciding the boundaries of Czechoslovakia is settled correctly, I will move up quicker than I ever imagined." He paused, as he often did when he talked aloud to himself. "The Hungarians want a piece of the Czech territory, and that will give the Führer reason enough to march the rest of the way into Prague. Privately, that is all the talk. We will let the Hungarians make their demands, and then we will proclaim that what remains of Czechoslovakia needs the protection of the Reich. By spring we will march into Prague, and I will be a colonel, at least."

"Will you also go to Prague?" Lucy asked with a slight pout in her voice. She had been considering escaping to Prague, but if what Wolf said proved true, she would have to find another place. "You know the baby is due to be born then."

"You will manage without me; I am certain," Wolf replied irritably. "Now fix me a sandwich. I only have half an hour, and then I must be back. We have not even taken time for lunch until now."

Lucy obeyed obligingly, grateful for the warning he had given her about Prague. Did everyone know what the Führer planned for the Czechs? Wolf had told her so casually. She frowned and asked a question in spite of herself. "What will the English say about it when we take Prague also?"

"They will say plenty, as always, but they will not do anything. As always."

17

Preparations

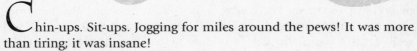

Chin-ups. Sit-ups. Jogging for miles around the pews! It was more than tiring; it was insane!

Jacob tied the spare bell rope to the banister of the choir loft and stripped off his shirt. Then he pulled himself up hand over hand and hung there, grinning down at Lori. "See? Nothing to it. Like the angels up Jacob's ladder, eh?"

She had done all the rest, but she would not do this. Heights terrified her. She would not climb, no matter what he said. "I won't."

He lowered himself down and dropped the last eight feet, landing upright beside her. "You will learn to do this, Lori, or you will not eat."

"Fine!" she said defiantly. "Then I *won't* eat! But I would rather die of starvation than by falling thirty feet on my head!"

"It isn't thirty feet." Mark tried to act as mediator. He had been doing that a lot lately.

"It's fourteen feet. Nothing," Jacob said. "I did not even use my feet or legs. You can use your legs if you—"

"I won't! This is the kind of stuff they make the Hitler Maidens do! Calisthenics! Burn books and spend your time developing muscles! You're as bad as any Hitler Youth leader! My arms and legs ache."

Jacob motioned with his head that Mark should leave. He could handle this himself.

Mark shrugged and left the auditorium, relieved that he did not have to climb the rope.

"Now, Lori," Jacob said in a patronizing tone, "sit down, will you?

Let me tell you . . . sit down." He directed her to a pew. "Relax a minute. We are adults. We can talk this thing through. There are reasons why—"

Lori did not want to hear his reasons. She was tired of his endless bullying. She had done everything he said because he acted as if it was important, but she would not climb the rope! "I won't."

"But you must learn." He stood behind her and rubbed her shoulders. "When we leave here—"

"You said we could stay forever," she protested. "I am not leaving until my parents return."

"Let's skip over that part." He did not sound as gruff with her as he had ever since they had been left here. "What I mean is, if we have to leave . . . suddenly . . . we need to know how to climb and how to run and . . . we won't be able to think about being tired, you see?"

He was telling her they could be pursued. They were certainly wanted by the men who held their parents! But she did not want to think about that, not today. There were things Jacob could not understand because he was not a woman. There were things about her body and her emotions that only Mama and her friend Susan knew about. She did not feel well. Jacob's hands on her shoulders helped her headache, but she would not climb the rope!

"I want to lie down," she said softly. "I don't feel like doing this today."

He pinched her hard. "You're too soft!" He sounded angry. "You will hold us back and get us all killed if we have to make a run for it!"

"Then *run*!" she cried. "And I will stay here!" She stood up and whirled to face him. "And don't touch me! I won't climb your stupid rope! I . . . I wish my mother was here! I want a hot bath and a cup of tea! I want to be left alone!"

She stormed from the sanctuary and took refuge in the ladies' room, the only place she could be alone. There she wept until she thought she had no tears. An hour passed, then two. Finally a timid knock sounded on the door.

"Lori?" It was Jacob.

She did not answer. Her eyes were bloodshot and puffy. She looked as though she had been hit in the face.

"Lori? Are you in there? It's Jacob."

"I thought it was the Gestapo!" She could not help saying it.

"Yes." A long pause. "Well, I was hard on you today."

"Every day you are hard on me!"

"I thought maybe . . . I was thinking that . . . perhaps," he stammered. She could almost hear him blush through the door. This was not at all like Jacob Kalner. "At home . . . there were times when Mother would want a cup of tea and an aspirin." He cleared his throat loudly. "And Father ordered us to be gentlemen. I have not been a gentleman. And I am, well . . . open the door. I made you tea."

"I won't climb your rope!"

"*All right* . . . I mean, not now. But here is your tea."

She raised her head and replied regally, "Leave it at the door. I don't want to talk to you no matter how sorry you are!"

It was a miserable, rotten thing to say to him on one of the few occasions he had been sensitive. She regretted sending him away, especially when he was just beginning to figure out that she was not an eleven-year-old rowdy anymore.

It would have been nice to talk to someone. To Jacob. To tell him how very much she missed her mother, especially at a time like this.

Opening the door a crack, she pulled in the tepid cup of tea. Two aspirin lay in the saucer, along with a stack of crackers. It was not Mother. It was not a long soak in a hot bath, but it was something, at least. This small kindness made her cry again. Maybe later she would try to climb Jacob's rope.

Shaved heads and filthy black-and-white-striped uniforms, a bowl of watery soup, and a place on the straw of a crowded bunk—within the walls of Nameless camp, all men were created equal. Entitled equally to suffer. Entitled equally to endure. Entitled equally to perish at the whim of beasts in military uniforms who considered themselves more equal than other men.

Grief was the great leveler of men—rich or poor, wise or foolish, or just ordinary. None of that mattered anymore. Even goodness at times seemed to be lost in a mottled shade of gray, blended into the mist of human misery. But for the most part, the difference between light and dark seemed distinct. Some men, like Pastor Karl Ibsen, were candles; other men were the wind that would snuff out their light.

From the high view of the watchtower these rows of striped uniforms did not seem human or distinct in any way from one another. But each faceless form was an individual of untold value and unmeasured worth. In this way the pastor saw his fellow prisoners. *A face. A name. A man. A soul.* He counted them all as worthy of love. He loved them all in the name of his Lord, no matter how light or dark the shadows that fell across their hearts.

In this terrible purgatory, Karl Ibsen found a flock that needed him more than all the filled pews in Berlin. For his own suffering he thanked

God, because many men found the truth while Karl suffered among them.

This morning the north wind penetrated his thin cotton uniform. His hands were broken and bloody from cold and from the work he did without gloves. He looked like any other man in the assembly yard.

Kapos with sticks in hand prowled the rows as the roll call was read. Sometimes for no reason at all they stopped to level a blow across the back of a prisoner. Cries and thuds punctuated the calling of the roll. It lasted for hours.

During this time, Karl prayed. The guards and their dogs could not see that he prayed, and so they could not stop him. Karl prayed for his wife, Helen. He thought of her in every pleasant way, and inwardly he smiled because her goodness was real and her love was eternal. He prayed for his children, for Lori and Jamie, that they would remember all he had taught them and not be afraid.

Beside him a man fell coughing to the ground. Karl stooped to help him and was kicked hard in the stomach. The man who had fallen thanked him, blessed him with a look, and then the SS officer kicked him as well. When the man could not rise, he was shot. His blood splattered on Karl's uniform.

Karl stood slowly. He wept silently, but he did not stop praying.

The members of Orde's Special Night Squad listened quietly to his report of his meeting with General Wavell. He concluded by restating the general's order that they confine their actions to defending their perimeter.

Larry Havas stood behind Orde in the little knot of men. He shrugged and remarked to Zach, "Just what we expected all along. Jews who strike back rock the British boat, if you know what I mean."

Captain Orde rounded on him savagely. "And just what do you propose to do about it?"

"Do about it?" queried Havas. "Me?"

"Is that your only response, Havas? 'Oh well, it was good while it lasted'?"

"But, Captain Orde, what other response can there be?" inquired Zach. "To continue means that we will soon be asked to make the short trip to Acre prison and then the even shorter trip to the end of a British rope!"

"That is the trouble with you Jews!" Orde stated heatedly. "Always so patient, worrying about trouble that might find you. You might as well go lie down on your bunks and wait for the Arab knife that cuts your throats, because it will come far more certainly than the British rope!"

Moshe watched the exchange in silence. With a dramatic change of volume, Orde suddenly lowered his voice to a bare whisper, so that all the men had to lean in to hear what was said. "My own neck is more squarely in the noose than any of yours." His words were barely audible, but his eyes flashed fire. Startled, Moshe realized how much Orde looked like the image of an Old Testament prophet.

"We cannot afford to think about what we are not allowed to do," Orde continued. "Instead, we must take full advantage of what we are permitted."

Quizzical glances flew around the group. No one dared to respond to the challenge in the flaming eyes to ask what he meant.

Orde answered the unspoken question. "You are permitted to go freely on the roads of the Mandate, are you not?"

"Yes, but what—" questioned Zach; then he stopped abruptly as Orde continued.

"And to defend yourself if attacked?"

"Yeah," grunted Havas. "So what?"

"So," concluded Captain Orde, "let's get busy defending ourselves."

Piano lessons! The steady ticktock of the metronome matched the patter of raindrops but clashed with the unsuccessful attempts of nine-year-old Deborah Harding-Smith to attack the musical scales one octave at a time.

"Once again, from middle C." Anna positioned the child's rigid fingers on the piano keys for the eighth time. "Try again, Deborah. One and two and . . ."

Deborah began again, banging down on the keys as if she were at war with the keyboard. The constant rhythm of the metronome had no more meaning to this exercise than the howling of an alley cat on a back fence. In fact, Anna often thought that it would be easier to teach a cat to dance the rumba than to guide this one child into the wonderful world of tempo. Tone-deaf and totally without rhythm, Deborah hated these hour-long lessons. The time here was wasted. She knew it. Anna knew it, although she did not say it. And everyone who heard this horrid banging also knew it. Everyone, that is, except for the child's mother.

Mrs. Harding-Smith believed her pigtailed daughter had the potential for great talent. She was, as yet, uncertain of what that forte was. *Maybe ballet?* Deborah had gotten stuck with one leg on the bar and torn her tights—not once, but twice. *Perhaps tap dancing?* Ah well, the poor thing could not remember heel from toe or hop from shuffle. The tap teacher had developed a nervous twitch in her right cheek and declared to Mrs. Harding-Smith that Deborah could not even march in step, let alone learn to shuffle-hop!

Deborah's untapped talent was not to be found in the art of dance. The search for Deborah's undiscovered genius had continued through cello, flute, and clarinet lessons, as well as several other instruments that wheezed, whistled, and bawled like dying animals. The piano was a last resort, Mrs. Harding-Smith confessed. It was difficult to make a piano sound like anything other than a piano, no matter how badly played it might be.

Anna supposed that this was meant to comfort her on the long journey through the land of fractured whole notes and stuttering scales.

This afternoon, Charles and Louis peered out from the hallway to investigate what had happened to the poor piano. Anna waved them away and sat down on the bench beside Deborah, who suddenly burst into tears of frustration.

The lesson became a time of consolation. The child sobbed in Anna's arms and confessed that she hated all musical instruments and that she would rather be playing cricket with her six brothers, or hiding out in the clubhouse, or anything at all besides this.

Anna knew how she felt. "Well, then, perhaps we should tell your mother together."

"Oh, no! Mother will be most unhappy! She will think I am an utter failure. I have not even learned to play the scales properly. I try, really, Mrs. Lindheim! I do try! I am not so absolutely stupid as all that!"

"So you want to keep trying, do you?" Anna asked as Charles and Louis peeked around the doorjamb again. She narrowed her eyes, a clear sign that they were intruding on an emotional moment.

Deborah wiped her nose on her sleeve and nodded miserably. Anything was better than facing her mother with another failure. "Yes, I want to try. I *will* try."

Anna felt sorry for the little girl, but after so many weeks, she was also sorry that the torment must go on to avoid the scowling disappointment of Mrs. Harding-Smith.

"All right then. Trying is the same was winning." Anna took a deep breath and stared at the big black notes on the instruction booklet. Pretty boring stuff.

Anna closed the book. "If we are going to go on, we must find *something* about the piano that you can enjoy, *ja*?"

"I like it when *you* play." Another big sniff.

"But what do *you* like about the instrument?" Anna danced her fingers over the keys. Beautiful, clear, and alive, the notes covered the serious conversation of the boys as they discussed the unhappy female on the bench.

"Well . . ." Deborah screwed up her face. "I can send my brother Harry signals on it when he is upstairs and I have to practice."

"Signals?"

"Yes. Mother thinks it is part of the lesson, you see." Deborah lowered her voice. "Mother can't tell one note from another." Her lips turned up in a sly smile. "So I send Harry messages. In code. I learned it from his Scout handbook."

Anna rather liked this new twist in the concept of music as the language of the heart. "And what sort of messages do you send?"

Deborah's eyes brightened; her face grew firm with determination and expertise. "You see, two dots, like this—" She banged hard twice on middle C. "That is the letter *I*. You see?"

Anna nodded. She was impressed—at least interested. "Go on."

"Four dots—" Deborah banged four times on the key of D. "That is the letter *H*. You see?"

The letter *A* was a dot and a dash. *T* was one dash only. *E* was one dot. Put all together, the message was *I hate*—Deborah went on to spell out two more complete words—*piano lessons.*

She could also signal things like *Mother is a crank today* and *Only ten more minutes and I can get up.* The potential for communication on the piano was endless, much better than the other instruments that merely squeaked and did not cooperate at all with Deborah's skill as a telegrapher.

At Anna's urging, the child went forward through the entire alphabet. Then as Anna played a series of chords in the treble clef, Deborah repeated the performance on one note with skill and undeniable talent. The result was a new composition, impromptu, and quite nice in its simplicity—something bordering on a simple jazz tune. Anna laughed and said she knew an American jazz trio who might perform Deborah's remarkable new song.

Half an hour later, Mrs. Harding-Smith returned to fetch her daughter. Anna and Deborah treated her to a duet, a jazz composition called "Telegraph Alphabet."

The mother laughed and cried and blew her nose loudly into her handkerchief. No matter that Deborah played one note only during the course of the song! Her child had *at last* discovered her forte! She was a prodigy in the true sense of the word!

Anna Lindheim closed the door behind her departing pupil and the ecstatic mother. She sank down into a chair with a sigh of great content-

ment. At last she had helped Deborah Harding-Smith find her true calling. No doubt the child would grow up to operate a telegraph key for
Western Union.

The storm passed, leaving behind an unusually clear night. Brittle star-
light outlined the silhouette of Parliament. Such grand beauty only rein-
forced the notion of those who believed, like Chamberlain, that Britain
was the center of the universe. Beyond the boundaries of her mighty empire, the stars seemed dull in comparison.

Tonight Theo and Murphy donned their formal dinner jackets. Anna
and Elisa dressed in elegant evening gowns. Charles and Louis eyed
them with childish envy and sat sulking in their pajamas beside the
radio.

Freddie Frutschy and his wife Hildy came up the steps precisely at
seven o'clock from their newly refurbished apartment on the ground
floor.

Charles loved Freddie, of course. So did Louis. And they also liked
Hildy very much. Hildy was also from Germany, but that had been a
long time ago, she explained in English. She spoke English with an accent much worse than the freshest immigrant, and yet she refused to
speak German to the boys. *"Great Britain my home ist. Und English now I
am speaking!"* Hildy was very happy in the new apartment, happy to
work as housekeeper while Freddie doubled as bodyguard and chauffeur for the household. *"Und happy she vas to sit on the babies also,"* she
declared.

As pleasant in temper as Freddie, Hildy had wispy gray hair, braided
and woven like pretzels on her head. Her face and figure were both
round. She wore false teeth, which clicked and clacked in her mouth
whenever she spoke her garbled brand of English.

The couple filled the doorway. "Ach, Eleeeza! Beautiful you ist tonight! Never mind you the boys about. Tonight a fine time ve ist having
for sure!"

Charles could hardly understand a word she said. He imagined that
her mouth was something like a telegraph key, and if he could only learn
Morse code, everything would suddenly make sense in her exclamations
of ticks and tocks and dots and dashes. In the meantime, no German
would she speak, and her brand of English was undecipherable.

The two boys reluctantly rose and gloomily embraced the two ele-
gantly dressed couples. Hildy dashed off to tune in the BBC to her favorite radio program. *"A pathetic British imitation of a pathetic American soap
opera,"* Murphy had described the show.

Elisa cupped Charles' face in her hands and leveled her clear blue eyes at his. "Don't send us away unhappy, Charles," Elisa whispered. "Tonight is a very important night. You must be happy for us to go to this meeting. Maybe we will be able to help those children we dreamed about. When you say your prayers tonight . . ."

"I will," he agreed. No need to say more. He knew enough about this topic that he could tell the grown-ups a thing or two. But tonight they were doomed to stay home and listen to Hildy's radio programs until eight o'clock, when they would be sentenced to bed by the extension of her stubby finger and a series of garbled clacks. "But I wish I could come too."

At that, a sympathetic Freddie hoisted Charles up on one broad shoulder and then Louis on the other. "Ah, come on, lads," he said. "We fellows'll leave the old woman to 'er BBC whilst we play with the tin soldiers, eh?"

Charles could touch the ceiling when he sat on Freddie's shoulder. Life seemed much more pleasant from such a great height.

The dinner party at the London home of Dr. Chaim Weizmann had an impressive guest list. Several sympathetic members of Parliament were in attendance with their wives—including Winston Churchill, Anthony Eden, and Harold Nicolson, who were known for their opposition to the Chamberlain appeasement policies. Weizmann, dressed in his black dinner jacket and stroking his scholarly goatee, leaned in to whisper in Theo's ear.

"There they are." He nodded his head toward the English politicians. "Our jury."

By this, Theo understood that every other guest had been invited to testify. Theo, in addition to his internment in a Nazi prison camp, had seen much in Berlin on Kristal Nacht. Anna had firsthand experience with the thousands of homeless refugees in Prague. Elisa had lived through the horrors of Vienna and could also testify as to the desperation of the children of Germany as seen through the lives of Charles and Louis Kronenberger. As for Murphy, he was an American. His perspective completed the circle of world opinion in favor of the rescue of the Jews of Germany. The roll call of witnesses included other prominent refugees from Hitler's new Reich. In all, a dozen Englishmen and an equal number of witnesses attended.

Testimony was given one on one as members of the jury were placed strategically between witnesses. The clatter of conversation hummed throughout each course of the meal, and Dr. Weizmann presided regally at the head of the long table. There was no need for him to direct the conversation. In an hour, over prime rib and Yorkshire pudding, more factual information was passed along than in several days of official meetings.

Over dessert and coffee, the discussion became more focused. Harold Nicolson, British writer, back-bench member of Commons, and staunch backer of Anthony Eden, spoke first.

"We are simply outnumbered," he said simply. "On both sides, labor and conservative, the debate was clearly sympathetic, but pathetic as far as the will to do anything at all."

Winston Churchill puffed on his cigar and morosely swirled his whiskey in his glass. "I heard the figure of ten thousand children from Germany and Austria mentioned. We took in as many from Belgium in the last war." His lower lip extended in thought. "You must not allow yourselves to be backed into a corner of anachronistic talk about moral responsibility and past obligations of Great Britain," he warned. "Talk is cheap."

"And that is coming from our finest orator," Anthony Eden quipped.

A twittering of polite laughter subsided into silence as the guests waited for Churchill to finish. Murphy contemplated the slouched bulk of the bulldog statesman with amusement and respect. He was, in physical appearance, the exact opposite of the handsome and dapper Anthony Eden. But both men shared the same views and the same disdain for the appeasers.

Churchill continued. "Lord Halifax—" he cleared his throat as if the name had stuck there—"has quite bluntly defined the interest of the government in ensuring that the Arab states would be friendly to us. In other words, we must not only invite the devil to tea but must serve up our friends to him on his plate."

"And our children," remarked Weizmann.

"Yes." Churchill cocked a watery eye at the leaders of Zionism. "If this goes unchallenged, then you might as well return forever to London and build a house with three floors in it. One could house the government of smashed Austria. The second, the government of Czechoslovakia. And the third, all your hopes of a Jewish homeland."

"Well and good, Winston," added Eden, "but what is to be done?"

"This meeting between the Arabs and the Zionists has been called to give the appearance that the government is really doing all it can do to maintain the peace in Palestine. They are, in fact, giving the Mufti everything he wants, like Hitler in Munich. Therefore, I could recommend that the Zionists refuse to attend *unless* the rescue of ten thousand children in Germany is immediately undertaken." He nodded toward

Murphy. "Such a reckless gamble should be widely publicized, of course, to demonstrate the desperation of the cause."

Silence filled the room. It was indeed a desperate move. To boycott such a meeting could mean losing everything. "There are seven hundred thousand Jews in the Reich," added one distinguished scholar from Heidelberg. "Only ten thousand?"

"It is the very number mentioned in the Commons debate," Theo interjected. He understood the reasoning behind the figure. "We will simply quote that number back to Chamberlain and Halifax as the number they mentioned."

Churchill raised a thick finger. "And as the number of children rescued from Belgium in the Great War, it is a precedent. We must ask ourselves if our fathers were more moral and decent than we are." At that he smiled briefly, knowingly, then sank back into the enjoyment of his reeking cigar.

Perhaps there was a method in the madness, after all. To rescue ten thousand was something, anyway. It was still not a Jewish homeland, still not a standing-room-only Zionist state. But it was ten thousand lives.

The other guests had left two hours earlier. The mantel clock in Chaim Wiezmann's study chimed 2 AM. Cigar smoke hung in a thick haze across the room.

Murphy's eyes sagged, heavy with sleep, as the conversation continued. Only Winston Churchill seemed entirely awake. Theo looked exhausted but attentive. Anna rested her head against his arm. Elisa looked pale and thoughtful as she listened to Winston's plan. She turned down Mrs. Weizmann's offer of the spare bedroom. The Lindheims were a family of concert musicians, she explained. Late nights were a way of life.

"Censorship in the Reich is a difficult problem." Churchill cocked his head toward Murphy, who could only nod his agreement. "How long did they keep your reporter locked up?"

"Three days. And now his reports are about the new construction sites and autobahns. Nothing meaningful. His phone is tapped. Every word coming out of Germany is screened by propaganda officials; photographs as well. Anyone transgressing the rules of the press is liable to be arrested and executed as a spy." Murphy smiled as he thought of Timmons, the ex-sportswriter. "Timmons is not cut out for it."

"Since we cannot get answers the normal way, the best thing for us to do is to ask questions." Churchill lifted his chin and stared at the clock.

"Time is running short for Europe, Murphy. People seem content to accept Chamberlain's version of the world. I propose we challenge that version on the radio. A political mystery program, if you will. The Trump Broadcasting version of *War of the Worlds*." He grinned. "We will ask about the fate of individuals like Anna's sister who have vanished, perhaps. And about policies. Nations. The plans of leaders. Questions may stir our people from their apathy."

"What about the answers?"

"We still have friends behind the gate in Germany. We must put the machinery in place to bring the truth back to us. I have some thoughts about how we might achieve that with the help of a certain piano teacher." He tapped his cigar on the ashtray. "Let Timmons send his reports about the autobahns. And let Herr Hitler wonder about how TENS gets the answers to our questions so soon. I think the censorship problem is about to be solved, my friends."

18

The Mouse and the Serpent

Money.

Never before had money been such a concern to Lucy. With enough money, she could break free from Wolf. Without it, Lebensborn became a certainty.

She remembered the whispered concerns of her mother and father as they struggled to feed nine children during the desperate days in Germany before Hitler had brought promise of order and prosperity to the German nation. With so many mouths to feed, Lucy had taken jobs as a housemaid and a waitress, with every pfennig pooled into the family finances. She had never minded giving up her paycheck to help the family. It had seemed natural and right; there were still younger brothers and sisters at home in Bavaria. Even now, Lucy faithfully sent home half of her salary and spent the other half on little luxuries for herself.

She looked at her paycheck. For the first time she would send none of it home to Bavaria. For the first time she would not walk by the shopwindows on the Kärtner Ring and pick out a new hat or handbag or pair of shoes to buy for herself. The check was for a hundred marks: twenty-five dollars a week. Lucy calculated that she would need at least a thousand marks before she dared to leave Wolf. Such a vast sum would take her two and a half months to save, even if she never spent a pfennig for anything!

She sighed and walked into the bank, wondering how she might acquire the needed sum in less than ten weeks.

The bank clerk, a sweet little man with big cow eyes, recognized her

and smiled. She had told him about her family back home and the reason for the weekly money order.

"*Guten Abend,* Fräulein Strasburg." He pulled out the money-order
book automatically. "Will you be sending your usual again this week?"

"No, *danke.*" She signed off the check and shrugged self-consciously,
knowing he would wonder what had happened to make her change her
pattern. "This week I will just keep the cash."

"All of it?" Surprise and concern raised his thick eyebrows in an arch
over his brown eyes.

"All of it, *danke,*" she replied with a smile.

He seemed almost hurt as he tucked away the money-order book.
"In cash?" This was most unusual.

"*Ja. Danke.*" She pretended to study the grain of the marble counter.
"*Ja,*" she said again, searching for a lie that would salve his curiosity.
"Mama wants me to send packages home now instead of money. The
products here in Vienna are still much better than in Germany," she
added with a conspiratorial whisper. Then she pretended to worry that
her words might be overheard. She winked at him, giving him the all
clear. "So. Heil Hitler, *ja?*"

At this revelation, he brightened, genuinely relieved. He counted out
the Reichmarks. "You are a devoted daughter." He slipped the bills beneath the cage. "*Grüss Gott.* Until next week then!"

Lucy tucked the Reichmarks into her handbag and strolled happily
out of the bank. She was glad that the little clerk had liked her illusion. If
he had known the truth, she mused, he would have said, *"You are a faith-
less lover and a terrible SS mother."*

She let out a sigh of relief. She would pick another line to stand in the
next time she came to the bank.

At the meeting in the big cathedral there were almost a thousand people,
Anna said. Charles wondered if he and Louis counted because they were
so short. He hoped that children did not count at the meeting because
that would mean there were really a lot more than one thousand.

Men stood at the podium and spoke. Women also seemed angry and
determined. Elisa and the string quartet played music and everyone sang
together.

When it was over, stacks of the yellow papers were handed out and
places were assigned for people to distribute them. Charles knew that he
counted then, because he carried a thick stack of yellow flyers on his
arm. He liked helping; it made him feel better.

It was cold this afternoon. He waited at the top of the long stairs that led down into the Trafalgar underground entrance. He and Theo were in charge of the handrail on the *up* side of the stairs. Anna and Louis were in charge of the *down* side.

The policeman told them they could not go down into the tube, even though it would have been much warmer than standing out in the wind. There were rules they had to obey about where a person could stand with a petition and how to hand out the handbills. A pastor and four others had been arrested in Blackpool, so everyone had to be careful. The government did not like this, but it was not like Germany. Charles was glad of that.

Crowds pushed up and down the stairs. Most of them looked the other way when Theo and Anna spoke to them. It was cold, after all, and no one wanted to stand outside and sign anything. Charles passed handbills to as many as he could. People folded them and put them in their pockets, and Charles hoped they would read them when they got home by the fire.

A man in a black coat and homburg hat stopped and put his face close to Charles'. He read the writing on the handbill and smiled a smile that was not altogether nice.

"Would you like to sign?" Theo asked. "For the children."

"You already got me," said the man. "But I could use a handful of your leaflets. Put them where they belong."

Theo thanked him and gave half of Charles' stack to him. Charles watched him walk down the sidewalk. He paused for a minute, shook his head, and tossed the leaflets into the garbage can. Then he walked quickly away before Theo could reach him.

The leaflets were ruined, covered by grease from a half-eaten sausage and ashes from a pipe.

"Over a hundred!" Theo looked angrily at the man who crossed the square. "A very small fellow."

Other people had been nicer. An old woman brought Charles and Louis peanuts and handed out their papers while they ate. Some days the sun came out; more people stopped to sign and talk than on the dark days.

This part of it was slow going, as Murphy said. But every day he wrote for the newspaper, and three times a week there were radio broadcasts that Murphy said could be heard as far away as the German Reich. He said he hoped the broadcasts gave Hitler indigestion, and Jewish people hope.

D' Fat Lady had a name, which Charles learned to say. "G'bye, Dell." He felt sad that the trio was leaving.

"You remember t' pray for ol' Delpha Mae, honey." She took Charles' face in her big hands and kissed his forehead. She could see the worry in his eyes. The Nazis did not like people who were any other color than white. What would they do to these black American singers as they toured through the Reich? "You listen to yo' daddy's radio station every Thursday, honey, 'cause ol' Delpha Mae gonna be sendin' you love through the wires. Huh?" She gave Louis a kiss. She called him Louie and shook her finger at both the boys. "We gonna teach old Beet-hoven a thang or two! Gonna teach them Nazis all about bein' hip!" At this, she threw her head back in a big laugh and hugged both boys one last time.

There were hugs for Elisa, Murphy, Anna, and Theo while the taxi driver loaded steamer trunks and Hiram Jupiter's silver horn for the trip to the ship.

Philbert, the piano player, gave Anna one last word of advice. "You 'member now, you don't *need* no music written down when you play! It's different *ever* time, Miz Anna! By the time we gets back t' England, I 'specs you gonna be playin' jazz as good as Fats Waller, and that ain't no jive!"

"We'll play a duet then." Anna laughed. Then with serious eyes she took Delpha Mae's hand. "God bless you. Be safe, *ja*?"

"Don' worry none 'bout us!" Delpha Mae said loudly. "We is too noisy to jest diss'pear! Them Nazis would cause a *war* if'n our program didn't come on the radio ever week like *clockword*!"

Charles figured she meant to say *clockwork*. *D' Fat Lady Trio Program* was broadcast every Thursday like clockwork over Trump Broadcasting Service. Ivory soap was the radio sponsor, and Charles had learned to sing the advertising jingle when he had been in New York. It was almost his favorite radio program, except for Charlie McCarthy. He liked the jazz because most of the times the lyrics were "Bippity . . . bop, bop, hey dad-dah!"

With such words in their songs, the trio did not need to know German. They had already made a big hit in Paris. Three months of live broadcasts from France to America had put Ivory soap in the same league with French perfume. The trio had wowed sedate society in London, and now Elisa predicted that Mozart and Schubert would be dancing the jitterbug in their graves.

As for the Führer, it was well-known that he publicly disapproved of modern music, even while he privately screened American musicals. In regard to black musicians, he considered them to be a curiosity, "like performing bears," and he looked the other way when groups toured the cabarets of Hamburg and Berlin and Vienna. TBS had specially arranged the tour of European capitals with Murphy overseeing the link-up through the BBC in London to New York. This was the only broadcast from Germany that did not require the approval of Nazi censors.

Delpha Mae was right. The group was so popular in the States that not even the Nazi leader would dare insult them or discourage a warm reception in the Reich. Besides, he rather enjoyed this contrast of the great German culture to that of the culture of the United States. Delpha Mae had heard Hitler's description of the corrupt and primitive music of "former slaves." She simply shrugged it off and said that she reckoned the trio would add a little color to the entire tribe of goose-stepping prison wardens! "Ain't that so?"

Delpha Mae was not afraid of anybody!

"You be listenin', you two!" she called as the taxi pulled away. "I'll blow you kisses from Vienna, babies!"

Wolf rummaged through Lucy's closet, at last pulling her most austere black dress from the rod—long sleeves, ankle-length hem, and high neck. It was the dress Lucy hated above all others.

"I wear that to funerals," she said angrily, "not luncheon receptions."

He tossed it on the bed. "This could be a funeral—your own, if you do not wear the dress."

"You told me he wanted to see beautiful German women. How can he tell if we are all made to wear black shrouds?" She pouted as she pulled up her stockings.

"Haj Amin Husseini is a Muslim leader in exile, expelled by the British. He is here as a guest to the Führer. His idea of beauty does not include low-cut dresses and bare ankles and shoulders. Women are meant to be covered—veils and such."

"Then what's the point? How will he be able to tell beauty? Take him on a tour of Rome and let him look at the Sistine Chapel. Michelangelo painted some lovely nudes."

"Vatican City will not appeal to the leader of the Muslims in Jerusalem." He buttoned his tunic and smoothed his hair. "He is more interested in touring prison camps for Jews than seeing great paintings, I hear." Wolf watched her in the mirror as she dressed. "The Mufti considers women as window dressing. You may smile, but don't talk."

"Like a basket of flowers," she said cynically. She did not like playing this role for the Mufti. She had heard he was barbarous and effeminate at the same time. Haj Amin was nothing like the sheik portrayed in the movies by Rudolph Valentino. Rumor among the secretaries in the Foreign Ministry said this Mufti fellow was actually more interested in pretty boys than in women. The thought made Lucy's skin crawl.

This was one reception she wished Wolf had not asked her to. He explained that the Reich was courting the Arab factions in the British Mandate with the aim of acquiring Palestine as a colony of the Reich. The Jewish problem was as vital there as it was in Germany itself. And now those self-righteous Englishmen were campaigning to reopen the gates of Palestine for ten thousand Jewish waifs. British officers were leading Jews into battle! Haj Amin had come here for some reassurance that Germany would make such immigration impossible, as well as silence Jewish guns, Wolf told her. The Führer desperately wanted to drive the wedge deep between the Arabs and the British in Palestine. The Jewish issue provided an ideal wedge, as long as it did not also damage relations with Germany.

Wolf believed that Lucy could not fully understand these lofty matters. But she understood the politics of dividing one group against another. Such tactics were used every day in friendships and marriage. Jealousy, dissatisfaction, anger—all these things could be used in getting what one wanted. Arabs and Jews had lived side by side for centuries. Now Hitler wanted Palestine; Haj Amin wanted Palestine. Together, Haj Amin and Hitler would have it—a simple matter of the eternal triangle, not to mention strange bedfellows. The Nazis and the Muslims had crawled into bed together, and together they plotted the end of the Jews.

What is so difficult to understand about that? she asked herself later as she caught her first glimpse of Haj Amin arriving in his black Mercedes at the Hofburg. He had a light complexion and blue eyes, which no doubt made it easier for the Nazis to accept him. Whispers around the room told of the Mufti's Crusader ancestors. He wore long robes and a fez on his head. He was small boned and indeed glided with a feminine walk into the room.

He took Lucy's hand as she moved through the reception line. He smiled, appreciating German beauty, no doubt. Lucy smiled back without speaking, feeling queasy at his touch. She attributed the reaction to her pregnancy and the strange excitement of coming near to someone so important. But then again, there was something about this man that reminded her instantly of the poisonous snakes she had seen in the reptile cages at the Schönbrunn Park Zoo. Nothing at all about him even vaguely resembled Rudolph Valentino.

The afternoon was a social occasion. All the women were dressed like Quakers, and the men like peacocks. Haj Amin's arrival had been well publicized in the state press as well as in the international press.

Haj Amin stood before the journalists of the world and said quite firmly that this drive for the immigration of ten thousand children into Palestine would have to be silenced. Otherwise those Englishmen who ruled Palestine with such tyranny would be startled at the violence they faced from the Muslim populace. There would be no peace, he warned. There would be no peace conference between Jews and Arabs and the English until this idea of ten thousand homeless Jews in Palestine was stamped out once and for all! *No immigration!*

Lucy listened to the BBC at night when Wolf was not at home. Some, like Churchill, also saw the snake inside Haj Amin. Churchmen and plain people all said something must be done quickly, but it sounded to Lucy as though nothing would be done in the end. The success of Jewish fighters in Galilee was discussed at length. That, too, seemed doomed to failure.

At times Lucy walked past the ruins of Jewish shops or the long bread lines where the Jewish women came with their children. She wondered what would happen to these people. They looked like sad-eyed mice huddling in the corner of a reptile cage. The jaw of the snake was unhinged, and through the clear glass Lucy watched them being devoured whole. Everyone watched. There was no attempt to hide anything. But what could anyone do?

Lucy did not like asking herself that question. Why should she do anything, after all? Maybe she was one of the mice. How could she help anyone when she could not even help herself?

The smoking truck sputtered its way through the village. The men of Hanita knew this place sheltered several Arab terrorists from across the Jordan. Only two days earlier the terrorists had sniped at another Jewish settlement, killing one man as he drove a tractor and seriously wounding the first of his friends who had run to help him.

Orde's Special Night Squad had tracked the attackers back to this village but done nothing further—nothing until now, that is.

Moshe had no trouble looking genuinely nervous as he wheeled the truck past the village in the gathering twilight. "Come on; come on," he muttered to the complaining engine. "Don't break down here!" Missing the right front fender and headlight and sporting four unmatched tires, the ancient Dodge flatbed was used to haul seed and stock fodder around Hanita, but was seldom trusted off the settlement's property. Its sagging springs were even now loaded with a neatly stacked load of grain sacks.

Moshe's shoulders hunched over the steering wheel as he urged the truck to continue running with all the strength of willpower he could muster. He threw a glance sideways as he clattered past the headman's house. Against the doorjamb leaned a keffiyeh-crowned man with a hawklike nose and a permanent scowl because his lower lip was missing.

Moshe thought the man looked mean enough to have bitten his lip off himself. The man narrowed his eyes as he watched Moshe drive by, then spat loudly enough to be heard over the rattling engine. The view in the cracked rearview mirror through the missing rear window showed Moshe that the terrorist had abruptly ducked inside the house.

Relieved at having successfully passed the village, Moshe thought ironically that the villagers would probably be as pleased as the Jews of Hanita to see the last of this man.

A scant quarter mile beyond the Arab community, the narrow dirt track began a sudden steep grade. Midway up the climb out of the wadi lay a hairpin switchback that could only be turned by successively going forward and back a few feet at a time—a turn that would slow down any traveler.

Moshe painfully maneuvered the complaining truck around the corner, gears clashing. The truck's whole body shuddered like a prehistoric beast dying. Giving a last bellow that ended with a slowly spinning whine, the truck's engine died. Only halfway around the turn, the truck stood squarely across the road.

Moshe jumped out of the cab and hastily grabbed a rock with which to block the wheels before the truck rolled backward into the wadi. Then he backed toward the truck's hood, all the while staring intently down along the road. He raised the hood on its lone remaining hinge and propped it open with the stick tied there for that purpose.

He was busy for a moment, reattaching the two spark-plug wires that had become disconnected. He might have done it faster had he watched his hands instead of the road, but his hands were shaking as he wiped the grease from them onto the legs of his coveralls.

When he straightened up, he was not surprised to see three shadowy forms in checkered keffiyehs striding toward him up the road. They came boldly, making no attempt at caution or quiet. The man with the disfigured face took the lead; the other two flanked him a few paces behind. All three carried rifles slung over their shoulders.

Partway up the hill they stopped as they saw Moshe gazing down at them. "What's the matter, Jew?" called the leader. "Has your machine breathed its last?" The other two men snickered into their beards.

"Just a little trouble," replied Moshe in carefully measured tones.

"More than you think, dog," said the lipless one. "You are in a puzzle. If you run like the cur you are, I will shoot you down like I did that Jew farmer the other day. And—" he paused ominously— "if you stand still, I will cut out your heart." He reached into the sash knotted around his waist and drew out a short gleaming knife.

Moshe mumbled something, but in a voice too low to be heard. "What was that, Jew?" called the leader of the terrorists, stepping a few paces nearer.

Moshe's lips could be seen moving, but the three men still could not make out his words. One of the mutilated man's companions called out mockingly, "He must be praying!" The trio advanced a few more steps.

In a voice suddenly so loud that it made the three stop in their tracks, Moshe called out, "You are right! I am praying *right now!*"

As he shouted the last two words, Moshe lunged under the front axle of the truck. On the truck bed, a tarp that had covered the top of the load of grain sacks was thrown off. Zach and Larry Havas stood up, German-made rifles in their hands. The weapons lay across the barricade of sacks pointed down the slope at the startled Arabs. Havas' first shot dropped his man in his tracks.

Zach Zabinski fired, missed, then worked the bolt and fired again before his mark had finished shrugging the rifle off his shoulder. The second terrorist also crumpled in a heap on the road.

The leader of the cutthroats didn't even try to bring his rifle to bear. Instead he threw himself forward at the first shot, screaming his anger and defiance. He brandished his dagger overhead as his charge carried him almost to the side of the truck before Havas and Zabinski each fired again, both shots striking the man. The impact of the blows spun him completely around, so that his robes twirled in the twilight like the frenzied dance of a religious fanatic.

A moment later the hillside was quiet again, and Moshe crawled out from under the truck. "I cannot tell you," he said, "how glad I am you fellows have been practicing."

When they returned to Hanita, Orde met them at the gate. "How did it go?" he asked dryly.

"No trouble at all," replied Havas, grinning. "Of course, we had to defend ourselves once, but honestly, it was no trouble at all."

Alfie did not even bother to duck tonight when he spotted the light of the old watchman come around the corner of New Church. The watchman never looked for anyone in the tombs. He only whistled and hummed and checked all the boards on the windows and doors. He would not have been very good at playing hide-and-seek. He did not know any of the good places for hiding. He walked very slowly, shuffling his feet. This was not the other watchman who was at New Church before. Alfie did not like the new man's face. His eyes were squinty and his mouth was turned down. He had a little mustache just like Hitler, and he wore an armband with a crooked cross. If it had not been for that, Alfie might have tried to make friends with him. But Alfie especially did not like the armband.

Soon enough the watchman went away. Alfie was glad. He went down the stone steps into the underground room. It was all dark; Alfie did not light his candle until the watchman had come and gone each night.

He felt along the stone bench for his matches and the candle. He had practiced, and now he could light the candle with only one match. Mama had let him have the broken candlestick for his clubhouse when he had asked her. The light made the room seem warm, and he whispered thanks again to Mama with the same happy feeling he had when she had given him the candlestick so long ago. Maybe Mama had known how much he would need it. Maybe he had known it too, in a way, even though he had not thought about it then.

The smooth stone walls shone golden in the light. On the right and the left were benches made out of stone. Alfie made his bed up neatly and smooth on the right bench. Stacks of sardine cans and cans of beans and peaches sat on the floor below the left bench. Alfie organized them in rows that looked like a town with buildings and streets, and even a park. Sometimes he stacked two cans of peaches up to make a tall building like the Opera House. With sardine cans he made the Brandenburg Gate. He put his tin soldiers on top and liked his city very much. He used the empty cans for houses where people lived. His apartment was all shiny and bright because he took the labels off the empty cans. And over there was Friedrichstrasse and the Jewish church like it used to be, and then New Church where everyone came and sang and prayed and Pastor Ibsen talked about good things like Jesus loving children no matter how smart or not smart they were.

The Hitler men had not liked that talk. They stood in the back of the church with angry faces when Pastor Ibsen talked about God looking inside at souls to see who was really perfect and who was deformed. Alfie played out that Sunday morning again and again, because he remembered how good he felt that Pastor stood up for Alfie and the other children who were being taken from their families and sent away out of the sight of the German people. That day a lot of other Christians came to New Church. The Hitler men wrote down their names on lists and said they had not heard the last of this!

Alfie made his tin Hitler men stomp away and climb to the top of the shelf to report to Hitler; then they slipped and fell all the way to the floor. Sometimes he liked to make up his own ending.

The story he liked best of all was the one he performed tonight. In the back of the bean-can New Church with the candle for a bell tower, Alfie put *this* place. *His* place. Home with Mama. It was a sardine can with lots of sleeping tin men in it. Alfie was an infantry soldier in a handsome blue uniform. Sometimes his Alfie fought off troops of Hitler men who came to take him. Sometimes he tapped through his imaginary city and visited people and shops. Tonight Alfie put the tin-man Alfie to bed and sang songs from New Church and prayed and pretended that it was dark even though it was not really dark because of the candle. Last of all he put the general on his tin horse and then put them both on the candlestick.

"I am Jesus, king of everything," the general said. "And you don't have to be scared, Alfie." Then the candle and Jesus swooped through the air.

"Here I am!" the tin Alfie said, waking up. "I want to fight with You! Make me smart like other boys, and I will not be a dumbhead! I will fight the bad men!"

Jesus flew down and the candle was bright on the silver can where Alfie lived with Mama. The horse rode slowly into the can, and Jesus touched Alfie with His sword. "You are smart!" Jesus said. "And I will make you fight good for me!" And Alfie was not a dumbhead anymore.

"Please wake up Mama, too!"

The sword touched sleeping Mama and she woke up and hugged Alfie. She was so glad to see him that she hugged him and hugged him, and Alfie had trouble getting away to knock the bad men off the Brandenburg Gate and rescue Werner and Dieter and Heinrich.

Alfie scooted back to look at his little world. He would be glad when things really happened the way he imagined. He stared hard at the pretend Alfie who stood before Jesus. He wished he could really be smart and fight a good fight for others the way Pastor had fought a fight for him.

"How did I do, General Jesus?"

Well done, Alfie.

Then Alfie lifted the horse and rider back in the air, and they flew away to watch everything in Berlin from heaven.

19

Night Visitors

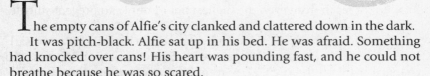

The empty cans of Alfie's city clanked and clattered down in the dark.

It was pitch-black. Alfie sat up in his bed. He was afraid. Something had knocked over cans! His heart was pounding fast, and he could not breathe because he was so scared.

"Mama?" he said to the darkness.

A deep sound of breathing answered him. For the first time Alfie thought about ghosts.

"Who is there?" he shouted. He was afraid to reach for the candlestick. He was afraid to run for the steps. Whatever was there stood between him and the steps. He heard it! It kicked his city and maybe crushed his tin men with its big feet!

"Is it . . . Jesus? Jesus, I hope it is You! *Jesus?*"

Alfie was shaking all over, just like when he figured out that Werner was dead and that they would kill him too. He pulled his blanket over his head and scrunched way back in the corner, hugging his knees and pressing his face against his legs. He tried not to cry, for then it would hear him and get him.

"Go away!" He took a deep breath and tried to sound brave. "This is my place!"

More cans clattered down from the shelf. The breathing made a soft rumbly noise. Alfie closed his eyes tight, expecting a blow.

A can rolled across the floor. Then something pounced and landed lightly on the edge of the blanket. Alfie gasped and screamed in terror. He struck out and hit something soft and furry. With a hiss and a meow, it whisked up the steps and away.

By the light of the candle, Alfie twisted open the sardine can. It hissed, and the aroma of the fish filled the place. He went up the steps where the cat had run away and placed a sardine just inside the iron gate.

He dripped a little juice a few steps back and laid the next sardine on the marble floor. He decided he would not give the cat more than two sardines unless he came down the steps. Alfie broke a third sardine in pieces and left one bite on each step all the way down into his room.

Animals were nicer than people. Alfie remembered what the lady said on the day after Berlin was smashed. It would be nice to have a friend!

He prayed as he laid the little trail across his room and climbed back into his blanket. He put the sardine can right on his chest and left the candle burning.

Bare lightbulbs hung from the ceiling of Barrack 7 at Nameless camp, high out of reach from even the highest tier of bunks to prevent suicide by electrocution.

In Barrack 7, however, there had been no suicides since Pastor Karl Ibsen had come among the prisoners. Sometimes smiles were exchanged between the men. They were kinder to one another than the prisoners of Barrack 14, where stealing and beatings were rampant. The difference was duly noted; it was not liked by the camp commanders.

Prisoners were not supposed to act humanely toward one another. The retention of dignity was a sign of inner resistance. Even silent resistance sent a tremor of fear through the ideology of oppression, the mastery of strong over the weak. It raised terrible questions. Who is really strong? And who is really weak?

Karl Ibsen and Richard Kalner shared a place with ten other men on the top tier of bunks. There was just enough room for two men to lie side by side like sardines in a can. Their heads faced out toward the narrow aisle; they were not safe from the blows of their captors even in sleep.

The lights blinked once, a warning that all prisoners must now be in place for lights out. In the most remarkable minute of each day, one man on each bunk recited a Scripture for the group to think on before sleep. The ritual had begun with Karl and Richard on Bunk 49. It had spread from tier to tier, embraced by many and rejected by some, until these brief Scripture lessons became the high point of each day. Men who had not spoken a word of Scripture since bar mitzvah searched their memories to recall passages memorized in their youth. Those who had never read one word from the Bible sought out others from across the barracks.

"It is my turn to say something tonight. Have you a short verse I can learn?"

"The joy of the Lord is your strength."

"Look upon my suffering and deliver me."

There was no lack of supply, it seemed. Newcomers who scoffed at first soon found themselves as eager as their comrades to learn a new verse. After a while no one could remember who had started the tradition.

Karl did not admit that this was something he had picked up at a church camp when he was a boy, or that he had memorized complete books of the Bible one verse at a time.

"May my tongue sing of Your word, for all Your commands are righteous."

From the bunk below, Karl heard the quaking voice of a young man who had come from Austria a week before. He declared he was an atheist and asked Karl for the shortest Scripture in the Bible. Now he repeated that verse in a mocking voice: *"Jesus wept."*

Silence below. Then, "Why did He weep?"

"Because He knew what men could do to one another."

"He saw us here. It broke His heart."

A longer silence followed as each man considered the tears of Jesus. There was no great theological debate, no need for it. The Lord's tears spoke to the heart from the shortest verse in the Bible.

Throughout the barracks, guards with rubber truncheons shrieked for silence. The lights went out. Then the young atheist who had offered the Scripture in jest wept also.

Since the church picnic last summer, Lori had often daydreamed about being alone in a quiet place with Jacob Kalner. She had even imagined what it would be like to kiss him. Now such thoughts seemed foolish. She glared at him with resentment and anger.

The tiny bellows room of New Church was cold. Lori's teeth chattered as they placed the pew cushions on the floor to serve as mattresses. The heavy red velvet draperies from behind the altar had been taken down and would serve as a blanket for the trio. They dared not attempt to keep the furnace burning or sleep in a more comfortable room in case the Gestapo returned for a surprise search of the premises. The bellows room was the safest place, Jacob reasoned. At the first sound of trouble they could kick the cushions and the drapery into a corner among a stack of other items that had fallen into disuse around the church. And then they could slip back into the bellows to hide. Comfort was of small consideration compared to safety.

This thought in mind, they climbed into their makeshift bed. Jacob lay closest to the door. Lori lay next to the bellows and Mark slept in the center. It was still early evening, but not even light from the streetlamp penetrated the black cubicle.

Lori lay awake a long time as she listened for imaginary footsteps in the church beyond. Her breath mingled with the frigid night air in a steamy vapor. Jacob and Mark breathed with the even cadence of deep, untroubled sleep. Lori took some comfort in their ability to sleep. It was hard for her to close her eyes. Hard to give up watchfulness, in spite of the fact that they had rehearsed and drilled their escape a dozen times. *What if they come and we do not hear them?*

Every pop and groan of the rafters became the imagined footstep of a Gestapo officer coming to search the tiny church for fugitives. The wind against the roof, dry leaves tapping on the windows—the slightest sound became the harsh whispers of their pursuers. Even beneath the heavy fabric of the curtain, Lori trembled with fear. Mark curled warmly at her back. Jacob slept against the door so he could hear if they came. But he slept so soundly! *What if we do not hear them in time?*

She thought of her family and prayed for them one at a time. But those thoughts made her so sad that she considered slipping out of the church and marching to the nearest Gestapo office to give herself up. It was better not to think too much. Better to be afraid instead of locked in despair for Mama and Papa and Jamie. And so she let herself tremble, let the churning fear keep the sadness away.

It was very late when her eyes finally grew heavy with the exhaustion of terror. At last she drifted off into an uneasy sleep where the sounds of Mama's arrest replayed over and over again in her dreams. Somewhere far off, she thought she heard the thin, high wail of her brother's cry as he was carried away: *"No! No! Mama! Don't let them take me! Mama!"*

Then she felt an urgent tapping on her head! *The signal!*

Jacob wordlessly slipped from beneath the blanket, on his feet in an instant. He pressed his ear against the door and then, without explanation, tore the heavy fabric off Lori and Mark and tossed the cushions against the wall.

Lori jerked wide-awake at the first sign of danger. Without waiting to listen, she grabbed Mark by the arm and guided him back into the giant bellows of the pipe organ. Only seconds passed before Jacob followed into the cramped space. Lori wiped her face with the back of her hand. Her cheek was wet. She had been crying in her sleep.

She listened, trying to hear what had awakened Jacob, trying to make out the imminent danger that must be ascending the steps to the organ loft.

But she heard no sound except the thump of her heart in her ears, the rapid breathing of her companions.

Jacob exhaled loudly, as if with satisfaction. "All clear," he said in a voice that seemed too loud for the tiny hiding place.

Neither Mark nor Lori dared to believe him. *How could he know?*

He said even loudly, "Come on. Back to bed! Just a drill!"

Lori groaned with audible relief. All this fear wasted on a drill! What gave him the right to say when they would have a drill? She had just fallen asleep, and now she had to do it all over again!

"We have drilled enough!" she said angrily as she dusted herself off. "I just washed my face before bed, and now I'm all dirty again!"

Jacob grabbed her by the arm as she reached for the doorknob. "You're not going anywhere. I told you. Use the toilet before we go to bed, because once we're here for the night, we're here!"

"You can't make laws about such things," she argued angrily. "Unless you're a . . . Nazi!"

"I told you—," he began.

"You did not tell me you would wake me up in the middle of the night for nothing!" She pushed past him and jerked open the door. He did not try to stop her, but set to work reconstructing their bed.

"We needed a drill," he muttered to Mark. "You don't go running off to the toilet every time we have a drill, now do you, Mark?"

Mark was too tired to reply. It seemed like a very long time since they had been able to sleep a whole night through.

Lori grasped the cold metal banister and worked her way cautiously down the dark stairway to the foyer. Groping along the wall, she found the door of the women's room and slipped in.

They had agreed that lights must never be switched on in the church, and so she moved blindly to the sink and splashed ice-cold water over her gritty face and hands and arms. She could not find the towel; she shook off the drops and wiped the dampness on her slacks, aware too late that her clothes were also filthy and she would have to wash her hands again.

Silently fuming at Jacob, she repeated the whole process one more time and then searched for the towel. Then she heard it . . .

In the pitch blackness of the tiled room, Lori heard the sound of shallow breathing. She stood rooted at the sink, blinking in the darkness toward where she knew the mirror would be. Was that her own pale face staring eerily back at her? Was she imagining? Why could she not move?

Her mouth went dry with fear. She held her breath, hoping that perhaps she had only heard an echo, her own echo against the tiles. But it was not so. The breathing was real; human, but not human. She opened her mouth and tried to speak the name of Jesus. But her lips could not form the word, so she simply stood there, clutching the cold porcelain of the sink.

There could be no doubt that whoever . . . *whatever* . . . was there with her had heard her clunking around. Why did it not speak? Why was the breath so shallow and . . . so *frightened* sounding? She drew a breath. Was it Mark? Had he slipped down here ahead of her to frighten her as a horrible prank, to teach her that she must obey Jacob?

Resentment gave her courage. "Who . . . who is there?" she demanded.

A little cry answered her, resounding off the tiles of the little room. "Lori? Sister? Lori?" It was the unmistakable voice of Jamie, sniffing through tears and calling with joy all at the same moment. *"Lori?"*

"Jamie!" She said her brother's name again and again as she patted the wall in search of the forbidden light switch. "Oh, Jamie!" she cried, no longer caring who heard her. It *was* Jamie! The light slammed against their eyes, making them both squint and blink as they took in the sight of each other in astonishment.

Jamie was dressed in the black uniform of the Hitler Jugend. His shoes were new and brightly polished, and he wore a heavy warm coat and gloves. His clothes looked new and strangely dark against his fair skin and hair.

He embraced her, holding tightly to her as he explained his escape from the Hitler Youth dormitory after dinner and his return to the dark and deserted church by way of a streetcar. "And then I came in through the window! And I was sitting in the basement for a long time, but then I had to use the toilet so I came this way and then I heard something . . . something . . . I don't know. I thought maybe a ghost or Gestapo. I ran in here and hid up on the toilet tank, you see, but then you came in. You didn't turn on the light . . . I thought the ghosts had followed me!"

She stroked his back gently as he rambled wildly on. And then, mindful of the lights, she reached up and flicked them off again. Only then did Jamie fall silent and let her simply hold him close.

"We must be careful of the light," she said softly. "I don't think they'll come back—not with all the signs. But we cannot go turning lights on, or someone will notice." She smiled in the dark, touching the fine, soft hair of her brother as Mama used to do.

"Where is Mama?" Jamie asked after a moment.

"They took her. I . . . I don't know where. Or Papa either."

"I saw our auto," Jamie said, as if he were telling of meeting an old friend. "It is parked not far from the Kalners' flat. The streetcar passed it, and I looked at it very hard. It was Papa's auto . . ." He sighed heavily. "I wish I had gone with Papa. Oh, Lori! What could have happened to them?"

Lori held her emotions in check. She was the older, the more responsible. She would not cry like a little baby, even though she wanted to. She had asked herself the same questions a thousand times, but she had no way of knowing the answers. "They will let them go," she replied in her most reassuring voice. "You will see. Mama and Papa will be released in no time. The Gestapo won't hold them. They can't. Papa hasn't done anything. Mama is innocent. Don't worry, Jamie."

"Are you alone?" he asked, drawing away and stiffening at the sound of footsteps against the flagstones of the foyer.

A muffled voice called through the door. "Lori? Are you all right?"

"Jacob!" Jamie said triumphantly.

Hand in hand the two went out to tell him Jamie had come home.

Alfie called his new cat Joseph, because his coat had so many different colors. Alfie knew the names of colors—orange and yellow and brown and tan. And Joseph had a little white on his pink nose and three white paws.

Alfie was glad that Joseph had come to live with him and keep him company. He did not mind sharing the sardines. Joseph was very fat but did not eat a lot. He was no trouble and slept on Alfie's feet every night. Joseph helped keep Alfie warm.

The best thing about Joseph was the way he purred and buzzed all over when Alfie stroked his soft fur, almost like laughing. It made Alfie feel happy inside that the cat liked him.

At first Alfie worried when Joseph hopped up the steps and slipped out between the bars of the gate to disappear over the fence of the graveyard. Alfie hung on to the bars and looked out to the very spot where Joseph had jumped. He watched the place for hours and hoped that Joseph would come back. But Joseph sneaked back another way, and suddenly Alfie felt him rubbing against his legs and buzzing hello.

After a while Alfie quit looking at the spot where Joseph jumped over the fence; he decided that Joseph was just playing a trick on him. Alfie gave Joseph an extra sardine every time he came back and let him lick the tin while he stroked his back. Alfie hoped Joseph would not go away forever. Such a terrible thought made Alfie's heart beat fast with fear. He didn't want to have to get used to loneliness again.

"You are such a good friend, Joseph," Alfie said to the cat. "Will you still come back when I run out of sardines? There are not very many cans left, but I will feed you all the same. But you must not forget me when there are no more sardines to eat."

Joseph purred as though food made no difference to him. He smiled a cat smile and cleaned his whiskers and lay down in a ball on Alfie's big feet. Alfie sat very still for a long time because he did not want to disturb Joseph. He did not wiggle his toes or say anything at all, even though he was thinking how much he loved this new friend and how glad he was that Joseph shared his warm coat even though there were not many cans of sardines left.

Lucy hoped to slip out of the room before Wolf awakened. She dressed in the dark, ran a brush hastily through her hair, and groped in the top drawer of the bureau for her Mass book. Today was the day of her patron saint, St. Lucy. It was also Lucy's birthday—not that she expected anyone to remember. As a final gesture of an innocent past lost forever, Lucy longed to sit in the pew of St. Stephan's Cathedral and hear the familiar words of the one Mass she remembered well.

She quietly slid the drawer back into place and put a scarf over her head as she inched past the bed where Wolf lay sleeping like a guard dog dozing on the threshold.

Her heart beat faster as her coat brushed the side of the bed. *Help me; help me get out, and I will light a candle and—*

Wolf's hand shot up and clamped hard around her wrist, pulling her down to her knees beside him. "Where are you going, little fox?" he asked with a too-sweet voice that betrayed his anger at being awakened.

She cried out with pain at the strength of his grip. "Please, Wolf! You're hurting me!"

"Where are you going at this hour?" He did not reach up to switch on the lamp. He could not see the Mass book she held up in the blackness as proof.

"I . . . I am going to confession! To early Mass!"

"Or have you been somewhere and are just sneaking back into the room?" He twisted her wrist. "Eh? Have you been out with someone?"

"Wolf!" The pain shot up her arm. She thought her wrist would snap. "No, Wolf! I am going to church! To Mass! Turn on the light, and I will show you!"

He hesitated, then switched on the lamp without letting up on the pressure of her wrist. Blinking against the brightness, he peered at the little leather book she continued to hold up like a flag of surrender. A cross, an open Bible, and the Communion cup were stamped in gold on the cover. He snatched the book from her free hand as she moaned softly, trying not to argue with him. *"Parish Mass Book and Hymnal,"* he read; then he flipped open a page marked by a red ribbon. He laughed as he read the writing at the top of the page. "St. Lucy. Virgin. Martyr! *Innocence!"* He roared with laughter, released her, and hurled the well-worn book against the wall.

Lucy sat in the pool of light rubbing her wrist as he lay back on his pillow, laughing at the idea of his Lucy sneaking off to honor such a saint!

She did not raise her eyes but remained, shamed and humiliated, on the floor. "I . . . always go to Mass on this day," she managed to say, although the words nearly choked her.

"Well, you have nothing in common with this dead Catholic; let me tell you!" Lucy had never seen Wolf so amused. "St. Lucy's Day! Virgin! Martyr! Innocence! Nothing you could claim!"

She felt some desperate need to explain, to stop his ridicule. "It is . . . my birthday, Wolf. You see . . . I was not trying to . . . I mean, I know I am not . . . should not go, but every year . . . I have never missed a year."

He jabbed her under the chin with his thumb, lifting her head with the painful pressure until her eyes were forced to look at his mocking smile. "Your birthday is it, St. Lucy? My innocent virgin! My long-suffering martyr!"

Tears stung her eyes. She held her breath, not wanting to dissolve into weak emotion in front of him. In one instinct of self-defense, she slapped his hand away and scrambled to her feet. "All right! I know what I am—I am the creation of your holy Reich! I know who I belong to! But I am going to Mass because it is my birthday. Even whores have birthdays!"

His mouth still curved upward in a smile, but he shrugged and lay back, surprised at the sudden show of fortitude. He waved a hand as though brushing away a fly. "Go on, then. You women! All the same. You and your church! Every prostitute from the highest level in Berlin to the lowest level in Vienna has a crucifix above her bed."

She picked up the book and moved toward the door. She did not want to give him even an instant to change his mind and order her back to bed.

"Be back before eight o'clock!" he shouted after her. "And bring me a pastry from Demel's on the way back!"

She slammed the door behind her as if she had not heard his words. Then she ran down the dark stairs and out into the cold, deserted streets of sleeping Vienna.

Lucy was late. She stepped off the nearly empty streetcar on the opposite side of Stephansplatz and jogged quickly across the slick cobbles toward the Riesentor, the giant gate. She hoped the entrance was unlocked. Breathless from running, she threw herself against the massive doors beneath the first arch. They did not yield. She ran to the center arch and pushed. Again, the door resisted her.

It would be a small Mass, Lucy knew. St. Lucy was not a very important saint, as saints go. *The priest will probably be in some little side chapel,* she reasoned, running down the stone steps and making her way to the side and rear of the towering edifice.

Clambering down a flight of steep steps, she pushed against the tarnished bronze handle of a wooden door. The hinges yielded, opening in welcome. Lucy lunged into the church and found herself in a small, nearly deserted niche where a handful of old people knelt to receive Communion.

The priest did not look at her as he held the host and blessed it, but certainly he must have heard the tardy worshipper clatter in!

Lucy stood rooted, cradling the tiny book in her arms. *Too late! I am too late even for this day!* She knew the words by heart, but she dared not utter them. She had not been to confession, had not laid the hell of her sin before the black-frocked priest who now ministered to the ones who had been on time. *"Princes persecute me without cause, but my heart stands in awe of Your Word. I rejoice at Your promise as one who has found rich spoil."*

Yes, Lucy knew the words. She had no need of the Mass book to read from today, but even as she listened, she knew that for her to speak such words was blasphemy! To speak the words of an innocent martyr, unabsolved, would heap more darkness on her soul. Lucy stood in silence. When the priest had passed down the row of kneeling communicants along the altar rail, he looked up at her questioningly.

Lucy simply stared back in confusion, and then she hurriedly shook her head and inclined it toward the door as if to say she had stumbled in by accident. A convincing performance. The priest glanced away toward his early congregation and did not notice Lucy even when she stepped back into the shadows and turned to slip out the way she had entered.

Names of the missing drifted across the frontiers of Germany first by the hundreds and then by the thousands. Businessmen and scholars, former politicians and clergymen, all had been swallowed up in a single night.

Those in the free world could not hope to discover the fate of all of them; they could only hope to alter the fate of a few.

The list for tonight's TBS broadcast at the BBC in London contained only ten names—German priests and pastors who had been arrested on Kristal Nacht and had not been heard of since. Murphy carefully interviewed anyone who had known these men in the pre-Nazi days in Germany. Each page of the typed script bore a photograph of the missing clergyman and some biographical information, including family members and the possible reason for the arrest.

The program would be beamed from London to Amsterdam and then into the heart of the Reich. If it reached the right ears, perhaps there would be answers.

Two and one half minutes was allotted for each man and his family. An average of thirty seconds per name.

Murphy reread the short descriptions and wondered how it was possible to cram an entire human life into two and a half minutes.

The inner circles in Berlin knew that the original concept of the order came from Reichsmarschall Hermann Göring himself. Göring had no real sympathy for the weak and ineffective German church, but his sister was quite open about her disapproval of Nazi tactics against the clergy-men. Her vocal expressions of that disapproval were an irritation to Göring. At last he decided, "Anything to shut her up!"

The case was brought personally to Adolf Hitler with the explanation: "The foreign press is not as concerned about our treatment of the Jewish question as it is about the crackdown on the clergy. Such a move would also quiet the murmurs from the Vatican."

The Führer listened and remembered that his own strong resolve was borne out of his days in prison. Too much pressure against the German churchmen might, in fact, create a diamond out of a lump of coal.

Based on that conclusion, a plan was formulated and the command was issued from the highest authorities in Berlin.

Pine boughs scented the cold morning air. The clean, sweet aroma cleared Karl's head of the foul odor of nights inside the prison barracks.

Three dozen men worked on the line, stringing thick rolls of barbed wire on the inner perimeter of the compound. Within a week the wire would be electrified, they were told. Even to touch the wire would mean instant death. But for now, bloody hands and nicked clothes were the only penalty they paid.

The layers of wire seemed formidable enough without electricity, Karl thought. Even if a man somehow managed to get past this barrier, two more lay beyond it—not to mention the machine-gun towers above.

He scanned the mile of fence that followed a gentle slope down and then a level stretch for another half mile before the fence turned a corner. The camp was enormous. How could they expect to fill it? Why was it so big? And who were the potential prisoners waiting on the Nazi lists?

Karl gazed at the towering white clouds piling up over Polish territory. In the distance, he could hear the shrill whistle of the German express train as it slipped over the Polish border on its way to the free port of Danzig. Karl hesitated just a second too long for the young guard who watched him.

"What are you looking at?" the guard demanded. He did not beat Karl, probably because of Karl's vocation. A few Nazis still hesitated to beat a pastor.

"I was listening to the train whistle," Karl answered, as if he were carrying on a normal conversation on a street corner in Berlin.

"A lonely sound," the young dark-haired guard said as he lit a cigarette.

"A lovely sound," Karl contradicted as he returned to his task. "A free sound."

The whistle blew again, and a flock of birds rose up from the trees that bounded the track on the German side. In a spiral swirl they circled and then swept across to the Polish side of the frontier. *The sky has no boundaries*, Karl thought as he watched and envied their flight.

"Karl!" Richard's voice came as an urgent reprimand, a request that he pay attention to their job. Maybe the guards thought twice about beating Karl, but Richard's bruises were evidence that they did not hesitate at all to club him down for any imagined offense.

Karl looked back, first at the sharp barbs, then at the bloody nicks in Richard's hands. With every drop of blood spilled here at Nameless, Karl thought of crowns made of woven barbed wire and iron spikes driven through innocent hands. The image somehow made this suffering more bearable.

"Karl!" Richard whispered again, raising his eyes for Karl to follow his gaze.

Four soldiers tramped toward them through the mud. Only their eyes were visible beneath heavy helmets and warm trench coats with the collars turned up. Their eyes were fixed on Pastor Karl Ibsen.

"You are Pastor Karl Ibsen?" asked the fellow with his rifle slung over his shoulder.

Karl did not stop his work, but replied with a silent nod.

"Then you will please come with us." They stepped apart, leaving him room within their inner square.

Richard's eyes met Karl's steady gaze. *So this is it. They intend to shoot you or turn you loose*," Richard seemed to say in that look. "God bless," he whispered as Karl turned away. The soldiers did not hear him, or they would have knocked him down with the butt of a rifle.

The camp commandant of Nameless was a small, waxy-faced man with worried, red-rimmed eyes. No one had ever seen him with his peaked cap off, and now Karl knew why.

The thin, balding head was covered with scabs. Except for the Nazi uniform he wore, the fellow could have easily been mistaken for a prisoner with an advanced case of ringworm or eczema.

He looked through the file marked with the name and number of Pastor Karl Ibsen. He scratched his ear. A dusting of dandruff flocked the shoulders of the proud black uniform.

Karl stood silent before the desk of the little man in an office that was no more than a shack warmed by an iron stove. He did not mind the wait, nor was he intimidated by the shabby little man in the grand uniform. Karl enjoyed the warmth. It was the first time since his arrest that he had felt any warmth penetrate his clothes and body. It made him pleasantly sleepy.

"So," the commandant began at last, "you are Pastor Karl Ibsen of New Church, *ja?*"

"Pastor Karl Ibsen of Nameless camp." Karl gave a gracious bow.

The officer was not amused. He wanted to get right to the point. His little nose twitched as the warmth of his stove began to awaken the stench of Karl's body.

"It seems there may have been a clerical error."

"Is there such a thing in the Reich?" Karl said, amused, guessing what was coming.

With a wave of his hand the officer dismissed the comment as a jest. He managed a wan smile. "Yes. Well, sometimes even the Reich can make mistakes, given the confusion and chaos of rounding up these vermin."

"Vermin?"

"The Jews. The Jews you were arrested with." He cleared his throat and studied the folder again. "It seems that one of the prisoners has reported that you had come to his flat in order to collect a debt he owed you. You were then arrested and brought here. If you are willing to swear to such a thing, you will be released . . . under certain conditions and restrictions, of course."

So, Richard had told his tale. He had lied for the sake of securing Karl's release. "Was the prisoner Richard Kalner?"

"Yes. The former professor. Richard Kalner."

"Where is my wife?" Karl jumped to the question uppermost in his mind. "Helen. My wife?"

"She is also . . . in detention. As is the wife of Richard Kalner. We will see to it that they pay you what you are owed. Jews cannot take advantage of—"

Karl raised a hand, interrupting the officer. "And what about my children? Where are they? Also arrested?"

"Naturally you are concerned." The officer seemed almost solicitous as he scanned the report. "Son, James, taken to Hitler Youth School in Berlin. Daughter, Lori . . . at large." His lower lip protruded as he said it again. "At large. Still . . . somewhere. Possibly with relatives?"

Karl did not reply. Each beloved face came up before him now as he considered his choices. And what were those choices? "You mentioned certain conditions and restrictions."

"Yes. I have been instructed to inform you that this is a simple matter, really. You simply sign a paper saying that you have been well treated and that you will not slander the Reich. Your future sermons must be submitted to the local authorities for censorship. No different than every other church in the Reich nowadays."

"And may I preach from any part of the Scripture that I feel led to?"

The officer laughed. Karl Ibsen surely was joking again. "Within the established guidelines of the State Church, you know."

"And what about those in my congregation who are of Jewish heritage?"

"Well?" The officer became suddenly impatient. What sort of foolish question was this? "What do you think? If just going into a house to collect a debt got you arrested, then what do you think?"

Karl did not have to think hard. "I want a public hearing," he said coolly. "I am a citizen of Deutschland, and I request a public hearing."

"But . . . you are . . . I am telling you—" He held out the slip of paper that Karl was to sign. *Good treatment . . . do not hold the Reich responsible* . . . "There can be no hearing, you see. If you sign this, you are free to go." He smiled hopefully. "All you must do is denounce your associations with these Jews and you are as free as any man in Germany."

"I was at the home of Richard and Leona Kalner because I owed *them* a debt."

The commandant laughed with relief. So that was what this was all about! "You do not know the laws? No Aryan owes any debt to a Jew. Your debts and my debts to the Jewish moneylenders are all erased, a gift from our Führer to the German people! So . . . it was all a mistake. You went there to pay this swine, and . . . well, here you are."

"Not that kind of debt." Karl gazed at the man with pity. Here was a creature who could be purchased by the Führer's laws.

"Debt. You did say you owed him a debt."

"The debt that love requires of all men; the debt that demands that we do good to others, not harm; that we not look the other way when the innocent are persecuted. I owe them much more than money. I owe them my life."

The eyes of the scabby little man hardened. He understood, and the words of Pastor Karl Ibsen convicted him. He did not like it. "What about your family?"

Again and again this terrible question had played in his mind. *What about Helen? What about Lori and Jamie?* Should he go against everything he knew was right for their sake? Would they hate him for staying here to minister as one dying man to other dying men?

"I love my family," he said.

"Then sign."

To sign was a denial of the Christ he served. Karl trembled as he considered it; he longed to take the pen and sign his name and walk out of hell. Instead he said, "Jesus died for my family. Should I not be willing to die for His children?"

"You are a fool." The pinched face grew more pinched. High moral issues disgusted him. Life and death were enough to deal with every day. "You can return to your home in time for church next Sunday, your wife and children at your side."

"I will spend my Sunday here," Karl said softly, "where Christ dwells among the suffering."

After a moment of hesitation, a rubber stamp slammed across the unsigned paper. "You are dismissed, prisoner Ibsen."

Sunday morning. Each week on this day, the emptiness of New Church haunted Lori. The colored glass of the high windows made patterns on the empty pews. Iron pegs in the wall where the Nazis had torn down the wooden cross seemed marked with bloodred reflections from the rose window.

The pews where row on row of families had stood together in praise and worship were empty. Papa was not in the pulpit, Mama not at the organ. No song. No Bible readings. No request for prayers of healing. Healing people. Or healing this broken land.

Jamie knew what Lori was feeling. He came to sit beside her in the choir loft. Together they smiled down at the memories that crowded the vacant sanctuary. He took her hand and they hummed softly, "A Mighty Fortress Is Our God."

First Mark came and sat behind them, then Jacob. Jacob sang the words of the song, although his voice was off-key. Lori smiled. She had always loved listening to Jacob's voice. She had pretended not to notice two years ago when it had croaked and cracked and eventually slid into manhood. It was wonderful to hear him sing; she would not tease him as she used to.

"Where do you suppose Papa is?" Jamie asked when the song was finished.

"Your father?" Jacob said, voice echoing into the rafters. "Maybe we don't know where he is, but I can tell you what he is doing."

Jacob was right. Pastor Karl Ibsen would be preaching or praying on this day, no matter where he was, not matter what they did to him.

"And your father will be helping the sick," Lori said, turning to face Jacob with a tender look. She caught him off guard.

Jacob nodded. Frowning against the emotion, he stuck out his lower lip. "I hope . . . they are *together*," he managed to whisper. "We should pray for them, especially today, I think."

The congregation of four joined hands, and for a moment the empty pews of New Church seemed full again.

Snow fell throughout the day, covering all of Vienna with the illusion of peace.

The charred remains of synagogues and shops lay concealed beneath a cold, white shroud. Jagged heaps of dynamited walls took on soft, smooth contours, easing the memories and consciences of those who passed by. It seemed as though no great synagogues had ever stood in the city. After the fires of Kristal Nacht died away, nature completed the eradication begun by the Nazis. Already the Reich and the world beyond had begun to forget.

Only the trapped, the imprisoned, the hopeless seemed to remember clearly the terrible vision of what the future held for the Jews of Germany.

Peter pulled the collar of his coat close around his chin. The north wind spit freezing flakes against his cheeks and obscured the end of the street in a white, swirling veil. It seemed the safest time to check on their home.

He tucked his hands deep into his pockets as he trudged past the boarded-up shop of old Frau Singer. Other pedestrians darted into buildings for shelter. Automobiles pulled to the curbs, leaving the streets nearly empty except for an electric streetcar that rumbled by. The car was nearly full of bundled-up passengers, and another half-dozen people waited at the corner ahead of him. Stamping cold feet, they glared impatiently toward the approaching car. A placard above each door proclaimed clearly, *Juden Verboten!* Even if he had the fare, Peter could not ride it. He looked away as it stopped for passengers. Pretending not to notice or care, he hurried past, envying the closeness and warmth of the Aryans inside it.

He traced the steps he had taken to the Fishers' apartment during Kristal Nacht. Nearly every shopwindow on this street was boarded over. Heaps of rubble still blocked parts of the sidewalk.

Peter looked up to the window from which the old man and his wife had been thrown. He shuddered, more from the memory than from the bitter cold. Then, with that image fresh in his mind, he hesitated at the corner, afraid of what he would find on the street where he had grown up.

Where once organ grinders, peddlers, and beggars had strolled beneath the facades of the stores and houses and long blocks of flats, there were only silence, emptiness. He shook his head, reprimanding himself for expecting to see friends and neighbors instead of planks and cardboard nailed across shop fronts. He told himself that no sensible person would be out on a day like this, that people still lived behind the boards that shut out the light from their homes and businesses. And yet the old neighborhood, once so alive in the shadow of the Turnergasse Synagogue, seemed haunted and strangely eerie.

He could not make out his own apartment building through the billows of snow. He hoped the windows of their apartment had been boarded over. He wondered about his collection of books. Boxes of novels and volumes of history had been donated to him by fleeing friends. Had they survived intact? He longed for a good book. The world could fall apart, and Peter would not notice as long as he had his books to read.

Quickening his pace, he strained to see. Thoughts of his little library drove away fear. Suddenly nothing seemed as important as knowing the fate of those books. For half a block he did not think about the friends he had watched being herded onto the Gestapo prisoner lorries. For two hundred paces he was warmed by the memory of summer evenings with a novel open on his lap as he had glimpsed this teeming street from the window of his bedroom. *Children playing, women gossiping below as they leaned on their brooms.* . . . Life had gone on even after the Nazis had come. But now . . .

Automatically he looked up at the telephone wire where the ragged tail of Marlene's kite still dangled. He had laughed at her when the warm winds had stolen the kite from her. She had stood in the street and wailed as Herr Temko rushed from his confectionery shop to console her with a piece of hard candy. Had that been only six months ago?

The remains of the kite flapped, tangled up on the wire, smashed and broken and torn to pieces—a grim reflection of the broken lives below.

Peter stopped midstride and gasped as his own building came into view. Only two charred walls remained of what had been a three-story apartment building. The window that had been his room gaped open with the harsh white sky behind it.

There was nothing to go home to. Almost the entire block was destroyed. Perhaps no one was left alive behind the boarded windows, after all. Perhaps those who had not fled or been captured were now ashes, like the books. Peter shook his head. *Ashes!*

Why had he not filled his pockets with the books, saved something at least? But he had not known, had not believed that it could come to this. No one was left from Turnergasse. Maybe no Jews were left at all in Vienna.

☙

Shivering in the cold, Lucy walked slowly past the Hofgarten green-houses near the Imperial Palace. She dug her hands deep into her pockets and tucked her chin down inside the collar of her coat.

Through the glass she could see the gardeners busy at work on plants that would be placed in flower gardens throughout the city. Sometime in March, the people of Vienna would go to bed on a winter's night and wake up to an instant spring. The world would bloom without anyone being aware of how it happened. Lucy had watched them planting the bulbs in the Rathaus Park—red tulip bulbs, a bent little man had explained to her. When they bloomed they would match the flags of the Reich. Hitler himself had imagined it and had given the command for a million bulbs to be brought in from Holland. It was likely to be a very pretty sight indeed, Lucy thought, and one she hoped to miss. By then, she would be somewhere else—far away from the gardens of the imperial city. Soon afterward, she would have a baby to hold in her arms.

It all seemed like a distant dream, and yet, as she touched her stomach through her coat, it seemed frighteningly real as well. A little someone to feed and clothe and care for. Lucy shuddered with cold and fear. She needed money. She needed a miracle.

It was a short walk from her office in the Rathaus to the six-story baroque building at Number 17 Dorotheergasse. Taking up an entire city block, the structure housed one of the world's largest last-resort banks for the financially desperate of Austria. First established by a Hapsburg emperor to benefit impoverished subjects, the place had stood since 1707 as the only government pawnbroker and auction house in Europe. Clients could present almost anything as collateral for a loan and walk out with at least enough cash to purchase bread for a day. Hitler, rumor said, might have starved to death without this service. Mozart had been a frequent visitor between symphonies.

The name clearly set in stone above the broad double doors read *Dorotheum*. The Viennese called the place *"Tante Dorothee"*—Aunt Dorothy—as if it were a benevolent relative they could occasionally tap for financial assistance. This sense of kindness and familiarity had been driven from the place, however, by the new Nazi overseers.

Desperate Jews arrived at the door with the wealth of their worldly goods. They left with only a small fraction of the actual worth. Diamonds, furs, precious paintings, and antique furniture all disappeared, swallowed down the maw of the Reich's financial need.

In her handbag Lucy carried her grandmother's silver crucifix, the only thing she owned of any real value. It seemed a small matter to part with it when she considered the value of what she carried within her.

Lucy looked to her right and saw a beautiful grand piano, upended and wheeled through a freight door. How many times had she heard Wolf speak of the bargains he had bought here at the auctions? Everything had been shipped back to his home in Prussia, she assumed, just as he would try to ship her baby back to Prussia. Precious things vanished easily in the Reich nowadays.

She squared her shoulders and walked in, careful not to look anyone straight in the eye. Austrian police stood guard in the foyer, their uniforms unchanged from the pre-Hitler days—with the exception of a swastika armband that branded them as loyal servants of the Führer. To her right, a guard sat at a large desk munching a bratwurst sandwich. *Information* read the placard beside his thermos bottle.

She felt suddenly nervous as she approached him. Fingering her handbag, she did not speak until he swallowed a big mouthful and looked up at her. His expression communicated impatience for her to get on with it so he could finish his lunch.

"*Bitte?*" she asked hesitantly as she gestured toward the long corridor with dozens of doors on each side. "I have something . . . to sell." She fingered her handbag and smiled nervously.

"Everyone who comes here has something to sell, Fräulein." He wiped his mouth on a clean linen napkin. "And everyone has something to buy, we say here. So. Where may I direct you? You have a piano in your handbag? Or maybe a radio?"

"No. A . . . this . . ." She pulled out the velvet-wrapped crucifix and showed him one end of the gleaming silver.

He seemed unimpressed. "I don't know. Fine arts, maybe. Or religious artifacts?" He shrugged. "Up the stairs to the appraisers. They will know best. Two flights up." He returned to his sandwich.

Lucy climbed the marble stairs. The office of the appraiser of religious artifacts was the first door to the left of the stairs. Lucy entered, surprised that no one was there except the appraiser himself, who busily scrutinized the gold work on an eight-branched menorah. Behind him on a desk lay dozens of such items—Jewish treasures, Lucy assumed. Were they sold for their weight in gold and silver? she wondered. If so, her crucifix seemed small in comparison.

She bit her lip and closed her eyes, asking forgiveness for what she was about to do. There was no other way. To sell the watch Wolf had given her would invite his wrath.

Lucy held the handbag against her heart and waited for the little man to finish his investigation. He glanced up at her, startled to see that someone had come into the room.

"*Bitte.*" He laid down his magnifying glass and smiled, revealing a row of gold-capped teeth that would no doubt be worth a fortune at the Dorotheum. "I did not know anyone had joined me." He cleared his throat. "Lovely, is it not?" There was, Lucy thought, a hint of sadness in his voice as he gestured toward the menorah. "From a fine Austrian family." He shrugged, as if to dare her to disagree. "The authorities wanted to melt it down. But it is worth much more than the metal." Rubbing a hand over his bald head, he shrugged again. "I have been here a long time. So? How can I help you, Fräulein?"

Lucy stared hard at the candelabra and the rows of tagged artifacts behind the appraiser. "I want . . . to sell . . ." She faltered. She did not want to sell the crucifix. "I *must* sell . . ." She started to open the handbag, then stopped and pulled up the sleeve of her sweater to reveal the Swiss watch. A few seconds ticked off. "This watch. Where do I find the appraiser for watches, please?"

The old man looked relieved. Certainly he had the saddest of all appraisal positions in the Dorotheum these days.

"Ah. Good. You have walked up one flight of stairs too many, I'm afraid. Next floor down. End of the corridor."

Lucy did not need to lie to the watch appraiser, but she lied anyway. "Money to send home to my parents in Bavaria."

It made no difference to him why she needed money. He simply considered the collateral and determined how much it might bring at auction. "Three hundred marks is the retail value," he informed her. "A very fine timepiece, but we have many fine watches coming in every day." He himself was from Bavaria, his accent like that of everyone Lucy knew from Munich. She commented on the fine clocks made there, and he smiled appreciatively. "For a citizen of the Reich, I am authorized to lend one-third of the value."

Lucy frowned and sat back in real disappointment. Was it worth facing Wolf for a mere twenty-five dollars? "That is not very good." She looked searchingly into his eyes. "My parents . . . you see . . . they are in desperate need of funds."

"Well then, if you sell it, I can offer you two-thirds of the price. If it brings more than that at auction, we deduct our fees and you get the rest."

"Yes," she agreed instantly. "Two hundred marks is good." It was not as good as Lucy had hoped, but she placed the sum in her handbag with the crucifix and hurried happily back to work. It was a start, anyway. And if the situation became truly desperate, she still had the cross that she could take back to the sad-eyed man at the Dorotheum.

In the meantime, however, she would have to think of a way to explain the missing watch to Wolf.

21

One Righteous Man

The envelope arrived through the mail slot of Red Lion House right along with the regular mail. From the outside it seemed harmless. Elisa, Charles, and Louis paid no attention to the large brown envelope sandwiched in with two letters from Leah Feldstein in Jerusalem. Nothing seemed quite as important as Leah's letters that arrived on the regular mail ships from Palestine twice a week.

Elisa opened them right away and read out loud. She skipped over some parts, but shared the most exciting stories with Charles and Louis.

> *"It is not as bad in Jerusalem as you might be hearing. Be sure to take the news about Muslim riots with a grain of salt, because living with a newspaperman you should know how things are exaggerated to sell papers!"*

This kind of jibe, directed at Murphy, made Elisa laugh. Things really were bad in Palestine, but at least Leah could still joke about it. Letters from Leah were the best part of the week.

> *"God never promised us that life would be without difficulties, but He did promise that we will overcome them as He has."*

Such words of encouragement like these made all of them nod and say again that no matter what happened, the best news yet was that they would all be in heaven together for sure!

Such words made Charles think about Mother and Father. It made him wish he could hurry and be with them, too. Sometimes he felt as if he were trying to straddle a creek—one foot in heaven and the other foot here with all the new people he loved. He missed Leah very much and thought of her in the Promised Land the way he thought of Mama and Father in heaven—except that Leah was able to write letters from Jerusalem. He wished his parents could also write letters from heaven. He asked Jesus to give them little messages since there was no post office in heaven.

When Elisa finished, Charles and Louis asked her to read the part again about Shimon cracking walnuts in Tipat Chalev with his plaster cast. They liked hearing about the way Jewish boys could go to their own schools and there were no Nazis to beat them up or make them get out. It was good to know that the same English uniforms Charles and Louis saw on the soldiers around London were also right in Jerusalem, protecting boys and girls from the Arabs who liked Hitler.

Leah added:

> *"Better than that, we are all part of God's kingdom. One family. One nation in His eyes. The people who want to destroy the world for their own reasons will find in the end that Darkness must always fall back in retreat when there is Light—even the Light of one tiny candle! Each of us must fight the Darkness in our own way. Some are soldiers who struggle against force. Some are preachers who raise their voices. Some pray. Some play music of praise. Shimon and I fight by simply remaining here in Jerusalem. God promised that we Jews would return to the land. Our battle is to believe His words and stay put, even though the Arabs would like to drive us back to the sea . . . ."*

Louis asked Elisa to read all of Leah's words. But Charles did not need to know everything. He clung tightly to the words of hope she sent to them in London:

> *"We will win! We will make it! Don't worry or be afraid!"*

All of this seemed to be written just for Charles, because sometimes he wondered if they would win. And he *was* afraid!

He drew pictures of the house on Red Lion Square and put his smiling face beside that of Louis in the crooked crayon windows. Leah would be able to tell which face was Charles and which was Louis because there was still a line marking the scar on Charles' mouth. That scar left from his surgery on his cleft palate worried him lately; his imperfection frightened him. After all, that scar made him different and hated in Germany.

Because of his mouth, his father and mother had died. He thought about that a lot, and only Leah's letters made him feel better. Somehow he, too, wanted to fight the Darkness, but the Darkness felt too strong for him. He did not talk about these things, but they rose up in him every day as he struggled to learn to speak. The fears were with him when he smiled and someone's eyes flitted down to the pink scar and then back to his eyes.

Elisa gave each of the boys one of Leah's letters to hold. They studied the stamp from this faraway part of the United Kingdom. Part of the same empire as London, but so very far away!

And then, just as she had done every day, Elisa divided up the remaining mail between the boys and they helped her open it.

Charles slit the big brown envelope, and the Darkness came into the room. It flooded over him, driving away the good words of Leah, making him remember in one glance the things they had run from. Color drained from his cheeks. His eyes were riveted to the picture that was only half out of the envelope. It was a black-and-white image of a man nailed to planks.

"Charles?" Elisa took the envelope from his limp hands. She gasped, and pain filled her expression. "Dear God," she said, tossing the envelope across the table and gathering Charles in her arms. "Oh, Charles! Charles! Who would send us such a thing?" She began to cry. She buried her face against Charles' shoulder and repeated his name again and again.

Louis had not seen the picture, and yet his face, too, reflected fear and grief. Elisa did not stop crying. Charles stared out the window. It was very bad, this picture, whatever it was.

Louis ran to the telephone and rang up Murphy at the office.

The SS commandant called Karl out from the long line of prisoners. "You have a visitor," he announced loudly.

A ripple passed through the ranks of men. No one had visitors. Such things were not permitted, unless . . .

"They will work on him," said the atheist. "He will go over to them. You will see."

He muttered the words at great risk. Others also whispered among themselves. The guards must have heard, yet they did not beat the convicts for resenting Karl Ibsen.

Karl marched off, surrounded by the four guards, to the office of the commandant. Richard watched as the striped uniform entered the office. "He will be back. You will see. He is the only righteous man I know."

Even with his eyes closed, Karl would have recognized the Rev. Gustav Dorfman by the scent of his hair pomade. Today, in preparation for this visit, Dorfman had groomed himself a bit more heavily than usual.

The distinguished pastor of the First Lutheran Church in Berlin was handsome, in a posed sort of way. In his late forties, he was tall and thin, his suits always tailored to meticulous perfection. His wavy gray hair was always neatly trimmed, always in place. This afternoon was no different.

Dorfman was well-known within the church long before Hitler came to power. Widely recognized and respected as a man of God, his mellow, fluid, convincing voice packed the pews of Germany's largest Lutheran church every Sunday. Karl knew him on a handshake basis only. He had not been surprised when Dorfman had been among the first churchmen to join the Nazi movement as the wave of the future, declaring National Socialist doctrine as "the hand of God to punish evil."

Dorfman did not offer to shake Karl's grimy hand. It was just as well, Karl thought. Dorfman waved the guards from the room and indicated where Karl should sit. This man expected respect and received it in some measure from those who followed his teaching. Karl, beneath the filth and stench of his ordeal, viewed this shallow, empty man with pity rather than respect. Some of the men in the bunks of Barrack 7 grasped more knowledge of the Scriptures than this self-proclaimed spiritual leader. The young atheist who had wept at the thought of the Lord's tears had infinitely more spiritual depth.

However, Karl was glad for the chance to sit down in the warmth. No doubt the Nazi who respected Dorfman's authority and the size of his congregation also believed that Karl would respect a clergyman as prominent as this.

Dorfman took the chair farthest from Karl. He smiled. Perfect teeth gleamed. Manicured nails drummed the table. "Well, Pastor Ibsen. Karl?" The voice was smooth. "Tell me why you are here."

"I was ordered to report to the office," Karl replied. "I assume it is to speak with you."

The perfect smile twitched. Was Karl playing a game? "No, what I mean to ask is, why were you arrested? And why are you still here in prison?"

Karl cut to the heart of the matter. "I was arrested when I attempted to help my friends . . . my brothers."

"And who are these brothers? You can't mean the Jews?"

"There are others as well, also brothers. But, yes, I suppose I am arrested for standing for the rights of Jewish Germans."

The phrase *Jewish Germans* sparked resentment in Dorfman. Jews were Jews in his eyes, and Germans were Aryans. He had been asserting that since his seminary days. "Karl," he said in a patronizing voice, "aside from the fact that the Jews have been scientifically proven to be subhuman, was it not the Jews who killed Christ?"

It was a trivial, ridiculous argument, laughable in its ignorance if it were not so dangerous and deadly. The reply came not from Karl, but from the Scripture verses he had memorized on his sixteenth birthday: *"Then the governor's soldiers took Jesus into the Praetorium and gathered the whole company of soldiers around Him. They stripped Him and put a scarlet robe on Him, and then twisted together a crown of thorns and set it on His head. They put a staff in His right hand and knelt in front of Him and mocked Him. 'Hail, king of the Jews, they said.'"*

Karl paused to respond to the astonished look on Dorfman's face. "These were Roman soldiers. You may check if you doubt me. Matthew, chapter 27: *'They spit on Him, and took the staff and struck Him on the head again and again. After they had mocked Him, they took off the robe and put His own clothes on Him. Then they led Him away to crucify Him.'"*

Karl managed a slight smile. "Sound familiar? Easter service. Seems to me that the death of the Lord was the reason He came to this earth. I know you discount the Old Testament Scriptures, but Isaiah 53 speaks of the Messiah being offered for the sins of all mankind. Not just Jews— even pure Aryans like you may be saved, a free gift from the greatest Jew who ever lived."

Dorfman's face clouded with resentment. How dare this filthy criminal quote Scripture to him, a leader in the State Church! So this was the result when renegade Protestants strayed from church doctrine. He pulled up his seminary teaching to counter this heresy. "The church leaders believed the Jews should be slaves to Christians. Martin Luther himself—"

"Is a sad example of the reality of human fallibility. Speak to me through the Scripture and we will have a match, Reverend Dorfman, but please do not quote Martin Luther to me. Or Saint Augustine. Or any of the rest. By now those men know how badly they erred. When the Day of the Lord comes, I do not want to be found quoting them."

The Rev. Gustav Dorfman called in the guards to return Karl to his rightful place among the sinners and tax gatherers of the Reich. Perhaps he would come again one day, but he had not been prepared to meet such a skillful adversary.

"You are still with us, preacher," called up the young atheist from below Karl's bunk. "What did you meet in there today?"

Karl sighed. "I met a man who was wearing the robes of a great religious leader when Jesus came to Jerusalem. He saw the Lord and hated Him because Jesus was truly righteous."

The young man called up to Richard. "What is he saying?"

Richard did not reply. He rolled over and fixed his dark eyes on Karl. "Tell him what you mean, Pastor Karl."

"I mean that the religious leaders who crucify the Lord exist in every generation. They have been present in every age. I met a man today I can only pity. In the end his suffering will be much deeper than ours."

The atheist's mocking tone was tempered by the edge of sadness in Karl's voice. "And yet you tell us that God loves even a man like that. Even the Nazis He loves, you say."

Karl considered the challenge. It was a real question, worthy of reply. Could a just God care even for evil men? "God sees them as they will be if they don't repent, Johann. He pities them. Remember your verse, *'Jesus wept.'*"

Winston Churchill looked more like a bulldog than ever. His lower lip protruded angrily as he scowled down at the photograph on the coffee table in front of him. He picked it up by the corner and then let it fall back again.

"It is good to see the sort of men we are dealing with," he growled under his breath to Murphy. "I shall take this image with me into battle at the House of Commons."

Murphy passed him a long list containing the names of prominent men and women arrested in Germany on the night of November 9. Included on that list was the name of Anna's sister and members of the Ibsen family. The list had been enclosed with the photograph of Thomas von Kleistmann. The implication was clear: The same sort of horrible death awaited those people who opposed Hitler unless they could be ransomed and released. Some names were already crossed off, killed by the Gestapo or yielded to Nazi pressure. Others were checked with a note that read:

> *Familes of these prisoners are also missing. Spouses and children are held responsible for the crimes of relatives and subject to the same punishment as the "guilty."*

This long list, obviously taken directly from secret Gestapo files, had been sent to John Murphy at great risk to whoever had sent it. The photograph had not been intended to harm Elisa or the children but to warn Murphy. The envelope was addressed to Murphy. It was not meant to be seen by anyone but him and those he trusted.

Churchill sighed and shook his head. Such a sight made even the Old Lion speechless. "Is the little boy all right?" He imagined the terror of a six-year-old in seeing such a thing.

"Charles has seen too much already." Murphy spread his hands in a gesture of helplessness. "There are a million Jewish and Christian Charleses living through this kind of thing, Winston—the children of men who are willing to die for the right even though nobody on this side of the line seems to care." He stared at the image of Thomas and suddenly felt sorry that they had never met. "They must have someplace to go. *Now*. No more talk. It is too late for talking." He slammed his fist down on the list. "Here is the picture of reality. This is the evil England is making peace with!"

Winston Churchill's eyes brimmed with emotion and resolve. "Bring Charles to the debate in Commons. For the sake of the ones he left behind, he must hear the final debate on the refugee question in Palestine. Even if we do not win, Murphy, one child must be a witness to his generation that we did battle against this blinding darkness."

This time Wolf was not late to Café Sacher. Lucy kept him waiting—not too long, only five minutes; but she made certain that her entrance was noticed. She did not look toward their corner table as she swept into the room. She played to the eyes of other men, certain that Wolf would notice their interest as well.

He stood and pulled out her chair. His face displayed his jealousy as he resumed his place and finished off the wine in his glass.

"You are late!" he snapped.

She displayed her empty wrist. "The catch on my watch broke. I lost it today somewhere on the Ringstrasse."

"Lost it!" He leaned forward. "That was a very good watch! Expensive."

"Not good enough, or it would not have broken."

"You will not get another one."

"Then I will be late, won't I, Wolf?" She could see that she was having an effect on him. His tanned complexion reddened with anger toward her. She knew she must be very careful in her game. "I thought of you . . . of who I belong to . . . and when I looked at my wrist, the watch was simply gone." She shrugged. "I was disappointed, of course. But, you see, I think of you even without it, Wolf."

At this, he softened a bit. The hard line of his mouth curved up at the corner as he pondered her compliment. "Then you do not need another one."

"I need nothing at all to remind me." Her voice was soft as she leaned in toward him and touched the back of his hand. "After all, I carry a little Wolf inside me."

At this, his indignation vanished entirely. She had played her cards well, and he rewarded her with his approval. "In that case, maybe you should have a new watch so you will never again keep *this* Wolf waiting, *ja*? I got the other from an old Jew on Franz Josef's Kai. He was selling out. Said it was the finest. He was lying, no doubt, and I would have him arrested—"

"Will you?" She tried not to let her concern show as he directed his anger to the old Jew who sold him the watch. Would her lie cause the arrest of an innocent man?

"The fellow is already arrested. Rotting away somewhere."

"Because of me?" She was horrified.

He laughed. "Such concern, Lucy! No. The fellow was accused of trying to smuggle diamonds, I think. Something like that. A fabricated charge, but reason enough for his entire stock to be Aryanized. I could have gotten your watch for nothing had I seen it coming." He poured himself more wine. "That will teach me to trust a Jew."

Lucy's conscience was relieved. She had not been the cause of an old man's arrest. Of course, the old fellow was in prison anyway, no matter what the reason. Still, Lucy decided she would be more careful about her lies to Wolf. She sat silently, feigning interest as he continued his monologue of hatred against the Jews of Vienna.

"They are worse here than in Germany, as a rule. At least at home they acted the part of German citizens. I had not thought much about them at home. But here in Vienna! It is no wonder the Führer hates them so. They laughed at him when he was a hungry student in this place, and now he is laughing at them."

The waiter placed onion soup before them. He inhaled the aroma and then cautiously took a spoonful. He might as well have been talking to himself, but Lucy continued to hold him with her gaze, to nod and smile at all the right pauses. She had learned to be the perfect audience.

"Some fellow in the Gestapo is tipping them off, we think. We come to the door of a prominent Jew and find that he has slipped out the back the night before. Several rich ones have gotten away. Who knows what they have smuggled out with them? Himmler has taken the case away from the Gestapo and put it into my hands. I will find him, whoever he is."

"Well then, you will gain another rank before the baby is born," she said brightly, flattering his dreams of glory.

"Yes. Yes. That is true." He sipped another spoonful of soup. "I have narrowed the field down to half a dozen." His eyes narrowed as he pictured the suspects and savored the flavor of an arrest. "Himmler says that ruthlessness is a quality to be admired when duty calls for it. And so I will cultivate that. Himmler will notice such a thing. Not even friendship matters compared to the good of the Reich." He directed his preoccupied gaze to Lucy as if he had just noticed her presence across from him. "You see how important this is to me." The eyes hardened. "You would not ever betray me, lie to me. Would you, little fox?"

She managed an indignant laugh. They had discussed this before. Wolf was not speaking of political betrayal or loyalty to the Nazi cause. "No man could come close to you," she replied coyly. "Here, I promote you! You do not need to arrest any traitors to please me. I promote you to general of my bed. No, field marshal! Or, more true, you are my Führer, the leader of my country, Wolf."

He relaxed a bit, sitting back and swirling the deep red wine in his glass. "I did not like the way men looked at you when you came in."

"I cannot help how they look."

"Or the way you looked at them."

She shrugged. "Soon enough men will look at me and say, there goes another mother for the Reich!" She patted her stomach. "They can look all they like, and I will still be pregnant with your child."

"When you begin to show, then you go to the Lebensborn," he announced sternly, though seemingly satisfied with her reply. She had managed to fend off the attack once again.

Lucy considered the warning and the growing life within her that would soon enough lead her to her own imprisonment at Lebensborn. The thought of gaining weight made her cautious about eating. She only nibbled at the vegetables and did not eat the roast at all. And tonight, for the first time ever, she refused even a taste of Sachertorte.

Homemade British leaflets in support of the immigration of child refugees dominated the conversation over dinner at the Führer's table. BBC broadcast appeals to the British people had brought minimal public response, and the Führer was convinced that the hypocrisy of the English leaders ran in the grain of the common people. No one wanted a homeless, filthy tribe of paupers invading their cities and homes. This effort, he insisted pleasantly, would fail like all the others.

"The voice of dissent is always stronger than the voice of weak Christian charity. And this is what makes our race strong. We are the only people on earth who are not swayed by the weakness of this false mercy. Let the English talk and weep and plead! Those idiots! What is the difference?"

Himmler picked at his vegetables and remarked, "It is a pity we have emptied out the insane asylums, yes? We might have sent them ten thousand imbeciles in answer to their leaflets!"

The guests laughed at the idea. "Let the English hypocrites see how far their mercy extends when it comes to drooling idiots, eh, Himmler?"

It was too late to speculate on such a marvelous practical joke. The do-gooders did not seem to have room for healthy children, let alone inferior ones. The German institutions had been cleaned out, but it would have been a great joke to send over a batch of imbeciles and cripples to these whining English nannies.

There was, of course, a slim possibility that some British aid might be extended to refugee children. If that was the case, Himmler said sternly, steep fines would be levied on the parents of such children and they would leave the Reich without so much as one mark tucked into their shoes!

This information would no doubt slow the beating hearts of compassion and silence the criticism. Mercy would put on a more practical face and show up this sentimental nonsense for what it was.

The Führer based his actions on the basic premise that all men were equally motivated by greed and selfishness. This time would be no different.

Joseph, cat of many colors, was sick. He did not eat his sardine. He lay curled on his blanket in the corner and watched Alfie, who watched him back unhappily. Joseph panted when he breathed and made his mouth into silent meows of pain.

Alfie was afraid. He hugged his knees and studied Joseph in the candlelight. It looked as if the lid was closing on his furry friend. The long soft tail flicked nervously. Joseph did not move his tail like that unless he was unhappy. Things were very bad tonight.

Twice more Alfie laid the sardine beside Joseph, but the cat looked away. It was no use dragging the ruby necklace across the floor. Joseph did not want to play. He would not pounce on it or smile his cat smile at Alfie.

"Don't die," Alfie moaned. "Please, Joseph. Everyone here is dead but you and me. Please get well, Joseph." Then he reached his hand out to pet Joseph, but the cat growled at him and showed his teeth. He did not want to be touched. He only wanted to lie there and hurt while Alfie watched him sadly.

22

Life amid the Gravestones

From the bell tower of New Church, Mark and Jamie could clearly see the brown-clad workmen as they drove the posts into the soil of the flower bed outside the iron gate.

"What does it say?" Jamie squinted and tried to make out the lettering of the sign.

"It is the same as the one in front of the synagogue, I think," said Mark. "So now we know why they wanted to close your father's church."

"But Papa told them he liked New Church where it was." Jamie remembered the day his father had been approached by the government officials with an offer to relocate New Church and build a new building. "Papa told them that New Church was not so big and maybe not new anymore, but that it had stood through two hundred years of storms, and he would not move." Jamie frowned. "They did not like it."

"So they got it anyway." Mark read the sign.

ACHTUNG! ATTENTION! A GLORIOUS NEW CENTER
OF GERMAN CULTURE WILL BE CONSTRUCTED ON THIS
SITE, BY ORDER OF THE MINISTER OF THE INTERIOR.
TRESPASSING FORBIDDEN. HEIL HITLER!

"You suppose that is why they arrested Papa?" Jamie wondered aloud. "And why they burned the synagogue, too?"

"Your papa was arrested because of us," Mark replied impatiently. "Because we're Jews. And the Nazis burned the temple for the same reason. If they want a house or a church or a store or a whole city, they don't ask anybody. They just take it. That is what my father said the day they arrested him. They wanted our fathers because they are friends. The church doesn't have anything to do with it."

When the public-works truck drove off, the boys clambered down the spiral steps, relieved that they could report no one left within earshot. But Lori and Jacob were already arguing in the basement over what was left of their food supplies.

Jacob tossed a can of tinned beef down with a clatter. "Once I even thought I liked you. Now I see you are the most stubborn girl who ever lived."

"And you are nothing but a bully! It is no wonder you got into a fight every time you walked into the street! You can't even get along with—"

"With *you*? Ha! *Impossible!* I wish I had taken Mark and run the opposite direction!"

Mark and Jamie exchanged looks of disgust. This sort of discussion had become a daily occurrence—whispered anger followed by steely silence between Lori and Jacob. Jacob thought he should be the boss. Lori argued with him about everything from sleeping arrangements to how much each person should eat each day in order to preserve their food supply. After all, she reasoned, she had been the one to discover the case of meat tins.

"We cannot go on forever." Jacob sat down hard on an empty wooden crate. "You think that night watchman isn't going to come inside some night and catch us by surprise?"

"Not with all your drilling!" Lori exclaimed.

"You want to stay here for the rest of our lives?" Jacob grabbed Mark by the sleeve of his sweater and pulled him close, as if choosing sides for a battle.

"And if we leave, where will we go?" Lori demanded.

"Prague, where your father said we should go all along! There are people there. That pastor he knows. I say we get out of the church!" Jacob was adamant.

Lori gestured at the tin of beef and the boxes of Communion wafers. "But we can make it last another month if we're careful."

Jamie looked at the boxes of flavorless wafers and grimaced. "Breakfast, lunch, and dinner," he said mournfully. "And besides, we can't—"

Lori interrupted him. "My mother and father will certainly be released by then. How would they know where to find us?"

"We can sneak out the basement window," Jamie interjected.

"Brilliant." Lori silenced him with a dark look. "Doors and windows chained and padlocked. The Nazi seal across every door. Sneak out the window and go where?"

"Prague, I'm telling you!" Jacob shouted, arguing over the heads of Mark and Jamie.

"We are safer here!" Lori insisted.

"No . . . ," Mark began, trying to tell Jacob and Lori.

She would not let him speak. "With those signs no one will come snooping. We can wait it out. Even if it takes longer than a month, we can wait! We have water. Coffee and tea in the kitchen. If the Gestapo comes again we will hear them rattle the chains and have time to hide." Her voice was so full of pathetic hope that Mark and Jamie exchanged looks. *Wait until she hears . . .*

"Besides," she continued, "they would take one look at us and arrest us on the spot. We look like we have been mining coal. Or rolling down a mountain. You think we would not be noticed dressed like this?"

This much of her reasoning was accurate. She was the only one among them who looked halfway clean. She even washed her hair in the dark bathroom once a week.

Mark caught their reflection in the glass of a cupboard. They looked terrible, smelled worse. Their clothes clung to them. Their hair was combed, but badly in need of a trim. They looked precisely like boys who had been hiding out for nearly a month.

Mark eyed Jacob, hoping for help to silence Lori. "They are going to tear down the church," Mark blurted out.

"That's right!" Jamie added. "We saw a new sign. They are going to build a cultural center. Over the synagogue, too."

Disbelieving their grim report, Lori simply glared at them and shook her head.

"We aren't making it up," Mark protested. "We saw the sign."

Jacob cuffed his brother angrily. "You were in the bell tower again!"

"But, Jacob!" Jamie backed up as Lori and Jacob suddenly became allies against the two younger boys.

Lori grabbed Jamie by the shirt and yanked him to her.

"You were in the bell tower?" she echoed. "They could have seen you!"

"They're going to tear down the church!" Mark cried as Jacob shook him again.

Finally Jacob and Lori heard it. "Tear down—" Lori's anger and disbelief turned to concern. She raised her head as if to listen for the sound of a wrecking ball against the silent stone walls of the little church.

"What did you see?" Jacob demanded.

They told him once again, repeating the words of the sign.

Lori finally spoke over their heads to Jacob. They were almost friends again. "They warned my father that New Church would not stand in the way of the master architect's plan." A smile of bitter amusement came to her lips. "I guess you were right, Jacob. We have to leave."

"Yes." Jacob's voice held no pleasure. "I . . . I'm sorry. About this. About your father's church."

She chose to ignore his sympathy. She decided yesterday that she loathed Jacob Kalner. She did not know what she had ever seen in him in the first place. She did not want him feeling sorry for her now. Her cool reserve surfaced again. "We will have to wash our clothes and underwear."

Jacob grasped his trousers at the waist as if to keep her from taking them. The arguing began again. "Nobody is getting my trousers off me," he scowled. "I saw the SS herding those poor schmucks around the streets in their nightshirts. Not me. If they get me, it will be with my pants on."

"Go ahead and stink then, Jacob Kalner!" Lori argued. "But stay away from the rest of us! The Gestapo will smell you from Albrechtstrasse and say. '*Himmel!* Somebody must have died in New Church! Better go have a look!'" She lifted her nose haughtily and stepped back a few paces to make her point. "But the three of us will be clean, at least. They will not track us by our scent when we leave! We will be washed!" She wrapped an arm protectively around Jamie, who looked back at her suspiciously. "Won't we, Jamie?"

"Well," Mark replied, out of reach of Jacob's long arm, "at least we won't stink like Max!"

At that, Jacob's eyes narrowed in anger and he shook a meaty fist at his brother, who dodged him and joined Lori's camp.

"We will sleep in the choir robes tonight. And we will be clean enough to walk out of here and go to a movie," Lori finished triumphantly.

At this, Jacob's eyebrows went up and he smiled slightly. He would try a different tactic with Lori. If she insisted that they all be clean, there was another way to do it. "Or we can burn these clothes," Jacob said. He appraised Jamie, who squirmed uncomfortably beneath Lori's hand. "We will send Jamie back to your house. He can break in and get us whatever we need. I can wear your father's clothes—"

"No!" Lori said. "I *forbid* it! Jamie is not going out until—"

"I have some money hidden." Jamie darted back to Jacob's side. "I was saving it for Christmas. I can get that and clothes and—" His face flushed with the thought of such an adventure. "And the extra set of keys for Papa's auto!"

"He will be caught!" Lori wailed. "I am the oldest! I will not allow it!"

Jacob looked at her stonily. "And if he is caught? What then? They will take him back to the Hitler Youth School. And he will be fed and have a place to sleep. But if any of the rest of us are arrested, what then? I am sent to Dachau. You, you pretty little Aryan, will be sent to an SS breeding farm and produce little blond babies for the Fatherland and the Führer."

Jacob's last statement was too much for Lori. She burst into tears and ran sobbing up the basement steps. *Let them do what they want!* She was tired of fighting, tired of making decisions for these hateful, terrible boys!

Even the boarded glass of the windows rattled when she slammed the door. Slamming doors was forbidden by Jacob. Lori had the last word, after all.

Once she was gone they made plans without her. At least, Jacob made the plans and the little boys agreed to them.

Jamie would sneak out of the church and raid the parsonage four nights from now when the moon was dark. He would bring back clothes, money, jewelry, and the spare keys to Pastor Ibsen's automobile.

During a Nazi Party rally in Berlin, the foursome would make their break. It would be a simple matter, Jacob explained to his compliant comrades, as long as nobody made any mistakes.

The prisoners of Nameless camp recognized the black, mud-splattered Mercedes of Rev. Gustav Dorfman as it passed the main gate. No one was surprised when special roll call was ordered before evening meal.

Caps off, the men were forced to stand in the cold drizzle as Karl Ibsen was once again called out from the ranks.

"You must be an important fellow, Prisoner Ibsen, to have such a visitor."

By now the other prisoners did not blame Pastor Ibsen for this obvious attempt to drive in the wedge between him and them. They did not blame him that there would be no shelter or soup for all the camp until battle was done between Ibsen and Dorfman.

Karl left them, confident that they would pray for him, hopeful that he would not be kept away long. They were his brothers. Together they huddled on a precipice of survival. They were learning that great battles were won when their prayers silently went up for one another. Although the guards led only Karl into the office of the commandant, several hundred hearts went with him.

Gustav Dorfman came prepared. Dorfman had excelled in theological debate in his seminary days. He had learned early that winning an argument often hinged on simply putting the right emphasis on the correct syllable. From the pulpit, his melodious voice resounding from the rafters, the emphasis he put on certain words and verses had led a congregation and then an entire church into error.

In the days following Dorfman and Karl's first conversation, the men in the barracks had questioned Karl:

"Can this man Dorfman really believe what he preaches, or does he say it just to keep the people in line with the government?"

Karl had thought about that question deeply before he attempted to answer. In the mud and suffering of Nameless camp he had looked at the prisoner uniforms: striped like prison bars, all the same. *Then God said, "Let us make man in our image."*

So this was the image men like Dorfman saw of the Creator. They made the image a slave to their own ideas—identical, faceless, without color. Dorfman's god served the masters of the Reich. The basest clay had set out to change the image of the Potter.

"Dorfman's heart and mind were convinced of his own righteousness before he ever read one word from the Scriptures," Karl had answered. "He has seen what he wants to see in God's Word. He believes what makes him feel best about himself."

"But how can he not see the truth?" asked Johann, who had found truth in the tears of Jesus only a few nights before.

"He is like a color-blind man gazing at the shining lights and colors of a prism. His view of God is gray. There is no love or brightness or beauty there, only gray. He has clothed God in a drab gray uniform. He has dressed the heart of the German people in that same uniform and ordered that they march in step. Look at their belt buckles, Johann. *Gott mit uns*—God with us! Pity them. They have never seen the glory of a rainbow reflected in one teardrop of the Lord! But you have seen it, Johann. So have I. Never mind that they try and make all men look alike and talk alike and think alike and march in step. They have failed before they began, because we are all splashed with the colors of God's great love for us. Let your heart run and skip with the joy of it, Johann! God sees the colors of your soul, even in this place. From the least among us, He counts us beautiful, made in His image."

This truth caused Karl to grieve for the grayness of Gustav Dorfman's soul as the man flipped open his Bible and smugly began his debate in support of conformity to the government policies he proclaimed in his church.

"So, you want God's word on the subject? Let us begin. Romans, chapter 13, is one that every Christian must heed. A command." He began to read aloud the words that Karl knew by heart. "*Everyone must sub-*

mit himself to the governing authorities, for there is no authority except that which God has established." He followed the words with his finger. *"Consequently, he who rebels against authority is rebelling against what God has instituted, and those who do so will bring judgment on themselves."* He paused and gestured toward the window where the guard towers were clearly in view. *"Rulers hold no terror for those who do right. . . . For he is God's servant to do you good. But if you do wrong, be afraid, for he does not bear the sword for nothing. He is God's servant, an agent of wrath to bring punishment on the wrongdoer."*

Karl closed his eyes for a moment, then looked again at the bristling guard towers. He could clearly see the outline of the gray soldier and his machine gun trained on the backs of the men waiting in the field.

"A suitable passage for der Führer to seize upon. This has often been used as a club with which the ignorant have been beaten into submission to evil."

"The reason you are here is that you have disobeyed the God-given authority of the land. That authority is the Führer."

"The reason I am here is because I have obeyed the law of God that is written in that same chapter in Romans. *'Love your neighbor as yourself. Love does no harm to its neighbor. Therefore love is the fulfillment of the law.'"* He paused. There was enough within those verses for several weeks of sermons, but his friends were standing in the rain, after all. "I saw firsthand the Nazi government's treatment of neighbors on Kristal Nacht."

"You call these Jews your neighbors?" He flipped to another passage. "The Lord Himself has said to the Jews in Matthew 21, verse 43: *'Therefore I tell you that the kingdom of God will be taken away from you and given to a people who will produce its fruit!'"* Triumphant, Dorfman laid the book open on the table.

Karl simply quoted the rest of the passage. "Verses 45 and 46: *'When the chief priests and the Pharisees heard Jesus' parables, they knew He was talking about them. They looked for a way to arrest Him, but they were afraid of the crowd because the people held that He was a prophet."* Karl inclined his head slightly, as if amused. "Chief priests and religious leaders throughout the generations have often sought ways to silence the true Jesus. They have arrested or condemned those who preach His word. And then they are afraid that the simple people in the crowds who hear and believe will turn against their authority. The first day they accused Jesus, the simple people in the crowds were Jews." Karl shook his head slowly at the expression of anger on Dorfman's face. "He was speaking to men like you, Gustav Dorfman, in Matthew 23: *'Everything they do is done for men to see. . . . They love the place of honor at banquets and the most important seats in the synagogues; they love to be greeted in the marketplace and to have* men call them Rabbi. . . . Woe to you, teachers of the law and Pharisees, you hypocrites! You shut the kingdom of heaven in men's faces. You yourselves do not enter, nor will you let those enter who are trying to!'"

Dorfman jumped to his feet in outrage. Like the Pharisees, he was indignant that Karl Ibsen was talking about him. "You! How dare you!"

"Not me! Hear the words of our only teacher . . . a rabbi! A Jew! The Messiah! Hear His words to you, Gustav, and tremble: 'Woe to you, teachers of the law and Pharisees, you hypocrites! You travel over land and sea to win a single convert, and when he becomes one, you make him twice as much a son of hell as you are.' Listen to the voice of the Lord, Gustav! 'One of them, an expert in the law, tested Him with a question—'"

"That is enough."

"'Teacher, which is the greatest commandment in the law?' Jesus replied, 'Love the Lord your God with all your heart and with all your soul and with all your mind . . . first and greatest. . . . And the second is like it: Love your neighbor as yourself. All the Law and the Prophets hang on these two commandments.'"

"You are insane," Dorfman said in a low, menacing voice. "Insane to talk to me like this! Do you know the power I have here? They will do what I tell them. If I say you are a hopeless case, then—"

"It is you who have lost your hope, Gustav. And you, and men of the church like you, have hidden the true Messiah from the People of the Covenant. From the Jewish people. You think God is not watching? Jesus is still there, still true and loving beneath all the molten gold you dip Him in! Hang Him in the churches, persecute the race from which He came, claim that you are the new Israel! But I tell you, He is not in your church, Gustav. No, He is here in this camp. He walks—alive— among the suffering! He has not forsaken His Covenant or His people Israel! I heard His voice, and it calls me to obey Him . . . not you! Not your dark and twisted Führer!"

Karl stood to face Dorfman. Filthy and stinking in his uniform, his eyes revealed more life than those of this withered man inside his perfectly tailored suit.

Dorfman tried to speak. He looked at the Bible fearfully. Had he ever heard the warning of judgment before now?

Karl spoke. "Jesus wept because of men like you. He also died for all of us, Jew and Gentile alike. But I pity you more than most men, Gustav, because you have poked your bony finger in the eye of God, when you should have stopped to touch His hem and mingle your tears with His."

"Are you finished?" Dorfman backed up a step, regaining some of his aloofness. "No. I do not need to *ask* you if you are finished. I *tell* you.

This is the last . . . last chance. I am ordered to say . . . if you repent your stubbornness . . ."

Karl smiled sadly. Dorfman still saw gray.

"You will not convert me to your cause," Karl said. "I will pray for you, however. You are in deep water. I would not trade places with you for all the riches of the Reich."

"No!" Alfie cried, his eyes growing wide with terror. Something very bad was happening to Joseph. The soft white belly of the cat tightened, and he growled miserably. And then Joseph jerked his head around to his tail and made a moaning sound.

"Joseph!" Alfie called the name of his friend. Tears splashed on the stone floor beside the untouched sardines. "Don't leave me alone, Joseph," he begged.

Again the cat moaned and his stomach tightened, and it seemed as if Joseph's insides were coming out. Alfie shrank back in the corner and watched what must surely be the last breath of his little friend. He sobbed and called for Mama and then for Werner. He wished he had not run away from the hospital; it might have been better to go with Werner than to be so sad and alone!

Then something amazing happened to Joseph. He licked and licked at the little something that had come from inside him. He did not seem to hurt anymore for a while. And that little something between Joseph's paws suddenly moved and made a tiny squeak and said *meow*!

This terrible thing was not so terrible. It was a kitten! It was wet and skinny and very unhappy looking, but it was alive. Joseph cleaned the little yellow thing and then looked proudly at Alfie. *What did you think?*

Alfie wiped away his tears and dropped down on all fours to look closely at the kitten. Joseph let him look, but growled when Alfie tried to poke it with his finger.

"Joseph," Alfie said happily, "you are a mother!"

The yellow kitten nuzzled close to Joseph and, finding a faucet in the soft fur, began to nurse. Alfie had seen this before with his dog. He had seen puppies eat supper this way, so he was not surprised. He had not touched the puppies, either. Mama had not let him watch them be born, and he had always supposed that his dog had burped them up. This was something new. Alfie did not go to sleep all night as Joseph had four more kittens. A fat gray one, a little tiger-striped one, and one just the same colors as Joseph. The last one, black with white paws, did not move when Joseph cleaned him. He just lay there between Joseph's paws, very still and small. Joseph nudged the kitten away and turned his attention to the other ones who squirmed and squeaked and wiggled against Joseph's belly.

Alfie looked at the black-and-white kitten. It was no bigger than Alfie's finger. He asked Joseph's permission to pick it up, since Joseph did not seem to want it.

He placed it in his hand and sat back against the wall. It was wet and cool against his skin. Its little mouth opened in a gasp for breath—still living, but not for long. This kitten reminded Alfie of the boys in the ward of the hospital. Weak and thin, it could not compete with the row of strong and healthy kittens squirming against Joseph's belly.

"Ah, little cat." Alfie held it up to the warmth of his breath. "I would call you Werner if you would live."

The tiny body twitched, and Alfie ran his finger gently over the paper-thin ribs. Back and forth he stroked the kitten. He held it close to him and spoke gently to it while his finger licked it in place of Joseph's tongue.

"Live, little Werner," Alfie whispered over and over throughout the long night.

The ribs rose and fell as the kitten lived on by the will of Alfie. Its damp fur dried into a fragment of fluff. The pink nose twitched, and the white paws began to stir weakly.

Alfie put the tip of his little finger into the mouth of Werner. The snap of suction rewarded him. Only then did he lower the kitten for Joseph to see again. The mother cat purred her gratitude and nuzzled the kitten. Joseph even allowed Alfie to find Werner a good faucet and plug him in for his first warm meal.

Peter had not left Herr Ruger's apartment since he discovered their home was destroyed. Nor had he allowed his mother to go out. Marlene, who had left her dolls at home, complained incessantly about the fact that she could not so much as look out at the snow, let alone go play in it. Self-centered Marlene had turned ten while they stayed at Herr Ruger's, but still could not believe that anything had happened out there since she had not been affected by it. No one had hurt her, and so, no one could have been hurt. This punishment of remaining in Herr Ruger's apartment was the only unhappiness she could perceive. Her whining left Peter on the verge of throwing her out the window.

Baby Willie was Peter's only salvation. A constant source of entertainment, the seven-month-old babbled and cooed and crawled and drooled in happy laughter when Peter held him high over his head or played peekaboo or crawled after him in a game of infant tag.

Thankfully, Peter's mother had brought an entire basket of diapers along. Laundry lines crisscrossed the front room of Herr Ruger's elegant apartment. Clean diapers were placed on the radiators to dry. Socks and underwear draped on a line running from the dining room to the Queen Anne armoire like pennants on a ship.

Herr Ruger's flat had become a kind of ark for the little family. Kitchen cupboards were well stocked. Warmth hissed and rattled through the steam radiators. No one had knocked on the door or telephoned. News blared over the radio with typical Nazi Party fanfare. Herr Ruger had not returned to claim his home from the little band of fugitives, and so they stayed on, eating the food cautiously, warming their hands gratefully, sleeping soundly in beds that were not their own.

Marlene, oblivious to all danger, finally shattered the tranquility of their imprisonment.

Her serious dark eyes locked on a piece of paper, she emerged from Herr Ruger's bedroom. "Mother, I have written a poem about the snow. It is very good, I think. And I have decided that I will be a poet. I will write a verse every day until next year, and then I will have an entire book." She handed the paper to her mother with a flourish.

"Well, read it to me," Karin Wallich said, handing the paper back to Marlene.

Marlene shot a sullen look at Peter, who was prepared for the worst. "No," Marlene declared. "Peter will laugh at me." She reverently placed the paper back in her mother's hands.

Karin smiled benignly with the kind of patient look that mothers have when they must interpret a child's genius out of chicken scratchings. Her lips moved as she read silently. "Why, Marlene, this is really—" Then Karin Wallich's smile faded. The praise died on her lips. Color drained from her cheeks at what she held in her hand. She managed a whisper. "Marlene, where . . . where did you . . . get this stationery?"

"From Herr Ruger's desk drawer," the child declared blithely. "But do you really like my poem?"

"Show me!" Karin was on her feet now.

Peter stood in automatic response to the alarm in his mother's voice. "What is it?" He took the paper from her hand.

His eyes focused past the scrawled letters and ink blotches to the embossed letterhead of the sheet. The eagle of the Reich clutched a broken cross in its talons. Beneath that was the insignia of the Gestapo, the Vienna address of Gestapo headquarters!

Peter roughly grabbed his sister's arm. "Where did this come from?" he demanded, giving her a shake.

She began to cry. "It was in the desk. All I wanted was some paper. There was lots of it. Lots and lots. He would not mind a few pieces of blank paper. He would not even miss them."

"Show me where you found it!" He propelled her into the gloomy bedroom. A large credenza with a fold-out writing desk stood open. A stack of clean white letterhead stationery lay in an open drawer. Peter and Karin hovered over it, staring at the ominous emblem in disbelief. Neither of them dared to touch the paper, as though the insignia itself might harm them. Marlene whimpered her innocence in the background. They seemed not to hear her.

"Gestapo," Peter whispered.

"Where could he have come by it?" Karin could hardly speak.

"Stolen? Perhaps he has stolen it."

"If the apartment is ever searched . . . if he has stolen Gestapo letterhead stationery! Why . . . they will *arrest* him! They will execute him!"

"But why would he have it?"

"They will say he is a forger."

"Maybe he is." Peter frowned. He pulled open another drawer. The credenza had not been opened before. They had left the tiny drawers and compartments alone, just like the chest of drawers. Personal things, the belongings of Otto Ruger, had not been looked at. Herr Ruger's privacy had been respected . . . until now.

Inside the second drawer lay a framed photograph of Otto Ruger. The image made Peter gasp and blink with horror. Otto Ruger in a Nazi uniform. Smiling beside Gestapo Chief Heinrich Himmler, who was speaking to Adolf Hitler on the steps of the Vienna town hall.

Karin slowly picked up the photograph and held it for a moment, then tossed it back into the drawer as though it had burned her hand. "*Mein Gott!* Herr Ruger . . . he is . . . *one of them*!"

A chill filled Peter, the same terrible fear he had felt during his walk through Vienna on Kristal Nacht. Suddenly the apartment felt heavy and dark around him, as though the walls had ears and eyes. *Like creatures on exhibit in the zoo,* he thought.

"We must not stay here," Peter said firmly, taking the photo from the drawer and looking closely at Herr Ruger as if to be certain that there was not some sort of mistake. *No. No mistake!*

"I always thought he knew too much. A strange character, our Herr Ruger. Showing up with news of your father after the arrest. He has planned this. He has lured us here. Probably there are listening devices to hear us talk, about your father and—" She lowered her voice and looked wildly around at the walls. "What shall we do, Peter?"

He put a finger to his lips, feeling the same paranoia. He pulled his mother into the bathroom and turned on the water to cover their conversation.

"We cannot stay here. You are right. This is some sort of trap. Not just for us, but for Father." Peter was convinced of it. "It is only a matter of time before they come for us here." He slammed his fist against the sink. "We have been idiots! We *trusted* him!"

Karin looked at her image in the mirror. She appeared years older than she had two months ago. Older than even a week before. She felt as if someone else was living through this nightmare. "Hurry, then," she said wearily. "I will pack our things. Clean up. We can be ready in half an hour. But where will we go?"

Half an hour later, the face of Peter's mother was still pale and drawn, a colorless contrast to her red hair. Then Peter caught a glimpse of his own reflection in the bedroom mirror. His skin was as pale as hers. His red hair stuck up. He, too, looked frightened.

Karin closed the door so that Marlene could not hear.

"What are we to do now?" she asked hoarsely.

"The entire neighborhood has been cleared," Peter said again as if to convince himself of the truth.

"I do not know what prison your father is in, where they have taken him. If anything happens, how will we know? And if he writes us, how will we get his letters?" Tears brimmed in her eyes. She seemed not to be thinking about Herr Ruger anymore or the possibility of listening devices planted in the walls. Peter hoped she would not cry.

She looked at their luggage, remembering again why their clothing was packed. But they had no home to return to; the old neighborhood was dead, stamped out in one night.

"The Nazis could not have arrested everyone. There must be others like us. If we could find them, get away from here before Herr Ruger returns . . ." She wrung her hands and paced back and forth in the bedroom as Peter sat silent and thoughtful in the overstuffed chair beside the window.

He lifted the edge of the shade and peered out toward Frau Singer's shop. They had not seen any sign of the old woman. What had become of her?

Peter closed his eyes and tried to think what his father might have done. No answer came to him. He drew his breath slowly and gazed out over the snow-dusted skyline of Vienna. In spite of the cold, two birds perched on the telephone wire just outside. Peter traced that wire to another and another. Telephone wires and electrical wires intact throughout the city. With a half smile he turned and looked first at the telephone and then at his mother.

"Well, why don't we just ring someone up?"

She looked at him as if he had gone mad. They had not even dared to lift the receiver, for fear the lines might somehow be connected to some unknown Nazi at the telephone exchange. Once, when Willie had pulled the telephone off the table, they had both rushed to pick it up, and had stared silently at the thing as if a Gestapo officer might crawl out of it.

"Ring someone up?" Karin frowned at Peter. "You mean just like that? Telephone someone?"

"If the lines are still working—and I can't see why they wouldn't be. The Storm Troopers broke windows and furniture, but they did not pull down the telephone lines."

She opened her mouth to protest, but closed it again and sidled up to the phone. Her fingers rested on it, questioning the wisdom of such a brash move. After all, if the walls were bugged, certainly the telephone would be as well. "Maybe it doesn't matter," she said, finally picking up the receiver. "Who? Who should we call?"

"Frau Singer." Peter looked out the window again as he mentioned the name of the old corset maker.

"But her shop is closed."

"Everyone's shop is closed. That doesn't mean she won't answer the telephone if it rings."

"But is she there?"

"Call her and see." Peter continued smiling down on the little corset shop as his mother dialed. He could hear the ring of Frau Singer's phone. Once. Twice. And then . . ."

"*Guten Abend.* Singer's corsets and—"

Karin Wallich cried out in astonishment. Could it be that easy? "Frau Singer! It is you!"

"And who else should it be? But who is—?"

"Karin Wallich. Oh, Frau Singer!"

"*Mein Gott! Himmel! Mein Gott!* We thought you were gone forever! Some said you slipped over the border into what is left of Czechoslovakia! Karin Wallich! But where are you, my dear? You are not calling from Prague?"

Peter put a finger to his lips, warning his mother not to mention that they had been in the apartment of a Gentile just across the street. Such juicy news would no doubt make the rounds and somehow end up in the ears of a party official.

"I am in Vienna," Karin answered with relief.

"With the children, my dear?"

"Yes. With Peter and Marlene and little Willie."

"Are you well?"

"Much better now. We thought the wind had blown everyone away."

The old woman's laugh crackled over the line. "A strong wind blows from these Storm Troopers, but even the Nazi wives need corsets! They have broken my shopwindow, but as long as I have my two hands I can make what they need."

The color returned to Karin's face. She smiled easily at the old woman's resilience, and the smile melted years from her face. Peter laughed to see it and slapped his thigh in delight. *All this time . . .*

"It is so good to hear your voice, Frau Singer." Karin winked at Peter. "We thought we were the only ones left."

"They arrested nearly all the men between sixteen and sixty. I was certain Peter would be taken as well. They destroyed the soup kitchens and left the women to clean up. There has been little to eat this past week, but today the first funds came from the Refugee Children's Committee in London. There will be food again tomorrow."

Karin covered the mouthpiece and whispered happily to Peter, "The soup kitchen will be open tomorrow! Imagine!"

There was much news to catch up on, but the telephone was not the way to do it. The thought came to Peter and his mother at the same moment, and their smiles faded as quickly as they had come.

"Yes, well, I really must not keep you any longer, Frau Singer," Karin said abruptly. "Perhaps we will see you soon."

As the old woman stammered her farewell on the other end of the line, Karin replaced the receiver. Enthusiasm was tempered by caution once again. Should they go to Frau Singer's apartment and ask for shelter? The place was only across the street from Herr Ruger's window. Perhaps they would put the old woman in danger by going there.

Wolf was proud of the thick Persian rugs he had acquired for the apartment. He had sent a number of similar purchases home to East Prussia, but these two he kept out purposely.

The designs were of rare intricacy. There was a special name for each design. Lucy could not remember exactly what Wolf had told her about them except that they were exceptional and valuable. He had picked up the whole lot from a confiscated Jewish house not far from here.

On the cream-colored border of one of the carpets were four reddish brown spots. They matched the color of the woven wool background, but the spots were some sort of stain.

"Blood," Lucy said firmly.

"Chocolate," Wolf said, unconcerned.

"It looks like blood to me," Lucy insisted. "And I will not walk on blood."

"Jewish blood."

"I . . . I don't care whose blood it is! I cannot bear to have it in the apartment, Wolf! How can I sleep with a stranger's blood in the house?"

"You are squeamish for the daughter of a farmer. Didn't you ever see the slaughter of a hog? Not much different than the slaughter of a Jew!" He laughed as she clutched her stomach and turned away.

"Stop it! I will not have even one drop in my house! Can you be so thoughtless?" She pretended to be near to tears. "I am expecting a baby! Can you be so heartless as to play such a cruel game with me? Such matters affect the unborn, you know."

Wolf's mocking smile vanished. He looked at her apologetically and shook his head. "I was only joking. Just teasing you! I am sure it is chocolate." He laughed nervously.

She shook her head defiantly and sank down onto the couch. "I don't believe you! And what if it is? I will look at the spots and imagine—" She gestured toward the second rug, which was smaller but just as beautifully patterned. "And how can I know they are not both stained with someone's blood? Look at the color!"

Wolf considered the rich deep red of his treasures and regretted that he had pushed the issue so far. "So, have them cleaned." He shrugged, then frowned. "But carefully. There are ways, you know. They must not ruin the color." At that, he put his arms around her and pulled her close to him. He expected a reward for agreeing with her about cleaning the Persian rugs. Normally he did not give in to such frivolity.

Lucy remained stiff and unresponsive to his touch. He kissed her, but she did not soften, as if the horror of the rugs had made her into a statue.

"What is it?" he asked.

"Roll them up," she commanded. "I cannot . . . not when those things are open like that. Roll them up so I will not have to look at them."

Wolf nodded impatiently and acquiesced to her desire, certain that when he yielded, she would yield to him.

⌐⊘

Frau Singer's shop was only across the street, but it might as well have been on the opposite bank of a raging river. Once again Peter looked out past the edge of the shade and then back to the luggage by the door.

Only two scuffed tan leather suitcases and a box of diapers remained of their possessions.

Baby Willie sat on top of the diaper box and drooled as he chewed intensely on a rubber duck. He was the only member of the family who was not waiting nervously for the sun to slip away so they could escape Herr Ruger's apartment.

Mozart, Herr Ruger's cat, eyed the baby coolly from a window ledge. *The cats will be glad to see us go,* Peter thought. *Then they will no longer have to dart past this tail-grabbing human kitten who seems to have invaded every corner of their house.* Peter had already decided to let the cats out when they left the apartment. It would not do to have Herr Ruger return home to starved pets and a stinking apartment. Perhaps the cats would hide out in the alley and come home when they saw their owner in the window.

"Another half hour, Mother," Peter said. They had a plan of escape. Down the back stairs, out the rear door, and then once around the block before they returned to Frau Singer's place.

"I should have asked her first," Karin fretted.

"It is better this way," Peter replied as he eyed the wall clock next to the photograph of Hitler. "She will not turn us away."

"I will be glad to go." Marlene pulled up her socks and sat primly on the edge of the sofa as if waiting for a train. "There is nothing to do here."

Peter was about to reply that he was certain Marlene would be unhappy no matter where they were, but the sound of footsteps made him forget it. There was no time to move, no time to speak. A key scratched in the door lock and then, as the cats leaped from their perches and ambled toward the door expectantly, Herr Ruger entered.

He looked up briefly, accepting the fact that there were people in his apartment. Then, stamping snow from his boots, he doffed his Russian beaver hat and entered.

"Peter!" He seemed genuinely relieved as he stooped to scratch beneath Mozart's chin. "And Frau Wallich! Are you coming or going?"

Karin Wallich was on her feet in an instant. "We were just leaving." she said through a cracking voice. "Only stopped by to—" She gestured at the cat.

"No, no!" Herr Ruger glanced at the luggage, then at Willie on the box of diapers. "Have you been here a while? I was hoping to find you."

Peter moved toward the suitcases. "We are on our way to a friend's house." He placed the apartment key beside the telephone. "And so—"

Herr Ruger straightened slowly, his fair skin flushed pink from the cold. Golden red hair fell over his forehead much like the dark hair of Hitler in the picture. He smiled at Marlene as though he was puzzled by this strange welcome and the haste of Peter and Karin Wallich to leave. "You do not want to go so soon, do you, Marlene?" he asked. "I have just arrived home. I would like a cup of tea. Do you know where the tea is, Marlene?"

"Oh yes," Marlene blurted out, basking in the attention.

"Then perhaps you would fix me a cup of tea before you leave."

Karin's shoulders sagged as Marlene hurried to comply. It had been simple for Herr Ruger to discover that they had been in his apartment long enough for Marlene to know where the tea was kept.

He picked Willie up and held him on a thick, muscular arm. "Have you found your way around all right, Willie? You do not seem to be in such a hurry to go."

The baby smiled and batted him on the chin. Herr Ruger grinned. He eyed Karin. "Children are seldom frightened unless they are given a reason." He paused, gestured for her to sit, and then pulled up a rocking chair and continued to hold Willie. "So, I can see clearly that you are not like Willie. You are afraid of me." He cleared his throat. "I am blunt. Straight to it." He directed his gaze to Peter, who sat rigid and silent on the sofa. "You did well, Peter. You were invited to come here. Have you been comfortable?"

Peter looked hard at him, remembering the picture of Herr Ruger standing beside Himmler and Hitler. He tried to pretend he had not seen it. "We . . . that is . . . I remembered you said we should come if—"

Karin interrupted, "And so the night of the riots . . . our own apartment building was burned to the ground."

Herr Ruger nodded. "Yes. I saw it. So, you have been staying here. Why are you leaving?" he pressed on.

"We have other friends . . ." Peter shrugged, carefully avoiding looking into Herr Ruger's searching eyes. Such eyes seemed to know everything.

"Then who will watch my cats?" Ruger smiled. He stood and placed Willie into the arms of Karin; then he raised a finger, instructing them to remain where they were. With that, he disappeared into the bedroom and re-emerged holding the photograph they had discovered. Hanging it on an empty nail beside the clock and photo of Hitler, he turned to face his guests. "My pride and joy, that photo," he said. "You see how close I am to the Führer. How trusted I am."

Karin trembled. Peter did not look at the terrible picture. He stared at his hands, picked nervously at his nails. "You are wise to be frightened by me," Ruger finished ominously.

"What . . . do you want with us?" Karin breathed.

He answered with a question. "Have you told anyone you were here, Frau Wallich?"

A look passed between her and Peter. They had not even told Frau Singer. "No one."

"Good." Herr Ruger smiled. "So, Karin, you look enough like me to be my sister, wouldn't you say? And Peter might be my nephew. It is the hair, you see. The red hair. I spotted it in the file photos."

"Gestapo," Karin whispered, searching his face. "You are *one of them.* Why are you . . . why have you done this? Why? You know what we are. Surely you know what has happened to my husband."

Herr Ruger's face hardened. A strange half smile played on his lips. "Yes. I know what has become of Michael Wallich."

"What? *Where is he?*" Peter begged. "Where is my father?"

"He is dead, Peter." The smile remained. His eyes looked cold and unfeeling as he announced the news.

In the kitchen doorway, Marlene cried out and dropped the teacup onto the floor. "Mama!" she wailed. "Papa is dead!" She ran to her mother, who sat dry-eyed, unsurprised, as if she had known it all along.

"We wish to leave this place. Are we allowed to leave?" Karin's tone was emotionless.

"You mean leave this apartment? Or leave Vienna? Or Austria?" Ruger questioned, staring at the weeping little girl who clung to her mother.

Peter angrily jumped to his feet and shouted, "All of that! We want to get out! *Out of here!* Do you understand that?"

Herr Ruger put a finger to his lips, then gestured toward the ceiling. "The neighbors, Peter," he warned, still smiling. He sighed. "I am working on that. Getting you all out, I mean. There is a place I know in the Tyrol. Maybe there. But the snows have closed the passes already. You will have to stay here a while at least."

Silence filled the room for a few minutes, except for Marlene's sniffling. Karin stroked her hair. Baby Willie tangled his stubby fingers in her curls and pulled.

"Why are we here?" Peter asked wearily. "Why have you brought us here? Why help us if you are one of them?"

Herr Ruger shrugged. "It is not so simple as us and them, Peter." Now Ruger looked very sad. "You must call me Otto. Uncle Otto. Do you understand? I am your Uncle Otto Wattenbarger from the Tyrol. Do you hear me, Marlene?" He caught the eye of the little girl. His stern voice stopped her tears. "I am Uncle Otto. And you will say nothing more than that, even to your mother."

"We do not have the option to leave here, I take it?" Karin's tone now became hard and resentful.

"That's right. It's gone too far, Karin. Sister." He turned to Peter. "Have you ever been to a Catholic church, Peter?" he asked, as though it was the logical progression of their conversation.

"No. And I will not—"

"Will not?" Otto raised his chin in amusement at this defiance.

"You are in this as deeply as we are," Peter spat. "I supposed you are not in danger if we are caught?" This was an open threat.

"Do not be ungrateful, Peter" Otto replied, as though the words made him sad. "Or I will simply kill you myself and say you had it coming." He clapped his hands together. "Now. We must begin our catechism. You must learn to pray. Learn how to address a priest properly. And how to speak to the saints. All the saints." He seemed very pleased. "But first, Marlene, you must make me another cup of tea."

Nightmares came fresh and vivid every night now for Charles Kronenberger. It did not matter that Elisa and Murphy left the light on and spoke of only happy things to him and Louis. Charles was still afraid. Would the bad men who had followed them to Vienna and killed Father also come here to London? The Englishmen did not seem very angry about the things Hitler was doing. Maybe they would not stop him if he found out where Charles was and remembered that this was one little boy who had gotten away from him.

Such fears came to him against his will. In the quiet of his new home, he would remember the frightened voice of his mother as she begged the Gestapo not to hurt Father. He would see the fist rise and fall across her face as she fought to keep the doctor from taking Charles to the clinic. He would hear once again the clink of metal surgical instruments on the tray, and then he would awaken with a cry to find Elisa at his bedside.

Sometimes, when the grown-ups did not know he understood, he would listen to them talk in English about what had happened on that dark night in Germany. The names of his father's friends were among the many arrested. Pastor Karl Ibsen. Charles knew the name well. Pastor Ibsen had helped his father fight when the Nazis said only perfect people were welcome in the Reich. He had spoken up for other boys and girls like Charles. Somehow he had survived a long time. But now Pastor Ibsen, like everyone else who protested, was gone. Timmons had wired

Murphy from Berlin. Murphy had closed the door and told Elisa and Theo and Anna. But Charles listened at the keyhole and heard what the grown-ups said. That night the dreams were worse than ever, and Charles thought that God had sent the dreams to punish him because he had been bad and listened.

Eyes looked worried even when faces smiled at Charles and Louis. Louis could speak more clearly than Charles, and so he asked the questions out loud. But Charles had just as many questions as Louis did. *What happened to the other children like me who are still in Germany? Will they get to come to England, too? Who is left to speak for them since Pastor Ibsen has disappeared? Will the Nazis come to London? Will they kill me while I sleep? Will they hurt Elisa if her baby is not perfect?*

Last night, as Charles lay in bed with his eyes closed, bits of Murphy's voice had drifted up to him.

"Not only is Ibsen missing . . . closed the church . . . your Aunt Helen and the children vanished. . . . Timmons is looking into it, but . . . hopeless. Dangerous situation . . . euthanasia . . . one hospital emptied overnight . . ."

Charles fell asleep after hours of staring at the closet door and wondering if Nazis were in there waiting to empty out his bed forever, too.

The next morning Murphy promised it would be a special day for Charles and Louis. Mr. Churchill had gotten Elisa, Louis, and Charles permission to sit with Murphy in the press gallery of the House of Commons. Despite the lack of visible response to all appeals, the English government might find some way to help the refugees, Murphy said, and it would be a good thing for Charles to see how they would do it.

Charles put on his best brown tweed jacket and knickers. He combed his hair carefully and examined the pink scar where his mouth had been broken. His lower lip still stuck out a bit farther than his upper lip, but the doctor said they could fix everything until no one would notice. Even so, Charles thought that someone might see where his mouth had been imperfect. Charles knew what sorts of things happened to imperfect children, and it frightened him. For the first time since his trip to New York, he wrapped a scarf around his neck and carefully pulled it up to conceal his mouth. Until that pink scar healed, he decided, he would hide it from the Nazis. He would hide it also from the Englishmen who liked the Nazis. Otherwise, maybe he would just vanish, too, and someone whole would get the new bed and toys he'd gotten from Mr. Trump.

His serious blue eyes looked back from the mirror. In his mind, Charles warned himself, *Do not get too happy, Charles. You were happy with Father in Vienna; then the Nazis came. Everything could go away and then you would feel worse.* He would not tell Elisa anymore that he was scared, because that made her worry. But he would be careful all the same. It did not pay to feel too happy.

"*Guten Tag*, Pastor Ibsen," the camp commandant said pleasantly, as if greeting him at the door after Sunday service. "Did you hear us singing hymns in chapel this morning?"

Pastor Karl stared straight ahead at the wall map of Poland. He had heard the singing, yes, and the sound of such music coming from the mouths of men like this had sickened him. He did not reply.

"We sing quite well, I think." The commandant tapped a cigarette on his desk and then held the open case toward Karl if he would care to smoke. Cigarettes were highly prized by prisoners. The commandant was hoping to thaw the ice of this stubborn, iron-jawed churchman. "You do not smoke?"

Karl stared over the officer's head toward the blue sky shining through the window behind him.

The commandant lit his cigarette and rocked back in his squeaking desk chair. "There has been a change in policy," he continued in his too-pleasant voice. "You are to be relieved of your work among the other prisoners."

A pause. Karl let his eyes flit down to skim the pockmarked face of the officer. "I told you. I will not sign your paper."

The commandant laughed. "Such strength of character we consider admirable. Of great benefit to the German people, if it is channeled properly."

"You will not cut a new path for this stream," Karl said softly.

"A man of conviction. A true German. A son whom the Fatherland does not wish to lose." He waved his hand in the direction of Hitler's glaring portrait. "Clemency has been offered. You are a Christian. A man of God. You should have a time of rest. A time to think and read and bathe."

At the mention of a bath, Karl's eyes flickered with an instant of longing. In a split second he mastered that basic desire for cleanliness and masked his face with resolve again.

But the commandant had seen that desire. It made him cheerful. "I see you approve."

"I prefer to remain with the others," Karl said, regretting having shown even that brief weakness.

"We would not think of it. The Führer has given the order personally that you are to be treated well. You are a man of God, after all."

"I am a Jew," Karl said, as though declaring his nationality. "Let me go back."

The cheek of the commandant twitched in a flash of impatience. But he also mastered his emotion quickly. He shrugged. "You are as Aryan as Adolf Hitler. We know this. That is why we are patient. You have been among the Jews too long. It is natural that you—"

"I am a Jew," Karl said again, firmly.

The commandant was determined not to lose before he had really even begun the process of winning back Pastor Ibsen to the German fold. He spoke to him as though speaking to a child. "Your race entitles you to a gift from the German people whom you have served as pastor. A little time out of the cold. It is cold." He tapped the ashes of his cigarette. "You still have friends in high places in Berlin, you see. People who wish to see you back home where you belong, preaching as you did before." It was a lie, meant to personalize the offer of warmth and a bath and a day of rest.

Karl saw through the lie. "I have only one friend in high places, and He is not of this world."

The commandant mashed out his cigarette and smiled less easily at this reply. "You are not above the law or the commands of the Führer. He is the highest authority in the land, and so we shall both comply with his offer of clemency." He pushed a button on his intercom, and two armed guards immediately appeared to escort Karl from the office, across a snow-dusted gravel courtyard to the empty shower room used by Nazi soldiers and officers.

Karl hesitated a moment at the step and looked up to see five hundred of his fellow prisoners, row on row, beyond the wire fence. They were turned so they might clearly witness the mud-coated pastor enter the building and emerge thirty minutes later as clean as any free man in Berlin.

24

Never Give In to Fear

Rain crackled down on ten thousand black London umbrellas. The broad picture-postcard view of Parliament and the river Thames was obscured from Charles as he clung to Elisa's hand and dashed up stone steps and into echoing corridors filled with people. His child's view was not of majestic stone arches and polished floors, but of a forest of pinstriped pants and ladies' coats and dripping galoshes in the cloak room. This place where Murphy said the English ran their empire was very confusing.

Charles was afraid of being lost. Such a crowd and such noise reminded him of Vienna in the open square before he had lost Father forever. The big people did not see that he and Louis were down below and in danger of being stepped on. The endless babble of their voices was unintelligible. Charles tried to hear only Elisa's words.

"Up those stairs to the gallery? Mother and Papa came early . . . they'll be sitting with Dr. Weizmann, not in the press gallery."

He held desperately to her hand as she inched her way through the mob. Keeping his eyes on her face, he could see that she was attempting to smile pleasantly, although her eyes seemed worried. Murphy had said he would meet them here. But how would Murphy find them in such a busy place? The current of the crowd moved forward toward the steps.

"Hold the banister." Elisa looked down at Charles. Her blue eyes matched her hat and dress, light and pretty like sunlight beaming down through a dark wood. Charles smiled back from beneath his scarf.

Then behind them a voice harumphed and called out, "Mrs. Murphy! Elisa!"

Charles knew the voice. It was Winston Churchill. Elisa stopped on the bottom step and turned. She raised her hand to wave, and Charles grasped the fabric of her dress. He did not take his eyes from her face as she looked toward the voice.

"Did you bring the little men?" Churchill asked. He could not see them either, so Charles raised his hand to mark his place on the lower step. People pushed impatiently past them, but they did not yield.

"Good morning . . . a day of hope for us all," Elisa called.

Charles heard no hope in her voice. Still, his stomach churned with excitement. He did not think about the crush of trousers and shoes. There was something wonderful at the top of the stairs!

A big belly towered above him. The full-moon face of Winston Churchill beamed down. Watery blue eyes twinkled out from heavy lids, and the great man's lower lip jutted out in a crooked smile. Churchill bent at the waist and extended his hand first to Louis and then to Charles. "How do you do? Master Louis Kronenberger. Master Charles Kronenberger."

"How . . . how . . . do you . . ."

Churchill focused his attention on Charles. "I am pleased you could come, young man." The chin jutted out in thought as he laid a thick hand on Charles' head. The face moved closer until that was all Charles could see. Churchill pushed the scarf down, exposing Charles' mouth. "There. That's better."

Charles noticed that Churchill's lower lip also stuck out farther than his upper lip, and he smiled.

"A smile to give me strength," Churchill said. "You must remember, young man . . . *never* give in to fear. Never, never, never give in! I shall look for you in the gallery."

Another quick shake of the hand, and the big face was gone. Once again they turned their attention to the steep stairs. Charles did not think about putting the scarf back in place. He did not think about the pink scar on his lip. Something good was about to happen, and he let go of Elisa's hand and charged up the steps ahead of everyone.

An electric atmosphere permeated the hall of the House of Commons. Elisa could feel Murphy's tenseness as she took her place beside him in the press gallery. Several rows to her right, the faces of Anna and Theo reflected the same deep concern as the expression of the Zionist Chaim Weizmann beside them. Anna managed a smile and a small wave to the boys. Elisa wished they could have sat together; that she might have been able to hold her mother's hand the way Charles clung to her now. Elisa felt very young and small as she considered the importance of the

coming debate. Thousands of lives depended on the results. The riots in
Jerusalem Leah reported about in her letters seemed to put all hope in
jeopardy.

"Winston was looking for you," Murphy whispered.

"He found us." Elisa looked over the rail of the gallery as members of
Parliament took their places on the long benches. Prime Minister Chamberlain and his cabinet cronies sat facing Winston Churchill and the opposition party.

Charles leaned against the rail and waved shyly at Churchill, who
spotted him immediately and managed a lopsided smile of acknowledgment for his smallest fan. Charles nudged Elisa and pointed downward.
There was the fellow who would not give in. *Never give in!*

How grateful Elisa was that Winston had taken the time to seek out
Charles and whisper such brave words. If the Old Lion had clapped her
on the back and directed his comments to her alone, it would not have
meant half so much as his kindness to Charles. She noticed that the
child laid the scarf over the back of his chair as though he had brought it
along by mistake and should have left it in the cloak room.

Murphy also saw the discarded scarf and shared a sigh of relief with
Elisa. "So what did Winston say?" he asked, his eyes lingering on the
scarf.

"He said, 'Never give in to fear.'" Elisa repeated the words as if they
were a prayer for Charles and for everyone who was threatened now.
Such brave words made her think of Thomas and the photograph they
should never have seen. The sight had made her fear—for herself, for her
family, and for the many thousands who lived within the shadow of
such brutality. Yes, she was afraid, but she would not give in to it. There
was too much to do. They could not be paralyzed by threats.

The bulldog face of Churchill turned upward one more time to the
gallery. He winked and gave Charles the V-for-victory sign.

And then the battle began.

Elisa found herself more concerned with the reactions of the boys
than with the debate. Louis fell asleep in his chair after a restless hour.
But Charles sparked with interest, although he could not have understood most of what was being said. His eyes were intense. He stared hard
at Winston Churchill, frowning when the statesman frowned, nodding
when Churchill made a comment on the proceedings.

Elisa noted that Charles' lower lip jutted out in imitation of Churchill when Colonial Secretary Malcolm MacDonald took the podium.
When the same look of defiance as Churchill wore showed in the child's
eyes, Elisa knew that Charles had found his hero. A sense of gratitude
filled her eyes with tears.

MacDonald began to speak, and his words rang out the death knell for those trapped in Germany. But Elisa, like Charles, had heard a sermon on the steps of the Commons. A one-line lesson in courage had been etched on their hearts.

"The tragedy of people who have no country has never been so deep as it is this week," MacDonald began.

"Hear! Hear!" cried Churchill and a handful of others.

"But I must sound a word of warning . . ."

Murphy leaned close to Elisa. "Here comes the blow."

"When we promised to facilitate a national home for the Jews, we never anticipated this fierce opposition by the Arabs."

Charles sat forward on the edge of his seat. His small, pale hands were clenched in tight fists on his lap as he listened and tried to make sense of what was being said.

Yes, it was true that the Jews had made the desert bloom in the Mandate. Yes, it was also true that the Arabs poured across the border at a rate of thirty-five thousand a year to enjoy the benefits of that progress. But it was equally true that they had now begun to fear Jewish domination. The riots of the Mufti's men were purely a matter of protest against further immigration. England was being forced to pay attention. How could the persecuted souls of Germany settle in a place where they would surely be slaughtered?

The men on Chamberlain's side of the room cheered MacDonald as he finished. Such reasoning made sense. If the Jews went to Palestine and were slaughtered, then they were Britain's responsibility. If they remained in Germany, the blood was on the hands of Hitler. No one liked responsibility!

Churchill's turn came. Louis slept on, while Charles rested his chin on the rail to drink in every word and mannerism.

Churchill studied his notes in silence. Then his glasses came off again, and he shoved his notes back into his pocket. He would speak from the heart. In one final loving call to courage, he raised his eyes to Charles. The look was steady and unwavering, as though he were speaking to every child still suffering within the Reich. All of them watched him. Every mouth was marked with a thin pink scar, but every heart was guileless and innocent. A million young faces looked down through the eyes of Charles Kronenberger and asked for help.

Perhaps, Elisa thought as she observed the silent understanding that passed between the great man and that small boy, Churchill had invited Charles here as a witness to his own heart.

A minute later the voice resonated in the hall with measured cadence: "People . . . children . . . are dying, meeting grisly deaths from day to day.

Only two weeks have passed since the Night of Broken Glass devastated the persecuted of Germany, and we have already forgotten their misery! People are dying. While here—" he swept a hand toward Chamberlain— "all that is done is to have debates and pay compliments and above all run no risk of making any decision to help!"

The faces of the opposition stared back with open contempt as he spoke.

"Never give in," Elisa breathed. Her heart beat faster as she realized just how unpopular these words were. How much this man risked to speak out!

"In regard to our pledge for a Jewish homeland, it is obviously right for us to decide now that Jewish immigration into the Mandate should be equal to Arab immigration each year. My honorable friend has put the figure of Arabs crossing the Jordan at thirty-five thousand a year. Jewish immigration should be equal. It is just! If the Arab gangs refuse to accept this, then we should consider our obligation to them discharged!"

The outcry of the opposition drowned out the voice of Winston Churchill. Someone behind Chamberlain howled that the reason for the troubles in Palestine was the presence of the Zionists! "The Arabs could be managed if it were not for the Jews! After all, that is why the Arab gangs attacked—"

As the crowd shouted Churchill from the podium, Elisa regretted that Charles had come here after all. But then she looked at him. He brushed his blond hair back defiantly and raised his chin. His blue eyes blazed angrily and he stood up, holding his hand high in the air for Churchill to see. Little fingers were raised in an unmistakable V sign.

Churchill inclined his large head in thanks. *Never give in!*

It was truly the winter of Munich, the season of defeat and appeasement of evil, Elisa thought as she listened to the uproar of seared consciences. But here blazed the bright flame of one candle that had been passed on to another fragile wick. The battle must be won now, one life at a time.

The outcry of those opposed to the immigration of children to Palestine began to die away. But a louder, more insistent sound penetrated the high windows of the Commons above the gallery.

Horns and voices mingled. The faces of the MPs reflected confusion, then concern. The unmistakable outrage of a massive crowd could be heard.

"Send Parliament to Berlin!"

"No room in Commons!"

"Commons concentration camp!"

At a stern nod from Prime Minister Chamberlain, MacDonald

stepped to the podium. The roar of the crowd extended from the streets in an unending wave.

"There you have the voice of the people of Britain! Our honorable friends may see by their outrage that we must consider the needs of our homeland first! There is the British reply to those who would embroil us in a conflict that—" His words were almost drowned out by a fresh blast of horns from small boats and barges on the Thames.

Elisa lowered her head with a heartache at such a demonstration against a hand extended to help the innocent.

Charles sat up and smiled, not comprehending the meaning of it. The light from the windows reflected on his face.

Louis woke up and frowned at the din. "What is it?"

On the floor, MacDonald continued. "The people have spoken, and now it remains for us to respond to their wishes."

At that, a small elderly man in a dark suit hurried across the floor to whisper in the ear of Prime Minister Chamberlain. Chamberlain's face reflected concern, then astonishment. He gazed up at the vibrating windows as if trying to understand.

"They want the kids," Charles said, holding up his fingers to Churchill again.

"No, Charles—" Elisa started to explain.

Then the stirrings among the men on the floor stopped MacDonald midsentence.

More blaring horns. Voices shouted from bullhorns as the prime minster rose and MacDonald stepped down.

"It seems . . . ," Chamberlain said with a croaking voice, "we are asked not to venture out. There is a . . . demonstration, you see. People. Fifty thousand?" He looked over his shoulder at the messenger, who nodded. Yes. At least that many.

They packed Parliament Square and blocked the traffic of St. Margaret Street. Rushing through the gates of New Palace Yard, thousands had stormed the entrance of Westminster Hall, threatening to invade the House of Commons itself! A young clergyman had climbed the statue of Oliver Cromwell to lead the cheering crowd.

A chant began outside: "Let them come! Open the gates!"

Churchill raised his head. Had he heard right? A slow smile spread across his face. Fifty thousand British men and women had taken to the streets! And now their voices joined the few within the government who had cast a vote for mercy.

"LET THEM COME! OPEN THE GATES!"

A few men stood up and stared at the windows. They gaped at one another. Clearly they had misjudged. Could it be?

Murphy patted Elisa's hand and hurried down the stairs and out into the lobby. The crowd had pushed its way in. Their shouts resounded from the high vaults of the ceiling. Over the arched doorways of the lobby, the mosaic saints of the Kingdom gazed down serenely at the sight. Signs dripped wet from the rain:

SUFFER THE LITTLE CHILDREN TO COME UNTO ME!
THERE IS ROOM AT THE INN!
OPEN THE GATES!
LET THEM COME IN!

The faces of the thousands who crammed in, blocking the doorway, were not angry, merely determined. Blue-coated bobbies did not push them back into the rain. They faced the arched doorway leading to the Commons chamber. The thick oak panels did not keep their voices from penetrating the room.

As the masses waited outside, an emergency bill for child refugees from Nazi Germany passed within minutes. Ten thousand British families willing to take children filled a list in one day. There was a waiting list of others who longed to help.

The people of England had spoken, indeed.

The drab gray metal door was only one of fifty identical doors off a long, sterile corridor. There was no sound in the hallway except for the tramp of boots and the clanking of keys as cell number 17 was unlocked for Karl.

He stood outside, stubbornly refusing to enter until two guards nudged him firmly forward and banged the heavy door closed behind him.

It was a redbrick cell, constructed by civilian workmen to guarantee the strength and security of the structure. The cell had a concrete floor carpeted by a layer of straw, with a small drain hole in the center and a toilet in the back corner opposite the cot. The only illumination came from a lightbulb screwed into a ceiling fixture far out of reach. Ventilation was provided by a barred window eight inches square.

As the sound of retreating guards echoed hollowly beyond the cell, Karl stared at this example of the Führer's mercy. This was, indeed, the cell of a favored prisoner. According to rumor, the former Austrian Chancellor Schuschnigg was somewhere in this cell block. Other high officials of the Nazi Party had been brought to such a place when they fell out of favor with the Führer. Often they stayed just long enough to reconsider the error of their ways and appeal for pardon. Sometimes pardon was granted. Sometimes it was not.

Karl's eyes lingered on a small, rough wooden table at the head of the cot. On it were books, blank stationery, and a pencil for writing. For an instant his heart rose. *Is that a Bible on the table?* He rushed forward to retrieve a leather-bound volume from among the stack of pamphlets.

Selected Readings from the Holy Bible. Karl opened it and skimmed through it briefly. His joy left him. The readings, pulled from the context of their original place in the Scriptures, were arranged under headings such as Duty to Authorities and What God Says about the Jews.

The title page of the twisted collection was emblazoned with a swastika and the symbol of the new Nazi state church. Shaking his head, Karl tossed the book onto the cot and picked up a pamphlet containing the virulent anti-Semitic writings of Martin Luther's old age. The spirit of antichrist, it seemed, had been compiled in each of the booklets and writings selected to occupy Karl's hours in the cell.

Better to be filthy and stinking and hungry in the barracks with other men than in this place, Karl thought. For the first time since his arrest, a sense of loneliness overwhelmed him. He thought of Helen and Lori and Jamie. He remembered Christmas as it had been last year and the years before—the reading of the Christmas story from his precious uncut Bible, the sound of voices raised to sing in praise of the little King born in a stable, the aroma of Christmas supper, and the delight on the faces of his loved ones as they unwrapped their gifts. Later, when everything had been cleaned up, Helen had lain in his arms and they had loved each other with the gentle passion grown from years of friendship, of knowing each other. And the children had slept a contented sleep.

Such memories rushed in on Karl with pressing grief. He dropped to his knees in the straw and moaned softly. How much better to work beside other suffering prisoners! To struggle day to day, moment to moment, with cold and hunger and bleeding hands and then to fall exhausted on a plank bunk and sleep! There was no mercy in this clean, bare cell. There was no comfort in the carefully chosen passages of the books left for him to read. In the barracks he had been comforted by giving comfort to others.

In this place there was no one to encourage, no one to help, no man with whom he could share his ration and say, "I am here for this reason. . . ."

In this cell, there was only Karl, and he knew that loneliness was the fiercest fire of all to try his faith.

The bathroom had been converted into a darkroom. Otto posted a sign on the door forbidding entrance until the passport photos were developed.

After rinsing the pictures, he placed them in the bathtub to dry. Otto brought them out for viewing after supper, and ignoring the moans from his subjects, he declared that the photographs were perfectly dreadful, just as all passport pictures were meant to be.

Willie was too young to be required to have his likeness on official identity documents. Babies changed too much from one week to another. Not even the rabid fanatics in the Nazi Ministry of the Interior expected that.

"His papers will be simple," Otto said cheerfully. "I can have them back in a matter of days."

"So what? He is not going anywhere without the rest of us." Peter watched lovingly as Willie pulled himself up to stand along the side of the sofa. He was trying so hard to walk! He looked at Peter as if to see whether Peter was proud of this latest accomplishment.

Otto did not answer Peter's statement. The truth was, it might be necessary to separate the family, to send each one out of the Reich a different way. Until that time, Otto was exploring the possibility of moving Willie and Marlene to families in Vienna who might be willing to shield Jewish children.

"How long will it take for my passport?" Marlene looked down unhappily at the pouting image of her face. "I won't show it to anyone."

"You'll show it when they ask you for it," Peter challenged. "Or they will arrest you and drag you off."

"But it doesn't look like me," she whimpered.

"Yes, it does. Ugly." Peter regretted saying it before it was out of his mouth. His mother insisted he apologize. Marlene made a face at him. Typical.

"We had better get our papers soon," Karin said to Otto. "Or I know two children who are likely to wake the dead with their arguing." She apologized to Otto. They had moved in on him, disrupted his life, and now he had to endure the bickering of Marlene and Peter. She knew he would be glad to be rid of them all.

"I will be glad when you are safe," Otto said quietly as he gathered up the pictures.

Peter eyed him from the sofa, where Willie happily pounded his big brother's leg, begging to be picked up. "Why are you doing this?" Peter asked.

"Maybe because I don't want to hear you and Marlene fight anymore." Otto smiled, trying to make light of the one unpleasant fact of their confinement.

"That's not what I mean," Peter said, picking up Willie and receiving a slobbery kiss. "I mean why—from the start—have you put yourself in danger for us? You don't owe us anything."

"Your father was a good man," Otto replied. "He died so that a lot of other men could live. This is just my way of fighting back. One small thing I can do. There are other men who also admired your father. I am getting help with your papers. You will seem as Aryan as Himmler himself when we get through." He still seemed cheerful, hopeful. "Just try, you and Marlene, not to kill each other before we get the details worked out."

Orde had not come to the evening meal at the Hanita mess hall. He had not spoken to anyone at the settlement all day. Moshe and Larry Havas walked together across the dark compound. The lantern in Orde's tent was still glowing. His shadow paced the length of the tan canvas, then back again.

"You think we should ask him if he wants to come listen to the radio?" Havas asked tentatively.

Moshe shook his head. "You ask him if you want to. Not me. As a matter of fact, I want to sleep in another tent tonight. He is in one of those black moods."

Havas shrugged. "You can bunk with us if you don't mind the snoring."

"Better than growling."

The music from the old Philco radio echoed pleasantly in the mess hall. It was American music from some big band at a New York hotel, someone said as Moshe and Havas took seats near Zach.

"Very mellow stuff," Larry said. "Too mellow. Depressing. What we need is a little Tommy Dorsey to wake us up."

"What we need," said Zach quietly as he stirred his coffee, "is for Captain Orde to snap out of it! He is like a dark cloud hovering over the entire settlement. We speak to him, and he grunts. Smile and wave, and he scowls. I was so happy this morning when I heard about the child refugee transports. I asked him what he thought about it. Ten thousand kids to England, and I thought he was going to hit me." Zach shook his head. "What do you think, Moshe? You bunk with him."

"I think you should shut up. Here he comes." Moshe jerked his head as the door swung back and Orde strode in. All conversation stopped dead. No laughter, nothing but solemn awareness that the cloud was sweeping across the hall toward Zach.

Moshe did not look up. It seemed to him that the head of every man

and woman in the room pulled in between hunched shoulders. Like
a herd of tortoises, no one wanted to take the brunt of Orde's mood.

Zach pretended not to see Orde until he sat down beside him.

"Shalom, Orde."

"That means peace," Orde remarked sourly.

"Hello. Good-bye. Whatever." Zach tried to sound cheerful. It was
the wrong move.

"What are you so happy about? Still gloating over ten thousand children going to England?" Orde scowled.

"Well, no. Although it is better than leaving them in the hands of the
Nazis."

Orde glared hard at him. "Let me tell you what this means."

"Do I have a choice?" Zach still feigned lightness.

The cloud darkened.

"You have been sold out by the British! Those kids are not coming
home here to Zion! No, they are being torn away from families to be
spread around like so many chicks from a hatchery! You have been paid
off! Ten thousand children in England, and the Zionists will be expected
not to bring up the issue of immigration again! Haj Amin and Hitler
have won! The price for the nation of Israel is ten thousand children."
He was fuming, his face flushed with anger. "There is dancing in Berlin
tonight. The Mufti and the Führer are dancing on the graves of your people, and you expect me to smile?"

No. No one expected him to smile. But the feeling was that it would
have been better if he had stayed in his tent.

·"At least we can be happy that those children are saved," Larry ventured.

"*Saved?* They are consigned to the obscurity of wanderers and orphans! *This* is where they belong! *This* is the promised homeland for the
People of the Covenant, and I tell you, we will do everything to bring
them here!" Orde thumped the table. "Do you understand me? We will
not be purchased with the lives of child hostages! We will fight here, and
everyone from England to Hitler and the Mufti will wonder what has
gotten into us Jews in Palestine!"

"Don't forget, Orde," Zach said gently, "it is you who are on our side,
not us on your side." Nervous laughter rippled through the room.
"Come on; we are in this fight as one." Zach shrugged. "Although at
times you out-Zion all the rest of us put together." He laid a hand on
Orde's arm. "That makes you the most dangerous man in Palestine to
the Mufti because you will fight, and to us Jews because you are a Christian who is fighting for us. And for Zion. It is a miracle we speak of
among ourselves. It makes us think, you know?"

"Yes." Orde stared at his clenched hands and slowly relaxed them. "And we have the promise of His Word to back us up." He stood abruptly. "Well, then . . . I am tired. Shalom."

That was all. He left the settlers staring at one another, wondering at the odd man they called Hayedid, friend. Moshe bunked with Larry, much preferring the snoring.

25

Treasures

The porter, a young peasant—thick-necked, short, and well-muscled—had dark features that made Lucy wonder if he was a Jew. He assured her he was Hungarian. After all, Vienna had been the capital of the Austro-Hungarian Empire. Many swarthy people who were not Jews lived in the city, and many Jews who were not swarthy. It was all very confusing to Lucy, at best.

Not wanting trouble, Lucy had checked his papers before she hired him. There was no *J* stamped on the page denoting a Jew. Only then did she offer him two marks for carrying the rugs for her.

As she instructed, he followed at a discreet distance, the rugs rolled and slung easily over his broad shoulders. He carried them as though they were not at all heavy and kept up with her quick pace.

When they reached the Dorotheum, Lucy turned to make certain he was still behind her. Their eyes met, and he stopped and looked away. It was important, she had told him, that no one realize she was so impoverished that she must sell these priceless family heirlooms.

Lucy slipped in and climbed the stairs, pausing at the first landing to watch him enter after her and follow. A broad nod of her head told him that he was doing well. He followed her up to the fourth floor and found the appraiser's office identified by the sign *Persian Carpets*.

Once inside, the young man dropped the cargo where she pointed. Lucy paid him, gave him a pleasant smile of farewell, and hoped she would never see him again. He checked the coin in his hand and left without comment. These days it was common for people to sell off family possessions. His expression, which seemed to convey his amusement that such old rugs had any value at all, caused Lucy a moment of genuine uneasiness. Suppose she had paid two precious marks to have the things carried, and then they were of no value? Suppose her ruse of faintness over the sight of brown chocolate stains was for nothing? She certainly could not repeat such a performance to gain Wolf's permission to empty the apartment of its furnishings.

Her palms were damp and cold by the time the appraiser turned his attention to her. He perched his spectacles on his nose and looked first at her and then at the rolled-up rugs beside her on the floor.

"Ah!" He smiled. "Kurdistani."

How did he know this from the bottom side of a rolled-up rug? "Yes," she agreed as if she knew. "Are they . . . ?"

He was already stooping beside them, feeling the texture and examining the closeness of the threads. "And a very fine example, too!"

This answered her question. "Family heirlooms," she said with just a hint of tragedy in her voice.

The appraiser glanced up at her with a start. "Yes, I know." His voice was flat. His eyes narrowed slightly. "I knew the family."

She stared blankly at him. She was caught, and she knew it. Drawing a deep breath, she stared out the door and imagined this little man questioning her and calling the Gestapo. She thought of what Wolf would say.

Swallowing hard, she attempted a maneuver. "Not my family," she said softly.

He straightened and faced her with a hand on his hip. He dared her to lie, dared her to tell him that she knew the people who had once owned these rugs. His defiant and angry look pierced her defenses. "Would you care to explain?"

"I purchased them." She raised her chin. Why should she explain anything? "Now I need money."

"Surely you have a bill of sale for such fine merchandise." His gaze was steely, as if he spoke for the family they had been taken from.

Lucy looked desperately at the door. She wanted to run, to disappear into the crowds of the city. Tears, genuine tears, glittered in her eyes. "No. I have no bill of sale. I know nothing about these except they are supposed to be of value . . . and the truth is, I need money. I . . . they belong to my fiancé . . . that is, he acquired them. I don't know how he got them, but he did."

"Is he a thief?" The appraiser seemed unmoved by this breakthrough of honesty.

With a shake of her head she replied, "No. He is an SS officer." She hesitated. "And he is not my fiancé. And . . . I need . . . the money." Her words had fallen to a choked, pleading whisper.

The man reached around her and closed the door. Then he turned to face her. He was considering what this liar with the stolen carpets of his Jewish friends had to say.

He swept a hand toward the carpets. "These were taken . . . *stolen* . . . from the home of my friend. He asked that I might keep watch for them, just on the·chance that they might show up." His lower lip protruded. The muscle in his jaw twitched angrily. "There are several others."

"No." Lucy was pleading. "He . . . he shipped them to Prussia."

At this news the appraiser gave her a sad, disgusted look. "Thief or SS officer—what is the difference?" He shrugged with resignation. "I could be arrested for that. And you, no doubt, would be arrested for stealing these from your SS thief. Therefore, you have something on me. And I have something on you. We are equal before the law." He gave a slight bow from the waist and managed a smile.

"I would not report you," she said. "I'll take them back and no one will ever—"

He held up his palm to silence her. "It is too late for that. You brought them here to sell them. Therefore, I will tell you that there is a reward for them. Not a big reward, considering their great value, but then, my friends have lost a great fortune here in Austria and elsewhere. So the reward is small. Two hundred marks each."

"Two . . . hundred . . . marks? Each carpet? That is four hundred." Lucy gazed at the rolled treasures in astonishment. She had not guessed! Could not have imagined! "But . . . won't the Reich steal them back again?"

He smiled briefly. "No," he said flatly, the simple word fraught with meaning. "My friend is out of the country on business. But I am authorized to pay the sum, and he will reimburse me. Therefore, you are in agreement with the reward?"

Lucy bit her lip, then frowned. Perhaps she had chosen the most valuable thing in the apartment to steal. "Well, I . . ."

"You will think of something to tell him. A bright Fräulein like you." He was already counting out the money, and the matter was settled.

Without questioning Otto, Karin Wallich had sewn their passport photos into the lining of his heavy, double-breasted, camel-hair coat. It was a fine overcoat. Worth a lot of money.

Otto did not wear it as he entered the Dorotheum; it was wrapped in paper suitable for storage. This was a wise procedure if a man wanted to pawn his best coat. Otto had also tossed in a handful of mothballs for good measure.

He entered the Dorotheum at the same moment as the tall, beautiful, blond woman and her porter. He held the door open for them both and smiled at her obvious attempt to pretend that the rugs over the fellow's shoulders were not hers.

Otto knew this woman—or at least he knew *of* her. She was the mistress of Wolfgang von Fritschauer, now comfortably housed in the former flat of Elisa Lindheim—all thanks to Otto. It paid for Wolf to keep on Otto's good side.

His eyes lingered on her shapely legs as she ascended the steps. The rug bearer was also noticing the striking beauty of his employer. Heads turned everywhere in the Dorotheum. No doubt it was difficult for a woman like that to do anything without being noticed.

Otto had heard Wolf boasting about those Persian carpets. They were his best bargain in Vienna, Wolf said. So what was Wolf's mistress doing hocking the carpets? Maybe she just needed the money. Then Otto smiled at his own curiosity. After all, someone might look at him and wonder why he was pawning his overcoat.

At first the news of a home in England for refugee children sounded like an answer to the prayer of every Jewish mother in the Reich.

Peter watched his mother's face as she listened to the distant BBC broadcast. At first her eyes reflected joy; then the slow realization of separation from her children etched pain deeply into her expression.

"Those who may apply for the child transports must meet the following conditions. Applicants must produce a certificate of health demonstrating that the child has no physical or mental impairments—"

"That leaves Marlene out," Peter joked, but his mother did not smile. Marlene shot him a black look, although she could not fully understand the English words.

"Applicants between the ages of infancy and sixteen will be considered. Passage through Poland to the Free Port of Danzig must be secured, and all economic conditions imposed by the government of the Third Reich must be complied with."

Those conditions included the payment of all fines and taxes owed by the parents of the children to the Nazi government. Papers must be current. Children of criminals against the Reich would not be allowed to emigrate.

At least twenty other conditions had to be met, but Peter did not hear them. Peter's father, Michael Wallich, was considered a criminal by the authorities. This one issue alone shattered any hope that they would be allowed to leave Vienna. They were hiding out precisely because they had no money to pay the additional fines that had been levied on them. Without cash to pay off the Gestapo, no papers would be issued. Beyond all that was the question of purchasing train passage to faraway Danzig.

Peter patted his mother on the back. "Well, Mother, you see? You can't sell us, and you can't even give us away! If you had any money you could pay someone to take us to England but—" he shrugged—"it looks like you are stuck with us, yes?"

The pain did not leave Karin Wallich's eyes, even though she managed a smile for Peter.

All the sardine cans were empty.

"I'm sorry," Alfie told the mother cat, Joseph. "I don't have anything left but one can of peaches. I know you don't like peaches."

Joseph did not seem to mind. She flicked her tail and fed her kittens, then ran up the steps and disappeared. When she came back, she cleaned her whiskers as if she had just eaten a sardine and she fed her kittens again.

Alfie would have liked to eat, too. He saved the last can of peaches for two more days and did not open it until his stomach felt as if it were chewing itself.

Now there was nothing left at all, and Alfie's stomach hurt again. He sat still because his head was spinning. The kittens were fat and round. Joseph had lots of milk for them and did not ask Alfie for sardines. This made Alfie think that maybe Joseph knew where to find food on the outside.

Joseph licked her babies clean while Alfie stacked his empty cans. He put his tin soldiers on top of one another but felt too weak to play with them.

"I am hungry, Joseph," he said. "Do you know where food is?"

The cat smiled a wide cat smile and licked her lips. She got up from her blanket and shook her babies loose. Then she walked toward the steps. *Yes,* she seemed to say, *I know where there is food.*

Alfie stooped and scooted all the kittens back into one wiggling heap on the blanket. He put a diamond ring in his pocket in case he might need to trade it for food.

Joseph waited patiently for him at the top of the steps and then dashed out from the gate while Alfie fumbled with the lock.

It was daylight, clear and not too cold. They sky shone blue behind the jumble of bare branches, and Alfie looked up at the sky and laughed.

It had been a long time since he had been out of the dead-Halder house. It felt very good to have sunlight on his face again.

He followed Joseph, who strolled toward the stone wall surrounding the churchyard. The wall was taller than Alfie's head, but the cat jumped over it easily. Alfie went back to the secret opening through the fence and crawled through. He took a deep breath and looked around to see where Joseph had gone. She sat on a stone bench beneath a tree. She waited for Alfie, then bounced across the grass and along the sidewalk in front of New Church.

Even though Alfie was hungry and light-headed, he smiled and waved at passing cars. It had been so long, and today was a better day than the day the men had put up the boards and signs all over New Church. Things looked almost normal except for the black heap where the Jewish church had been.

There were city sounds and clanging trolley bells and people walking into shops up the street. Joseph looked over her shoulder at Alfie, her fur shiny in the sunlight. She walked straight toward the ruins of the Jewish synagogue, and Alfie saw a line of people waiting to go into a building just behind where the church had burned.

Alfie breathed a deep breath. He smelled food. Joseph smiled at him. He picked her up and held her as he crossed the street.

He took a place at the end of the line. The faces of the people did not look very happy. There were not very many men—mostly women, and a lot of children, and some old men. All of them looked at him strangely; they knew he was different. Alfie was sure that they could see he was a Dummkopf.

"Is there food here?" he asked a pretty woman in a brown tweed coat and a black scarf. Her eyes were sad. She reached over and stroked Joseph's head.

"The soup kitchen is open," said the woman. "You have a pretty cat."

"Can I get food here?" Alfie's stomach growled. "I don't have any more sardines."

The woman looked down at two little girls who clung to her skirts. "This is the line for the children's transport."

"Where can I get food?" Alfie said. "I am hungry, and my cat said I could eat here."

She smiled slightly and stroked Joseph's head again. "You have a smart cat," she said. "Stay with me. I will make sure you get something."

"My name is Alfie. My cat is Joseph. She has kittens."

The lady smiled a little more, but Alfie could see that her eyes were still sad. "Where do you live, Alfie?"

He thought for a moment and decided it would not be good to tell her too much. "I live with my mother."

An old woman standing in front of the nice lady leaned in and whispered, "I didn't know there were any of them left on the streets."

Alfie knew what she meant, but he pretended not to notice the way the grandmother looked at him.

"Poor thing," said the young woman. Her children stared up at Alfie and the cat. They knew that he was a Dummkopf, but he smiled back at them in a friendly way.

"Would you like to pet my cat?" he offered. "Her name is Joseph."

"Are you going to England on the transport ship?" one of the little girls asked.

Alfie thought about it. "Yes, I will go."

"Mama, can he go?" asked the second girl.

The old grandmother shook her head and put a finger to her lips. "Only healthy children," she whispered.

She thought Alfie did not hear, but he did. She did not mean children who were not sick. Alfie knew that she meant no Dummkopfs could go to England on this ship.

"Maybe I won't go," Alfie said bravely, "because I do not want to leave my cat Joseph and her kittens. They would miss me. Maybe they would even starve if I was not here to feed them." Saying this made him feel better.

A short man in a torn sweater walked down the line. He handed out forms that everyone took and studied. Alfie took the white paper also and pretended he could read it. As the line moved closer to the door, people filled in the blanks and talked about what it said.

"Only ten thousand children . . ."

"It is something, anyway."

"Do you suppose there will be room?"

Alfie folded his paper and put it in his pocket. *No room for Dummkopfs*, he told himself. But it was all right. He was needed. Joseph needed him. God had brought him there to care for Joseph and to save little Werner's life.

Later, over a bowl of thin soup and a piece of bread, Alfie felt much better about things. He would come back here if they let him. These were Jews, he decided, and he was glad they shared their soup with him even though he was not smart.

The present site of the German Railways Information Bureau was at No. 6 Teinfaltstrasse in Vienna. It had been taken over, Lucy heard, from a

Jewish-run banking firm after the Austrian Anschluss. It was of suitable grandeur for the lofty aspirations of those who wished to travel within the ever-expanding borders of the Great Reich. It provided an atmosphere of elegance and prosperity as well as customary German efficiency.

Lucy stood outside and gazed longingly through the gold lettering. *Reichsbahnzentrale*. The eagle and the swastika were stenciled above. To the right, a large travel poster showed a photograph of a luxury hotel and spa in the newly acquired Sudetenland. On the left, an even larger photograph depicted a quaint row of old burgher houses with steep roofs and half timbers and a carved coat of arms on each door. The charming scene reminded Lucy of the lovely old houses in Munich. But this place was not in the Reich, in spite of the Teutonic appearance and the fluttering Nazi flag frozen in the corner of the poster.

"Danzig." Lucy repeated the name on the poster. "*Visit Danzig.*" It looked like a place she might want to visit, a place to hide. Everyone in Danzig spoke German. This made it more appealing as a destination than France, since Lucy spoke only German. She had wanted to run away to Paris, but it occurred to her as she listened to Wolf order dinner in a French restaurant that it would be impossible. Belgium and Holland were likewise ruled out. Wolf could speak half a dozen languages and never failed to seize every opportunity to do so in front of her. The effect was intended to make her feel small and stupid. In fact, it made her consider ways to get around her limitations.

The travel poster advertised *Free City of Danzig*—German to the core and yet not a part of Hitler's Reich. It was, Wolf had explained sourly to her one night, the last of the old-time city-states. Like the Vatican in Rome, it had its own government. It had once been a part of Germany, a part of Wolf's own Prussia. It had been vilely cut off from the Fatherland after the war, he said, to provide the one port to the Baltic Sea for Poland. The League of Nations administrated the two-hunded-square-mile port, but the customshouse was staffed by Poles. The police force and army were also Polish.

Wolf spoke about Danzig with fire in his eyes. He still considered it to be German, just like Austria and the Sudetenland. One day, no doubt, it would be reincorporated into the Reich. But for now, Lucy only cared that the language in Danzig was plain German and the politics were not. The swath of Polish territory separating Danzig from Germany would also separate Lucy from Wolf.

"Danzig!" She whispered the name hopefully and entered through the tall glass doors of the building. It still looked and smelled like a bank. Pillars of green-and-white-swirled marble supported the echoing ceiling. Clerks stood in cages behind the counters, and long lines of would-be travelers waited for the next available clerk. Oak racks along one poster-covered wall held timetables for steamship lines and railroads and attractive brochures depicting every possible destination within the Reich and without. Fresh new brochures had been printed immediately after the borders of Czechoslovakia had been eliminated. Under the heading of *Czechoslovakia* few pamphlets remained. A forlorn row marked *Prague* had been picked clean. Lucy supposed that many German officers, like Wolf, knew that the next destination on the Reich map was Prague.

She shuddered, glad she had decided not to travel to Prague. It would be swallowed up soon enough, and then what would she have done?

Just below *Czechoslovakia* and to the right were a dozen different booklets showing the glorious sights of Danzig. Lucy picked up one and thumbed through it. She looked guiltily over her shoulder, wondering if anyone in the bustling office could read her thoughts: *No SS maternity home for Lucy Strasburg! A tiny room and a job in Danzig!* She would say her husband had gone to sea, and when she had enough money she would go away too. Maybe she would take French lessons and learn to speak so well she could move to Paris after all.

She gathered up the pamphlets and shoved them furtively into her handbag. Then she walked to the rack marked *Railway Timetables* and then on to the one labeled *Shipping Lines.*

Exhilarated, she hurried out of the office. No one stopped her. No one cared that she might want to take a little trip and never come back.

She could hide her treasures from Wolf, and he would never know she was gone until it was too late. All his SS laws could not touch her in Danzig. Such matters were not addressed in travel guides, but Lucy knew that in the little port, *she* would be the mother of the baby she carried.

The news of child refugee transports whispered over the barely audible radio in the study of New Church. The four children sat in a tight semicircle around the receiver. They pressed their heads together and tried to breathe softly as the details and conditions for immigration were spelled out.

"Of course this changes everything," Jacob said when the news was over.

"It does not change anything," Lori insisted. "You heard all the regulations to get on one of those boats."

Jacob was adamant. He switched off the radio and scooted back on the floor to lean against the bookshelf in the darkness. "The regulations are—"

"No children of political prisoners," Lori interrupted. "That means us, in case you have not figured that out. They mean to hold us hostage here, threaten our parents with some harm against us. I have known that all along."

"The conditions are only for getting out of Germany and to Danzig with the official Nazi seal of approval on our documents," Jacob said.

"Which we and other hostage children like us will never get. Many are called, Jacob, but few will be going to England. The Nazis will never let us go."

"So what? They would not let us go to Prague either, and we have been talking and planning all day. Listen! If we can get out of Germany at one border, why not another? And if we can get to Danzig, maybe the English will let us get on one of their boats, out of reach of marching armies. The German army will have to swim the Channel before they take England. I want to put as much distance as possible between me and them!"

Lori sat silent, considering the logic of his reasoning. Maybe he was right. And yet, Prague was a certain refuge. Maybe Mama would be in Prague. Certainly the people there knew Aunt Anna and could contact her in England, tell her that Lori and Jamie were safe.

"Well?" Jacob demanded a response. "It's closer to the Polish border from Berlin. It makes perfect sense . . ."

She gazed intently into the darkness, trying to decide what they should do, trying to see what Mama and Papa would want them to do. One choice seemed as dangerous as the other. The Czechs were turning back refugees at every crossing. The Poles actually drove truckloads of prisoners to the German side of the frontier and deposited them in prison camps.

Lori had found an outdated map of Germany in her father's study and presented it as her credentials for participation in the planning meeting in the choir-robing room. Jacob accepted her offering with a reluctant nod. He did not want her to think a map would entitle her to make any decisions, especially not with word of the refugee transports from Danzig.

He spread the map on the floor, and they knelt down to study it. Jacob, on the south, had the best perspective. Lori, to the north, read the names of cities and nations upside down. Jamie stared silently from the east and Mark glared in the west.

Tiny dots, pinpoints on thin paper, linked by a grid of black lines. Ten thousand children would be passed from one dot to another.

The four sat in thoughtful silence for more than a minute as they considered what lay between the dot of Berlin and the dot of Prague.

"Look," Jamie said at last, tracing his finger along the thick black line of the main railroad from Berlin to the east. "It is only two and a half inches from here to the border of Poland. And another half inch to Danzig and the transports."

Lori reached across the map to touch Prague in the south. "But it is still only two inches farther to Prague. We should not think about Danzig. They will not take us on the ships to England. Papa said we should go to Prague; that is where his friends are, where the refugee children's headquarters are. Aunt Anna started that program. I'm not going to Danzig!"

Jacob leaned closer to the map. "There are more Nazi Storm Troopers between Berlin and Prague since the Sudetenland has fallen. It will be a more dangerous passage for us. And these things . . . here, where the Czech border used to be . . . these are mountains."

"Not very big ones," Mark said.

"But there will be snow." Jacob tapped the mountain fortifications that were now firmly in Nazi control. "Snow and Storm Troopers between Berlin and Prague. I say we head north instead. We reach Danzig. Call your aunt in England."

Lori drew back, sitting on her haunches and clenching her fists angrily. "You heard the rules. We do not qualify for those ships to England!"

"*To Danzig!*" Jacob's reply was firm. He was the leader. If it was up to Lori, she would simply sit in the church until the Nazis knocked it down on her head. She still hoped her father would come back! What did she know? "Yes. To Danzig. It is closer, and there will be fewer troops to get past."

Her chin trembled as she searched for words to express her outrage. "No! I am not going to Danzig! Papa said Prague, and so Jamie and I will go to Prague! If we *must* leave here, we should go where Papa wanted us to go. That way he'll be able to find us. Besides, *you* said we should go to Prague!"

Jamie's face reddened. He did not like his sister making decisions for him. This was not for a mere girl to decide. "I am going where Jacob goes."

"You are going right where Papa and Mama wanted us to go—the refugee center in Prague! Otherwise, how will they find us when—?"

"There is no *when*," Jacob growled in a low whisper. "Stop thinking they are coming for us! They are in prison, or worse!"

"Shut up!" Lori cried. Her fist came from the north and glanced off his cheek in the south. "You always think the worst!"

The blow did not hurt Jacob. He touched his hand to his cheek and smiled wryly at the attack. "You hit like a girl. You think like a girl."

His amusement only made her more angry. With a strangled yelp she threw herself against him, her fists pummeling his face and shoulders as he fell backward on the floor and raised his arms to shield himself.

Quick-thinking Mark rescued the precious map from Lori's scrambling feet. Jamie drew back in amazement at his sister's wrath. He had never seen such a thing from his sweet and gentle sister! Not ever! Now, here was Lori, slugging away while Jacob rolled back beneath the blows and tried to stifle his laughter.

"Join the Hitler Maidens," Jacob mocked. "They will teach you how to fight!"

At that, Lori's eyes widened. She hit him harder, but still he laughed at her as her fists bounced off the shield of his big hands.

"Anything! Anything is . . . better—" She reached for his hair and pulled. He gasped with surprise and grasped her arm, angry.

"You little—" He jerked her back and down to the floor, pinning her without effort while she kicked and called him a filthy Nazi commando, a Gestapo slime, and an atheist.

"You are rotten! *Rotten!*" she hissed, kicking her legs hard as he sat on her and held her arms against the floor. "Let me go! Let me—" Tears of hot anger spilled over. "I won't go with you! Not ever!"

Her knees struck him in the back, but he held her firmly in place. "Now you listen to me!" Jacob's voice was just as angry as hers. "You have been nothing but trouble! You whine about your parents—"

"When Papa gets back—"

"He's not coming back!" He gave her a shake, let her cry for a minute, then continued. "*So!* No one is coming to save us; do you hear me, Lori? It is up to us! We cannot survive if we argue—and you argue about *everything!*"

"You are . . . unreasonable!" The rage in her voice fell away to frustration and grief. "I cannot! I have not . . . you have not even let me have a bath! I want a bath! I want . . . my mother and father! I want to go to Prague so they will find us!"

Jacob glared down at his sobbing captive. She closed her eyes tight but tears still escaped. Her pretty face was red. Her nose was running. A flash of pity for her coursed through him. "Lori . . . ," he began gently, but did not let her up.

"And you are so . . . brutal! I am glad to know!" She tried to raise her arm against his weight. "You hear me? I am *glad* to find out how mean you are, Jacob Kalner, because I . . . I didn't know how *mean* you were!"

The blow hit home. Jacob had not thought of himself as mean. He had only been cautious and careful. His rules and regulations had been for their safety. Somebody had to be the leader, and it certainly could not be this sniffling female. "I am the leader," he said defensively. "Somebody had to be the leader, and it's me."

"You're a bully. Like Hitler! If you weren't Jewish, you'd be a basher, just like they are! And I'm glad I know the real you, because as soon as we get out of here I *never*—" she struggled against him—"I never want to see you again!"

Jacob eyed Mark and Jamie, who watched from a safe distance. Mark shrugged as if to say, *What do you expect?* Jamie scratched his head in embarrassment at his sister's outburst. Neither boy seemed to agree with her. "If I let up, will you promise not to—"

"I promise nothing!" she sobbed back.

He pressed harder on her arms, and she winced with pain. "Promise. And we will talk reasonably."

"Let me up! Bully! *Adolf Hitler!*"

Fresh anger flooded him at her words. He bent down over her, his nose an inch away from hers. "Take it back!"

She turned her face away. He pressed his lips against her ear and whispered fiercely, "Take it back, or I will—"

"You will what? Hitler! Hitler! Hitler!"

"I should throw you out of here. Turn you over to the SS! I'm glad to see what a stubborn person you really are! All this time I was thinking you were such a—"

"Such a what?" she demanded, raising a knee hard into his back.

"Such a pleasant person! I am only glad to have this time to get to know the real you, that's all! Not the kind of girl a man wants to . . . be trapped with . . . that's all!" He scowled up at the boys who still watched the struggle with amazement. He addressed them as their leader. "If we go to Prague, it would only be because I want to get rid of her, and she will not be gotten rid of any other way." He released his grip, but remained sitting on her stomach. She did not move for a moment. The print of his fingers showed red on the skin of her wrists. "You are a lot of trouble, but I will take you to Danzig with us anyway," he said. As she sneered back defiantly, he rose and stalked out of the basement, pausing only to gesture to his troops that they should follow and leave the mutineer to herself.

26

The Only Way Out

Over a hot cup of tea, Lucy studied the travel brochures and time-tables as though every word contained a happy prophecy about her future. Within each paragraph she inserted her own name. In the frame of every photograph, she imagined herself smiling in the sun on the steps of the old brick Marienkirche cathedral, or sipping a glass of white wine in a little café along Grosse Alle. She scrutinized the names of little shops housed in the gabled buildings of Langer Market. In one of those shops she would find a job and pass her days happily gazing out on that very street!

At this point Lucy frowned, sat back, sipped her tea, and looked away with a long stare of worry. *And what will happen if I do not find a job?*

She flipped to the part of the brochure that discussed in detail the currency restrictions for leaving the Reich.

> *The financial situation has made it necessary to limit the amount of currency of any kind that may be taken out of Germany. The maximum permitted as this is published is 200 marks.*

The cold chill of reality set in. She stared bleakly at the rates of exchange. Two hundred German marks was equal to just under fifty dollars. One American dollar was equal to one Danzig gulden. Legally she could take not one penny more than that amount out of the Reich. To attempt to do so would result in arrest for smuggling and instant imprisonment after the first customs check.

Lucy had seen firsthand how thorough the Nazi customs officials were. Some months before, she had witnessed the arrest of a Jewish couple who had concealed currency in the lining of their coats.

The memory made Lucy blink. Jews, she knew, could take only ten marks from the country. She had thought their arrest was only right as she had watched them being led away. But she was considering the same crime against the state. Her cheeks reddened with a flush of shame at her former self-righteousness. She had raised her head in disdain as the pale woman had begged the officers to let them go. How unfeeling Lucy had been then when Wolf had haughtily uttered, *"Jewish swine! Trying to steal from the Aryan people!"*

With a shudder of regret, Lucy pulled her attention back to her own troubles. *Hotels. Danziger Hof, 100 rooms (6 with baths), 2–3 guldens per day.*

"No," she muttered aloud. All her funds would vanish within two weeks at that rate, even if she gave up eating! "There will be no sipping of white wine in a café," she sternly warned herself as she skimmed down the list to the bottom. *Continental, 35 rooms opposite the Main Station. 1 gulden per day.*

There was nothing in the booklet any cheaper. Lucy mentally marked the place and resigned herself to the fact that even before she found a job, she would have to search for a boardinghouse where meals were included with a room.

Such restrictions made the matter of counting her assets seem foolish now. What was the purpose of selling her watch and rugs and her grandmother's silver crucifix if all the cash would be confiscated anyway?

With a sigh, Lucy pushed away the brochures and timetables. She stared, unseeing, across the rooftops of Vienna. Perhaps this was all futile. Maybe she was, indeed, destined to be a prisoner in the elegant Lebensborn. Perhaps she should simply resign herself to giving up the baby. Certainly Wolf's arrogant self-assurance in this matter was his knowledge that she was trapped. How could she leave Germany? And if she did leave, how would she survive?

Her tea grew cold in the cup. She wanted to ask God for help, but she dared not. Why should she expect her prayers to be heard?

Once again the vision of Stephanie Bridge and the cold waters of the Danube coursed through her mind—a vision as easily imagined as the streets of Danzig. Perhaps it was the only way out, after all.

The obvious distortions and lies published by the State Church and pronounced by men like Gustav Dorfman did not threaten Karl Ibsen. He knew the Scriptures; he could recognize in an instant where whole passages had been lifted out of context and mutilated to suit the aims of the Nazi Party. Reading the booklets and inwardly debating their twisted contents became a game with him, a mental and spiritual exercise. If other Nazi clergymen came to debate him in his cell, he would be ready for them. He could reply with the whole truth of God's Word. At first, this confidence had made him smile. All these years he had preached the importance of memorizing the Scriptures not by isolated verses but in the context of their whole meaning. He had not foreseen how valuable that lesson would be to him. But then, he had not ever imagined being locked in a tiny cell with no other company than a stack of printed lies.

The theology of the Nazi church was not the big lie that attacked Karl in the darkness of the night. The battle was much more subtle and much more dangerous.

As dawn crept through the tiny window of his cell, he lay beneath the thin blanket on his cot and listened once again to the whisper: *Once I was of use to God. Now what good is my life? What testimony do I have in this utter silence and loneliness?*

Karl could hear the distant whistle of the train to Danzig. The counterpoint of the prison loudspeakers echoed in the clear morning air.

He closed his eyes and pictured the groaning awakening in the barracks, the shouting guards, the growling dogs. The whisper came to him again: *You stayed here to help them. To minister to the suffering of this place. And here you are, locked in a cell. You are somewhat warm. You are fed. You have paper on which to write. And you are of no use to anyone here.*

Outside in the corridor, Karl could hear the rattle of the approaching meal cart. He would get thick, lukewarm porridge, a slice of bread, and a cup of tasteless coffee—an elegant meal compared to the breakfast given to Richard Kalner and the others in the barracks.

Karl sat up slowly as the meal slot at the bottom of the door slid back and the tray was shoved through. He stared at it, wishing he could give some of the abundance to those who needed it more than he did. The voice inside grew louder: *Maybe there was some reason for being a martyr when you could minister to the others. But this is pointless! You are separated from your family. You are more silent than you would be if you had signed the Nazi paper! At least you could do something if you left this place! Why not sign what they want and leave? You serve no one in this place.*

The meal slot shut with a clang. He stared at the food tray angrily, resenting the luxury of a meal that denied him the right to say, *I am here for Christ. I stay among the suffering and the hungry to serve my King, to share the comfort of God's love with others in need.*

A sense of guilt hung over him as he prayed over his meal. He ate it all, every bite, with the awareness that every morsel was precious. At the far end of the corridor the cart rattled back, picking up empty trays. Karl took his pencil and wrote the note he had written every morning since he had been placed in the cell: *Let me go back to the people I have come to minister to. Pastor Karl Ibsen*

He never received any acknowledgment of his request. The official answer of the Nazi state church was that it was not suitable for any Aryan to minister to a Jew. Karl knew that answer from the booklets. They were all lies, and yet, still, he listened to the whisper: *Why not tell them what they want to hear and go free?*

After lunch, Moshe lay back on the cot and watched Samuel Orde scribbling away at the desk against the back wall of the tent. It was not a desk, really, but two planks laid out on sawhorses pilfered from the Hanita workshop. It served its purpose.

When Orde was not training the young men of the Yishuv to fight like Englishmen, to march sixty miles a day and survive hardships in the desert, he spent his off-hours writing about it at this desk.

Does he ever sleep? Moshe wondered drowsily. His feet ached from last night's hike over rough terrain. His back and neck felt as though he had been trampled by a herd of elephants. He wanted only to stretch out and sleep. But there was Orde—writing, writing, checking notes like a bank executive, putting sections of paper to one side and shuffling other sections together.

The stack of manuscript pages grew day by day. While some members of the Special Night Squad returned to the plow during the daylight hours, Orde plowed through his magnum opus.

Moshe had come to find out what it all meant. "What is it?" he asked at last.

"A training manual for the army of the future nation of Israel. And for the Haganah to use until there is an official army, of course."

It was an answer, but Moshe had not been asking *that* question. He wanted to know what drove Orde to work so hard. Why did he love the thought of Zion, the Jewish homeland, so much that he dedicated all his life and training to moving it nearer to reality . . . or at least to helping keep the dream alive in these perilous times?

"No." Moshe tried again. "I mean, why are you doing it?"

Orde did not lay his pen down or turn around. He kept writing as he spoke. "It seems important for you to have a training manual, one particularly fitted to this terrain and these fighting conditions. Also, it seems important that I put down on paper what we are fighting for—the specific promises God has given in His Word about Israel and the return of your people to the land." He paused for an instant, the pen held just above the paper, poised to continue. "Also . . . I have the feeling I may not be here with you much longer."

This was not exactly the reply Moshe had wanted either. The ominous foreboding in Orde's voice made Moshe sit up in alarm. "Don't say such things, Hayedid. It is bad luck," he said. He had already lost his brother and did not relish the thought of losing his English friend.

"Luck has nothing to do with it." Orde laid the pen down and turned to look at Moshe. His expression was kind, as if Moshe's concern had touched him.

"I am trying to ask you . . . not just about this book of yours but about why you do this? Why do you care so much what happens to the Jewish people? You must be one of a handful. Other Englishmen resent the way you help us, resent your faith. We all see it, even when you slap a man for coughing when we are on a sortie, even when you are so harsh with us that we think we cannot walk another step. You keep on walking yourself, and so we must follow where you lead us. How do you have the strength? And *why*?"

"Ah. So that is your question, is it?" Orde seemed amused by this burst of emotion, confused though it was. "I can tell you this, Moshe . . . I keep walking to get back to Hanita so I can write this book for you!"

"You could get killed," Moshe challenged. "The Mufti calls you the most dangerous man in Palestine. There is a great reward for your head. Quit joking with me, Orde. I want to know why you are so interested in us!"

Something deeper filled Orde's eyes. He considered the question. "Your Messiah came through the root of Israel. He says His Covenant is with you forever, for a thousand generations. The Lord submitted Himself like a lamb of sacrifice to pay the penalty of my sins. Mine. Samuel Orde. My many sins He took on Himself."

Tears—real tears—shone in Orde's eyes. "I am *so grateful* for His love and kindness. I really believe that He considers the People of the Covenant His own dear children. Satan desires that the promises God made to the Jewish people be broken, that you also be slaughtered like lambs. No Jews. No Israel. Because then God would be a liar."

Orde frowned. "Is that possible? Could evil stamp out the Covenant? I don't know. But there is a battle going on here to do just that. And I am a soldier. I understand battles; fighting is what is right. So I am here. This is a spiritual battle between good and evil, light and dark. Some men will fight it with prayers and words of peace. I am called to fight with my sword, as David fought the Philistines. It is the least I can do for my King.

He died for me. Should I not be willing then to die for His beloved people?"

Moshe had no response. He had a thousand questions, but maybe he did not want to hear the answers Samuel Orde would give him. And so he lay back down and closed his eyes and pretended to sleep while the scratching of Orde's pen continued for hours.

The tickets came to Otto's box in a sealed envelope direct from the Berlin headquarters of the Abwehr, military intelligence. Inside was a note on the letterhead stationery of Admiral Canaris himself.

> *Officer Wattenbarger,*
>
> *Congratulations on a job well done in Vienna. These tickets were purchased in advance with great difficulty. Our hope is that you will find some relief from the cares of duty in these most enlightening shows.*
> *Admiral Canaris*
> *Chief of Abwehr*

There was no mistaking Canaris' meaning. The job well done was the matter of getting the cyanide tablet to Michael Wallich before the Gestapo staff butchers could make him talk. Michael's easy death had saved the neck of Canaris and every other high traitor to the Nazi cause. Canaris owed a debt of gratitude to Otto, but much more to Michael Wallich. A handful of tickets seemed a pitiful reminder that Michael had risked everything for a democratic Germany and lost.

Otto fanned the tickets out on his desk, twelve in all. Two for each Wednesday night performance over the next six weeks.

The seats for the raucous American jazz performance had been sold out in Vienna for a month. And now they were coming to Vienna. Posters and leaflets were everywhere.

D' FAT LADY
FAMOUS AMERICAN JAZZ TRIO
DIRECT FROM PERFORMANCES
NEW YORK—PARIS—LONDON—BERLIN

Every high Nazi Party official and officer in Vienna was scrambling for seats—anything to provide some relief to the endless concerts and Strauss waltzes morning, noon, and night.

Tickets to hear American jazz, for Otto and a guest—pure gold, no doubt, worth a trunkload of fine china or a fine Persian rug. This was a strange and extravagant gift, considering that tickets were being resold now on the black market for many times the original price. Otto had heard yesterday that a certain SS officer had procured two seats by jailing an Austrian furrier until he agreed to pay bail with his tickets.

Otto gathered them up and stuffed them into the envelope. He was not particularly fond of American jazz. Reselling the tickets could make him mildly rich, but he also knew that Admiral Canaris was a frugal man. Such a wildly expensive gift said more than a mere thank-you.

Light from the lamp over the dining table glinted in Karin Wallich's red hair. She ladled up the soup and smiled tenderly at little Willie when he flapped his arms enthusiastically at the prospect of supper.

Taken all together—the soft glow of her hair, the warm and tender look from mother to child—the effect was stunning. Otto looked away quickly, uncomfortable to discover that the widow of Michael Wallich was a beautiful woman. Desirable. He did not look at her face again throughout the meal. She did not speak to him except to answer his questions in monosyllables. Perhaps that distance was better kept intact.

Peter, who did not like Otto, still managed to carry on conversation: science, art, great books he had read. The boy was obviously as brilliant as his father. Such intelligence added to the personal risk for him. Intellect in a Jewish child was interpreted by Nazi doctrine as sly and devious.

The truth was, Peter made suppertime bearable for Otto. He pulled his mind away from . . . other things.

And so it was a surprise to Otto when he raised his eyes from Karin's hands and asked her, "Do you like American jazz?" An odd question to ask right in the middle of passing the bread.

Her mouth curved slightly upward. Almost a smile. "No," she replied.

Silence descended as Peter considered the reason Otto would ask such a question. Whatever the reason, Peter did not like the tiny smile on his mother's lips.

"Ah. Well . . ." Otto stammered and averted his eyes. He was glad she had answered no; otherwise he might have done something insane and actually asked her to go out with him. For an instant he had forgotten why she was here. Forgotten why she could not step out into the sunlight or go shopping. The men in charge of Michael Wallich's case had said:

"Husbands tell wives secrets."

"Certainly the woman knows what he knew."

"If she is still in Vienna we will find her."

"But how to make her talk?"

"She has children, doesn't she? Hang a child by its thumbs, and there is no mother in the world who would not . . ."

Otto stared at his spoon. The memory of that conversation made the color drain from his cheeks.

"Are you all right, Herr Wattenbarger?" Karin leaned forward with concern.

He had told her she was in danger because of Michael's activities. He had not told her everything—not about the danger to the children or the fact that they were the weapon the Nazis could use against her. That was why the rule had been made about the children of political prisoners not being allowed on the child refugee transports to England. The children were held hostage. The children assured that imprisoned mothers and fathers would do or say anything they were told.

"Herr Wattenbarger?" Karin rose from her seat and took a step toward him. *"Otto?"*

She had never called him by his Christian name before. The sound of it jerked him back to reality. "I . . . had a moment. Not feeling well . . ."

Everyone was staring at him, even baby Willie. Otto looked at the baby, then at the delicate face of the mother. The Gestapo was right. They could probably break Karin to pieces and she would not tell what she knew. *Ah, but to hurt baby Willie—one blow to that sweet face, the twist of his chubby arm . . .*

Otto managed a nervous laugh as she put her hand to his forehead. "I am not a fan of American music either."

"If it affects you so badly, I would not mention it," she said. "Do you need to lie down?"

Her hand was cool. He put his hand to her arm in a gesture of appreciation for her concern. "I'll be all right. Just a long day. Thank you."

This much conversation between Karin and Otto sparked a smoldering look from Peter. The rest of the meal was eaten in silence.

Ronacher's Establishment had been known as the most prominent place of amusement among the wealthy of Vienna before the Anschluss. Located at No. 9 Seilerstätte, just off the broad boulevards of the Ringstrasse, the place had always been packed with barons and dukes and a fair mix of their female counterparts.

The clientele had changed since the coming of the Nazis. Now peasant boys who had risen through the ranks to become high Nazi Party officials sat in the velvet chairs of the elegant supper club. The food was still the best in Vienna. The entertainment was the most lively and modern in Europe. Backstage, electronic equipment was in place to broadcast live shows to other cities in Europe.

Tonight, holding tightly to Wolf's arm, Lucy walked through the double doors of Ronacher's and into the room she had only dreamed of as a child. Never had she imagined herself here at the finest nightclub on the Continent.

The glitter of medals and jewels did not hide the fact that most of the audience had humble beginnings like Lucy's. Wolf looked over the other guests with a distinct air of disapproval. Noting table manners and wild laughter and the copious amounts of liquor being consumed, he leaned forward and muttered to Lucy, "All the plow horses have come wearing their racing silks tonight."

Once his disdain had intimidated her. It had also impressed her. Tonight she merely smiled back at him.

"Those of us raised on a farm have a certain respect for the plow horses. I think that these would be better called sows' ears, Wolf darling. Sows' ears who have come to Ronacher's in hopes of turning into silk purses, yes?" She beamed.

He swept his arrogant eyes over her and took her hand. "And what are you, my little peasant?"

"A fine broodmare, I think. Deserving of good food and comfort so my master may have a more pleasant ride."

Once again she surprised him. He appreciated wit, even in a farm girl. He had not suspected she was capable of such repartee.

"Give me a strong colt, Lucy, and one day I might give you Ronacher's as a gift."

"This one seat is enough." She turned her head toward the stage and dance floor where D' Fat Lady Trio would soon begin their performance. "I know how difficult it is to get tickets. I am the envy of everyone in the office, Wolf."

Champagne corks popped at nearly every table. Wolf ordered French champagne, the best on the list. Then he proceeded to name the various politicians and military men around the room. He knew the minute details of their low beginnings, and he recited facts with the attitude of an aristocrat scraping manure from his riding boots. Suddenly he paused in his monologue and laughed out loud at the sight of a red-bearded man seated at a table next to the stage.

"And will you look at that!" Wolf poured himself another glass of champagne. "There is the follow you wanted to meet, the man who managed to find your apartment. And that peasant has the best seat in the house, too!"

"Gestapo?"

"Special investigations."

"He seems young." Lucy eyed the broad shoulders of the man dressed in an outdated blue serge suit. He was seated with a buxom, plain-looking young brunette in a cheap black dress right off the rack. Both of them looked out of place, and the woman seemed a bit drunk as well. She babbled on incessantly while the man with the red beard sullenly stared at the curtain.

"I wonder who he arrested to get such seats," Wolf said. "It pays to know this man, I tell you. Apartments. Furniture. Furs." He flipped the sleeve of Lucy's new coat. "Well, I manage all right. But look at Otto, will you? Sitting there without pretense in his blue suit. And all the medals and diamonds in the room do not have as good a seat as he has!"

There was, at least, some respect in Wolf's tone as he said this.

"Otto?" she asked.

"As much a peasant as you, but no racing silks, eh? Like the Führer. Yes, that is what I admire in the Führer. His plainness. A plain brown uniform. He does not attempt to conceal what he was, like Hermann Göring with all the tinsel on his chest. A plain and honest man, Hitler. He knows something about duty."

Wolf was speaking to himself; Lucy might as well have not been there. The man named Otto was simply a jumping-off place for Wolf's Prussian monologue about duty and discipline and the Aryan way of doing things.

Very boring stuff after the tenth time. Lucy tuned him out. She preferred staring openly at the tasteless display of new and stolen wealth that adorned these hopeful sows' ears.

Wolf had finished off almost an entire bottle of champagne by the time the curtain came up and D' Fat Lady Trio blasted away at every vestige of aloofness, duty, and Prussian reserve.

This black woman, with her wide smile and a glittering dress plastered to her enormous body, rocked the place like a Munich beer hall. Even dressed in their finest, the peasants who attended this performance could not conceal their origins.

Lucy loved it. And when D' Fat Lady singled out the reserved and austere Otto, she laughed and applauded wildly with the others. Stiff and grim-faced, Otto was hauled into the spotlight, caressed and crooned at to the tune of "I'd Rather Be Blue." She twirled his hair around her big black finger, wrapped a silk scarf around his waist to pull him close. Only when he blushed a deep red and smiled with embarrassment did she finally let him go. He headed for his seat, and she pulled him back again!

It was delicious. Lucy only wished she might have seen such a woman pull Hitler onto a stage in his plain brown wrapper! Could the Führer blush? Lucy wondered. And would Wolf still admire him if he actually showed some human emotion?

This strange question replayed in Lucy's mind as she turned to watch Wolf's response to the show.

His eyebrows raised slightly, he smiled at D' Fat Lady as she wrapped the silk scarf around Otto's neck. But Wolf's smile was not pleasant. Lucy had seen this smile a thousand times, cold and filled with resentment and mistrust as the black hands tied a big bow in the bright pink scarf.

With a shrug Otto bowed slightly and returned to his seat amidst thunderous applause. Lucy thought she could see envy on the faces of the men around the room. After all, they had worn their medals to catch the spotlight. But the plain blue suit now wore the racing silks.

Wolf's eyes narrowed as the applause died away. "That will teach him to get tickets so close to the front." He was not amused.

D' Fat Lady gave a deep bow, then straightened up, clicked her heels together, and raised her arm silently in a rigid Hitler salute. Then after a long pause she smiled and said in accented German, "That is how high my dog can jump!"

The crowd roared with laughter. The woman across from Otto nearly fell off her seat. Only two men in the room did not smile. Otto's face was hard as he removed the scarf and tucked it into his pocket. Wolf simply glared at D' Fat Lady and poured himself the last of the champagne.

Otto emptied his pockets onto the bed. The note D' Fat Lady had slipped him during the evening's performance was tied into one end of the scarf.

Instructions were simple. Each week he would stop by the box office of Ronacher's and pick up a fresh program sheet. He was told to tune in to the BBC broadcast on Monday night at eight o'clock. A number of rhetorical questions would be asked. Otto would listen, and then through information channels, answer those questions as specifically as possible—names, dates, future plans of the Führer in central Europe. All these things must be reduced to a series of dots and dashes inserted along the dotted border that framed the picture of the jazz trio on the program. Simple telegraphic code. After that it was a matter of enjoying the Wednesday night show at Ronacher's and leaving the program on the table.

Otto burned the note and flushed its ashes down the toilet. As simple as this all sounded, Otto knew what even a single scrap of paper left lying around could mean if the plan fell apart.

The highest sources in the German command were involved. They would provide him answers, he was certain—information he could not possibly be expected to know. Other things he would find out on his own.

For the most part, however, he played the role of courier between the head of military intelligence and the American jazz trio. It was an odd arrangement, indeed, but Otto had long ago ceased to be surprised by methods of passing information.

27

Breaking the Silence

Winston Churchill's bulk seemed to take up most of the glass sound booth at the BBC. After seeing him at his fiery best on the floor of Commons, Anna thought how much he now looked like a caged bear on display.

A sheaf of notes lay in front of him. To his right a cork bulletin board held the photographs of Helen and Karl, Lori and Jamie, as well as eight other prominent Germans who had spoken out and now had vanished.

The warning light came on. Thirty seconds to airtime. Churchill nodded slowly, cleared his throat, and glanced through the questions he must put to the world, and to one man within the Reich in hopes of getting necessary answers.

The link to New York was strong—no sunspots or unpredictable atmospherics dulled transmission to the West. The link to Europe, however, was weaker. Blank spots were reported in transmissions to Amsterdam, Prague, and Paris. There was no way of checking the reception in Berlin and Vienna, since the BBC was supposed to be banned there. Murphy did not look worried as he raised his hand to signal ten seconds.

Anna gripped Theo's hand and prayed that the question would be heard and an answer would come quickly about Helen and Karl and the children.

The red light blinked on as Murphy's hand lowered. Churchill looked up, then down, and began.

> *"I avail myself with relief at the opportunity of speaking to the people of the United States and to people whose hearts are free in spite of imprisonment. . . ."*

He sounded awkward and uncomfortable in these opening lines. Anna prayed for him. Everything must be right and strong!

> *"I do not know how long such liberties will be allowed. The stations of uncensored expression are closing down; the lights are going out in men and in nations alike. Let me, then, speak in earnestness and truth while time remains. . . ."*

Baby Willie played with a pan and a wooden spoon in front of the radio set. Peter thought that his baby brother preferred music to the forbidden speech of the Englishman Churchill. But these words were better than food to Peter, who sat beside Otto and leaned in to hear the speech.

Otto took endless notes, pausing to run his pencil down the page as Churchill moved from one question to another.

> *"Have we gained peace by the sacrifice of the Czechoslovakian republic?"*

Otto underlined this question and the next one as well.

> *"The question which is of interest to a lot of ordinary people is whether that sacrifice will bring upon the world a blessing or a curse."*

Otto underlined the word *curse* twice. He held up his finger sternly to silence Marlene as she strode cheerfully into the room and demanded that music be put on.

> *"We must all hope it will be a blessing, that as we averted our eyes from the process of liquidation of a country we will be able to say, 'Well, that's out of the way. Let's get on with our daily life.' But we in all lands must ask ourselves, 'Is this the end, or is there more to come? Has any benefit been achieved by the human race by submission to organized violence?'"*

"Why do you listen to this, Uncle Otto?" Marlene chirped. "Boring stuff. And aren't you supposed to be a Nazi?"

Peter gave Marlene his most deadly look. She stuck her tongue out at him and retreated to her room to sulk and mumble.

Peter's mother brought tea. She sat down at the far end of the table and fixed her attention on Otto. It seemed to Peter that he had seen her look at his father with that same odd mix of respect and fear, during similar moments when Michael Wallich also scribbled notes, or when he had talked in hushed tones to strangers who came to the house.

Peter had not paid attention to the undercurrents then. Now they pulled him along as well.

The words of Winston Churchill whispered in the dark study of New Church. Lori held tightly to Jamie's hand and wished that Papa could hear this man.

> *"We are confronted with another theme. It is not a new theme; it leaps upon us from the Dark Ages—racial persecution, religious intolerance, deprivation of free speech—the conception that a citizen is a mere soul-less fraction of the state. To this has been added the cult of war. Children are taught from their earliest schooling the delights and profits of conquest and aggression. A whole, mighty community has been drawn into this warlike frame. They are held in this condition, which they relish no more than we do, by a party several million strong. Like the Communists, the Nazis tolerate no opinion but their own. They feed on hatred. They must seek a new target, a new prize, a new victim. The culminating question to which I have been leading is whether the world as we have known it should meet this menace by submission or by resistance. . . ."*

Then the speech took a remarkable turn. Suddenly Winston Churchill began to speak about the men in Germany who had chosen to resist the Nazi ideology and had paid for it with the sacrifice of homes and work and even lives. Some of those men had simply disappeared without a trace. Their families were also missing.

He recited names, told stories of individual courage. And then, as Lori held her breath, she heard the story of her own father flood the room.

> *"Involved from the beginning against the euthanasia and infanticide practiced in the Reich, Pastor Karl Ibsen and his entire family have simply disappeared from the scene in Berlin. His home has been turned over to the state. His church is condemned. His wife and children have not been heard from!"*

"Here we are!" Jamie cried. "Hey, Herr Churchill! We are still here!"

In the mess hall of Hanita settlement, the words of Churchill were translated into half a dozen languages. Orde simply sat among his men and listened without comment—until this moment.

"We shall meet this aggression with resistance," he replied, as though Churchill were there among them. He smiled and scratched his head thoughtfully. "Is he talking about Hitler or Haj Amin, do you think?" he asked with a wave of his hand. "Ah well, all dictators have the same boot maker from hell. Some wear bigger boots than others, but the effect is identical, eh?"

No one was listening to the BBC anymore. Did Hayedid, their friend and commander, mean that they were to go out again? Moshe noted the eager faces of the men who had flocked to the settlement with just such a thing in mind.

Orde glanced at his watch. "Winston would be the first one to agree that resistance does not mean self-defense alone, lads. There is no moon tonight. Are you well rested?"

Anna had not stopped praying for the impact of Churchill's speech to reach the ears of those who needed to hear. Karl and Helen, along with a handful of others, represented the few who had been willing to speak out. Not enough people had joined them, and now the question remained: What could only one righteous man accomplish?

Churchill's voice resounded with the same stirring sound that he spoke with in Parliament. He finished:

> "It is this very conflict of moral and spiritual ideas that gives the free countries their strength. You see these dictators surrounded by their masses or armed men and vast arsenals. They boast and vaunt themselves before the world. Yet in their hearts is unspoken fear. They are afraid of words and thoughts! Words spoken abroad, thoughts stirring at home, in churches and schools—all the more powerful because they are forbidden—terrify them. A man chooses to speak what is right and decent; a little mouse of thought appears in the room, and even the mightiest of dictators is thrown into panic. And so that one man must be silenced. They make frantic efforts to bar words and thoughts. Men and righteousness are made to suffer. . . ."

Yes. Karl and Helen Ibsen were made to suffer. Thousands of others suffered now as well. At the end of the broadcast, Churchill appealed for anyone with information about the missing families to contact the Red Cross or the local offices of TENS. Then the red light winked off, and it was all over. No applause—just Winston Churchill in the glass booth mopping his brow and gathering his papers.

"Don't even think about it," Jacob warned Lori as she looked thoughtfully at the telephone on her father's desk.

"But you heard it!" she cried hopefully. "They said to call the TENS office! I know about that. It is the American newspaper office. My cousin Elisa married the fellow who runs it in London, and—"

"London!"

"There is an office here in Berlin. A reporter who works for them called Papa once." Lori continued to stare at the forbidden telephone as she talked. The more she said, the more reasonable it seemed that they should contact TENS. "Listen, no one knows where we are, no one in the world but us! Now the BBC has broadcast our names and asked for help in finding us. Oh, Jacob! We can call, and they will help us."

He was adamant. "They will help us into prison. Or worse. You think the Gestapo is not interested in us as well as our parents?"

"Not you or Mark. They did not mention you! Just me and Jamie! So let me call and tell them where we are."

"And in five minutes there will be a Gestapo prison van at the curb! You are dreaming!" Jacob was angered by her foolishness. "No one is going to get us out of here but us! If it had made any difference, we could have called the British Embassy, told them we were coming in for tea and political sanctuary! Lori, wake up before you get us killed!"

"Let me telephone! Maybe Elisa's husband can help."

Jacob took her by the arms. "Now you listen to me and understand what I am telling you!" He gave her a shake. "Do you know why our parents wanted us out of the country? out of harm's way? I'll tell you! Because on their own, without us to worry about, they can hold up against any pressure. Torture, death even! They were not afraid for themselves! They were afraid for us! For what the Nazis can make them say and do if we are threatened!"

Tears tumbled down her cheeks. "The law of family guilt." She knew about it. This law above all others in the Reich kept the people in line. Papa talked about it, calling it the most cruel law of all. The law of hostages.

"Let me tell you what your father and mother could not stand! They could not bear seeing you . . . hurt." The Reich had devised a thousand ways to hurt a young woman like Lori. They would not have to break her arms to break her father. Consigning her to an SS brothel or to duty as a breeder for the SS Lebensborn would be enough. There was much more, but Jacob did not speak these things. The thought of them terrified him for Lori. He knew how Pastor Ibsen would react, simply because Jacob also wanted to protect her. It was a responsibility that had made him more stern than loving with her, perhaps—but the truth was, he cared deeply what happened to her.

"I . . . I just want everything to be all right again." Lori bit her lip and tried not to cry in front of him.

Jacob pulled her close against him, wrapped his arms around her as he had longed to do every day since they had come here. Laying his cheek on top of her head, he closed his eyes. He had to fill the shoes of her father now. He had to think logically and protect her even from herself if she was not able to think clearly.

"You know that man who searched the church? A Gestapo agent. I am certain of it. He was looking for you, Lori. I felt it when we were hiding." He stroked her back. She did not pull away from him. "I thought that if he found us I would have stayed and fought him until you got away." He frowned, hoping he was not telling her too much. "It is you they want. You and Jamie. My brother and I are Jewish. It is natural that we oppose them. But you see, your father is one of them, and it cuts them to the core that he will never really belong to them. A Gentile and a true Christian. Your father is more a threat to them than you can imagine. And you, Lori, are the only way they can get to him." He lifted her chin and searched her face. "Do you understand what I am saying?"

She nodded hesitantly and then leaned her head against his chest again. She had needed an embrace, and she was grateful for his show of tenderness.

All three boys were snoring. Lori got up quietly and tiptoed out of the bellows room. She felt her way down the stairs and along the corridor to Papa's study. Closing the door softly, she sat on the floor and pulled the candle and matches from her pocket.

To strike even one match after dark was forbidden by Jacob, but there were no windows in Papa's study, converted from an old storeroom ten years earlier.

The match flared. Lori touched the flame to the wick of the candle, then sat for a while as wax dripped in a little heap on the stone floor. Tall shelves of books ringed her, but not one could tell her what she ought to do now.

Everything Jacob said made sense, yet Elisa's husband was the head of TENS. Would they ask for information if they did not have some plan for helping the Ibsen family?

They could have called a hundred people in Berlin and asked for help long before now. Lori had not done so because Jacob trusted no one. But *this* . . .

She carried the candle to her father's desk and unlatched the secret cubbyhole in the back of the center drawer. The address book was still there. She opened it and made this her gauge for making a decision.

"TENS." She thumbed through the sheets containing her father's neat printing. *"Timmons,"* the entry read. *"TENS. Adlon Hotel, room 122, telephone 3-6677."*

From there it was an easy reach for the phone.

At the rattle of the key in the lock, Karl Ibsen sat erect on his bed. It had been a long time since he had seen a human face.

The heavy door groaned in protest. Arthritic hinges opened reluctantly.

Framed in the doorway stood another prisoner—black-and-white stripes, eyes downcast, the thin six-foot frame stooped with the same suffering Karl felt. The face and features had been ravaged by that suffering.

At first Karl did not recognize the man. Then he gave a small cry of joy. A hand shoved Pastor Nels Ritter into the cell, and the door clanged shut behind them! Karl's prayers had been answered!

"Nels!" he cried, embracing the silent brother.

"Hello, Karl." The voice of his old friend was altered, joyless. But no matter! They were together in their suffering for Christ! They had spent years upholding each other in prayer, and now they were brought to this moment.

Karl wept with relief. Nels looked coolly around the cell. He stood with his hands clasped in front of him.

Nels did not seem pleased to see Karl. Arrested for opposing the laws and the enforced infanticide of sick babies in the Reich, Nels had always been a fighter. Karl knew instantly that something had broken in him; and was it any wonder? But together they could stand the pressure. Here was a gift of God that would make the Nazis wonder what power they were facing!

"Sit, Nels," Karl said gently, as though speaking to a child.

"No." Nels stood in the center of the cell. He did not embrace Karl.

"Nels? It's all right. Whatever they made you say—look at me, Nels. I know your heart. God knows."

"Don't you want out, Karl?"

"Yes. Of course. Yes."

"You know you don't have to agree with everything they say."

"What do you mean?" The first joy ebbed away. Nels had been sent here to convince him. "Please, Brother."

"Don't!" Nels raised his hand, a gesture like an axe being raised. "We don't have to say what they tell us *always;* just avoid saying what they don't like."

"Is that what you are going to do?"

"I am going home to my family. And you should do what they want and go home to your children! You think you are Peter or Paul? John on Patmos in solitary confinement? You have children? And . . . they . . . *need you,* Karl!"

"Yes." Karl sank down on his cot, crying openly. In all his weeks of solitary, he had never felt so alone. "And I need them. They are praying. Helen is praying—"

"Helen can't pray, Karl," he blurted out. *"She is dead!* You hear me? Helen is dead. Give it up and go home to your children! Helen, Helen . . . is *dead!"*

The rattle of night-squad gunfire had silenced the last sporadic firing from the walls of the Arab stronghold. This did not mean that the fighters of the Islamic holy war were dead. No. They had simply melted away into the labyrinth of Palestine's deserts.

Captain Samuel Orde followed Zach Zabinski to the toppled stone fence, where a dead man lay sprawled out.

"I thought you should see this." Zabinski shone his flashlight down at the face of the dead man. Blue eyes stared blankly up past Orde, the jaw slack in the relaxed grin of death. The hair was blond and the ash-colored skin was fair.

"European," Orde remarked. He shone the light into the man's mouth, illuminating three gold fillings. "His dentist doesn't live in Cairo; I can tell you."

"What do you make of it?" Zach asked grimly. "Tonight it seemed . . . different somehow. More organized. The grenades . . ."

"German made," Orde commented as he tore away the blood-soaked robe of the dead man. "Must have been the Nazi imitation of Lawrence of Arabia, eh?"

Zabinski smiled grimly at the joke. Captain Orde could make a joke at the oddest moments! "Not a successful one I would say, eh?"

The wound went clean through the heart. The foreign soldier died before he hit the stone he lay on. He wore black trousers beneath the robe, and heavy hobnailed boots. Orde had little doubt where the man had come from, but just to make certain he raised the limp white arm.

"Look at that, will you?" whistled Zach. "What do you make of it, Captain?"

A small tattoo of twin lightning bolts next to the letter O marked the soft underside of the dead man's arm. "Come, now. Are you telling me you've never seen this before?" He let the arm fall back.

Of course. It was stupid even to comment on such a thing. Quite obvious, with all this business of secret signs and sacred mottos and dark rituals. Even his blood type.

"He's an SS."

"Well done." Orde sniffed with disgust and wiped a fleck of blood from his hands with a handkerchief. "One of the master race in the flesh. Only now he's just dust, eh?"

"Quite dead."

Orde walked away a few paces and called to his men. "Load the bodies in the truck, lads!"

There were twelve dead among the Arab fighters. Reports from the Arab Higher Committee invariably denied that any Jihad Moquades were ever required to take the quick road to Paradise while fighting the Jews. News of actual deaths might dampen the enthusiasm of even the most dedicated Holy Struggler. Orde, therefore, continued his practice of hauling the bodies of his foes to the nearest Arab police station, where he dumped them off with a note pinned onto their clothing: *I should have stayed home.* This always had a sobering effect on potential Jihad Moquades who might have otherwise happily joined the marauders of the Mufti's terrorist forces. Attacks tended to slow down for a few days after Orde conducted his own body count in this manner.

"I'd send this one back to Hitler with a note, but I'm sure der Führer would find a way to blame the Jews of Germany." Orde stepped over the body and made his way to where his men held three prisoners at gunpoint.

A tiny mouse of independent thought had appeared within the great halls of the German Chancellory, and the Führer was trumpeting his fury at Churchill's broadcast.

It was not Churchill's reference to Czechoslovakia or racial persecution that angered him; it was the fact that once again the obstinacy of Pastor Karl Ibsen shook the fist of spiritual warfare in the face of the whole Nazi Reich.

Hitler's blue eyes turned black with rage. His translator wondered if the Führer's pupils had dilated completely or if some other dark presence had simply taken control of Adolf Hitler's human body. It made Doktor Schmidt shudder as he relayed the challenge of the British statesman.

Minister of Propaganda Joseph Goebbels did not look up to follow the pacing German leader. Goebbels was frightened. As propaganda goes, the news he had for his Führer was not good.

"Report to me the progress we are having with the reeducation of the German clergy," Hitler demanded. He paced and turned, snapping his fingers impatiently as he brooded.

"Reverend Gustav Dorfman is solidly with us, publicly denouncing the falsehood of the pastors who remain stubborn."

"I do not care about Dorfman! The man is something I can clean off my shoe! Yes, he is with us because it benefits him! What about the others?"

Of course there were others. Goebbels calmed the Führer with stories of those who had recanted their former views of National Socialism and now applauded its mission from God. Many now stood in their pulpits, reinstated, ready to preach according to the doctrine of the state.

"We have had particular success with a Protestant pastor, Nels Ritter. He is quite vocal on your behalf now, Führer, and he was quite close to Pastor Ibsen in the old days."

This news did not cheer Hitler. He spun on his heel and fixed his dark stare on Goebbels. This was the mouse! This was the name and the man he feared. *A truly righteous man*, they said. *A man who could not be compromised!*

"And what about Ibsen?" he demanded. "When shall I have my broadcast? When will he tell them in England what they must hear? When will he say that we are right and just? Tell me where Ibsen is!"

"In a prison at the border. We are making progress, mein Führer. He remains unchanging in his stubbornness. He does not know of the interest in his life from the West, of course—nothing to encourage him in his obstinacy. He is . . . we are slowly breaking him, Führer."

Hitler lowered his chin and glared out from beneath his forelock. He swept it back with his hand. "Break him quickly, Goebbels," he ordered. "I want him on the radio, repudiating all that Churchill has said. He will say that we are good and just in our battle. He will say that the Almighty has blessed our cause! I want him to say it out loud! They make him a martyr, and he is not even dead. They wonder where he is; well, we will let them hear his voice speaking on our behalf!"

"Such things take time."

"Time?" Hitler raged, striking out at Goebbels. "I do not have time to waste. They focus on this insect of a man as if he matters. And through his voice we are accused of crimes. You know where he has stood! I want every one of his stands reversed in our favor! I do not care what you do! You and Himmler. Only do not kill this man! I want him on my side." Suddenly Hitler remembered the faces of Ibsen's family: Helen, Lori, Jamie. "I told you we would use his family as a last resort. So. Now it is time to move on. Tell Himmler! Make Ibsen beg for the lives of his family! Make him promise anything for their sake! I want this matter settled!"

28
Betrayal

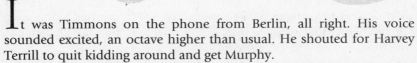

It was Timmons on the phone from Berlin, all right. His voice sounded excited, an octave higher than usual. He shouted for Harvey Terrill to quit kidding around and get Murphy.

Harvey waved at Murphy across the din of the newsroom. Murphy thumped Adams on the back and took his time sauntering back to his own office.

"It's Timmons from Berlin," Harvey said laconically. "Frantic, as usual. Says he has something for you about Elisa's cousin."

Murphy's eyes widened. He shoved past Harvey and lunged for the phone. "Timmons? Timmons! This is Murphy!"

No reply. Murphy thought he could hear voices in the background behind the usual long-distance static.

"Hello! Hello, Timmons? What have you got? Are you there, boy?"

The sound of guttural laughter sifted across the miles. Maybe Timmons was talking to someone in his room. Had he called and then left the phone hanging off the hook?

Murphy tried again, this time with a more formal tone. "Hello? This is Murphy. TENS London on the line."

Heavy static intruded into the connection; then suddenly a voice broke through clearly. A thick German accent replied cheerfully. "Ah. John Murphy. The newsman? *Ja.* This is Officer Alexander Hess. Write the name down, *bitte*, in case you should need it. No doubt you will have questions. Your embassy may relay them to me personally at the Reich Ministry of the Interior. Gestapo, *ja?*"

Murphy stammered, trying to keep the man on the line. "What? Is this a joke? Let me talk with my employee. This is a private conversation. Put Timmons on the line."

"*Nein*. No private conversations here, you know, Herr Murphy." Hess laughed. "I regret to inform you that your reporter is detained for questions, possibly conspiring to harbor fugitives from the law. Yes? You understand? Okay, then. You have questions? Call the Ministry of the Interior."

At that, the receiver clattered and clicked dead.

People at the soup kitchen had begun to ask too many questions, like, "Why doesn't your mother come here?"

Alfie told them that she was home sleeping, and then they said, "It must be the sleep of the dead, because she is always sleeping."

Such things made him feel nervous. As the time came closer for the children to leave for the transport, sometimes Hitler men would come to look at documents and take people away. So far Alfie had managed to slip out before they stopped him. But they were at the soup kitchen and looking for people to close the lid on.

It was time for soup, but Alfie did not go. He had not gone the day before either, and he was hungry. There was no way to get around it. He would have to buy food and bring it here or he would starve, and the kittens would not have anyone to watch over them.

Alfie picked out his jeweled necklace. In the center it had a green stone as big as his thumbnail with diamonds shining all around it. *Such a pretty thing ought to buy a lot of sardines*, he thought as he shoved it into his pocket.

He decided he would go to the grocery store around the block from New Church. Sometimes he and Jamie had gone there to buy chewing gum or hard candy. The grocery man knew them and was nice sometimes, when he was not too busy.

Alfie's stomach was rumbling by the time he hurried across the busy street, then past the shoemaker's and the toy store and the ladies' dress shop where Mama had gone shopping for her clothes. He stopped for a minute in front of the window like Mama always used to do. He could see himself in the glass and imagined her standing beside him.

"Hello, Mama," he said. "I wish I could buy you a dress." But he knew that Mama would want him to buy food instead, and so he walked on, rounding the corner to where Niedermeyer's Grocery was.

Herr Neidermeyer was dusting the top shelf with a feather duster as if nothing had changed at all since the last time Alfie had been in. He did

not look up at Alfie, which meant he was busy thinking and would probably not be nice today.

That was all right. Alfie did not need help. He got a basket and went
right to where the sardine cans were stacked up high. Alfie took a lot.
Then he scooped in some cans of milk because the kittens would be
needing to learn to drink milk properly from a bowl. They would not always be babies crying for their mama.

After that, Alfie got a loaf of bread and some chewing gum and
peaches. He had enough to fill two boxes. He could carry two boxes
without trouble. Mama used to send him to the store because he was big
and strong. She would call ahead and place her order, and Alfie would
go pick it up.

Alfie put the basket on the counter by the register. "Hello, Herr
Niedermeyer."

The feather duster went up like a flag. Herr Niedermeyer looked as if
he were seeing a ghost.

"*Mein Gott!* Is it . . ." He snapped his fingers, trying to remember
Alfie's name. "I have not seen you in a long time! Good heavens! Not
since—" He frowned. "What is all this?"

"Food," Alfie told him. It was strange that Herr Niedermeyer did not
know what Alfie had in the basket.

"You want all this?"

"If it will fit in two boxes for me to carry."

"It has been a long time since you were here with that other little boy.
What was his name?" Niedermeyer began ringing up the items on the
register. One by one he put them in boxes.

"Jamie."

"Ah, yes! The Ibsen child." A strange look crossed his face. He was
thinking of something unpleasant. Alfie watched his eyes squint down.
"Do you know where Jamie is?" he asked.

"I think they took him away."

"Yes, but he got away and men have come round looking for him. If
you see him you will tell me, won't you?"

Herr Niedermeyer was being nice, after all. He pushed the keys on
the cash register, making a lot of numbers behind the glass window.
Alfie stared at them.

"You have money?" Niedermeyer asked. He did not like the way
Alfie looked at the numbers. Alfie had never bought anything but chewing gum before.

"Yes, I can pay you. If it is not enough, we can put something back."
Alfie dug in his pocket and placed the jeweled necklace on the counter.

The grocer opened his mouth in astonishment. He looked at the necklace and then glanced from side to side to see if anyone else was looking. He scooped it into his hand, mumbling something all the while.

"Not enough? You want to buy half the store?" Then he went pale and scared-looking. "Where did this come from?"

"I picked it up in the street. Pretty, isn't it? My cats like it, but I am hungry."

"You did not steal it?" Niedermeyer whispered and let it drop into his pocket.

"No. If I did, I did not mean it." Alfie stacked the boxes on top of one another.

The grocer was staring hard at him. "You . . . I remember now. Jamie's friend. The Dummkopf. They took you away, *ja*? To—" He did not seem nice anymore. "You caused all sorts of trouble for that pastor, too. I remember! It is quite clear now. And they took you to the Sisters of Mercy asylum, and . . . how did you get back here?"

Alfie felt scared. Herr Niedermeyer looked angry, like people looked when they would shake Alfie or hit him on the face. He picked up the boxes and started to back away. "I am going home now."

"Home? Home where?" Niedermeyer mumbled something about a reward. "Wait!" he called to Alfie. "Wait here. I'll get you some candy. I . . . just a minute!"

Alfie stopped just inside the door. "Only a minute. I got to go home."

"Sure, sure." Niedermeyer grabbed a pack of mints from the rack and put it on top of the boxes. "Now just wait; I have a surprise for you, *ja*?" He hurried through a curtained door just behind the register.

Alfie heard him dial the phone and ask for the police, please. Herr Niedermeyer was calling the Hitler men to come after Alfie!

The bell above the door jingled as Alfie slipped out. He carried the boxes down the alley and ducked to hide behind garbage cans. Alfie did not move when the green police car wailed up in front of Niedermeyer's Grocery. He listened to the men talk about Alfie and Jamie and how Herr Niedermeyer had always suspected that the Dummkopf was stealing while the other diverted his attention. He was certain that the Dummkopf ought to know where Jamie Ibsen was because the two had been fast friends. He wanted to know if he could have the reward if they were brought in.

Alfie stayed in the alley until long after dark. It was only a short walk back to the churchyard, but now he was afraid. They were looking for the Dummkopf! And looking for Jamie!

From now on, Alfie knew he would have to be very careful.

Goebbels stammered as he faced Gestapo Chief Heinrich Himmler and Special Agent Alexander Hess.

"I did not tell him about the situation with Ibsen's family. He was too angry, Heinrich. You know how he can be."

"The official records show that Helen Ibsen died in prison. The Führer need not know anything but that. And as for the children, Officer Hess has good news for us today." He motioned to the round-faced plainclothes officer who tugged his earlobe thoughtfully. He looked more like a pleasant, balding shopkeeper than a Gestapo officer.

"We know the children are in Berlin," he said casually. Such momentous news, and he acted as though it were nothing.

"Berlin? *Where* in Berlin? With whom?" Goebbels asked incredulously. All this time, and the Ibsen children might have been walking past him in the street.

"Where? We do not know exactly." Hess shrugged.

"Really, Heinrich," Goebbels protested to Himmler. "This is not good news. The Führer is demanding action with the family of this man."

"Just listen." Himmler was cool, confident.

Hess began again. "We discovered them quite by accident. We had the lines of the American reporter Timmons tapped. Usually there is nothing of interest coming or going over that line, but there was a phone call. A young woman. The girl Lori, we are certain. She thanked Timmons for the broadcast. She said that she and her brother and the children of—" he checked his notepad—"Richard Kalner were all together. Here in Berlin. Timmons agreed to meet them. The man is a dolt. He cannot possibly grasp what it means to them." Hess broke into a slow, sleepy grin. He yawned as though bored. "We have men stationed at the place of rendezvous, near Brandenburg Gate. Timmons offered to pick them up in an automobile. Anyway, they do not know what this Timmons looks like. We detained him about an hour ago. I will take his place and meet them."

Goebbels wiped his thin face with a white handkerchief. This was great news—the clear hand of Providence! So at least part of the Ibsen family would be available for use to convince the recalcitrant pastor of his error. Goebbels hoped to have the broadcast arranged quite soon, after all.

The inside of the streetcar was illuminated by three lightbulbs in the ceiling. By this light, passengers could read the advertisements above the windows and the latest rules and regulations about who could ride and who could not. *NO JEWS ALLOWED* was stenciled in unnecessarily large letters above the driver and then again on the fare box.

With the rain outside, the car was crowded almost to capacity. Lucy took the only remaining place beside an old woman just behind the driver's seat. There were many Nazi uniforms on board, but the old Austrian woman next to Lucy still carried on a loud and animated conversation directed at the nervous driver.

"And so"—she gestured toward the sign about Jews—"you see, it is this sort of thing I am talking about!" She did not seem to notice when Lucy sat beside her and the car lurched ahead. "Look! Look at what they have posted all over my Vienna!" She clucked her tongue for the shame of it. "All my life I have lived in Grinzing, which as you know is just outside the city. And now I come to shop and I hardly recognize the shopkeepers anymore. Everyone is leaving, and can you blame them?"

The driver glanced nervously in the rearview mirror to see a dozen grim, stern faces beneath peaked Nazi caps looking back toward the old woman. The man was sweating. It would have been humorous had it not been so dangerous.

Lucy peered out the window at the darkening city in an attempt to ignore the indignant monologue against the Germans who stomped in and took over everything so that a native could not even find her way around anymore! Coins and currency were different! Even the names of places around Vienna had been changed to honor the conquerors! "It is a crime." The old woman's lower lip protruded defiantly, and Lucy felt sure she was purposefully speaking loud enough for everyone on the car to hear her.

The streetcar clacked past the Stadtpark and stopped. Uniformed passengers got off, but not before giving the old lady an icy stare. New German passengers got on, took their seats, then sat rigidly as she began her tirade against the government all over again. In spite of the cold air rushing in from the open door, the driver wiped beads of heavy perspiration from his forehead.

Lucy simply stared at the passing lights and sights of the city. Just ahead, across from the canal that wound through the park, loomed the enormous central railway terminal. Lucy's head turned with involuntary longing as they passed it. Somewhere at the end of the line was the freedom for an old woman to complain on a streetcar without fear! Between that magic place and this, however, stood uniforms and stern faces and rules and customs inspections that would take Lucy's survival money and pitch her into prison in the bargain. The thought of such a journey made her shudder more than the open defiance of the Austrian woman who blasted the Nazis with such disregard.

"And now you will see what I am talking about!" The old woman nudged Lucy and held up a ticket stub for everyone in the public car to see. "Look here!" She shook the stub at a round-bellied Wehrmacht officer who managed to retain a complacent, cow-eyed look of innocence. "You see what you and your Führer have done!" She held the ticket higher. "I bought this streetcar ticket to travel to Am Heumarkt! But I thought you renamed it Adolf Hitler Platz, and so I bought the ticket for Adolf Hitler Platz! Now he tells me that the place you renamed Adolf Hitler Platz is really much farther up the route, and so here I am!" Her sagging cheeks reddened with rage as she fixed her gaze on the innocent officer. "I have spent too much on this ticket! It may be only a few pfennigs to you, but it means a lot to an old woman!"

So that was what this was all about. As simple as that. She had paid fare for a place up the line and now would lose the unused portion of the ticket. Relief flooded several faces.

The Wehrmacht officer stood up, managed a smile, and clicked his heels politely as the car stopped at Am Heumarkt.

"A simple error," he said on behalf of the Reich. "The driver will no doubt refund the unused portion and then, perhaps, you will know that we Germans have come to make life better for our brothers and sisters in Austria, *ja*?" At that, he plucked the ticket stub from the old woman's fingers and presented it to the startled driver. "Refund the fare to Adolf Hitler Platz, if you please."

"*Danke! Danke!*" the old woman said. "So gracious, so polite, so just!" Two copper coins were promptly refunded, and the old woman limped down out of the streetcar.

As other passengers boarded and counted out their change and pulled their tickets from the roll, Lucy Strasburg conceived the answer to her dilemma.

"Wait!" she cried as the doors banged shut. "My stop! I'm getting off here, too!"

With an exasperated roll of his eyes, the driver opened the doors and let Lucy off to rush past the mumbling old woman. Just across a narrow bridge lay the train station—and, she hoped, the solution to her financial problems.

Haj Amin Husseini, exiled Grand Mufti of Jerusalem, defender of Islam and herald of jihad, advanced majestically to meet Adolf Hitler. Haj Amin was dressed in a flowing blue cape over an expensive white silk robe. His perfectly starched white tarboosh sat poised above his red-bearded face like a crown of state. Of the two men, Haj Amin looked more like the monarch of an Aryan nation than did the dark-haired, drably uniformed Hitler. Even so, Haj Amin was coming to beg favors of the German Führer, and both men knew the reality of the relationship.

Haj Amin touched his fingertips to his forehead, his lips, and his heart in a sweeping gesture of salaam. Hitler bowed in acknowledgment, then extended his hands in welcome. The Führer directed the Grand Mufti to a pair of formal chairs drawn up before a stone fireplace. Haj Amin's retainers had not been permitted to enter with him, and with a short wave of his hand, Hitler dismissed his own aides as well.

Haj Amin spoke first in excellent German. "Herr Hitler, how it pleases me to meet you at last. Your assistance to our struggle is such clear evidence of your far-seeing wisdom."

"And how is that struggle progressing?" inquired Hitler quietly, even though he already knew the answer.

"Well, extremely well! Of course you know my poor troops have neither the equipment nor the training to even compare with your legions, whom we strive to imitate. But with additional funds—"

Hitler interrupted. "It has come to my attention that the efforts in the north of Palestine have suffered some setbacks. Even some of our . . . advisors . . . to your cause have disappeared. Can you explain this?"

"It is the perfidious British," replied Haj Amin, bristling. "They say they will not tolerate these Jewish murderers, but they wink at this man Orde and his gang and commandos."

"So because of one man your campaign falters?" asked Hitler, fixing his gaze on Haj Amin's eyes.

The Mufti shifted uncomfortably in his chair. He had noticed that the Führer had not said "our campaign." "We have placed a price on his head. It is only a matter of time until—"

The Führer answered kindly, but his firmness admitted no further argument. "You are in error. No Jews, no British must be allowed to think that resistance is profitable, or even possible. They must be allowed no time to reflect on what one man can do."

"But how can we stop him immediately?"

"Isolate him. Have your envoy tell the British that the sole reason for the Arab riots is their wayward officer. Tell them that there can be no peace until he is removed, that there cannot even be peace talks until he is out of the way." The Führer's voice was patient, instructive.

Haj Amin blinked. "But we have used the peace-talk issue to prevent further Jewish immigration to Palestine."

"Exactly," Hitler confirmed, as if recognizing a bright pupil. "They have met one demand. Now is the precise time to escalate those demands. Tell them it is not enough."

"I see; I see," nodded Haj Amin. "And if they refuse to discuss the matter?"

"Promise them unending demonstrations, riots, and bloodshed, and then have your representative walk out of the room!"

"And will the British sacrifice one of their own, their best fighter?"

"My friend," said Hitler jovially, "you must study the lessons of the history of your own region more thoroughly. The British are in the precise spot to bring you his head on a platter, if you know how to ask for it."

Later that evening the Führer of the Third Reich and the Grand Mufti of Jerusalem appeared together publicly. They spoke of mutual admiration and cooperation in overcoming mutual problems. The Führer and the Grand Mufti posed for photographs together as Herr Hitler presented a personal token of friendship to Haj Amin. It was a bulletproof vest.

It had been a discouraging week for Otto. His notebook carefully hidden away, he had taken all the names and facts from John Murphy's broadcast with him to the offices of the secret police.

Claudia, the thick-trunked, surly secretary in his outer office, scowled at him reproachfully when he gave her two names to look up in the cross files.

Returning an hour later, she smiled at him and tossed the folders onto the *IN* basket. "These priests," she said. "Somebody twists an arm, and they howl they didn't mean to offend the Führer! Ach! They are neither one with us nor steadfast in what they are supposed to be. Not worth the bullet to kill them nor the food to feed them, eh?"

Without comment, Otto leafed through the records. Both men, painted so sympathetically by Murphy, had confessed the error of their ways and recanted their foolish stubbornness against the Reich. Blessed saints for the Nazi cause now, they were both being restored to their pulpits. No doubt they would soon be making public statements that would make the newsman look like a fool around the world.

Otto shuddered at what the Ministry of Propaganda could do with this. The people in England and America would have to choose their martyrs carefully. Many men would gladly praise the devil and go free than suffer even a small discomfort. Otto knew this to be true from personal experience. Tragically, it seemed to be the most self-righteous men who yielded first when proper pressure was applied. Somehow they convinced themselves that they could still serve God and the Reich at the same time. Claudia's cynicism about the clergy was correct. The only ones they fooled were themselves.

Three more from the original list had recanted by the end of the week. Two elderly priests had died within days of their imprisonment. This left three men unaccounted for, somewhere within the vast prison system of the police state.

On Wednesday morning Otto called the Berlin Gestapo headquarters with the rumor that two children matching the description of Karl Ibsen's son and daughter were reported in the Vienna area. Would a complete file be forwarded immediately in the event the two were captured? His fabrication worked. The file was sent by air. By noon a thick folder lay on Otto's desk.

> IBSEN, KARL HENRY. Doctor of Theology. Age 41 years. Married 1914 to KOENIG, HELEN IRENE—deceased, Ravensbrück, November 28, 1938.

The file provided pictures of the couple and their children, facts, and data going back to 1933. The information painted a portrait of integrity and courage. Otto read it throughout the afternoon. It was also a record of suffering and tragedy.

The wind blew hard again, shaking the radio antennas high atop the BBC in London. Murphy paced nervously, raising his eyes at the sound of the wind. Would the Vienna broadcast penetrate the weather closing in over Europe?

The performance was supposed to be recorded and rebroadcast to the States at a later time. If the American public was deprived of their weekly jazz ration, there was no telling what sort of backlash might come to the advertising sponsors. These European performances had made a smash hit back home. Billed as *D' Fat lady Trio in Ivory Palaces, Brought to you by Ivory Soap,* the official figures showed that sales of the floating soap had jumped by 50 percent since the tour began. No other jazz trio would do. Americans wanted the music straight from Europe's ivory palaces.

The American radio listeners were not the only ones praying for a clear connection to Vienna tonight. In the studio with Murphy sat Winston Churchill and the head of the British Secret Service. Anna, Elisa, and Theo lined one side of a long table opposite a small, mousy-looking telegrapher who had come with the intelligence chief.

The questions asked by Winston Churchill on his own radio broadcast were about to be answered, entirely in the syncopated rhythm of D' Fat Lady. These questions had been carefully formulated by members of the Foreign Office as well as British Intelligence, the plan conceived by Anna Lindheim and a certain piano student who preferred sending coded messages to practicing her scales.

The great recital was about to begin.

"He will be sending the signals entirely in the bass," Anna explained patiently to the telegrapher, who could not imagine that this system would work. No uncensored news had come out of Germany for years, and he did not believe that an American black man at the piano could break that barrier.

"I told you," he said dryly, "I am no musician. If it is in the bass or the basement or the attic, I still cannot tell one note from another. Just write down the little dots and dashes as you hear them, and I will translate the code for you."

"It will be recorded, Anna. If we miss anything, we can play it back," Murphy explained. "You can do this."

Elisa came along as a backup musician. She also had a notebook open. Provided Philbert could play the rhythm of short dots and sustained dashes as the German contact wrote them down, there seemed to be little chance of a foul-up. Of course, there was this matter of the weather. Now that Timmons had been arrested by the Gestapo in Berlin, it seemed more important than ever that this work.

The phone rang. Murphy snatched it from its cradle. His face reflected relief, then delight. "The connection is through!"

Moments later, recording technicians in a glass booth in another part of the building began to record the thunderous applause that greeted the trio as they stepped onto the stage of Ronacher's in Vienna. The technicians did not know how important their efforts would be tonight. Like the telegrapher, the rest of the world would hear the music they had come to recognize and love. But Anna heard the first staccato message of the piano even before the applause died away.

"Four dots. Break. Two dots." The telegrapher read over her shoulder. "That spells *Hi*," said the man sourly.

As the tinkling keys continued in the background, D' Fat Lady greeted her listeners. "Well, hello-o-o-o-, my babies! And hello-o-o-o, Charlie and Louie, wherever you is! D' Fat Lady gonna sing ever' song fo' you tonight!"

More applause. Anna, as well as Elisa, could hear the tuneless background music of the piano continue to tap out a constant, unwavering code. No matter that the notes might be played from one octave to another; it was there! Unmistakable. Half note. Half note. Quarter note. Break. Half note. Half note. Half note. Break.

"From the ivory palaces of Vienna, Ivory soap presents . . ."

Quarter. Half. Half. Quarter. Break. Quarter. Half. Quarter . . .

"And here's a song that'll tell the folks back home jest what we is a feelin' . . ." At that, the full, rich voice of Delpha Mae broke into the familiar tune of "Ain't Misbehavin'."

The piano never missed a beat. Half. Half. Break. Quarter. Half . . . The date *March 15* was spelled out. And then the name *Prague*. Followed by *Invasion*.

Churchill had asked what had been gained by the sacrifice of Czechoslovakia. The answer that was relayed from German High Command: S-C-O-R-N.

And was this destruction of the one central European haven for minorities a blessing or a curse?

C-U-R-S-E.

Could peace, goodwill, and confidence be built upon submission to wrongdoing backed by Nazi force?

N-O. Y-O-U M-U-S-T F-I-G-H-T O-R D-I-E.

And so the messages came, clearly more troubling than any that had come out of the darkness of the Reich until now. Prague would fall on March 15. All the sacrifice of Munich meant nothing. More suffering was yet to come. Hitler intended war. No matter what he said publicly, there was always one more reason for him to march forward, one more manufactured injustice that he would right with his iron fist.

"Puttin' on the Ritz" mentioned other players in the drama whom Churchill had not named in his broadcast. H-A-J A-M-I-N . P-A-L-E-S-T-I-N-E A-T-T-A-C-K.

How far was far enough for the Führer? After Prague, what would come upon the world? Then Poland. The excuse would be Danzig. Then Russia. Then France. Belgium. Holland.

A-L-L W-O-R-L-D.

Twenty minutes of doom was passed through the light, joyful music of D' Fat Lady. In between every telegraphed announcement of Nazi intentions of conquest and terror, the audience applauded. The message was clearly in the air, filling their heads, but nobody heard it!

At last the name of Karl Ibsen was tapped out in the sweet melody of "Taking a Chance on Love." Before the song was finished, the pen had fallen from Anna's hand. She leaned her head on Theo's shoulder and cried as word of her sister's death in prison reached her for the first time.

Tiny drops of wax on the floor. Jacob picked at them absently while they listened to the syncopated rhythm of D' Fat Lady Trio over the radio in Vienna.

He could not catch the strange lyrics, but the beat made him tap his toe and think of England and America and child-transport ships leaving Danzig for freedom in England.

Lori had been strangely preoccupied all day long. She seemed not to hear the music. Perhaps she was still considering making a phone call to that reporter.

He dug his thumb into the wax, scraping it off the floor. *Candle wax?* Jacob looked toward Lori, studying her profile. Her eyes were downcast, her mouth in a tight line. She had not looked him in the eyes all day. *Why?* "There is candle wax on the floor," he blurted out.

She jerked her head up. A moment of fear and guilt crossed her face before she mastered it. Yes, it was guilt. No use trying to pretend. "So?"

"What did you do?" He sprang to his feet and looked at the desktop. *Drops of wax.* And then at the dial of the telephone. *One tiny drip.*

In a flash Jacob knew: She had gotten up and come down here in the night. She had found the number and called. For a moment he wanted to grab her and shake her. Instead he towered over her. Why did she not look at him?

"Tell me," he said in a quiet voice as the music played in the background and Mark and Jamie gawked at them without understanding any of it.

"All right!" she replied defiantly. She jerked her face up. "I called. So what? I called, and the Gestapo did not come! Jamie and I are going to meet the reporter at the Brandenburg Gate. Come if you want. Or don't come. But you are not telling us what to do anymore!"

Jacob stepped back from her. His arms hung limp with fear and resignation. "There is not one newsman in the whole Reich who does not have a tapped telephone. If you go to meet this man, you condemn yourself . . . Jamie . . . and your parents to defeat—maybe death."

The look on her face was adamant. She knew he would say these things. But the plan was all worked out. She was going, and he would not stop her!

D' Fat Lady crooned something gentle—an American love song, Jacob supposed, but it was lost on the listeners of New Church. He was certain that if she left, it would be the end of her. He would never see her again. Pastor Ibsen would end up leading a Nazi congregation in the praises of the holy Führer.

"When are you leaving?" he asked.

Momentary surprise flashed in her eyes. She had not expected him to give in so easily. "Tonight."

Jacob glanced at Jamie, her accomplice by birth. Jamie shrugged as if to indicate he had no choice.

"What time do you meet this fellow?"

"Midnight."

"Very cloak and dagger, Lori. Commendable. You think the police won't notice a young woman getting into a man's car at the Brandenburg Gate at midnight?"

"Well, I didn't want to say where we were! If you and Mark don't want to go, then fine. I respect that. I did not give away our hiding place."

Jacob sighed with exasperation. He glanced around the room and fixed his gaze on the closet. The lock was conveniently on the outside.

"Jamie!" Jacob ordered. "I am the leader. You are not going."

Jamie nodded agreeably. He never wanted to cross Jacob. "Sure," he said, too quickly.

Lori shot him a venomous look. "Traitor!"

"No." Jacob reached down and grasped her wrist. "He is smart. And so am I." He yanked her to her feet and in one quick motion threw her into the closet and locked the door.

She screamed at him and pounded her fists against it. "You can't! Let me out! Let me go! I will call him again!"

Jacob jerked the phone line out of the wall. He crossed his arms and stared at the door. "You can come out for breakfast. We have been through too much, Lori Ibsen, for me to let you get hurt now. Whether you like it or not, I am your father and your brother for the time being."

"I hate you!" she screamed. "Let me out!" The shouts dissolved into tears.

Jamie smiled at Jacob. "A smart move. Papa would have done the same."

"The apple does not fall far from the tree," Officer Hess remarked to the commandant of Nameless camp. He brushed his finger across the pictures of Lori and Jamie Ibsen and then touched the picture of their father. "They look very much like him; don't you think?"

The commandant smiled sourly. "In such a place as this, one's appearance changes drastically."

"As should one's state of mind. But you have not been able to alter the state of mind of this pastor," remarked Hess in an accusing tone. "So, the Führer has asked me to take charge of the situation here as well."

"I thought you were on the job of finding the little apples from Karl Ibsen's tree." The commandant took offense at the accusation of failure in Hess' words. Hess had not yet met Ibsen and so did not know what he was up against. "Found them yet, have you?"

"It is a matter of time. But we don't need them. Not now. Ibsen is just a man like any other. Soon he will be marching in step, singing in tune."

"So you think?" The commandant scratched his scabby head. "He is your patient, Herr Doktor."

Karl's arm and two of his fingers were broken. He wrapped them the best he could in strips of cloth torn from his blanket. Still, the ache was unending. It kept his mind focused. *Fear not them which kill the body. Fear not them which kill."*

Again and again he repeated those words. When the new SS officer strode into his cell, Karl was not afraid of what he might do to him. He would welcome an end to this. The torture had not ended since the hour Nels Ritter had left him.

Officer Alexander Hess played the role of one sympathetic to Karl's situation. He had a chair brought in, and he sat across from Karl and talked gently to him at first. "All right, you have made your point. But you cannot win, Pastor Ibsen." The round, shop-clerk face seemed sad. "Look at you! I was just looking at your picture. You and your wife, Helen." He paused while the knife found its mark. "And your children. Lori and Jamie. Beautiful children. They haven't changed. Only taller."

Haven't changed? How did this man know? Had he seen them? talked to them? The knife twisted. Karl dared not answer.

Hess continued. "They miss you, of course. They cannot understand why their own father has abandoned them."

Silence. An ache filled Karl's heart, a pain much greater than the broken bones.

Hess extended the photograph of the family. Helen, sitting in the sunlight, her arm linked with his! And Lori and Jamie hugging each other. Karl's hand lay on Jamie's shoulder—this same hand with the broken fingers. Karl could remember what it was like to touch the faces of his children.

He caressed them with his eyes instead. His throat tightened with emotion and longing for that moment, and he prayed that God would help him not show his longing to this new man. A miracle. Karl's eyes remained dry and his breath even.

Fear not them which kill the body . . . oh, God! They use love to try to kill my soul!

"Why don't you just admit your errors? Then all will be well again. You can see your children. Embrace them."

"I cannot embrace anyone," Karl said. "My arm is broken."

"Bones heal. Broken hearts do not. You are leaving your children as orphans. By your choice."

"The Lord . . . says . . . He will be father to the fatherless."

A flicker of anger flashed through the officer's eyes. "You have suffered here." He maintained his patience. "I am certain they have made it very hard for you."

Fear not them which kill the body.

The officer continued. "But are you willing for Lori and Jamie to suffer—maybe to die—for the stubbornness of their father?"

Could words so cruel be spoken in such a gentle voice? Such a question should have been asked with a chorus of shrieking demons. If Karl listened, he could hear the wailing of hell behind that question.

An answer, Lord! An answer! Fear not! Fear not them which kill the body, but rather fear him which is able to destroy both body and soul in hell!

Karl closed his eyes and listened to the answer in his heart. He looked up at Hess, who sat smiling. "My children are both saved."

"But they are not safe."

"They are safe."

"They are in the hands of men who may use them as weapons against your stubbornness. Are you willing—"

Karl jerked his head up. He had heard the Voice tell him what he must ask. "You say my children have grown?" He smiled.

"Life in the Hitler Youth is very good. Good food, exercise, and . . . they are well. For now."

"May I see photographs of them?" Karl asked. He saw surprise cross the officer's face.

"Photographs?" The officer pointed at the picture of the family. "There you have—"

"I want to see how they have grown."

"Well, I . . . that is, we—"

Karl smiled. "You cannot provide me with photographs because you do not have my children. No, Lori and Jamie are not in your web."

"You will see—"

"My children are saved," he said again. Then he closed his eyes and did not hear the rest. He listened to the sweet whispers and was unchanged. Unmoved. Unafraid.

The din inside the vast railway terminal was deafening. Voices, hissing train engines, and loudspeakers emitted an echoing roar.

The ticket lines were all long. From the bits of conversation gleaned from around her, Lucy guessed that nearly everyone here was trying to get home for the holidays.

The queue inched slowly forward. It was thirty minutes before Lucy finally found herself face-to-face with a ticket clerk.

She hesitated a moment too long with her question, and the man burst out impatiently, "Yes? Well? Well?"

She carefully gauged how she might ask the question without rousing the man's curiosity. There was certainly something illegal in what she hoped to do. The trick was not getting caught.

"Yes. For Christmas, I want my brother to come to Vienna to visit me," she began.

"Yes? Well?" He wanted only details necessary to sell her the ticket so he could get on to the next customer.

"He will not come unless it is a round-trip ticket back to Bavaria."

"Round-trip, Bavaria . . . that would be Munich. The fare is—"

Lucy interrupted him. "What I need to know is this: If I convince him to stay on with me in Vienna, might I obtain a refund on the unused portion of his ticket?"

There was nothing to think about. "Certainly. Return the unused portion, and you will be refunded. Yes." He paused as he figured the fare. When he looked up through the wire of his cage, the beautiful blond woman had vanished.

Seven hundred marks. Lucy laid the bills out on the bed in neat piles of twenty mark notes. It was not the full one thousand that she had hoped to have, but it was enough, and much more than the limit she could legally take out of the country.

She patted the money with the joy of a child who had been saving a long time for something special. "Danzig!" she said aloud as she slipped the notes into a long brown envelope and then into her purse. A shudder of excitement and relief coursed through her.

On the radio in the front room, martial music blared as a prelude to some official Reich announcement. The people of the Reich and the people of France had just signed a mutual nonaggression treaty. Lucy paid no attention to the details. Soon she would be out of Germany, and she had found a better place to hide than France. "Danzig," she said again as she hurried out the door and made her way back to the bustling railway terminal.

The lines were longer, the clatter more resounding; the movement of people through the building seemed constant.

Lucy took care not to stand in the same line she had when she asked her question an hour before. She had too much at stake to risk the first man recognizing her.

The ticket clerk, an Austrian civil servant with a drooping mustache and a cap so old that the visor was cracked, smiled at her through the cage. The smile seemed to say that he had been around a long time and was not threatened by the German workers who had been brought in to replace so many.

"A long wait, eh? And how can I help you, Fräulein?"

"Danzig." Lucy pulled her envelope out and laid it on the counter.

The ticket seller looked down his nose at the envelope. "Danzig, *ja*. You are traveling alone?"

The blessed question filled Lucy with happiness as she answered it. "No—I mean, what is the fare?"

"How many tickets to Danzig, *bitte?*"

Lucy had forgotten the most important bit of information. "Well, they must be round-trip tickets. From here to Danzig and then back again to Vienna, if you please."

"And how many are traveling?" The man was not impatient. Travelers were often a bit confused about travel plans. But he could not tell her how much until she told him how many.

"How much for each passage, *bitte?*" she insisted. "I need to know if I have enough for all of us, you see."

That was a different matter—counting her pennies. Of course, there must be cash enough for each traveler, or someone would have to stay behind. "Round-trip. Vienna to Berlin to Danzig. Back the same route." He checked a printed sheet. "If you get a Polish travel visa, the cost is only sixty-five marks, Fräulein."

A Polish visa. Lucy had forgotten all about that. "Polish visa." She said the words carefully, as though she did not understand.

He answered patiently. "*Ja*. You must, if you enter Danzig overland through Poland, go to the Polish consulate and obtain a travel visa. That is the least expensive manner of travel."

Lucy did not care about least expensive. This was, after all, merely a banking transaction for her. She would put all her extra money into round-trip tickets. At the first stop, she would cash in the unused portion and convert it to ready cash.

"What is the other way?" she stammered too eagerly.

He seemed amused. He cocked a bushy eyebrow and leaned forward with advice. "Many people do not wish to be troubled with the Polish visa. Yes. I understand." He smiled, revealing tobacco-stained teeth that gave him the appearance of an old horse. "If you purchase a ticket directly to Danzig only, you may go in a sealed car across the Polish frontier and never have to go through Polish customs. And then, Fräulein, you do not need a visa."

"That sounds like a very good idea. How much?"

"One hundred marks," the old fellow said. "And will all want to travel together?"

The line behind Lucy was restless with the slow Austrian way of doing things. There were impatient murmurs as she counted out the bills. "Five round-trip tickets," she said, figuring that she could easily carry out the extra cash and never be questioned by the German authorities.

"You will be traveling when?"

Her smile faded. "When?"

"It is important to know when you will come to catch the train." His smile widened. "Otherwise you will miss it."

She exhaled nervously. "I . . . might I make the decision later? We have not all settled on the date yet." She looked toward the platforms as a train chugged slowly out from the train shed. For an instant she thought how easy it would be to buy her tickets and get on the train right now. But she had not packed. She had brought no clothes. No baggage.

The ticket seller stuck out his lower lip and gestured toward the number of his cage. "I will write out the tickets, Fräulein. And when you decide, make certain you come to my counter the day before. We will fill in the date, *ja*?"

She nodded gratefully and slipped the money to him as he filled out all the details on the tickets. Everything but the actual date and time. As he finished, the amusement in his eyes faded to a serious concern. "Good luck, Fräulein," he whispered. "This counter, remember. *Grüss Gott.*" The voice was so low that only Lucy could hear it above the noise of the terminal. Until this moment she had not guessed that others fleeing the Reich currency regulations might have tried the same method of concealing the funds.

Slipping the tickets into her handbag, she raised her hand in a half-hearted Heil. A question ran through her mind: *Is it safe?*

"This counter *only*, Fräulein," he said. "Remember." With that warning, he looked past her and called loudly, "Next!"

There was so much to do. Ten thousand homeless children were coming to England soon. Stacks of letters and applications piled up on every table at the Red Lion House, and even higher stacks cluttered the house of Anna and Theo.

"You would think we could have no time for grief," Elisa said to Anna.

Charles heard them talking in low, sad tones as he walked through the front room toward the stairs with Louis. The two boys sat on the landing just out of sight and listened. Things had been gloomy indeed since the broadcast of D' Fat Lady in Vienna. Charles and Louis had been ecstatic about their names being mentioned over the radio. They had run up to hug everyone when the adults came home. But Anna had only hugged them tightly, the way mothers hug when they do not want to cry but might do it anyway. And then she had really cried.

Louis put a finger to his lips to warn Charles not to make a sound. They might get to the bottom of this somber mood that had undermined all the excitement.

"We can't give up on Lori and Jamie, Mother," Elisa consoled.

"No. But the message said they were in hiding, being hunted as well. I was hoping they made it to the charity in Prague. But there has been no sign. And who knows what will become of Karl now that Helen is dead? We must pray that he does not give in to them, Elisa. He is . . . a man like your father. You know how deep the goodness goes. The kind of man that evil men envy and destroy." She paused. "I was just thinking about that family. All of you children playing in the backyard. You were more like a big sister to Lori than a cousin."

"I played with her like a little doll—and she was."

"Helen and I used to watch you both and imagine what it would be like to be grandmothers together, in Berlin, to take our babies for long strolls in the Tiergarten, to the zoo." Anna's voice broke. "I wanted to tell her you were expecting . . . she was the last of my family. Somehow having her gone makes me miss my mother and father as well."

"Not the last, Mother. We must think of Jamie and Lori and not give up hope. There was that message from Timmons in Berlin."

"Yes." Anna sounded stronger. Louis exhaled loudly with relief as she lightened her voice.

Elisa abruptly held a hand up to silence her mother. "Charles? Louis?" she called. "What are you up to?"

"Listening," Louis said honestly. And that was the end of the conversation.

Elisa and Anna returned to the forms and endless applications, all from mothers hoping to send their children far away to safety.

The evening gown was too tight. Lucy strained to hold in her stomach as Wolf tugged at the gaping zipper.

"You cannot go the concert in this," he said impatiently.

"I will wear the other one," she said. "The red one you like so well."

"You look like a prostitute in that!" he snapped. "The general is visiting from Berlin. The entire commission will be attending tonight. How would it look if I show up with a fat-bellied whore at my side?" He glared at her stomach, which did not show her pregnancy at all in every-day clothes. Only in the skin-tight evening dresses was her condition no-ticeable.

"Well then, I will keep my coat on." Lucy fought to keep the emotion from her voice. She had been looking forward to the concert of Christmas music at the Musikverein. It was the only occasion Wolf had invited her to for the holidays.

"You will not keep your coat on," he sneered, "because you are not going. You are too fat. Fat pregnant women belong at the Lebensborn. Generals expect their junior officers to be discreet about such matters. That is why the Lebensborn has been provided. I have not been discreet."

Lucy did not push the argument further. Better to let the matter drop before Wolf arrived at the conclusion that she should be confined at the Lebensborn immediately. Lately he had become more and more impatient and irritable with her.

"Then I am not going." She shrugged as though it did not matter. Slipping out of her dress, she pretended to look at herself in the mirror. She was, in fact, watching Wolf look at her. Out of the restrictive dress, Lucy looked no different than always. She hoped that Wolf noticed; that thoughts of sending her behind the walls of the Lebensborn would vanish as he appraised her. She turned to face him. "You know I do not dress to please your generals, Wolf," she chided. "And if you prefer me this way, then I simply will not dress at all."

The seductiveness of her tone melted his impatience with her. He grabbed her by the wrist and pulled her close. "No one else must be able to look at you." He kissed her.

She pushed him away and raised an eyebrow in surprise. "Who would look at a mother of the Reich?" she teased.

"Everyone looks at you. Don't pretend you don't know that." He held her wrist too tightly, and she did not struggle.

"Then maybe you should keep me pregnant from now on." She smiled.

"I intend to try."

"But tonight you have already succeeded and so you do not need to stay. You will be late," she warned.

He kissed her hard, angrily.

"Your general will not approve if you are late to the concert."

He pushed her away and stepped back, examining the soft, subtle roundness of her belly. "Too many Sachertortes," he remarked. "Put your dress on. You may go with me." He glanced at his watch. "Hurry.

We have a stop to make." He smiled again, as though he had some secret triumph he would not share with her.

"What should I wear? What would please you?"

"The red dress." He changed his mind just that quickly. "It is near Christmas. Red is a suitable color."

Wolf cradled a bottle of champagne in his arm. The bottle was wrapped in red cellophane and tied at the neck with a red bow. He placed it on the seat on his car between him and Lucy.

She supposed that the champagne was for some general or other, but she was wrong.

As they drove through the snowy streets of Vienna, Wolf explained. "You remember the task I have been given? To find the leak among the Gestapo staff? To find the one tipping off the Jews?"

Of course she remembered. Within the context of that conversation Wolf had spoken of ruthlessness and duty as one quality. She had heard a threat to herself on that night. "Have you found him?"

He jerked his head in reply. Lucy studied his profile as the lights of decorations on the city hall gleamed through the windshield of the car. The brilliant Christmas decorations of Vienna seemed an unreal contrast to the subject they spoke of. Lucy looked away as a streetcar loaded with Christmas shoppers rumbled past. The smoke of burning fires rose up from the open-air bazaar in the park in front of the Rathaus. Everywhere were uniforms. Nazi uniforms. All those in civilian clothes wore swastika armbands plainly visible on the arms of their coats. Every building was draped with enormous swastika flags illuminated by blinking lights. This was Austria's first Christmas under those flags. Somewhere in all this, Lucy imagined the man whom Wolf now pursued. Did the fellow browse through the stalls of the Christmas bazaars? Or was he off somewhere saving a Jew and sealing his own fate in the bargain?

Such thoughts made Lucy depressed. She did not smile and nod as usual when Wolf explained how he had managed to track down his culprit.

"A friend of mine—as a matter of fact, he is that fellow who managed to find your apartment for me." Wolf laughed. "You said it right. It pays to cultivate the Gestapo, especially if such cultivation leads to the arrest of a Gestapo traitor and a promotion for me." He patted the champagne bottle. "And so, just to be certain, we will drop in on him tonight. Bring him a gift of our gratitude. If there are Jews in the apartment, so much the better."

She looked at him stupidly. "But it is nearly Christmas."

"So? What has that got to do with anything, my soiled dove?"

He was right, of course. The season of the year had nothing to do with being ruthless. On the contrary, arrests had been stepped up during the holidays.

"It just seems strange to bring him a gift, and then—"

"We will not arrest him tonight," Wolf said irritably. "As a matter of fact, we must hurry so we are not late for the concert. There will be time enough. He will not expect it. No, I know this fellow. He will not see the handcuffs until they are on his wrists."

30
Social Call

On this block of once-elegant flats, even the glass of the streetlamps had been broken. Boarded windows made the place look like a neighborhood of ghosts as lights glimmered out from between the cracks. The worst had been done here to the Jews of Vienna. Those who remained clung tenaciously to the remnants of their lives.

Wolf's black car turned the corner onto a street less marred by Kristal Nacht. Here and there was evidence of what had been, but for the most part, the buildings appeared normal and unscathed.

It was easy to spot which home or shop was owned by a Jew. As Wolf slowed and pulled to the curb, Lucy looked with interest at the nailed-up shopwindow displaying a freshly painted advertisement:

MADAME SINGER,
CUSTOM-MADE CORSETS AND UNDERGARMENTS
IN THE LATEST PARIS FASHIONS
OPEN

Lucy had heard of the Jewish corset maker. Even the wives of Germany party bosses bought her undergarments. Lucy made note of the address.

To her surprise, Wolf parked at the curb in front of Madame Singer's shop. He set the brake and took out a silver hip flask. Without explanation, he took a deep swig of the strong-smelling stuff and washed his mouth with it. He opened the door and spit into the street.

"He must think we are a bit drunk," he cautioned, handing Lucy the flask. "Drink."

She sipped tentatively and grimaced. The liquor burned her throat and brought tears to her eyes. "Terrible."

"American whiskey." He snatched up the wrapped champagne. "Otto will not feel threatened by our dropping in if he thinks we have drunk enough to disregard our manners."

At that, he slipped out of the car and came around to open the door for Lucy. This sort of propriety had first attracted her to him. Unlike the peasant boys of her village, Wolf had seemed the very model of chivalry. She had not suspected that underneath the public Wolf a private one lurked—a Wolf who differed very much from her first impressions.

She took his arm, and he held her securely as they walked toward the entrance of the white stone apartment building across the street. His eyes turned upward to the lighted window of an apartment that looked down onto a small courtyard. Through the tan window shade, Lucy thought she saw movement, and a surge of fear coursed through her. Behind that shade Wolf believed there were Jews hiding—enemies of the Reich, Communists and Socialists, bent on the destruction of the German people. These were the types of criminals he spent his life pursuing, and now Lucy was part of the hunt.

"Remember," he warned as he opened the door of the lobby. "We have had a bit too much to drink. We just happened by. Smile, my fox, and the huntsman may have a reward for you tonight."

Lucy smiled and held tighter to Wolf's muscled arm as they walked across the black-and-white tiled floor of the lobby to the antique elevator cage. "Are they dangerous?" she whispered.

"Smile," he said again, and the whiskey on his breath reminded her of the charade.

If anyone in all the world had a little sister more stupid than Marlene, Peter could not imagine it.

He hurried to button his trousers as the knock sounded on the door a second time. His mother lay in bed with a headache. That left Marlene and Baby Willie only a twist of a doorknob from disaster.

"Wait!" Peter whispered harshly as he stumbled from the bathroom.

Too late. In an instant, Marlene threw open the door and stood gaping in dumb horror at an SS officer and a woman in a red dress and a fox fur.

Baby Willie squealed happily and crawled toward them as Karin emerged too late from the bedroom.

"Who are you?" The officer's words slurred slightly as he peered at

Marlene and then into the flat. His smile faded. He squinted drunkenly at the number on the door. "Well, Lucy, have we got the right place?"

The woman did not reply. She looked at the baby on the floor and then at the frightened little girl in front of her. The smile remained frozen on the woman's face, but there was something in her eyes . . . *something* . . .

Peter composed himself. He forced himself not to look at the twin lightning bolts on the collar tabs of the black uniform. Pulling up his suspenders, he nudged Marlene out of the way.

"This is the apartment of my uncle," he said. "Otto Wattenbarger." *Confidence.* The terror they all felt must not be evident to this man.

"Otto! Yes!" The officer pushed past Peter into the apartment. "Then this is the right place. I thought so, Lucy. I told you this was it."

The woman hesitated, looking embarrassed; then she entered as well. Peter could smell alcohol on their breath. He did not close the door but stood beside it as the officer stepped over Willie and leaned close to stare at the photograph of Otto beside the Führer.

"Yes! Here he is! I told you this was it!" Wolf held up the champagne bottle. "For Otto. Where is he?" He patted Peter on the shoulder, not waiting for an answer before he plunged on to another question. "And who are you?"

Karin stepped out of the bedroom and stooped to gather Willie protectively in her arms. "I am Otto's sister." She extended a hand. "Karin Ruger. These are my children. Otto did not tell us to expect company."

"We were just in the neighborhood. Came across this bottle of champagne, a fine vintage. A little something for Christmas." He glanced toward the woman, who was not looking at anyone. "Right, Lucy?"

As if on cue, the woman looked at Karin as though she were surprised by something. "Yes. A gift for your brother. He managed to help us acquire our flat, you see . . . and—" Her eyes seemed to lock on Baby Willie, whose red curls framed a round and brightly joyful face. At her look, the baby tucked his chin shyly and laid his head against his mother. His thumb went to his mouth in a gesture so innocent that the woman's look became tender and human. The expression seemed out of place in the red dress and fur and perfectly coiffed hair.

"Well, maybe we should wait for him." The SS officer headed for the sofa and sat down, then patted the place beside him for the woman.

"Our manners," the woman said. "Forgive us. Wolf . . . you have not made an introduction." She did not move to sit beside him.

The officer nudged back his peaked cap. "Right. I am Major Wolfgang von Fritschauer, at your service. And this is Fräulein Strasburg."

"Fräulein Lucy Strasburg," the woman added with a touch of embarrassment in her voice. "We were just on our way to a concert . . . and I . . . have wanted to meet Herr Wattenbarger to thank him. Are we disturbing . . . ?"

Of course they were disturbing everything and everyone except for the baby, who considered them with a coy interest as he slurped happily on his thumb. Karin shook herself into action. "Would you like coffee? My brother may be a while, he said. Business, you know." She was already moving toward the kitchen, gathering the still-gawking Marlene up and shoving her ahead. "Come help me, Marlene."

Peter closed the door. They were not leaving after all, these intruders. The Fräulein sat down and crossed her legs, which poked out from a slit in the dress. Her shoes were also red. The major helped her off with her coat and tossed it over the arm of the chair. His boots were tall and perfectly shined. Peter had seen boots like that, proud and brutal boots, kicking his father, kicking other men. Peter had not imagined ever getting within range of SS footgear with a smile on his face.

"My mother will prepare your coffee," he said, sitting stiffly in a chair opposite the couple.

"You speak with a Viennese accent," the officer said pleasantly. "Otto did not tell us he had relatives here."

Peter shrugged. How was he supposed to reply to that? Had the officer also noticed that Karin's accent was quite different from that of Otto, her supposed brother? "You are not from here." Peter turned the conversation back to the officer.

"Prussia. Northern Germany."

The fellow looked Prussian, Peter thought, hating him politely. The military bearing, close-cropped blond hair beneath the peaked cap, ice blue eyes peering with arrogant amusement from beneath the visor, straight Greek nose—all like the statue of a god come to life. Peter pulled himself into a straighter posture and nodded.

The woman spoke with the low accent of Bavaria, but she seemed the female counterpart to this Prussian Adonis. Smooth chiseled marble in a red dress, she was perfect as long as she did not open her mouth to speak.

But she did speak. Her broad peasant accent was not so lofty as that of the officer. "You did not tell us your name," she urged. That look appeared in her eyes again—human, almost pained.

She was more difficult to hate, but Peter managed. He knew what she was, sitting there in her red dress showing her perfect legs. The officer did not keep company with such a woman for her intellect. An ignorant Bavarian peasant, so low that the only way she could raise herself was to hold on to the coattails of the devil. An insane urge ran through his mind. He wanted to ask her if the apartment Uncle Otto had found for her was in a Seventh District brothel. The thought made him pale.

"You have a name?" she asked kindly, and Peter knew that she was not drunk like the officer.

"Peter," he replied, trying to avoid staring at her legs. It was hard to concentrate. She was looking right at him, the way his geography teacher had looked kindly at him when he got the answer right.

"Peter! Well, I have a brother at home named Peter also. And you look about the same age. How old are you?"

"Fifteen," Peter lied. He did not want to give her any more information. Why did she ask such cheerful questions? He was afraid she would ask him about school, and then what would he say?

"Do you go to school, Peter?"

Yes, he had gone to school until *they* had invaded Austria. Now schools were closed to him and Marlene, to all Jewish children. How he longed for school! "Yes. The new Hitler Jugend school in our district has just opened. I will go there after the holiday break."

She seemed surprised at his answer. "Oh," she said, and he felt confident that he had fooled her.

"You Austrian children are quite behind the children of Germany," the officer remarked, eyeing him critically. Did that perfect Greek nose smell a Jew nearby?

"Uncle Otto says it will not take me long to catch up. Who knows, maybe I will also be an SS major one day." The game gave Peter a dangerous thrill.

The officer's expression became momentarily thoughtful. "Such a thing would please your uncle, I am sure."

"My brother Peter is also in the Hitler Youth," the woman blurted out. "I have an older brother as well, in the Pottsdam garrison. Everyone is in the military, now days, *ja?*"

At her interruption the officer became instantly surly. He looked away as if her friendly attempt at conversation disgusted him. His look made Peter pity her.

"The Wehrmacht for some. But the SS for me," Peter said. "It is the motto, you know. '*Meine Ehre heisst Treue*. My honor is loyalty!'" Peter repeated the motto enthusiastically. He raised his arm. "Heil Hitler!" he said, as if it were "amen" to a prayer.

"Heil Hitler," repeated the officer with a sneer fixed on his face. He no longer looked drunk. "Your uncle has taught you well. No doubt *we* will have to catch up to *you* in the Hitler Jugend." He stood suddenly, leaving the bottle of champagne lying on the couch.

Karin, looking worn, brought the tray of coffee into the room. Marlene followed meekly behind, carrying Willie and not looking at anybody.

"You are leaving," Karin said. It was not a question. Peter hoped the unwelcome guests did not hear the relief he knew was inherent in the comment.

"Yes. We are late. Nearly late for the concert." The officer did not seem drunk at all now. Every movement was clipped and preoccupied. "Come, Lucy." He snapped his fingers as if the woman were a dog to follow after him. She rose, looked at the baby, and then at Karin and the coffee cups on the tray. "Your son is a very bright boy. I am sure he will do well in the Hitler Youth."

Karin smiled with genuine relief. "I do hope so. Thank you for coming. Come again when you can stay longer. I will tell Otto you waited for him."

"Heil Hitler," Peter said again in confident farewell, and everyone repeated the words except for Willie, whose thumb returned to his mouth.

Again and again the Wallich family replayed the encounter with the SS major and his woman. Beginning with Marlene's stupid mistake, they progressed through the first moments of their terror at the sight of lightning bolts and the fancy dress of the beautiful woman from Bavaria. Everyone remarked at Peter's remarkable composure as he fended off questions and fabricated a future career in the SS!

When they came to the end of the story, they all howled with laughter. Even Marlene laughed after sulking for a while, saying she could not help opening the door.

Hours later Otto came home, his cheeks red from the cold. He carried little gift-wrapped packages in the deep pockets of his trench coat. Laying them out on the coffee table, he said he should have gotten a tree, but they would not be here long enough for that, anyway.

Then he listened to the story of the champagne bottle. He frowned and stared at the red bow tied around the neck. He asked questions about their behavior, nodding in approval at Peter's replies.

"They did not suspect anything; I am certain," Peter said.

Otto drew a deep breath and sank down on the sofa to consider what he had heard. "The day after Christmas I am driving you to Czechoslovakia myself. You will have to make your own way from Moravia to Prague, then on to Danzig. You will be out of harm's way there." Again he stared at the champagne bottle. "You must accompany me to Mass. If we are being watched, it will be expected that my sister and her children go with me to Christmas Mass. Yes. They may be watching."

Later as everyone was sleeping, Otto gently shook Peter's shoulder and called him into his room.

"Listen," Otto whispered, "there is something you need to keep for me . . . and for your family." He opened his wallet and produced a pawn ticket for the Dorotheum. He gave it to Peter, then stuffed a handful of bills into an envelope. "If something should happen to me—"

"What do you mean?" Peter spoke too loud.

Otto put a finger to his lips to silence him. "Just *listen*, will you? Maybe it won't be necessary, but if . . . if I can't make it home . . . *this* is your ticket out of the Reich." Otto grasped his arm. "Take this to the Dorotheum. Pay off the loan."

"What is it?"

"Just pay off the loan, and bring the bundle back to your mother. She will know what to do."

Peter's drowsy expression changed to one of sadness as he looked down at the pawn ticket. "I . . . hope nothing happens because of Marlene being so stupid."

"That's enough," Otto sighed with relief. "Just a precaution. Now go back to bed."

The holiday concert was held in the gilded hall of the Musikverein. Lucy listened to the music with a dull ache inside her. Later, at the dinner in the gold-and-white hall of the Imperial Palace, she sat between a Russian and a Frenchman who talked around her. Did anyone notice that she hardly smiled?

The clear, bell-like voices of the Vienna Boys' Choir brought tears to her eyes. Red and green candles decorated the tables. The great Christmas tree evoked an awed murmur from the crowd when it was unveiled. But it did not seem at all like Christmas. She had difficulty playing the role of Wolf's carefree courtesan.

Wolf was not pleased with her as they drove away from the brightly lit palace. "You were surly tonight!" he growled after they passed the guards and he could be himself again.

"I learned surliness from an expert teacher."

He slapped her—not hard, just a startling backhand across her full red lips. "I will teach you," he said menacingly. "I should have left you home."

"You needed me to help you spy." She daubed a speck of blood from her lip and smiled. "Terrible criminals they are!"

She had never mocked him openly before. He took her words as a challenge. "You saw what they are!"

"Yes, I saw. A frightened woman and three children."

The simplistic response made Wolf laugh incredulously. "You couldn't see that they are Jews?" he cried. "Yes, they were afraid! And I knew the minute the girl looked at me that these are Jews. Probably rich ones. I knew we had them before we even went into the apartment!"

Lucy had also known and had pitied the little family and longed to ask them not to hate her for what was about to come upon them. *It is not me! There is nothing I can do about it! I am just along for the ride!* She wanted to get to know the boy named Peter, who had looked at her with such polite scorn. He was a Jew; she was the mistress of a Nazi. Both were prisoners.

"They weren't Jews," Lucy argued. "I don't think they are Jews or smugglers or any such thing! Not black marketeers or . . . or anything like that. I believe them. This Gestapo man has his sister visiting for the holidays and—" She paused for effect. "Really, Wolf, I would be careful until you are certain. You might arrest the sister of a Gestapo agent, and then he would find a way to take back our apartment."

At the streetlamp Wolf gave her a withering look. He clenched and unclenched his fingers around the steering wheel. Had she succeeded in planting a doubt? "I have told you before to keep your mouth shut, you Bavarian slut! You chatted with that boy like he is an old neighbor in your village, and now you tell me maybe they are not Jews."

"I'm simply saying you should check the story. Have them watched for a day or so." She pouted, staring out the window. "I just think you should be careful. How would it look on your record if you arrested the family of a Gestapo agent after coming drunkenly to their door and imagining you smelled Jews inside?"

Wolf pressed hard on the accelerator to show Lucy his displeasure at her. He had not been drunk earlier, but now he definitely felt the endless rounds of schnapps and wine. Her words made him doubt, and he did not like to doubt what he had been so certain of only a few hours before.

"They are Jews. Otto is no doubt taking bribes to protect them. He should go to prison right along with them."

She mocked him again. "Oh? The Reich has prisons for babies, does it?"

He ignored her remark as they moved slowly toward the domed Burgtheatre, which was bathed in floodlights and draped in banners. He snapped his fingers. "Ha! He could be living with her, eh? She is an attractive sort. A racial charge would knock him into the clink and toss away the key."

Lucy snorted in scorn at such a wild thought. "Or, she might be his sister. In which case you will be court-martialed for slandering a loyal servant of the Reich."

"Why . . . why do you argue with me?" Her way of undermining his every idea made him furious and frustrated. "You are a fool to believe such a thing. The woman might pass for an Aryan. And the boy and the baby. But that girl—Jew was stamped on every feature."

Lucy shrugged as if the matter bored her. She grew more silent and sullen as he mumbled his theories as though they were fact enough to hang this Otto Wattenbarger fellow. Well, she had warned Wolf. Was it her fault if he did not listen? Maybe he would be the one arrested and then she could walk away from Vienna a free woman. She had not seen criminals in the flat—just a woman with weary, fearful eyes. Everyone had eyes like that in Vienna. "And so what if they are Jews?" Lucy regretted saying the words even as she blurted them out.

Wolf roared the question back at her. "If they are Jews . . . if they are not his family, as they claim, then a high-ranking party member is taking bribes to help rich Jews! Personally profiteering—and who knows what else he might do for money!" He glanced at her with all the disdain he could muster. "In a few days I will have your proof! Everything I shall need to send Wattenbarger where he belongs. You will see. Irrefutable . . . Jews in his apartment!" His cold blue eyes glinted steel and ordered her to be silent. Her involvement in the matter was finished.

The message came by early post to Murphy. He read it without surprise and passed it across the lunch table to Theo and Chaim Weizmann, head of the Zionist movement. The two had just been extolling the effectiveness of Captain Orde's campaign against the Arab gangs in Palestine. Orde and his training manual were the last, best hope for members of the Yishuv to withstand the pressures of politics and terrorism combined.

Re: The most dangerous man in Palestine

Dear Murphy,

I am disturbed to hear there are rumblings of discontent in several branches of the government with regard to the tremendous successes of our Captain Orde. No doubt those news dispatches he has written with anonymous pen were not in the least exaggerated. If anything, he has concealed most of his accomplishments beneath the dry jargon of a journalist. The truth is, however, that neither the Nazis nor the Arabs like our friend in the least! Messages have been sent—stern messages—that he must be taken out of the picture in the Mandate, or there will be no peace conference in London next month. The Arab Higher Committee has vowed that they "will not attend as long as Great Britain is supplying favor, arms, and ruthless officers like this Captain Orde to aggress against our peace-loving people!"

Thus spake the leaders of assassins, cutthroats, and butchers who write history with their own particular twist. They further insist that this Captain Orde is not a captain at all, but a full general incognito.

The last is a compliment, but believe me, no one within our government or the army is smiling or in any way pleased. Sam Orde is in trouble with the High Command. He has done too excellent a job. His results speak for themselves. There is talk that he may be posted back to England and given a desk job out of harm's way. A tragedy, although it may save him from assassination by the Arabs.

You may be losing a great correspondent in Jerusalem; England is punishing a loyal servant for offending those who would murder British subjects in their beds, and a great victory may be won for the Mufti. It reeks of appeasement once again. . . .

There was much more to the letter, but that was the meat of it. Theo placed the paper almost reverently on the table. "So the rumors are true."

"If we were a nation, Samuel Orde would be the head of the War Department. And no one would ask if he was a Jew."

Theo smiled cynically. "Oh, they would ask. And they would challenge his right to be there doing his best." He had lost his appetite.

Chaim Weizmann nodded at the reports he had heard about Orde from the Jewish Agency. "A fellow so single-minded and dedicated makes people around him a little . . . ill at ease, I think. A few thousand years back in our history, we might have called him a prophet."

"And stoned him."

"Or called him a great general."

"And made him king."

"There is a fine line that a man must walk in his success," Weizmann finished.

"He reminds me a lot of my brother-in-law," Theo said.

"Ibsen? The German pastor?" Weizmann seemed surprised by the comparison. "He is a soldier?"

"Why not? A true man of God fights Darkness with prayer and good deeds. A soldier in a right cause fights Darkness by drawing his sword and putting an end to men who kill without conscience. All Darkness comes from the same source. And all truth comes from God."

"Then we really are fighting a holy war." Chaim laughed.

"At times I hear invisible swords clashing above my bed and behind me as I walk down the street." Theo smiled, too, but his eyes were serious. "This aim of the Muslim Council and Hitler to kill the Jews is pure evidence in the flesh that the real war is between Light and Darkness. And every living human serves one side or the other." He looked squarely at Murphy, who had been silent during this exchange. "Maybe if Orde is posted back to England, you should point at his enemies and tell him to rejoice. Frankly, we can savor the fact that Herr Hitler hates us. It makes this life difficult, certainly, to lose everything one worked for. But that is not the point. When the devil looks at Sam Orde and Karl Ibsen, he shakes in his boots because he sees men who have not given in."

"A worthy aim," Murphy remarked. "Churchill said it to Charles."

Weizmann raised his glass in a toast. "As the poet said:

Here's to unknown generals of light,
unsheathe their swords of truth and right!
With prayers and deed together fight,
and put the evil hosts to flight."

"To Samuel Orde," Murphy said.
"To Karl Ibsen," Theo added.
"And to the unknown soldiers."

31

Christmas Eve

Lucy could not help raising her eyes toward the window of Otto
Wattenbarger's apartment as she ducked into the courtyard of Madame
Singer's corset shop.

An old basket maker and a maker of votive candles shared the same
courtyard. They stood talking over their Dutch doors and looked up
when they saw Lucy. Both men smiled and nodded, hoping that she was
a customer come for last-minute shopping on Christmas Eve. They
seemed disappointed as she passed them, pausing instead before the
closed door of the old corset maker.

"She lives upstairs," called the candle man. "Ring the bell and she
will come."

At least they were not jealous of the business Frau Singer attracted.
Lucy pulled the red-and-green braided bell cord. Upstairs she could hear
the faint jingle of the bell.

The window opened a fraction. "Coming! Coming!" the woman
called down. Then the window shut tight. The two men began to talk to
each other again about the things they had sold at the bazaar in the
Rathaus Park and how the Germans had nearly cleaned Vienna out.
Things were better since the Nazis had come, but how was anyone to re-
stock now that the merchandise was sold and shipped back to "the Big
Brother"?

Lucy pulled the collar of her plain brown woolen coat up around her
ears as she waited. It was cold in the courtyard; an icy wind whistled
down the steep eaves of the building.

"Ring it again," laughed the basket maker, and at that moment the stately, refined figure of Frau Singer appeared in the doorway. "So sorry, my dear." The woman spoke in a soft Viennese accent. She stepped aside and let Lucy come in from the cold. "I did not mean to keep you waiting. The teakettle whistled, the phone rang, and at the same moment you came."

Lucy stamped the clinging snow onto the mat and then smiled and nodded as if it did not matter at all. She wondered what Wolf would say if he knew she had come here to a Jewish shop. "You are the corset maker?" Lucy asked, looking around.

"I am Madame Singer." The woman extended her hand. "My stocks are somewhat depleted—" She waved her hand around at the broken shelves of what had once been the finest corset shop in Vienna. "I have moved everything upstairs for safekeeping." The face was kind, softened by a fan of fine lines at the corner of each eye that pleated when she smiled and nodded. "It does not really matter. My ladies still know where I am."

Lucy tried not to stare at the obvious destruction in the room. "I have heard that you are the best at your craft."

The old woman laughed. "Painless corsets," she said, and Lucy knew that the woman did not blame her for what the other Germans had done to her beautiful shop. "Painless corsets cannot be bought off a shelf now, can they? They must be fitted and handmade. That is why I am still here, my dear." She took Lucy by the elbow and directed her to a steep flight of stairs leading to her living quarters. "What are you in need of, a pretty and well-proportioned girl like you? A brassiere? Something for a strapless evening gown?"

Lucy followed her, feeling an instant kinship with the woman. She was so much like the women of her village—without pretense, welcoming everyone readily.

"I am expecting," Lucy said bluntly, "and I would like to keep my figure as long as possible."

At the top of the stairs, sunlight made rainbows through the beveled windows of the old woman's main room. Silk negligees hung on racks beside the tea cart. Bolts of silk and cotton lined up in a row on the fat, friendly, blue chintz sofa. An old-fashioned treadle sewing machine stood center stage in front of a warmly hissing gas stove. Brassieres lay stacked in neat lines on top of the lace-covered dining table. It was whispered that Hermann Göring's wife bought her underthings here. She had been angry when she heard that rowdies under her husband's orders had demolished Madame Singer's shop.

The old woman pulled open Lucy's coat and appraised Lucy's figure an instant. "Off with the coat, if you please," she ordered. "Let's see what we've got to work with."

Lucy obeyed, not feeling at all self-conscious. She held her arms out to the side as Frau Singer circled her slowly.

"Very good," said the old woman. "You are long in the waist and so will carry the child well. How far along are you?"

"Nearly four months."

At this information, the thin penciled arch of the eyebrows rose in surprise. *"Gottenyu!"*

Yiddish, Lucy thought. *The first signal that the old woman really was a Jew.*

"You hide this very well naturally!"

"I need some time . . ." Lucy faltered, unable to explain why she could not simply wear maternity clothes and waddle about like other pregnant women.

"Yes? This is not a time for corsets, my dear. Soon enough you will simply blossom, and there will be no hiding of a thing like that."

"I will lose my job," she said, a half-truth. "You know how they are."

Frau Singer eyed her with a knowing look. She did not need to say any more. "Well then, I will do my best. You will have to wear plain skirts and jackets straight at the sides, thus—" She demonstrated. "Bring your skirts, and I will adjust the waistline for you." She smiled and the lines fanned out across her face. "It is like a magician. Sleight of hand, all in the angle. I once helped the mistress of a duke remain out of confinement for the full term. Everyone thought she had just put on weight. Too many pastries from Demel's, they said. And then, poof! She lost the weight and had a baby boy suddenly appear on her doorstop. Or so she said. Everyone knew the truth, but that is really the way it happened."

Madame Singer did not ask questions; Lucy was grateful for that. Pins in her mouth, the old woman measured and hummed pleasantly as she figured how much of this fabric and that she would use. "We will make adjustments as your body changes, my dear," she promised. Then she fixed tea, and the two women sat at the window and chatted as the afternoon sky grew dusky. "I will not offer you a pastry," Madame Singer remarked in a motherly tone. "That would be too cruel, and someone would accuse me of making my customers fat so that I could sell corsets."

Lucy paid a remarkably small amount and promised to return in three days to pay the rest and pick up the special corset. She left the shop feeling refreshed, as if she had just had her hair curled and her nails manicured. No wonder the wives of the Nazi officials still patronized the little shop.

The candle shop and the basket maker's shop were locked up tight when Lucy walked from the courtyard. She looked up at the lighted window where the doomed little family lived, unsuspecting of Wolf's plans for them. A cold blast of air swooped down from the gables, and the warmth Lucy felt blew instantly toward the Danube.

Standing on the corner in the freezing wind, she held tightly to the scarf around her hair. The streetcar trundled past, but she did not run toward the stop. Still she looked up at the window. A cat sat on the sill, placidly looking back at her.

She could not explain why, but she found herself rummaging through her handbag in search of blank note paper and a pen. Leaning against the streetlamp, she thought of the sweet baby sucking his thumb, the frightened face of the chubby little girl, the weary look of her lonely mother . . . and the anger that seethed just beneath the surface of the boy named Peter. "Heil Hitler, indeed," she muttered, shaking her head. She wrote the note, then darted across the street and into the building. Wrapping her scarf close around her face, she planned to pretend to be on the wrong floor if they happened to catch her.

The groaning metal cage of the elevator lifted her up. Her heart pounded. She was breaking the law; she could be executed for such a simple act. And yet, who would ever know?

It was Christmas after all. Lucy hoped that someone would do something nice for her if she were in such a fix.

She pushed the brake button, locking the elevator, then folded the note, ran to the apartment door, and shoved the paper under it.

Lucy was back out on the street again, waiting at the streetcar stop before her heart slowed to a normal rate. Only then did she shudder at the thought of what Wolf would do and say when he found that the rabbits had escaped from his snare.

She looked back toward the lighted window of the apartment. The cat still sat silently on the window ledge as if nothing unusual had happened at all.

The holidays had come to London, filling the streets with more music and lights and smiling faces than Charles and Louis had ever seen in all their short lives. Together they climbed the Victoria Memorial in front of Buckingham Palace; from this perch they watched the changing of the guard. Red coats and tall black shakos on the heads of the soldiers made them seem like nutcrackers come to life! The clop of horses' hooves against the cobbles of the street was better than the toy cavalry horses sent from Macy's by Mr. Trump!

It was a magic time. Charles could not remember Christmas as a time of real happiness. All their lives they had lived under a shadow of fear that made the singing of carols sound brave and defiant, but never joyful.

A shadow reached here as well, but it no longer threatened the boys. Charles saw the sadness cross Anna's face sometimes. He knew what she was thinking without being told . . . she was thinking of the children in the photograph on her piano. Lori and Jamie Ibsen. She was wondering about their Christmas—where they were, where their father was now.

Charles understood such sadness. When his own father had been in prison, his mother had carried such thoughts in her eyes as well.

With so many children coming to England, they had much to be happy about. But Christmas would be much better if these two could come, too. Lori and Jamie were lost somewhere. Anna smiled and said Merry Christmas, but Charles could see the worry in her eyes.

Jacob hoped the Gestapo had forgotten about the Ibsen family and New Church. He had somehow imagined that people drove past and pictured the building as deserted and condemned. The urgency of fleeing had been lost in the midst of planning for escape. There was so much to think about. Every plan must have a backup; every eventuality must be explored and thought out. He worked his troops with calisthenics until even Lori could climb the rope as quickly as Jamie or Mark.

She was angry with him now, of course. She believed that he had destroyed their one chance of getting out of Berlin without having to climb ropes or scale walls or run for miles. But today she was proven wrong.

All the gear was packed and ready for the escape, stowed away behind stacks of Communion plates in the cupboards behind the baptistery. Jamie and Mark were playing checkers on a homemade board in the choir loft. Lori was sulking in her father's study. Jacob was studying maps.

Then the chains on the doors of New Church began to rattle. A terrible groaning sound reached their ears; the wooden planks nailed across the entrance were being pried loose.

Mark and Jamie were first into the bellows. Jacob waited at the top of the stairs and prayed for Lori to come soon. She slid to the base of the stairs. Clutching her shoes in her hand, she half crawled, half stumbled up toward Jacob. He pulled her up, dragged her to the bellows and into their cocoon just as the entrance doors swung open with an explosive clang.

Then, far away, they heard the echoes of footsteps and voices resounding throughout the building.

"They said not to waste anything . . ."

"You take that side of the building. I'll inventory the offices and storage."

"Wilhelm, take a look at the pipe organ! *Mein Gott!* We should be able to pull it out and install it in that new ice-skating rink planned for the—"

"*Nein!* The Reichskulturbund has put their stamp on it for the new opera building. Such a fine instrument! What a waste it has been in this place."

They were taking inventory—finding out what was usable in New Church before they knocked down the walls. Lori swallowed hard and tried not to cry. It seemed like the autopsy of a loved one. She found herself trembling with sorrow rather than fear as the fellow with the harsh lowlander accent examined the massive organ. Then the unthinkable happened. He switched on the motor that powered the bellows. The wooden support above them began to move down. Jacob raised his hands and braced himself hard to hold it up. His face grimaced with the strain of it, then the agony as wood cut into his hands and finally broke into splinters at his resistance.

Lori could hear the clicking of the mechanism and the tapping of keys and pedals. A terrible wheezing sound groaned from the pipes as the right bellows worked to do the job of both. Dust filled the space. Lori pulled her collar up and squeezed her eyes shut tight.

Just as suddenly, the storm ended. The electric motor whined off. The clear voice of the attacker called to his comrades from the other side of the partition. "Someone will have to look at this. I think there is something wrong with the bellows."

Mark coughed. Not a big cough. A strangled, garbled cough. Jacob clamped a bloody palm over his mouth. He coughed again.

"Listen to that, will you?" called the workman. "The thing sounds like it is dying!"

"They'll go through it next month," someone shouted up. "Just take a photograph and describe what you see. You're no Bach, anyway!"

For three hours the workers combed the building. When they finally left, Jacob rushed down to see if their supplies were still intact. They were there, tagged and moved to a larger pile labeled *Miscellaneous*.

The boom of the wrecking ball against the stones of New Church seemed very near.

All day the Wallichs practiced the things Otto had taught them. When to bend the knee and cross oneself, how to clasp hands properly and kneel and stand and kneel again, the simple Christmas carols they had known before. Such songs were always being played this time of year by the Beidermeier bands on the street corners. Before the world had fallen apart, Peter had seen his mother pass by a cold group of shivering musicians and drop coins into the open empty case of a trumpet player. The songs were the best part of the complicated ritual of Otto's Holy Catholic Church.

"St. Stephan's," Otto had remarked cheerfully as he left them this morning. "We will hear the Vienna Boys' Choir. Don't be nervous. It is not so very different from the synagogue."

It was going to be quite different; Peter was certain of that. His mother and Marlene practiced the lessons of Gentile worship with some enjoyment. For Peter, the requirements of passing for a Gentile rankled him to the core. He hated it all. He often considered striking out for the border on his own and slipping through the Nazi patrols into Czechoslovakia.

Relieved when Otto finally set the date for their departure from Vienna, Peter only regretted that he must now play out this charade of Christmas in St. Stephan's. It was easier for him to raise his hand and say "Heil Hitler" to an SS man and his bimbo than to bow the knee to the Gentile God. He hated their Christ. He detested the sign of the cross and all it represented. Such things, he believed, had taken his father. The sky had shattered on Kristal Nacht, and there was no God, no heaven there when he looked up. He learned the catechism like the pages of a survival book he would discard once they crossed the border of the Reich.

Peter eyed his sister with disgust as she primped before a mirror. "Uncle Otto" had bought her a new dress to wear to Mass. Her stringy brown hair was plaited and pinned like snail shells over her ears. She looked too fat, as usual, as she batted her eyes at herself and rehearsed the curtsey she must perform to priest and plaster saint alike. But Peter kept his mouth clamped tight. To tell her what he thought would be to call down upon himself a storm of wails and sobs and then the wrath of his mother.

"Didn't Uncle Otto buy a pretty dress, Peter?" she simpered, not turning away from her reflection.

He grunted a reply and turned away. Needing some moment of pleasantness, he scooped up baby Willie, who had crawled beneath the coffee table to chew on something.

"What have you got now, little street sweeper?" Peter sank down on the sofa and pulled a gooey slip of paper from his tight fist.

Willie tried to put the paper back in his mouth and squealed an indignant protest when Peter wrenched it from him.

"What is it?" Karin looked up from her studies at the dining table.

"Nothing. Paper. He could choke."

Karin nodded, then sank back into concentration over the Mass book.

As Peter wadded up the paper to toss it at Marlene, one word caught his eye. *JEWS*. The ink was smeared a bit, and yet here was Peter's true identity shouting back at him. He unfolded the paper, careful not to let the dampness smear any more letters.

> *JEWS,*
> *YOU MUST LEAVE THIS FLAT IMMEDIATELY OR BE*
> *ARRESTED. YOU ARE DISCOVERED.* GRÜSS GOTT.
> *A FRIEND*

Peter stared hard at the words as the blood drained from his face. The baby reached out for the paper with sticky fingers.

"No!" Peter shouted. He was shouting at the note, but Willie thought the harshness was meant for him and puckered his face to cry.

"What now?" Karin asked. "Peter, really, he is just a—" Karin's words stuck in her throat. The look of stark terror on Peter's face passed to her. She rushed to take the note from her silent, frightened son.

She read the words once, unbelieving, then again, then a third time as realization of their peril filled her. "Oh, dear God! What are we to do? What?"

Peter sprang to his feet.

Marlene finally turned away from her reflection to gape at her panic-stricken mother and brother. "What has happened?" she cried. Real tears filled her brown cow eyes. She could cry at the drop of a hat; this seemed more like the drop of the sky.

"Get your things," Peter ordered, looking at the door. Were the Gestapo even now entering the building? Did they climb the stairs or ride the elevator?

"But . . . but . . . ," Marlene stuttered. "But . . ."

"What about Otto?" Karin took Willie and held him to silence his crying. The room filled with terror, an electric spark that flicked from one person to the other and back again.

"He is probably already arrested," Peter said, grimly evaluating everything in the room to decide what to take and where they could run—tonight, of all nights.

"What?" Marlene stamped her foot and screamed.

Peter turned on her angrily. "I'll tell you what! Those people you let

in! That's what! You stupid little brat! You've hung us all, and your precious Uncle Otto in the bargain!"

His words were too cruel for Karin to stand. She stepped between
them and ordered them to gather their things quickly. *Now!*

"But what about Otto? What about Christmas at St. Stephan's?"
Marlene whimpered.

"No Christmas." Peter rushed past her to throw his clothes into a
suitcase. "We are Jews again."

Ten minutes later the little family had managed to cram all their belongings into a small suitcase and a satchel.

"What about Otto?" Marlene asked again. "We should warn him
they are coming."

"He knows already," Peter said, wanting to strike her for her stupidity.

"But, Mother," Marlene whined, "he will wonder where we have
gone!"

"Your brother is right," Karin said. "It is no doubt too late."

They switched the lights off. Karin placed the rumpled note into her
pocket. They would dispose of it far away from here.

Marlene threw herself at her mother, grabbing her around the waist,
begging to leave some word for poor Uncle Otto who had been so kind.

"Shut up!" Peter slapped Marlene across the head. "We are going
outside! Out of here! Do you know what that means? Only Jews weep in
the streets of Vienna. Now shut up."

"Go wash your face," Karin instructed her daughter with a voice so
weary that it was barely audible.

Marlene suddenly fell silent, as if Peter's warning had finally turned
off the spigot of her hysteria. She hurried to the bathroom, closed the
door behind her, and switched on the light while the others waited in
impatient fear.

Marlene looked again at her own reflection—the sad brown eyes, the
perfect hair now mussed by Peter's slap. The face was more angry and defiant than heartbroken. Marlene raised the note she had stolen from her
mother's pocket. She read the pretty handwriting and then, so Otto would
know why they left, she tucked the note into the frame of the mirror.

"Hurry!" Peter called to her.

Marlene splashed water on her red face and smiled as she emerged.

There had been no time to formulate a plan, yet Peter and his mother
said the same name at the same instant: "Frau Singer!"

The corset maker's house was just across the street, a few quick paces
from Otto Wattenbarger's door. Where else could they go?

Karin hesitated, aware of the danger in which they might place the old woman.

"There is no place else," Peter whispered as he took his mother by the arm and decided the issue. "You take one suitcase and Marlene. *Go!* I will bring Willie and follow by a different route."

The plan evolved just that quickly. Karin and Marlene slipped out the back door of the building. Peter, lugging his bundled-up brother and a satchel full of baby things, left by the front door.

He stopped outside on the sidewalk and tugged Willie's cap down around his ears. The baby shuddered and looked surprised by the cold air against his cheeks. Peter dawdled a moment longer, glancing nonchalantly along the shadowed facades of the buildings for some sign of a watcher. He saw no one, and he hoped that his mother and sister were not being trailed as they left the alley.

For just a moment, he considered walking directly across the street and into Frau Singer's shop. The green car of an Austrian Schupo passed by, and Peter thought better of it.

He tried to look lighthearted. *Big brother taking his baby brother out for a stroll to look at the Christmas lights of Vienna.*

"It is cold; isn't it, Willie?" Peter remarked, and the words rose up in frosty puffs as he walked carefully over the icy sidewalk.

As if in agreement, Willie tucked his head against the warmth of Peter's coat and gazed in wide-eyed wonder at the sights and sounds of the street. It had been so long since Willie had been out, Peter wondered if he even remembered the outside.

Peter talked constantly to Willie, indicating to this shop and that building as if the infant could somehow comprehend Vienna. The baby tried to suck his thumb through his mitten and got a mouthful of coarse wool for the effort. Only then did he begin to fuss. Peter tugged off the tiny mitten and let Willie have the precious thumb as they rounded the corner onto the broad Ringstrasse.

A brass band on the street corner played Christmas carols. Lights shimmered everywhere. In the windows of a thousand apartments candles were lit on the Christmas trees.

It was beautiful, but Peter was not part of it. He could not think of the beauty, only the danger he felt pressing at his back, threatening baby Willie—perhaps snuffing out their lives as easily as the candles on these trees would be extinguished. Stronger than any desire he had ever felt, Peter wanted to protect Willie from such a thing.

Peter stopped as a streetcar rumbled by on shiny wet tracks. He put down the satchel and shifted Willie's weight, kissing him on his ruddy cheek. Willie smiled at him without ever taking the thumb from his mouth. The baby did not know, could not realize, the desperation and love behind that kiss. Peter looked back to see if anyone followed them.

Beyond the enormous public buildings of the Ringstrasse, Peter could make out the spires of the churches of Vienna. Distant church bells began to clang joyfully, announcing the first services of Christmas Eve. Peter hefted the satchel again and hurried through the last-minute shoppers as he made his way back toward Frau Singer's shop. *So much for the Mass book. So much for Marlene's Christmas dress and her dream of being one of them!*

He had walked far enough. If they were being trailed, Peter had not spotted their pursuers. He exhaled a long, relieved breath and turned down the first side street. The noise of traffic at his back, he walked faster, in a hurry to be inside, to see if his mother and Marlene had made it safely to Frau Singer's flat.

There were churches somewhere, Lori knew, where families stood side by side in the pews and sang Christmas songs without fear of who might be watching or listening. Echoes of her own memories played in her mind as the shadows of evening dissolved into the darkness of deserted New Church.

No lights shone this year—no garlands, no manger scene or clumsy church pageant. No choir sang songs of praise and joy. Only four small voices whispered the soft melody of "Silent Night."

In memory of Christmas past, each of them had chosen something small from New Church to carry away. They wrapped their own gifts and laid them on the dusty altar. Lori read the Christmas story, and each of them prayed for their mothers and fathers and all the others who were not at New Church tonight.

The service completed, they opened their gifts. Jamie had chosen his father's silver filigreed letter opener, the one Pastor Karl had brought home from a pilgrimage to Jerusalem ten years before. Jamie held it up in the gloom. A faint glimmer of light struck its daggerlike blade. Jamie had always admired it, he explained, but Papa had never let him touch it. His prayer was that by next Christmas he could give it back to his father.

Mark had searched the church from top to bottom for something— anything—that might make a present for himself. He came across a packet of twelve yellow pencils and a box of clean white stationery with envelopes. It seemed an elegant gift to give himself from New Church.

Lori found her father's hidden Bible, the one that remained whole with both Old and New Testaments intact, even after the huge bonfires in which every vestige of the Jewish Scriptures had been taken from the churches and burned. As Papa had explained, the Old Testament held all the prophecies about the coming of Christ. Without them, the story was only half told, and told incorrectly at that. Lori was uncertain if any complete Bibles remained in Nazi Germany. But this last one she would take with her so she could read the words in her own language.

Jacob took the red velvet altar cloth, the one with the embroidered gold letters on it: *His Faithfulness Will Be Your Shield and Rampart.* Jacob did not say—tonight, especially—that he felt the need of a shield and rampart, even though that was the reason he had removed the cloth and folded it carefully. He said he liked the color of the velvet and he could not think of anything else to take. A nice memento, he explained gruffly. He would not allow any sentimentality to creep into his voice, although he was as homesick and heartsick as the others.

They sang one more carol, then sat in silence on the floor in front of the altar. Images of shining lights and roasted turkeys and Christmas trees played in each mind.

"Well," Lori said feebly. "Merry Christmas, then."

Jacob cleared his throat too loudly, the sort of sound that announced he had something to say. "One more present." He reached out for her hand and laid a small, oval, paper-wrapped something in her palm.

"But we weren't supposed to—"

"This is for you to use here." Jacob sounded strangely shy, like a little boy—maybe even hopeful that she would not throw the thing back in his face.

"Here? But we are leaving tonight."

"Well, I have been so . . . strict . . . difficult about certain things," he stammered. "Open it."

She held it up to her cheek. A faint floral smell escaped the wrapping. She tore open the paper and felt the smooth, round surface of a new cake of soap. Not just any soap, but the guest soap her mother had kept in the basement by the bathroom sink at home.

"Mama's soap!" she cried with delight. "But how . . . ?"

Jacob shrugged. She did not see the gesture of embarrassment. "I remembered it. From when I visited."

Jamie piped up. "He told me to bring it back."

"Oh! It is . . . wonderful!" She inhaled its fragrance. It seemed so long since she had smelled anything so wonderful. "I will take it with me and . . . find a bathtub!"

Jacob cleared his throat again. "Well I . . . that is . . . we thought maybe since it is our last night . . . maybe you might want a real bath now."

She laughed. A bath! After six weeks? Could there be a better gift? "But where?"

"We filled the baptistery for you," Mark said enthusiastically.

"It has been heating all day long," Jacob added in a matter-of-fact tone. "We will stand guard out here. The curtain is closed, so . . ."

The baptistery. It almost seemed a sacrilege. Lori hesitated as she wondered what Papa would say. "But in church—"

"We got the idea from Grandfather Kalner," Mark explained helpfully. "In a Jewish church, you see, that is where everyone used to take a bath. I can't remember the name, but Grandfather swore it was true."

"Well then—" Holding the sweet-smelling bar up to her nose, Lori hurried past the altar and through the door that led to the baptistery. She climbed the steps, not minding the profoundness of the dark.

The air was warm and steamy from the water the boys had prepared. This tank was something Papa had made as a special project for the church. *Heated water.* It was a wonder and a marvel—and a necessity, since old Herr Gruber had gotten baptized one Sunday and died of pneumonia the next from the shock of the cold water. Papa had not wanted to send his flock to heaven quite as soon as that.

Lori laid her clothes aside and brushed her toe across the warm liquid. She heard herself sigh with pleasure as she stepped down into the tank and let six weeks of bone-cold discomfort melt away. Beyond the curtain where the boys waited for her, she heard them laugh with delight at her pleasure.

She untied her thick braid and let her hair float on the water. Clutching the soap like a treasure, she lathered herself from head to foot. She held her breath and slipped her head under the water, surfacing only when her lungs began to sting.

"Why didn't we think of this sooner?" she called.

Did they hear her? It did not matter. This was nearly heaven, one memory she would have with her from New Church every time she took a hot bath!

And then, through the curtain, she heard them singing. They were caroling softly to her, apologizing in their own shy way for six weeks of harassment.

It was hard to remain unforgiving while floating in the scented luxury of a warm, soapy baptistery.

"Thank you," Lori muttered into the water. "I love you all."

32
Flight

The drive north through Palestine toward Hanita was long and dangerous. Sandwiched between armored transports, Captain Samuel Orde was grateful for the protection of the convoy. His vehicle was not government issue; Orde's enemies within the politics of the British military had seen to that. He was using transportation provided by the scrounging efforts of Larry Havas and maintained in what was wryly referred to as "operational order" by Zach Zabinski.

The car, of uncertain parentage, may not have had one original part left on it, but as Zabinski said, "It runs more than it doesn't." Orde was returning from an unsuccessful attempt to get his Special Night Squad supplied with more modern weapons, including explosives.

"Can't be done," he was told. "Out of the question." The belligerent Jews must not be given the means to take action against the Arabs except in strictest self-defense.

It did not matter that the Jihad Moquades, the Holy Strugglers, were provided with German-made weapons, or that they recruited mercenaries from nearly every Islamic nation in the Middle East. It did not matter that they were promised ten pounds a month if they lived, and instant admittance to Paradise if they died battling the hated Jews and the infidel Christian Britishers. What mattered was that British policy required nothing to be done to antagonize the Arabs any further. Offensive weapons for Jews? Unthinkable!

Orde was disappointed, but not surprised. His continued appeals for more equipment and official British sanction for his squads was partly a ploy. Orde reasoned that if he stopped asking, the political wizards would begin to question why. He did not want them to examine the stores of captured weapons with which the Jewish troops trained and fought. The convoy sped up slightly, taking advantage of a slight downgrade.

Captain Orde tried at all times to understand the minds of his Arab terrorist opponents. True, they fired their weapons wildly at times, expending more cartridges in an aimless show of emotion than Orde's troops would go through in a month of training and combat combined. But the sermons of their leaders acted upon them like a drug, driving out fear of death and making them a formidable foe.

Orde's little car eventually parted company with the convoy as he turned off toward Hanita. He mulled over the other reason for this trip, hoping that it might prove more successful than the appeal for arms.

In a recent action against Arab infiltrators, one Holy Struggler, an Iraqi, had been wounded and left behind. Through gritted teeth he explained to an interrogator that he hated all the British and all the Jews. He was angry that he had only been wounded, because he had lost both his ten pounds a month and his place beside the prophet Mohammed.

The Iraqi prisoner had warned darkly that the battle was only beginning. New men were coming from the north, he promised, more every day. Soon the stinking British would all be rotting in hell beside the cursed Jews. Haj Amin Husseini and the great German leader Hitler had both promised that it would be so!

Orde had transported the talkative captive to the British Mandate's government offices in Jerusalem. Hopefully, he reasoned, somebody in charge would figure out that there was more than just Arab unrest at stake here, that the only possibility of retaining a democratic toehold in the Middle East was the establishment of a Jewish homeland.

Orde downshifted as he rounded a corner and rolled into an Arab village that sprawled across the abruptly narrowed road. Maybe, just maybe, after the information was reviewed, the British government would realize that it was already at war with Germany. Just as in Spain, Nazi Germany was flexing its muscles, challenging a ruling government while pulling the strings of manipulation from just barely behind the scenes.

Captain Orde downshifted again, then braked as an Arab boy leading a donkey loaded with a bundle of sticks walked directly into his path. Orde instinctively thumped the steering wheel as if to honk, but the horn was one piece of equipment that had never worked.

Having made his sudden entrance onto the road, the donkey apparently decided that it did not wish to make as quick an exit. It stood with its ears laid back in an elaborate show of sulky displeasure. The Arab boy first tried to pull the donkey into motion; when this failed, he went behind the animal and gave it a shove. It merely shifted its weight from one leg to the other, but continued standing in the middle of the narrow lane.

Orde scanned the road to see if it was possible to go around the balky creature, but one side was bordered with a low stone wall and the other blocked by a roadside produce stand. Orde hoped that the proprietor of the stand would assist the boy in moving the donkey, but the owner was nowhere in sight. No one else seemed to be around either.

Orde did not want to get out alone in the middle of an Arab village, but he had nearly decided that he was going to have to help when the beast at last moved. The boy took a stick from the bundle on the donkey's back and tapped it lightly on a hind leg. Both boy and pack animal moved rapidly out of the street. As he slowly accelerated, Orde watched the pair disappear from sight; from behind the houses, the boy stared back at him. He had not given Orde a single glance during the struggle in the road.

Why is he watching me? Orde wondered. *And why did the boy suddenly remember the secret to making this particular donkey move after several minutes of struggle? It is almost as if he received a signal that it was time to move on.*

A tiny pebble of suspicion dropped into the pool of Orde's mind, and its ripples spread out through his every fiber. Orde's nerves and the hair on the back of his neck stood on end—a thin wisp of white smoke was coming from the back of his car!

At that moment Orde ceased to think, and his reflexes took over. He braked the little car hard and turned its wheels into the low stone wall for good measure. The immediate stop almost threw Orde into the windshield, but instead he used the momentum to lunge out the car door. He rolled over the stone wall, smashing his shoulder heavily as he fell.

The bomb planted in the rear of the car went off with a deafening roar. A great ball of flame rolled up as the gas tank exploded. His head covered by his hands and his face pressed into the dirt of Palestine, Samuel Orde could feel the concussion of the blast and the intense heat that burned his hands and the back of his neck.

Pieces of the auto began to rain down like shrapnel, but Orde was already up and moving. He ran in a low crouch along the stone wall, and miraculously, none of the spinning pieces of jagged metal touched him. He ran desperately, expecting any minute to be pursued.

By the time the frightened villagers came out to view the smoking remains of the assassination attempt, Orde was already more than a mile away, heading for Hanita. As he covered the ground in a rapid hike, he alternated between thanking God for sparing his life and apologizing for having been so stupid that he needed divine intervention.

Orde would never have forgiven such inattention on the part of one of his troopers, and he resolved to never again be guilty of it himself. *Especially not now,* he thought. *There are miles and many Arabs between here and Hanita.*

Not even a strong cup of coffee could remove the chill from Karin Wallich.

Peter stood by helplessly as his mother trembled uncontrollably beneath Frau Singer's thick eiderdown quilts. Every moment of fear she had felt over the last weeks suddenly broke loose. She did not cry. Peter would have liked it better if there had been tears in Karin's eyes, but there were none. She simply lay there, staring at the ceiling and shivering as though she lay in a pool of icy water.

"There now, Karin my dear. My *dear . . .*" Frau Singer stroked Karin's forehead. "You are safe now. No harm will come to you here."

Peter knew that Frau Singer's words of reassurance were only a whisper of hope. Harm could, indeed, come to them here. Nowhere in Vienna was any Jew safe.

Marlene huddled in the corner of the bedroom beside a large dark chest of drawers, her brown eyes wide with fright. Finally she realized the seriousness of the situation.

At last, Peter thought as he stalked past her, *Marlene figured it out!*

Mercifully, baby Willie had fallen asleep in a bed made up in the bottom drawer of the chest. Peter stooped over his baby brother and found some comfort in the fact that he could sleep so peacefully. He wanted to reach out and brush back the curl on his smooth forehead, but instead he contented himself with simply gazing at the child. Peter did not look at Marlene. He knew that if he looked at her, all comfort would vanish. He blamed her somehow for what had happened. He could not explain his anger, not even to himself, but he knew for certain that Marlene's actions had led to their discovery and the note and this.

He looked at his mother again. He wished she would cry. "We are finally at Frau Singer's after all, Mama," he whispered, hoping to remind her that they had wanted to be here all along. She did not acknowledge his words or even look at him.

Once more Peter gazed mournfully at her, then walked heavily out of the room. He picked his way around the bolts of material that littered Frau Singer's once-spotless front room. The light was out. A soft glow emanated from the gas heater. Peter went to the window and leaned against the frame. He pulled back the shade a fraction until he could see the street and the entrance to Otto's apartment building. Soon *they* would come. They would come in search of a mother and three children.

He did not have long to wait until the first act of the drama took place. They came on foot, the tall SS Major Wolfgang von Fritschauer and three other men. *The man who had come to bring their champagne and Christmas greetings!*

The sight of the major made Peter want to shout at Marlene to come and see what she had done! He wanted to shove her fat, simpering face through the glass of the window and scream at her. But he simply watched in silence. Was there any hope of warning Otto what he was coming home to?

At the thought, Peter's heart beat faster. Perhaps he could run down the stairs and wait across the street to call a warning when Otto came home.

The instant the thought came to him, he spotted two more men in the shadows flanking the doorway. No doubt others would be at the back door and still more watching from either end of the street. The awareness of how near they had come to their own arrest made Peter sweat as a wave of fear and nausea washed over him. The trap had been set only minutes after they had found safety. Now Otto Wattenbarger would pay the penalty for all of them.

Peter waited, hearing the kind murmuring of Frau Singer in the bedroom. He could not understand what she said. His attention fixed on the solitary figure of Otto Wattenbarger as he rounded the far corner. He passed beneath the ring of a streetlamp, his step cheerful, unsuspecting. He carried a shopping bag in one hand and a very small Christmas tree in the other.

So he decided we must have a tree after all. . . .

"Turn around," Peter whispered, desperately willing Otto to hear the danger. "Go back. They will not know it is you if you go back now."

The words made a round circle of steam against the windowpane. "Go back. . . ."

Otto walked on, unheeding the warning of Peter's heart. And then, for just a second, he paused and glanced up at the window of his flat. It was dark behind the shade. Mozart the cat sat like a black shadow on the sill. "Yes, it is dark!" Peter urged. "We are not there! Something has happened! Go back! Do not go home, Herr Otto!"

Another few seconds passed; then Otto started forward again. The spring returned to his step. Whatever whisper of dread he had heard was gone now. He did not notice the men in the shadow. He did not see the man walking half a block behind him. Propping the little Christmas tree against the door of the building, he shifted his shopping bag and stepped into the trap.

Peter groaned and hung his head as the glass door swung back, reflecting the men who waited in the street. A minute passed until the light behind the shade came on. Mozart jumped from his perch, and Peter knew that it was finished.

He shook his head slowly as he imagined the startled look on Otto's face, the accusation, the denial, the arrest.

Peter slammed his fist against the wall and leaned his head against the window frame.

A moment later he heard a sniffle. *Marlene!* She stood at his elbow, staring at his face when he turned to scowl down at her.

"It's all my fault," she said. "It's my fault; isn't it, Peter?"

For an instant he was filled with such hatred for her that he wanted to answer her with a smack across the mouth. He thought better of it. No need for that. He simply answered honestly. "Yes. Yes, Marlene, it is all your fault. Except for you we would have been on our way across the border tomorrow. Now we are trapped here." His rage almost choked him. "And now, because of you, they have arrested Herr Otto. Because of you, they will throw him into prison and torture him!"

Marlene gave a strangled sob and covered her face with her hands. She did not argue. She did not beat her fists against Peter in resentment. It was true. All her fault. Marlene sank to the floor with a groan and sat there very quietly in her pretty Christmas dress while Peter stepped over her.

Standing in the long queue of last-minute shoppers waiting for the streetcar transfer, Lucy at last considered the implications of her impulsiveness. The thought of warning anyone to run from Wolf filled her with a mix of giddy excitement and fear. She also felt strangely pleased at what she had done; it seemed like a Christmas present to the Jewish family. She hoped beyond reason that young Peter and his family had escaped and that the traitorous Otto, who had helped them, was also on his way to safety somewhere.

Perhaps curiosity made her board the streetcar back to Frau Singer's, or perhaps the warmth she felt when she considered her good deed. She did not consider the possibility that a raging fire of danger behind that good deed threatened her as well.

Lucy smiled as she stepped off the car in front of the boarded-up shop. She had already thought of a good excuse for her return: She would simply claim to have dropped her lipstick and then come back to look for it. Maybe she could look out the window of the old woman's apartment and watch Wolf enter in search of people who were long gone.

She did not need the basket maker to show her the way this time. Lights blazed pleasantly from the old woman's upstairs window. Most likely she was already working on Lucy's corset.

Glancing back toward the street, Lucy pulled the braided bell cord and waited. The old woman did not call down to her. Lucy rang again, a little longer this time.

At the first ring of the doorbell, a chill coursed through Peter's body. Cold perspiration beaded from every pore. It made no sense that such a simple sound in this safe place would blast away his composure like a cold wind. He had remained calm through everything until now. He told himself that they were safe and that he was glad to be away from the tyranny of Otto's lessons and warnings. He had said it did not matter that Otto was arrested as long as the rest were safe. These were, at best, fragile self-delusions that enabled him to accept what had happened. But the second ring of the doorbell shattered his hopes and plunged him into an abyss of fear for the first time in weeks. The sound of the ringing—urgent, insistent—demanded that the door be opened.

"It's the Gestapo," Peter said to Frau Singer as she rushed past him to peek out the window.

She paled visibly and repeated the word *Gestapo* as she peered down through the tiniest of slits.

The silence grew so intense that Peter could hear the old woman's breath against the fabric.

Then a distant, cheerful voice came from the street below. "Madame Singer! Madame . . . I have come back . . . I forgot something. Won't you let me in?"

Frau Singer let out an exasperated sigh. "Peter!" she explained, "Gestapo, indeed! It is one of my clients, and you have frightened the life out of me!" She cracked open the window and cupped her hand to call down, "One moment, *bitte*! I will let you in, just one moment!" The window slammed shut and the old woman whirled to face Peter. "Go back with your mother and sister."

Peter, chagrined by his cowardly reaction to a doorbell, glanced toward Willie, who still slept in the bottom drawer of a chest in the parlor. "Should I take Willie?"

Frau Singer clapped her hands at him, ordering him to leave the room. Willie was sleeping. He would be fine. There was a very cold client waiting downstairs for her to come, and Peter must stop this nonsense!

"Coming! Coming! Coming!" she called as she tramped down the steps of the side entrance of the shop.

The corset maker's pale face greeted Lucy as the old woman unlocked the door and stepped aside to let her in.

"I am sorry." Lucy began walking toward the stairs. "Have I disturbed your mealtime?"

"No, indeed. But, *Gottenyu*! It is Christmas Eve and you are back? You were just here. Your order cannot be ready."

"No, I . . . you see, I am certain that I dropped my lip rouge on the floor. May I . . ." She gestured up toward the apartment.

"I am watching the child of a friend. He is sleeping and . . ." The old woman hung back. She did not want to go upstairs with Lucy in tow.

"Just a quick look, Frau Singer. I am sorry." The woman took a conciliatory tone. "I got home and looked, and . . . it is the only color I have that will match my dress tonight."

The old woman gave a hesitant nod. Surely it was all right—just a moment to look. "I have not seen it. Of course my eyes for distance are not so good. If it is there, we will find it."

The parlor looked just as it had this afternoon—perhaps a bit more cluttered. The gas heater glowed red; the room was almost too warm. A little suitcase was beside the dining table—for the baby Frau Singer was watching, no doubt.

"It must be here somewhere." Lucy pretended to look around the floor as Frau Singer searched beside the sofa.

Lucy knelt and ran her hands over the carpet. Then she glanced toward the open bureau drawer, where little Willie lay soundly asleep.

Her eyes widened. She sat back on her heels and stared at the child. "The baby," she whispered. "How did he—?" She stared at Frau Singer, whose ashen face betrayed everything. Lucy crept nearer to the makeshift cradle. She reached her hand out as if to touch the red curls that tumbled over Willie's forehead. She had seen this child once, and she could never forget him!

Frau Singer stood very straight. She did not look at Lucy. She did not speak as she attempted to regain her composure. "The child . . . of a neighbor. A neighbor I . . ."

A strange smile played on Lucy's lips. She was glad they were here, but she wished they were farther away. No use to pretend she did not know. "Are they all here?" she asked with unconcealed amusement.

"All?" The old woman was still trying to pretend. She was not a good liar. "I cannot think what you mean."

"Willie." Lucy jerked her head toward the sleeping baby. "Peter. Karin is the mother's name, I think. And—" The name of the girl escaped her.

A shudder visibly passed through Frau Singer as she denied everything. No Peter. No Willie. No . . .

Lucy stood slowly and fixed her gaze on the bedroom door. Silence hung like a pall of thick smoke in the room. Lucy walked toward the door, only to be blocked by Frau Singer. "The toilet is not there," she insisted. "Please . . ."

Lucy reached out, grasped the doorknob, and opened the door.

The three of them huddled together on the bed. Karin lay beneath the blankets, dark circles of strain beneath her eyes. She wearily gazed back at Lucy.

Peter sat clutching his mother's hand, defiant and angry.

Marlene, who tried to hide behind Karin, was simply terrified.

"So you are here," Lucy said with a laugh. "Imagine!"

"What do you want with us?" Peter demanded as he stood to block the others from her view. "We have not hurt anyone! What do you want?"

For a moment Lucy thought he might strike her. Stepping back, she glanced toward Willie. "I wanted to see if you got my note."

His rage dissolved into astonishment. "*You?*"

Lucy bowed slightly. Peter stepped aside, revealing the grateful face of Karin gazing up at her. "I thought I might have a better look from here." Lucy shrugged, embarrassed by her lies. "Forgive me, Madame Singer. Your view . . ."

Frau Singer did not reply. She opened her mouth and closed it again.

No one could speak. Lucy backed up another step. Frau Singer shook her head as if she were coming out of a dream. "Do you still want your corset?" she croaked.

"Indeed," Lucy said. She looked at Peter and frowned. "What did you do with the note?"

Before he could answer, Marlene rose up on her knees and blurted out, "I left it for Uncle Otto. I left it on the mirror of the bathroom!"

Peter swung around and slapped her hard across the face. "Now Otto is arrested, and so will she be for helping us! You think that SS officer will not know her handwriting?"

Lucy felt giddy. She looked from the sobbing child to Peter. Finally she turned her eyes back on baby Willie who slept, undisturbed, through everything. She put a hand on her stomach and hoped her baby slept as sweetly now. The sky was falling. All her plans were crashing down around her head, and yet the baby must not be afraid . . . must not feel what she was feeling at this terrible moment.

Frau Singer took Lucy's arm, guiding her to a chair. "Sit. Here, before you fall down."

With the handle of his spoon, Karl Ibsen had scratched out a crude calendar to mark the day of his imprisonment. Although there was no mention of the date, no hint from his jailers, Karl knew that tonight was Christmas Eve.

Cold wind whistled around the corner of the redbrick building and in through the high window of his spartan cell. Karl closed his eyes, imagining the voices of faraway carolers on the wind. But it was just that . . . imagination. From there it was only a short step back into the memories of last Christmas.

Helen sitting at the piano in the parlor. Lori rearranging packages beneath the tree. And Karl hefting Jamie up on his shoulder to place the angel on the very top . . .

"Higher, Father! Lift me higher!"

In the darkness of the cell Karl laughed out loud, repeating the laugh of that moment. And then the laugh dissolved into a sob of aching loneliness. He pulled his knees to his chest and buried his face to conceal the sounds of his grief.

Where are my children now, Lord? Without their mother . . . without me? What will come of them? Oh, God! If the Nazis press me at this moment, I will say anything! God, do You hear me? Do not let them come here tonight!

No sooner had Karl finished that prayer than the sound of a key scraped and clanged against the lock of the cell door. As it was thrown back and light flooded the room, the exultant face of the camp commandant grinned drunkenly down at Karl. The strong smell of schnapps entered the cell with him. Four guards hovered in the corridor behind him.

"Well, Prisoner Ibsen! Happy Christmas to you! Of course, we do not call it Christmas any longer. No more little babies in the manger, *ja?* No one has even noticed the changes. Except maybe fools and old women. Which are you, Pastor Ibsen? A fool or an old woman?" The smirk of derision dissolved into unconcealed hatred. "Your stubbornness has cost me a leave. Every other commandant in the system got a break but me. We're waiting to welcome your two brats to Nameless, you see!" He kicked at Karl, causing a spray of straw to fly up in Karl's face. "Now get up!" He screamed the command, then whirled and left. Two soldiers with bayonets on their rifles rushed into the cell. They leveled the points in Karl's throat, prodding him to his feet.

Did they notice the dampness on Karl's cheeks? Had they heard that prayer somehow and broken in to mock it?

It did not matter. God sent a different answer to the heart of Karl Ibsen than the one he had expected. A sudden peace filled him as he staggered out and then down the stinking corridor. Would they kill him now? he wondered. He was unafraid of death. To die would be merciful . . . *to spend Christmas with Helen in heaven!*

They pushed him through three separate corridors, down a flight of metal steps, and out into a courtyard blazing with the yellow glow of floodlights. The wind tore through the thin fabric of Karl's uniform. He shielded his aching eyes from the searing light. His arm was slapped down by the butt of a rifle as the voice of the commandant screamed at him again. "*Achtung!* Prisoner Ibsen!"

Karl straightened to attention, eyes forward. Directly before him was a wooden gallows complete with three waiting ropes that swayed eerily in the wind.

"Death," Karl said with a half smile. Once again the butt of a rifle slammed into his stomach, knocking him to the ground.

He lay gasping for breath. The polished boots of the commandant strolled to his head. Karl could see the reflection of lights and gallows distorted in the shining leather.

"Yes, Prisoner Ibsen. Death." A short laugh. The reek of schnapps. "But not your death. Ah, no. The Führer does not want your death; he wants your approval. And if not your approval, then at least your acceptance, *ja*? You understand?"

Karl, still fighting for breath, shook his head. No. Not approval. Not acceptance. Not ever.

"And if I told you your children will be here tonight to dance from our little Christmas tree? Like angels on a string?"

Karl's head jerked up. He looked in horror at the platform where two figures were being led up the steps. *Oh, God! Not my children! Jamie! Lori!* His eyes focused on the prison uniforms. No. Not the children. No. These were men. Skeletons with striped rags covering their bones.

Another laugh. "Well, Pastor Ibsen. So you see we have our little joke to wake you up. Not your two little brats. Not tonight anyway. But . . . *your children*, all the same. Here you see we have brought two of your converts."

Karl struggled to stand. And again he was shoved down. With a snap of the commandant's gloved fingers, the bayonet was placed at Karl's throat.

"Now we will all rise for the benediction, eh, Pastor?" More laughter from all the guards. "Would you like to pray for your children who are about to die? Eh? For Prisoner Richard Kalner? For this young man beside him? Johann . . . Johann something. Ah, well, what's in a name?"

The courtyard seemed to be in motion. Karl swayed as he stared up at the faces of his friends . . . indeed . . . his family!

"Why?" Karl begged.

"Because you will not confess, Prisoner Ibsen. You will not take the oath of allegiance to our Führer. *You* are the reason they are dying."

Karl looked from the face of the commandant to the face of Richard Kalner. Hands tied behind his back, Richard stepped forward to the rope even as his gentle eyes sought Karl's face.

The doomed man shouted, "Home for Christmas, Karl!" Boots slammed into his legs and he tumbled down. Still he shouted. "Stay true! Stay true, Karl!" A final blow to the stomach silenced him.

Then young Johann cried out, *"Jesus wept!"* There was no more time to speak. A fist to the cheek and then the noose was dropped around the slender neck. Richard's limp body was dragged up and the second rope was put in place.

"But there are three ropes!" Karl cried. "Let me! Let me go with them!" He lunged forward, arms extended as if to embrace them. "Let me go too!"

"Stay true! *Auf . . . auf Wiedersehen!*"

The commandant raised and lowered his hand. The trapdoors sprung open beneath the two men.

And they danced from the barren branch of the Nazi Christmas tree while Karl Ibsen sobbed in agony too deep for sound.

The excitement of their imminent escape suddenly vanished from the face of Jacob. Even in the gloom of the church Lori could see his skin grow pale, as though he had seen a ghost.

She touched his arm. He gasped, startled, then managed to turn his eyes away from some horrible thought and focus on her concern.

"Jacob?" she asked gently. "What is it?"

It took him a moment before he found words. "I . . . I know what we are running from," he stammered. "But what are we escaping *to*?"

"Freedom," she answered simply.

"I was . . . it is Christmas, you know . . . and I . . . could not help but wonder . . ." He averted his eyes from her gaze. "Our parents. My father." He fought to explain. "I thought for a moment I heard him say my name." He covered his eyes with his hand.

Is Jacob Kalner crying?

Lori touched his cheek with her fingertips. *Tears.* She put her arms around him and pulled him against her. He laid his head on her shoulder and wept. He did not know why the tears came, but he cried all the same. He wept quietly so the younger boys sleeping a few feet away would not hear him.

In the solitude of his cell, Karl had no one to comfort him. He, too, wept quietly, keeping the satisfaction of his pain from his captors.

He did not question God any longer. God had not done this thing. God had not arranged for Karl to be here in this stinking cell or for him to preside over the deaths of Richard and Johann.

Karl stared at the redbrick wall opposite him and remembered the grief and troubles of Job.

"Curse God and die . . ." The wife of Job spoke to Karl now.

Karl replied aloud. *"Though He slay me, yet will I trust in Him!"*

And then the voice that whispered in his ear changed to an accusation. *"You* killed those men. One word from you and they would have lived! And the Nazis will do the same to Lori and Jamie! When they are captured, they will be strung up before your eyes!"

Karl groaned and covered his ears, but he could not shut out the voice. He cringed on the floor of the cell against the weight of the accusation.

"Lord!" he cried loudly, no longer thinking of the eavesdropping prison guards. *"Help me!"* Again and again he called out the name of Jesus. He could no longer recall the Scripture passages that had carried him through so much. *"Please!"*

Once again the warm peace filled him. He sat up slowly and drew a ragged breath. Tears stopped instantly.

And then he knew . . . he saw it clearly and he spoke, his voice strong. "I know who you are."

He waited, but there was no reply.

He spoke again. "You accuse me before the Lord, do you not? I know your name. The Accuser. Yes. I heard your voice. You wound me with your darts. But I tell you this!" He shook his fist at the empty air, certain that a dark presence saw his defiance. "My strength is in the Lord! In the Spirit of the Almighty! I have no faith in myself! You think you will have some small victory over the Lord if I give in? Is that what you think? Is that why you accuse me? I tell you that if I fail, then the Lord will have another and another who will fight for Him! Speak for Him! Remain true to Him!"

Karl's voice was ringing against the walls of the tiny chamber. The slit in the cell door slid back, but Karl was not aware of the eyes that watched him.

He shouted, "The Lord is my strength! I will not be afraid of you! Of what men can do to me! I know who you are! I know my enemy! I will fight you! *FIGHT YOU! And you will be ashamed!*"

He managed to climb to his feet. He raised his hand to the howling wind outside his window. "It is Christmas! God has come among us! The miracle is accomplished! *You! You cannot change it now!* The Gate is open!"

Through the loosened boards of the basement window, the sounds of the Nazi Christmas procession drifted into the cold underbelly of the dark New Church.

By the glow of one tiny candle, the fugitives checked one another's clothing one last time.

Jacob wore warm traveling clothes belonging to Lori's father. The trousers were slightly loose around the waist, but a belt and suspenders held them in place. Pastor Ibsen's hiking boots were one size too big, but this was remedied by two extra pairs of wool socks.

Lori was dressed in a red dirndl skirt trimmed in green lace. It was appropriate for Christmas, of course, but beneath her dress she wore Lederhosen, short leather pants, in case their flight should force them over rough terrain. She also wore her most sturdy shoes, hoping no one would notice that she did not wear her Sunday shoes with her favorite dress.

Jamie and Mark also wore leather knickers and wool socks beneath heavy alpine jackets and sweaters gleaned from Jamie's chest of drawers. They had only one pair of hiking boots; Jamie wore the boots, and Mark wore his old sneakers. Wisely, Jamie packed another pair of sneakers in his small rucksack, along with extra socks and woolen underwear, two more sweaters, and mittens for everyone. He had heard that Danzig was very cold this time of year. With all of that, he rolled up the black uniform of the Hitler Youth. He had wanted to leave it behind, but Jacob had grabbed it up and stared hard at it as though he heard some whispered message in its fabric. Then he had thrust it at Jamie and demanded that the vile thing be taken along.

Outside, the crowds sang more songs, but not songs of peace on earth, not songs about the baby in Bethlehem. Ancient carols of pagan legends filled the air of Berlin tonight as the torches of the masses lit the facades of buildings with a hellish glow.

"It is time," Jacob said, looking at the ladder they had made out of old boxes. The crates leaned against the damp stone walls of the belly of the church and led up to the broken window.

Lori held Jacob's eyes with her own fearful look before he blew out the little candle. He touched her gently on the arm.

"You go first," Jacob instructed Jamie. It made sense. If Jamie were caught climbing out the window, he would simply say that he had run away from the Hitler Youth and come here. They would take him back, but the others would have time to hide before the church was searched again.

Jacob hefted Jamie up and held the groaning crates steady as the boy cautiously picked his way up toward the sliver of light shining through the boards.

Seconds passed slowly before Jamie called down in an exultant whisper, "At the top."

The sound of creaking followed as he pushed against the boards, hesitated to look, then slipped out into the cold night air.

Jacob's hand sweated as he waited a full minute before Jamie called in through the boards: "All is calm!"

Jacob tapped Mark on his shoulder and sent him clambering up the pile next. The barricade creaked and the sound of singing increased as Mark escaped to the outside with Jamie.

"My turn?" Lori asked with hesitant excitement. Jacob could hear her voice shake at the thought of being outside again after so long. Did she also regret leaving their refuge in some way, as he did?

"Good luck," he said as he took her hand to help her up.

She did not move for a moment but stood there beside him, holding his damp hand. Then she stood on her tiptoes and brushed her lips briefly against his before she began to climb.

He listened to her breathe as she reached in the dark for handholds and scaled the fifteen-foot heap much more slowly than Mark or Jamie.

"Come on!" urged Jamie impatiently through the crack in the boards. "Hurry up, will you?"

At this she slipped and cried out as a box tumbled down, narrowly missing Jacob.

"It's all right," he assured her hoarsely. "Go easy, Lori. I will catch you if you fall."

He did not tell her that he would not be able to see her if she slipped and fell from the top of the dark pile. Probably he would be covered by the rubble before she hit him. All the same, his words seemed to reassure her. Seconds later she called down that she had reached the window and then she, too, squeezed out through the space.

"Come on, Jacob!" Mark chided him. *"All ist klar!"*

As Jacob scaled the heap with ease, it swayed precariously beneath his weight. He reached up, grasping the ledge of the broken window just as the boxes rumbled and spilled out from under his feet. He punched at the last of the boards over the window with his fist and then pushed through the space.

Their only retreat now lay on the bottom of the basement floor! There would be no going back. Mark and Jamie and Lori surrounded him as the rumble emanated up from the basement.

"The ladder has fallen!"

"We can't get back!"

"And so we press on," Jacob said, brushing them off and creeping forward from the wall of the church to the bushes that surrounded the building. The others followed—first Lori, then Mark. Jamie brought up the rear. Like a clumsy parade of waddling ducks, they crept through the flower bed, careful not to get their clothes dirty. They must not look the part of children who had escaped through a hedge and then a muddy churchyard!

Jacob peered from between the branches of the bushes. The graveyard was dark. Headstones, lopsided from the sinking earth, rose up as gray shadows before them. Crosses and square aboveground crypts made silhouettes like the unlit buildings of a deserted city. Beyond that was the iron gate they had passed through on Kristal Nacht, a lifetime ago.

He hesitated a moment too long for Mark, who tugged impatiently at his jacket. "Hurry! The *watchman*!" Mark warned.

But Jacob knew the watchman would not make his rounds of the desolate place until eleven o'clock—still nearly an hour away. He waved his hand, warning Mark not to attempt to instruct him. Then Lori gasped and pulled at his arm. Jacob looked up and saw the watchman's light swing around the corner of the church and leap from boarded window to boarded window at the far end of the building. Only a minute and the old man would be shining his light on the foursome!

Jacob broke from the bushes and ran for the cover of a headstone. He did not think of the knees of his traveling trousers as he lunged behind a tall black marble obelisk.

Like foxes breaking from a hedge, the three followed after him, each finding a gravestone to crouch behind. Jacob could not see the others, but he could hear them breathing, panting with fright as the footsteps of the watchman quickened and moved toward the bushes.

Do not breathe! Be quiet! Oh, God, make the fellow deaf! Jacob thought as he leaned his cheek against the cold stone and tried to melt into its inscription.

The watchman jogged toward the broken basement window and the loose boards that hung there. Someone had gone through them, broken the Nazi taboo!

The blood drummed so hard in Jacob's ears that he could not hear the others breathing against their own headstones. Like an evil finger, the light of the watchman probed the shadows surrounding New Church, touching the bushes and frostbitten plants, scrutinizing the walls of stone, less than ten feet from where the four lay curled in fear on the dirt of sunken graves.

I will have to kill him, Jacob thought as he closed his eyes as if to hide from the light! He was an old man, Jacob knew, but Jacob had never killed a man before. How to do it?

His fingers closed around a stone as the old man swept the light up the wall to an arched window in the main auditorium and then down again to the broken window of their basement escape hatch.

"*Himmel!*" cried the old man in alarm. And then again he whispered, "*Himmel!*"

33

Tor Auf!

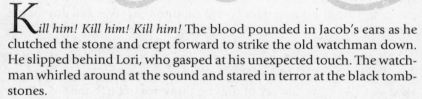

Kill *him! Kill him! Kill him!* The blood pounded in Jacob's ears as he clutched the stone and crept forward to strike the old watchman down. He slipped behind Lori, who gasped at his unexpected touch. The watchman whirled around at the sound and stared in terror at the black tombstones.

At that moment, a flock of upraised torches fluttered by in the street. The old man looked at them once and shouted for help. Then he raised his whistle and blew a shrill alarm, halting the torches. It was too late to kill the old man. Too late to run for the gate.

"Help!" The old man ran back along the path to open the gate. "Someone has broken into the church! Thieves have broken into the—"

Lori grasped Jacob's hand. Mark and Jamie scrambled to huddle with them.

Jacob watched as the torches seemed to multiply. They saw no retreat back into the church, no escape from the churchyard. It was over for them.

"I'll try to draw them away, " Jacob said. "Run for it!"

"No!" Jamie cried. "I know a place!"

With no more explanation than that, he leaped out from behind the tombstone. "Come on!"

They followed without question. No one else had any ideas. Lori fell in the mud. Jacob grabbed her arm and dragged her up. He held tightly to her as they ran blindly toward the back of the churchyard, toward the white family crypts that formed a tiny community for the dead beneath the trees of New Church.

Behind them the swelling voices of a mob surged through the open gate. They had only seconds before the light of the torches would pierce the covering safety of this darkness.

"Here!" Jamie cried as they reached the square stone crypt of the Halder family. "The key is above the gate!" He jumped up and tried to reach the ledge where the key was hidden. The lights behind them moved along the sides of the church, dipping down to examine every boarded window.

Jacob reached up and ran his hand along the stone ledge in search of the key. It was not there. Jamie cried out and shook the rusty iron bars of the crypt gate.

"It was here! The key was here!" His words were lost beneath the shouts of men who called out to one another and broke down the boards over the doors of the church. Their guns drawn, they peered into the darkness beyond the torchlight. The two swept their torches near the ground in search of clues. As the doors of New Church crashed open, Jacob dropped to his knees with Lori to sift through leaves and dirt for the missing key.

Jamie laid his face against the bars. The hiding place. So close. No one had ever found him and Alfie in this place. And now the key had vanished! Tonight, when hiding was not a game but a matter of survival—of all nights, the key of the crypt was not to be found.

Lori prayed as they searched. "*Tor auf!* Oh, Lord, please. *Tor auf!*"

The thump of footsteps circled the outside fence. No use trying to scale the stone wall. Too late now for Jamie to take them out through the break in the fence. Every escape was cut off.

"Lord," whispered Jamie, "*Tor auf . . .*"

In his restless sleep, Alfie heard the sound of leaves and footsteps. Whispered voices penetrated his dreams. The angels stood beside him again as they often had throughout the weeks. He felt their light through his closed eyelids. He did not open his eyes. They were there. He did not need to see them.

The kittens stirred in their box. They knew the angels had come back as well. Alfie did not need to wake up and check them. The dreams were too nice; he did not want to wake up.

"*Alf . . .*" The light glowed brighter as the angel spoke his name like Mama used to do.

"Yes?" he whispered with a smile.

"*Alf . . . they cannot find the key.*"

"Huh?"

"Tor . . . the gate." The voice was more urgent than gentle.

Alfie frowned in his sleep. The angel wanted him to do something. "What?"

"Alf . . . Alf . . . Tor . . . Alf . . . Tor auf! Open the gate!" The angel touched his face and told him to wake up.

Alfie breathed in deeply and opened his eyes as the bright light dwindled to a small star and vanished. He was awake. The sounds of scratching and whispered voices sifted down the steps.

"Where is it? *Where?*" It was the voice of Jamie. Clear as anything. It was Jamie!

Torches moved deliberately up the path toward the Halder crypt. Light scoured the other tombs and probed stones for signs of the living among the dead. The men who searched did not seem to be in a hurry. While shouts resounded from inside the church building, the flames of the torches sniffed nearer the crypt. Jacob rose from his knees and stood with clenched fists. He would fight them when they came, but it would do no good.

As they stood to face their fate, a large, clumsy hand reached out from inside the crypt and touched Jamie's shoulder. Jamie dropped to his knees in terror but did not cry out.

"Is that you, Jamie?" the old familiar voice of Alfie asked softly. "Are you playing hide-and-seek, Jamie?"

"Alfie!" Jamie could hardly whisper. *"Tor auf!* Open the gate, Alfie! Do you have the key?"

"I got the key, Jamie," the voice said too slowly. Then Alfie's giant hand pawed the air between the bars and, with unwavering accuracy, the key slid into the lock and the gate swung back.

The fugitives tumbled into the crypt. They scrambled between Alfie's legs as he slowly swung the gate shut and turned the key in an unhurried fashion.

"I'm glad you came, Jamie," Alfie said, his voice frighteningly loud.

"Shut up!" Jacob ordered.

Jamie was gentle. "We have to hide now, Alfie. They are—" He pointed at the swaying torches.

"Oh. Shhhh." Alfie put a finger to his lips and spread his arms wide to herd them to the back corner. "Down there. In the basement."

The square hole in the floor blended into shadow. Jamie slid down first, showing the others where to go. The blackness was heavy and palpable, the air thick with the smell of old sardines and mold. Alfie was last down the steps. He slid the stone hatch over the opening just as the voices of the pursuers swept into the crypt.

"I thought I heard—"

The hollow clunk of stone sliding into place cut off the words.

"Shhhh," Alfie said with a sound like escaping steam. The voices outside penetrated the stone floor. The iron gate rattled loudly. Lori leaned her head against Jacob's arm.

"Shhhh," Alfie warned again. A thin line of light penetrated the seam around the stone hatch. Within that square, the figure of Alfie stood framed on the steps. His face glowed with excitement, and he smiled as he stared at the light. The big, clumsy hand reached up to where the brightest beam gleamed through a chink. And then, as though he were brushing it away, it suddenly vanished and the blackness was complete once again.

Never was there such a Christmas tree as the tree in the center of the big room in the Red Lion House. Charles Dickens himself could not have imagined a more green or full or fragrant tree as he sat by the fire and wrote *A Christmas Carol*.

Or so Murphy said as he stood tiptoe on the stepladder and placed the gossamer angel on the top. Branches bowed down under the weight of candy canes and gingerbread cookies and a hundred colored lights that winked on and off as Charles and Louis watched with wonder.

The lights were new, sent from Mr. Trump in New York. He had purchased them at Macy's in New York and sent along a note explaining that the same sort of lights were used on the tree in America at the White House.

This bit of important information gave the lights an aura of magic for the boys. Charles and Louis had never believed in Santa Claus or elves working at the North Pole. Such fantasies had faded early as they had witnessed photographs of Hermann Göring dressed in a Santa suit, handing out gifts to good little members of the Hitler Youth. But Charles and Louis did believe in America and the White House!

Cabled all the information about the prisoner Pastor Karl Ibsen, the White House had made appeals to the German government on his behalf, and on behalf of his missing children. This lifted Anna's spirits. Every day she and Elisa walked across the square to the little church to pray for them. There was still hope, in spite of news of Helen Ibsen's death.

It was, at long last, Christmas Eve. The lights of the Christmas tree reflected on the polished wood floor of Red Lion House. Dinner dishes were cleared away and stacked. Everyone had tasted the puddings and pies, and the adults savored the very last of the Viennese coffee.

A warm fire crackled and glowed in the fireplace. Charles and Louis sat cross-legged on the hooked floral hearth rug as Murphy and Theo read *A Christmas Carol* in the very room where some said Dickens might have written the story.

Curled up on the sofa, Anna and Elisa listened to the story for the first time as well. Theo read the part of the narrator and sometimes paused to interpret the unclear passages from English into German for the struggling language students in the group. Murphy embellished the speaking roles with all the terror of Ebenezer Scrooge as he came face-to-face with the dark-hooded Ghost of Christmas Yet to Come.

Theo raised his eyes to make certain the boys had caught the meaning of the English words. The terrified expressions of their faces confirmed that they understood perfectly. He pressed on with the story:

> "They reached an iron gate. He paused to look round before entering. A churchyard! Here, then, the wretched man whose name he had now to learn lay beneath the ground."

"Kirchhof!" Louis uttered the word for graveyard.

At this point, Charles covered his eyes as if he did not want to see what Theo would read next. But the picture of the graveyard remained, so he uncovered his eyes again and held tightly to Louis' hand.

Theo continued with a slightly quavering voice.

> "It was a worthy place. Walled in by houses; overrun by grass and weeds, the growth of vegetation's death, not life . . . choked up with too much burying; fat with repleted appetite. A worthy place!"

Charles knew that the churchyard was not really a worthy place. This terrible graveyard of Christmas Future was a place so forsaken and forlorn that even the weeds died on top of one another for lack of rain. He squeezed Louis' hand and stared hard at the coals on the grate as Theo continued.

> "The Spirit stood among the graves, and pointed down to One. He advanced toward it trembling. The Phantom was exactly as it had been, but Scrooge dreaded that he saw new meaning in its solemn shape. . . ."

Louis' eyes grew wider, and he whispered the word for gravestone, "Grabstein!" He shuddered and leaned closer to Charles.

"The Spirit stretched his finger out toward the granite slab that
marked the former existence of a human being—"

This was a terrible time for the story to be interrupted by the sound of
the doorbell ringing like an angry bee. Everyone jumped. Charles
grabbed Louis around the neck and they both squealed. Then everyone
laughed and sat back and breathed easier.

The doorbell rang again.

"Probably carolers," Elisa said. She went for the platter of cookies,
and Charles raced Louis to the window to look.

"Not carolers," Louis said with disappointment. "It is some old beggar woman!" Their story had been interrupted not for music but for
charity. Murphy told them that this was just the sort of twist in plot line
that Dickens would approve of!

At first Anna did not recognize the woman who stood in the halo of
the porch light and pressed her finger so urgently to the bell. Her brown
coat was badly worn, torn at the sleeve and mended. Her hair was concealed beneath a tan scarf, her hands bare. Her shoes were run-down at
the heels and her woolen stockings were mended in several places.

Anna frowned through the window, pitying the beggar who had
come to the door on such a night. Then the finger pressed hard again on
the buzzer and the face turned to look up, beseeching heaven, praying
that Anna Lindheim would answer the door!

Anna gasped and put her hand over her mouth in an instant of recognition. The face of this once-beautiful thirty-eight-year-old woman had
visibly aged, but Helen Ibsen gazed at her as though from the grave.

"Helen!" Anna cried through the glass, and Helen's face broke into a
broad smile. Reports claimed she had died in prison in Germany, but
here she was! *Dear God, a miracle!* Helen Ibsen standing at Anna's door
in London!

Charles Dickens' *Christmas Carol* was laid aside, probably until next
year.

Presents did not matter. The lights on the tree in Red Lion House
seemed dim compared to the joy of the reunion of these two sisters. And
yet, tears were shed there as well. One of the Ibsen family was here, one
of four faces in the photograph on Anna's piano. This reality, like a
white-hot flame, turned their joy into a molten gold . . . beautiful and
bright but still untouchable.

Murphy thought they should call a doctor, but Helen asked only to
be taken to the home of Anna and Theo. She would be fine, she said. She
was only tired, very tired.

The three of them left and it was bedtime for Charles and Louis.

There would be presents in the morning, Elisa promised after prayers, because they were very good boys.

Long after the lights had gone out, Charles lay awake in his bed. "Louis?" he said softly.

"I'm awake too," Louis answered.

"Thinking?"

"Uh-huh. I was thinking about what surprise I want on Christmas morning. How about you?"

"I would like to see our mama again," Charles said. But he knew that miracles only happened sometimes, and this one would not be there when they awoke in the morning.

The teakettle shrieked. Helen turned toward it as though she had never heard that ordinary sound before. Her thick blond hair was matted, dirty. Anna ran a hot bath for her and brought her tea.

Clean clothes were laid out for her—a pretty blue dress that matched her eyes, real stockings, and slippers for her feet until new shoes could be purchased for her. She bathed and dressed.

For a long time Helen did not speak. She wept in Anna's arms and then sat quietly as she tried to remember everything that had happened since the night of November 9. And after she remembered, how could she sort it all out?

"I'm sorry, Anna." She sat up and wiped her eyes. "It has just been so long. A miracle, I suppose, that I am here. A miracle. But I would rather be back there with my children, and with Karl, you see."

Walking through Helen Ibsen's ordeal took a long time. First came the terrible night in New Church, the last time she saw Karl, and her arrest with all the others the next morning. Lori escaped, she thought, as did the Kalner boys. Again and again the Gestapo asked her where Lori was. She said she did not know, and they beat her until her back was bloody.

She showed Anna the still-pink scars of the lash. "But I prayed, Anna!" Helen said in a soft whisper. "I remembered the Lord and His silence. And I prayed."

Weeks in a cell had followed and then, without explanation, she had been released with three prostitutes—simply given her coat and her papers and turned out on the street.

"New Church is condemned. Leona Kalner has disappeared." A strange smile played on her lips. "It was so easy to leave Germany; it had to be a mistake. My papers were all in order. I caught the train to Prague. I hoped . . . we had told the children to go to the Protestant home in

Prague." Tears came again. "But they were not there. No one has heard from them. Oh, Anna, if they made it out, they would have gone to Prague!"

A series of small miracles had resulted in a visitor's visa to England. Helen was not Jewish, and she was the wife of a pastor. The British consulate had granted her a temporary visitor's visa the first afternoon. From there she got Anna's address and borrowed ship fare from a pastor in Prague. "I came on a freighter. I have not got enough money left to pay for a cup of tea."

Anna pulled her into her arms. Anna had not let herself believe that they would ever meet again on this earth. "You do not need money for tea, Helen. You must stay here. We will do everything we can. And we will pray!"

"Hey, Moshe, Zach, get a load of this!" Larry Havas sounded excited as he ran toward them, waving a scrap of notebook paper.

"What is it? Some news about Captain Orde?" asked Moshe.

"Have they made him king of Palestine or something?" kidded Zabinski. He stopped joking when he saw the grim look on Havas' face.

"What is it really?" asked Moshe again.

"Judith was monitoring British military radio traffic and she picked this up: Part of an army convoy was diverted to investigate the report of an explosion in an Arab village."

"So this is news?" demanded Zach. "Some Arab making pipe bombs has blown himself up?"

"Shut up and let him finish! Go on, Larry," instructed Moshe.

"The unit that checked it out found what was left of a car, but there wasn't anybody in it or around it."

Zach looked concerned. "And this was on the route Captain Orde would have been traveling?"

"That's just it: Orde had been traveling with that convoy until he reached the Hanita turnoff; he should have reached here by now!"

The first light of Christmas morning crept over the damp cemetery of New Church. Jacob cautiously raised the stone hatch to peer out and listen. He was grateful for the fresh air. He sucked it into his lungs voraciously, as though he had been under water for a long time.

Only hours had passed since their detection by the watchman, and yet it seemed much longer than that. Jacob had thought they would be well on their way across the border to Poland by now. But here they were, a few dozen yards from where they had begun, and in a much worse place than they had started from.

The advantage they had hoped to gain by leaving in the midst of a rally was now gone. Although all government buildings stayed open on Christmas Day, most of the shops closed their doors in some remembrance of Christmas Past. Traffic would be light. Chance of detection would be greater today than ever. Although Jacob could not see clearly from this place, he could hear the vague murmur of voices. There were still searchers around New Church.

Maybe tonight, he thought, letting the hatch slide down quietly into place. Maybe tonight they could sneak through the hole in the fence, separate, and meet at Pastor Ibsen's car!

Alfie played with the kittens and let Lori and Jacob talk. He was polite, like Mama taught him. He did not interrupt while Lori and Jamie argued with Jacob.

"We cannot take him with us." Jacob sounded angry.

"We cannot leave him here!" Lori's anger matched his.

"Maybe we cannot get out of here, either," whispered Jamie fearfully.

"We'll get out, all right." Jacob made a fist. "If they haven't found us now, they won't find us. We'll sneak out and follow our plan."

"We are taking Alfie," Lori said again.

"He is not in the plan." Jacob stared at Alfie. "Look at him. Sitting there with his kittens. He doesn't even know what we are talking about."

"If we leave him here, it is murder."

"To take him is suicide. There is too much at stake to take along this Dummkopf."

Jamie stood up and clenched his fists as if he wanted to fight Jacob. "Take it back!"

"Well, what else—" Jacob raised his hand to hold back Jamie's hitting.

"Shhhh," Alfie warned them when they got too loud! Maybe the men were still out there.

Jamie and Jacob looked at him. They lowered their voices again.

"He is smarter than you think," Jamie said. "And he saved our lives. *Your* life. If you leave him, you are leaving me and Lori, too, because we won't go without him. My father wouldn't leave him; I know that much! He would say that it is a miracle that Alfie was there to open the gate for us! And you don't spit in the eye of a miracle!"

Silence. Joseph the cat purred as Alfie petted her. Maybe it was time for Alfie to tell them about the angels and also about the grocery store. Which first?

"You have to be careful, Jamie," Alfie said, now that it was his turn. "The Nazi men are looking for you."

"How do you know that?" Jacob asked, a frown on his face.

"I went to a store to buy food, and the grocery man asked questions about you. Then he called the police and I heard them talking. They talked a long time. Don't go to the train station. Or the bus. They were going to pick you and Lori up." Lori grew pale and Jacob sat up straight. He smiled at her and raised his eyebrows as if he knew something she did not know.

Jacob stared at Alfie. "Maybe you're not a Dummkopf after all."

The words were mean, Alfie thought, but the sound of Jacob's voice was not.

Jacob sighed. "All right, then. Alfie is our miracle. We won't spit in his eye. We will take him; God help us."

Alfie was glad. "God will help us." And then he told them about the angels who had told him to open the gate.

34

Plan for Escape

Lucy awoke to the quiet gurgling of a baby. For a moment she could not remember where she was, and then it came to her with a flash of fear. *Christmas morning!* She had not gone home to Wolf last night. Surely by now he knew what she had done!

Strong, bitter coffee helped Lucy think. Cradling the cup in both hands, she inhaled the aroma. Somehow it calmed her. The girl, Marlene, begged her to forgive her for leaving the note. Strangely, Lucy felt no animosity. The child had simply forced Lucy to a final decision— a decision to do something good for the first time in too long.

"Wolf knows who you are—" Lucy leveled her eyes on Karin. "Wallich, isn't it? Karin Wallich?"

Karin replied with a single slow nod. Had Lucy ever seen such depth of sorrow in any woman's eyes? Such a look marked the face of Mary, the mother of Christ, in the fresco above the altar of Lucy's church in Bavaria. Such a thought crowded out all other thoughts. She imagined shouting at Wolf that he was hunting down the family of Christ! In the eyes of Karin Wallich, Lucy found the woman at the foot of the cross, watching the torture of the innocent.

"Fräulein Strasburg?" Madame Singer touched her gently, as if to draw her back into the present moment.

Lucy sipped her coffee. She must not let herself slip into such fantasies. They made her want to cry out how sorry she was for what was being done! Such images made her want to beg forgiveness. Like the prostitute Mary Magdalene, she longed to step into the fresco to weep beside the mother of the Lord. *It is the strain of the day*, she reasoned.

"Where was I?" Lucy pressed a finger to her temple.

"I am Karin Wallich," Karin replied. "And they know it."

"Yes." Lucy cleared her throat. "Wolf figured that out. And from there he came to the conclusion that Otto Wattenbarger was a friend of your husband. To arrest you and be able to condemn Otto as a traitor all in one day, Wolf will do whatever is necessary."

"We are not caught yet," Peter said.

"Thanks to you, Fräulein Strasburg," added Karin gently.

How kind and grateful were Karin Wallich's eyes. Lucy could not meet her gaze or respond to her thanks. "You are not safe yet. Please. You are only across the street. We must get you out of Vienna. Out of the Reich."

"Perhaps we can find a way to place the children on the transport list," Frau Singer offered.

"No. He will be checking every list." Lucy frowned. "Do you have your papers, Frau Wallich?"

Karin produced them, the old documents—the Wallich name, the photographs, the enormous *J* for Jews inscribed across the pages of the passport. "This is hopeless. You would be better off to burn these than to carry them."

"Otto took our photographs." Karin blinked back tears at the memory. "But no passports. He was going to . . . what does it matter now?"

Lucy opened her handbag and pulled out five tickets, train tickets from Vienna to Berlin, Berlin to Danzig. "Maybe . . . if we could find some other way to get you to Berlin. Catch the train there. Then it would not matter so much if you carry Jewish documents as long as they are in order. But Wolf will have men on every train platform looking for Karin Wallich. And Peter and Marlene. And Willie."

"Tickets to Danzig!" Peter touched one on the corner as though it were a ticket to paradise. "I have dreamed about a ticket to Danzig." He said wistfully. "And there it is. Magic. But no good to us."

"We can thank my dear Wolf for the tickets. I hocked his rugs at the Dorotheum to buy—"

"Hey!" Peter sparked and fumbled in his wallet. "Here it is. Otto gave this to me the night after you and Wolf showed up." He flashed it around the small circle of intense faces.

"A pawn ticket." Lucy took it from him. "Dorotheum. I guess I am not the only one."

"But you see," Peter explained, "Otto said if something happens to him—which it has—that I am supposed to go to the Dorotheum with this." He spread the fold of his wallet to display the bills. "The Nazis keep it open even on Christmas Day."

Lucy shook her head. "Yes, but there are Gestapo agents at every entrance picking up Jews right and left." She bit her lip. "I will go. If he has me arrested, you will have my train tickets. Somehow, maybe—"

"But, Fräulein—" Karin started to protest.

"You really should call me Lucy. We are in this thing together, Karin. Don't worry. Wolf will not have me killed. Not even tortured, I think. I am carrying his child, an SS baby. If I do not come back, you must remember that and not worry. He wants this baby, you see."

"If he's coming, he will have to understand!" Jacob paced the small space like an angry schoolmaster.

"Well, at least talk nice to him," Lori said.

"I *am* talking nice." With mock graciousness Jacob inclined his head to Alfie, who was trying very hard to understand the plan of escape. "Aren't I being nice, Alfie?" He did not wait for a reply. "All right, now. For the tenth time, tell me how it works, Alfie. Go ahead. Repeat it!"

Alfie's brow furrowed in thought. He wanted very much to get it right. "The train," he said doubtfully.

"Yes, yes, yes, and what about the train?"

"It will come to the border?"

"Yes. It will stop at the border check on the German side of the big fence." Jacob swept his hand over Alfie like a musical conductor pulling the notes from his orchestra.

"And what will happen on the German side of the fence?" Lori gently urged.

Alfie smiled at her. He liked it better when she asked him questions. "Nazi men with guns and dogs will look all over the train inside and outside for people who try and sneak by. Yes?"

"Good, Alfie!" Lori said. She shot Jacob a hard look.

"And then they will open the big electric gate, and the train will go through very slowly . . ."

"Yes"—Jacob resumed again—"into no-man's-land. And as the train slips through, we must each roll under the train and grab the metal rods on the bottom. Hold on very tightly, and it will carry us into no-man's-land."

Alfie nodded his head enthusiastically. It was a dangerous game, like jumping onto a trolley, but he could do it! "And the train will stop inside the no-man's-land, because there is another big electric fence on the Polish side!"

"Very good! And then what happens?" Jacob was looking relieved. Alfie seemed to have grasped their plan at last!

"When the train stops in no-man's-land, the Nazi guards get off the train and the Polish guards get on, yes?"

"Yes! And we slip on the train when the doors are open! Then the doors will be sealed, and the train will start up, and the Polish gate will open! We will ride all the way to Danzig in the bathrooms!"

Lori put a hand on Alfie's arm. "Now you see why we cannot take your kittens, Alfie! They would be hurt."

He looked at the kitten box and then at Werner kitty. "Except for Werner. I have to take Werner because he will die if I leave him. Jacob promised I could take Werner!"

"Don't get him upset," Jacob ordered Lori. "Why did you have to bring up the cats again?"

This addition of another person to their plans caused Jacob to want to rehearse everything again—walking to the car, seating arrangements, the trip out of Berlin on the autobahn. He rummaged through his knapsack in search of the road map. There were train schedules and a street map of Berlin and Danzig, but the road map was missing.

"The map!" he muttered angrily. "Where is it? Mark, did you do something with the map?"

No one had seen it since their last rehearsal. Somehow it had not made it out of New Church with the rest of the gear. Lori consoled him that perhaps it did not matter anyway, since he could probably sketch the entire map of northern Germany and then across Poland to Danzig by heart!

Jacob did not tell her that he had never driven farther than a few blocks in the city with his father, and around the Tiergarten Lanes after begging his mother to let him get behind the wheel. Somehow, staring at the straight wide lines of the autobahn on the road map had made him feel more confident. *Just get on the autobahn and drive straight to the border. . . .*

Yes, he had it all memorized, but all the same, the road map had been the closest thing to having his father sit beside him when he drove.

Jacob sat on the stone seat like the statue of The Thinker. He hoped the others could not see how frightened their leader was as the minutes ticked toward departure. He had put it off for weeks, but suddenly there was no more putting it off. *Key. Clutch. Gear. Starter. Gas. Autobahn . . .* They all believed he could do it, map or no map!

Lucy drew a deep breath to bolster her courage as she stepped out of Frau Singer's shop. The curbside where Gestapo cars had been parked was vacant, and the line for the streetcar was short. She climbed aboard and paid her fare, then sat to watch Vienna slide past as though in a dream.

Every policeman and every uniform on the street seemed a threat. She fixed her lipstick and brushed her hair, trying to act normal. She practiced a quick smile in her compact mirror and prayed that no one would see on the outside that her insides were churning like a paddle wheel on a Danube River steamer.

The bell clanged and the streetcar started forward, slowed, then lurched on again from stop to stop. Men and women got on and off. The men stared at Lucy curiously, as they always did. Some smiled, but she looked away, aloof. Now there were more reasons than the displeasure of Wolf to remain distant.

She stepped off the streetcar one block from the Dorotheum. Walking away from it, she turned the corner and doubled back to approach it from the opposite direction.

Those extra steps did nothing to make the uniformed guards at the doors of the Dorotheum vanish. The swastika flag still flapped noisily above the entrances. Her walk had served no purpose except perhaps to give Lucy a few extra minutes to compose herself before she entered the building.

She faced the stairs she had ascended to pawn the carpets. She knew which floor to go to for rugs and watches and even religious artifacts. But this ticket—what had Otto hocked? What department should she go to in this entire vast complex of rooms?

Lucy held the ticket in her fingers and frowned toward the stairs. Would it not look suspicious if she asked the concierge where she should take the ticket? He would ask her what item she wanted to redeem, and she could not even tell him what it was.

Her heart thumped wildly. People rushed past her, in the doors and out again. A man in a crisp blue uniform walked toward her. He was not smiling. She turned to go, but he called to her.

"Fräulein?"

Lucy stopped. She felt herself grow pale. He was staring at the ticket in her fingers. "I . . . I am . . ."

He took the ticket from her. "This is such a confusing place." He studied the numbers. "I get lost myself sometimes. Coats. Men's coats." He pointed down the hall. "Down there. You will see this number on the door, Fräulein."

"*Danke.*" She managed her most charming smile, the helpless-female one that always made men feel good about themselves and grateful to her that she allowed them to help.

Her composure regained, her confidence restored, Lucy took the ticket to *Men's Fine Coats and Clothing*. She glanced at the ticket before she handed it to a clerk:

Item: 1 Overcoat
Style: Double-breasted Camel's Hair
Size: 42 Regular
Quality: Excellent
Maker and Year Made: Robere, Paris, France, 1938

A dollar value had been put on this coat, of course. Lucy paid its redemption with the funds Otto had left with Peter. She gathered the package into her arms. The scent of mothballs was strong. An overcoat. Perhaps nothing more than an inheritance from Otto to Peter Wallich, whose own coat was ragged.

Or perhaps there was something else. The coat felt hot through the wrapping. Lucy wondered if everyone could see that the paper concealed something dangerous. She tried to hold it casually, as one would carry such an item home from the dry cleaners. *It is nothing. Just a coat.* But she hugged it to herself when she sat down in the streetcar. *Value? Maybe priceless.*

The remaining hours waiting in a tomb made Lori feel as if the walls and the Nazis were closing in on her. At last she wondered if her nerves would hold.

"It is Christmas Day," she moaned, "and look at us!" She closed her eyes and laid her head back on the damp stones. She missed her parents; she longed to sit in the sun again and laugh again, to walk in a street without being afraid.

From his place beside his city of tin cans, Alfie watched Lori. Mark and Jamie played with Alfie's soldiers and complimented him on the construction of towers and spires and tin-can castles. But Alfie was not listening.

It was Christmas! Alfie had forgotten all about that. He felt sorry for Lori and ashamed that he had forgotten about the presents he got for her and her mama. Lori looked worried and unhappy, as if she might cry. Her eyes were too pretty for crying, and so he told her to close them. He had a surprise for her.

Then he put the jewels in her hands. "Merry Christmas, Lori. Open your eyes." She gasped and looked at Alfie and then at the treasure. "I got them for you and . . . for your mama." He frowned. "Where is she?"

"I don't know, Alfie." Her voice was soft and nice, as it always was when she talked to him. "But where did you get such . . . things as these?"

"In the street." She liked them; he could tell. "I got them for you and your mama. And now maybe you can buy a ticket to . . . where are we going?"

"Somewhere safe." She patted his hand.

"The Promised Land? America?"

"Maybe. And when we get there we will buy a house for all of us to live in together. We will buy it with your jewels, Alfie, and no one will bother us again."

Alfie looked around at the dripping stone room that had been his home for so long. "I will like to live where there are windows. Clear windows to see through, and no bars—like it used to be. And my cat, Joseph, and her kittens will have a room all of their own." He looked at Joseph, who was feeding her babies. "I can take her, can't I, Lori?"

"No!" Jacob said from the steps. "We are taking you, but the cats are staying here! We're leaving tonight, like I said. The five of us, and no cats!"

Almost safe! Still no Gestapo vehicles in front of Otto's apartment.

Lucy hesitated a step to scan the street on either side. Clutching the package tightly, she lowered her eyes and walked toward Frau Singer's shop. These last few yards seemed more frightening than all the rest. It was here, after all, that Wolf would come. This small stretch of shops and apartments had been the focus of his attention for weeks. Possibly months.

No sooner had that thought crossed her mind than his automobile rounded the corner ahead of her, heading toward her. Unmistakable through the windscreen of the convertible she saw Wolf's grim face.

Run! Lucy's mind screamed to her. But it was too late to do anything but keep walking. He had already spotted her. The car sped up, sliding past Otto's building and screeching to a halt beside her.

Lucy managed a smile. She raised her hand and tried to look glad to see him. Maybe he had not seen the note in her handwriting on the mirror. Maybe he did not suspect that she had spoiled his hunt and flushed out the game before he had opportunity to fire.

"Where have you been?" he demanded.

"Where have *you* been?" she spat back.

"Working."

"All night?" she demanded, taking the offensive. "And what is her name, eh? Who were you working on? Is she pretty?"

Jealousy, even pretended, took him off guard. "Get in!" He slung open the passenger door and tapped his fingers impatiently on the wheel as she slid in beside him. "Working on my prisoner!" he said heatedly. Apparently he had not had much success, judging from the anger on his face. And did he know about her note?

"You should have called," she accused.

"The Jews got away. All the Wallich brood have gotten away. And now Otto denies that there were any Jews! He maintains that the woman was his sister, says they went back to the Tyrol! He is impudent in his defiance of us!" He banged a hand on the wheel, then made a U-turn and parked in front of the building. "Agent Block and his assistant went over the place with a fine-tooth comb . . . found nothing. I will search myself." The steely gaze turned on her. "So . . . you did not tell me what you are doing here."

She laughed. "You told me to have a corset made," she said coyly. "And I thought if I came, I might find you here . . . or *there*." She pointed at Otto's window. "I am sorry you have lost your Jews, Wolf. I do hope you find them again so we can go out for dinner."

Exasperated with her flippancy, he sighed and shook his head. "That would be nice."

"I need to visit the ladies' room," she said absently. "Do you mind if I come up with you? Too much coffee. Too much baby."

He shrugged. "Why not?"

Peter watched Lucy enter the apartment building beside Wolf. The SS officer seemed preoccupied, angry; but his anger was not directed at Lucy. She placed the bundle under her arm and smiled.

"What is happening?" Marlene asked contritely. "Is she coming?"

"She is with him. The officer." Peter rubbed a hand over his eyes in fear for her and astonishment at her self-control. "I don't think he found the note yet. He could not have found it. She would be arrested if he knew about it."

Behind him he could hear Marlene mumbling on the bed. He glanced at her. Tears streamed from her closed eyes. Marlene was praying.

She did not want to seem too eager to leave Wolf. Lucy wandered around the empty apartment while he dumped out drawers and pawed through Otto's belongings. Mattresses were slit open, carpets pulled up. *Nothing!* Wolf thumped the closet walls and broke the hanging rod in half in case something was hidden within its hollow center. *Nothing!*

Lucy stood patiently beside the radio as Wolf ransacked the second bedroom. She had found what she came for; it had slipped down between the wall and the sink. *A miracle!* Wolf tore through the bathroom;

opening the toilet tank, then using the heavy lid to break the sink from the wall.

Lucy browsed through the program for this week's D' Fat Lady concert. She thought of Otto at the stage. She pocketed the program, then, noticing that the radio dial was set to receive the BBC, she cranked the knob once.

Wolf gave a cry of frustrated rage. *"Nothing!"*

Lucy remained calm, complacent. "Wolf, darling, I'm going on to my errand now. You smash a while, and I'll meet you back home."

He appeared in the doorway, his shirt dark with sweat, his hair falling over his forehead, and his eyes wild. "I can smell it! They are Jews!" he shouted. "That Wallich woman! I know who they are!"

"Wolfie," she said patronizingly, "I hope you are right. Otto will not like what you have done to his flat . . . and after he found ours for us, too. This is not a way to return a favor!"

He threw a dish at her head. It crashed against the wall behind her.

She glared back at him. "All right! I have had enough! You are a child, and I am leaving! I will meet you at home when you are finished with this pogrom against your rival!"

Wolf lifted his chin. Eyes narrowed. "I will wait for you." The anger dissolved to confusion. "I . . . I need you tonight. It has not been . . . this has been a most difficult . . ."

Lucy's heart sank. He would wait in the car. *Oh, God!* She had to go back with him! *Another hour, another night of this!*

"How long will you be?" she asked quietly.

"Half an hour." He sounded contrite. The prospect of promotion was slipping away. The child she carried was now his best asset, the surest means of advancement.

"Then I'll meet you at the car." She hefted her package.

"Wait a minute. What have you got there?"

The answer hung in her throat for a moment. "Clothes to be altered." She walked past him and out the door.

"Where are they?" Lucy cried as she slipped into the shop of the reluctant corset maker.

"Mein Gott! We thought you were arrested!"

"Get them!" Lucy charged up the stairs. The parlor was empty. "Where are—?"

"In the bedroom. She is alone," Frau Singer called to Karin. "The package is here!"

Lucy tore the paper off the coat as the Wallichs pressed in around her.

"What is it? What?" She searched the pockets and turned it inside out. "What did he want you to get?"

Karin reached in and lifted the hem of the coat. She looked at the stitches that bound the silk lining to the camel's-hair fabric. Then with a soft sigh, she plucked scissors from Frau Singer's sewing basket and tore out the thread. Four brand-new, perfect official passports fell out onto the floor. Marlene's pouting image stared up from her documents. Ugly, yes. But beautiful. She laughed and picked it up. *Marlene Anne Ruger. Aryan.*

All right, so there it was. The priceless documents. Surely Wolf would suspect that such documents had been made. Perhaps he would have men on duty at every station to check photos and passports against the Gestapo pictures of the Wallichs.

"Listen to me." Lucy took Karin's arm. "I have to go with him now. But listen!"

Karin nodded; her smile of relief vanished. She could see plainly that it was not over. They were still across the street. "What should we do?"

Lucy frowned and ran her hand through her hair. She did not want Wolf to come looking for her. So little time. If he finished early . . . she groped in her handbag, pulling out the railway timetables. "Danzig . . . *Danzig!*" There it was. Two trains leaving Vienna. One tonight at 9:30. The other at 3:08 tomorrow morning. "You cannot leave together. They will be looking for four of you. Understand? Not even on the same train."

Karin blanched at the thought of separation, but agreed. "Willie and I?"

"No." Lucy said it before Peter could. "You and Marlene."

"But my baby—"

"The boys must stay together. If you are caught with a circumcised baby, they will arrest you, and . . . you know what that will mean to the child. No. You and Marlene. They will search you. No doubt of that. But they will see women, not Jews."

"What about Peter and Willie?" Marlene looked fearfully at her brothers. She was no longer thinking only about herself.

"They will go with me, as my nephews. I can handle these Gestapo types." Lucy spoke with a confidence that made everyone believe her. "You and Marlene leave tonight. Take your tickets to the ticket clerk in the third window of the central train terminal—the one opposite Stadtpark. You must see no other clerk but this one fellow. Can you remember?"

Peter was at the window. "Wolf is coming out."

"The third window!" Lucy repeated. "His name is Kurek. He has a drooping mustache. He will stamp in the date and time on your ticket. *Say it!*"

"Kurek. Third window. Central," Karin repeated.

"Wolf is standing by the car," Peter reported. "Leaning on the fender. Angry. Arms crossed."

"Yes." Lucy was breathless. "Peter. I will meet you at a quarter till three tomorrow morning—you and Willie—beside the drinking fountain to the right of the ticket window. Be there early. Kurek is off duty at 2 AM. You must get the tickets stamped before then! *Say it!*"

"Kurek. Third window. Central. Before two," Peter repeated. "Wolf threw down his cigarette. He is coming."

Lucy turned and embraced Karin Wallich, then slipped something into Marlene's hand. It was the note from the mirror. "Go now and rip it into a thousand pieces. Down the toilet with it, and no mistakes!"

Marlene smiled and ran to obey as Lucy hurried down the steps to meet Wolf at the curb.

35

The Last Pure Heart

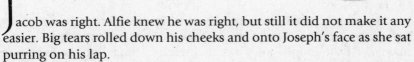

Jacob was right. Alfie knew he was right, but still it did not make it any easier. Big tears rolled down his cheeks and onto Joseph's face as she sat purring on his lap.

"I can't take you, Joseph," he said sadly. "You can't go with us. We are trying to get away from the Hitler men. These fellows do not like Jews like Jacob and Mark. And they don't like Jamie and Lori because they are real Christians." Joseph put her paws on Alfie's chest and rubbed her face in his salty tears as if she understood. "And they don't like Dummkopfs like me."

She purred loudly as though to say she liked Alfie a lot. This made Alfie blubber more.

"But the Hitler men don't have anything against cats. At least I don't think they do. I think they like cats, because cats are just cats and don't argue with them, you know?"

She purred louder.

Alfie looked up at Jacob, who was looking somewhere else and pretending not to notice Alfie and his cat, Joseph. But Alfie could tell Jacob heard them talking.

"You have to stay here with your kittens. They need you a lot. Except Werner." He frowned toward the little black-and-white kitten who tottered about on unsteady legs. "Werner is like me, Joseph," Alfie explained to the mother cat. "He is not as strong as your other babies, and so—" this was difficult to explain to a mother— "so Jacob says I can take Werner with me and take care of him. Otherwise he will die if I leave him."

Joseph did not seem to mind. She curled up on Alfie's lap and blinked sleepily at her kittens. *Maybe she understands and maybe she doesn't,* Alfie thought, but either way this was a very sad day.

Jacob let him pack some cans of milk and even sardines for Werner. Alfie had very little else to take for himself. He packed a few tin soldiers, especially Jesus and His horse. And then Lori held out the jewels Alfie had given her and told him he could use some of them to buy whatever he needed when they were out of Germany. This made him feel better. He promised Joseph that he would buy Werner a nice pillow to sleep on and lots of good food to eat.

Dressed in his black Hitler Youth uniform, Jamie ascended the steps of the crypt to reconnoiter. Jacob hoped their pursuers had given up after a day-long search and had gone home to hot cider and a warm fire by now.

The churchyard was pitch-black, although it was not late. He could not even see the silhouette of the church building as he peered out from the latch, listened, and then slid it back fully.

"Be careful," Jacob warned. Jamie inched past him and emerged in the upper chamber of the crypt. He crawled forward, clutching the key, and waited. No sound—only a slight breeze rustling dead leaves among the headstones. *So this is it!*

"Come on." Jamie fumbled with the lock. Clumsy in the dark, he could not open the gate.

"Tor auf!" Jacob demanded. Alfie took the key from Jacob and in one deft movement opened the gate.

It groaned back on its hinges. The fugitives huddled just inside the arch like partridges waiting to be flushed out. There was still no sound, no movement in the blackness. They slipped out and waited, moved forward a few paces and halted. Alfie locked the gate behind them. He reached through the bars and scratched Joseph's chin, then joined the crouching procession as it wound through the tombstones toward the break in the wall behind the gardener's shed.

Tonight there were no shouts, no alarms, no running footsteps or fluttering torches—only deathly silence. Leaves crunched beneath their feet; hands in the darkness reached out to make certain there were five in the line. Five together. Five slipping through the secret break one at a time.

It was easy, as easy as Jacob had envisioned it should be when they first thought of the plan. Still, their hearts beat the uneven rhythm of fear. Their breath came shallow, rising in little locomotive puffs of steam in the cold night.

One, two, three, four, five through the churchyard fence!

And Werner the kitten in Alfie's pocket.

Peter could not watch as his mother held the baby in a last embrace. He focused his gaze on bolts of cloth and the glowing gas heater, and finally on Marlene's brown hat. It was her best hat; it matched her coat and her eyes and hair. She was proud of it. Peter had teased her, telling her it looked like an upside-down soup bowl. Now he regretted saying so many mean things to her.

She was quiet and sad, not the usual primping, fussing little Marlene. Peter saw regret and sorrow on her face, and suddenly he wanted to tell her things he had not known he felt until this moment of parting.

Mama stood framed in the doorway of the bedroom, her arms full of Baby Willie. She rocked him and whispered quietly against his cheek, telling him things she might not ever have a chance to say to him again.

Peter knew there were things he must say to his sister, in spite of the fact she had been the bane of his existence. He took a step toward her. He towered over Marlene. She looked up at him with those chocolate brown eyes, a single tear poised in each eye, as if stuck there. Words were stuck also.

He straightened her hat. A shudder coursed through him. He wished she did not look so Jewish. He hoped that Lucy Strasburg was right. He prayed that when the Gestapo at the border checks examined Karin and Marlene they would see only mother and daughter, not two Jewesses.

"Do I look all right?" she ventured. "In my soup bowl?"

"Very nice . . . in your . . ." Peter swallowed hard. How he hated this emotion, this longing to hold on! It was so much easier to want to punch her! So much easier to cringe at every word. But now that *good-bye* might mean forever, nothing could shield him from loving her. Even her. Sister. Marlene. He could not say more. He reached out and pulled her close in a hug—awkward at first, then a warm merging of emotion they both felt.

"You know, Peter," she whispered, "maybe someday I will grow up . . . and be like Mama. And you will like me." Such hope filled her voice!

"Until then," he whispered, "you keep me on my toes, *ja?*"

She laughed and sniffed. Tears of relief came. "You and Willie will be careful? I'm not worried about me. I would rather something happen to me than you and Willie, see?"

"Nothing will happen to any of us, Marlene." He tried to sound reassuringly gruff. He patted her back. "Just believe that. We will meet at the Danziger Hotel day after tomorrow. Like we planned." He lifted her chin and kissed her lightly on the furrowed brow. "Don't worry. Just take care of Mama. . . ."

His words trailed away. He felt his head grow light. Mama stood at his elbow, pulling a string from his jacket, straightening his hair, stroking his cheek. He was almost grown now, and Mama was trying very hard to say good-bye to him as if he were a man. But the expression in her eyes when she looked at his face was the same as it had been when she looked at Willie. How he wished she could rock him, too, and whisper against his cheek! He wanted to lay his head on her shoulder and hear her say that everything really would be all right.

But now it was his turn to embrace her, to comfort her, to say all the things a man of courage must say. Papa would expect it of him! So why was he crying?

"There, there, Son," she said quietly, smoothing his hair and letting him rest his face against her shoulder. "You must not worry. We have not come this far to fail now. We will believe!" A mother was expected to kiss away her child's hurt. Even a child as tall as Peter.

He straightened and wiped his wet cheeks on his sleeve. "Yes, Mama." He cleared his throat. "We will meet at the Danziger Hotel. And don't worry about Willie. I will take good care of him. You know he is as happy with me as anyone. You and Marlene . . . have a safe trip, then."

Peter watched them from the dark window until they boarded the trolley, paid their fare, and sat perfectly framed in the lighted car. Marlene smiled, excited about making such a long trip. Then those brown eyes began desperately searching the facades of the buildings, finally fixing on the window where Peter stood in the blackness. The small gloved hand rose; fingers curled slightly down in farewell, and Peter saw her lips move: "I love you, Peter."

They had planned even this. Lori walked alongside Jacob. She held his hand and talked to him about last Christmas as they strolled along the sidewalk.

Jamie and Mark flanked Alfie, who looked out of place between them. He towered over them both. *The sore thumb*, Jacob thought, praying that they would not meet any old acquaintances on the streets of downtown Berlin tonight.

The neon lights and blaring traffic assaulted their senses after weeks of enforced silence and nights without light. Lori tried not to look spellbound; she kept her eyes on Jacob's face, pulling at his sleeve when he, too, gawked at the marquee of a cabaret that blinked on and off in red and yellow lights.

"Where is the car?" he called to Jamie when they were out of earshot of three drunken middle-aged couples.

"I think . . . just up there—" Jamie jerked his thumb. "But maybe not anymore. Who knows?"

Alfie knew. "Pastor's car?" he asked with a broad, childlike smile. "I saw it. It needs a wash." He raised his nose in the air as if to take his bearings in the cacophony of the city streets; then he pointed. "It is still there."

Lori squeezed Jacob's hand to slow him down. Let the trio cross the street first. They must not walk too close together. There was a policeman on one corner. And there was another.

The five had to walk separately; if policemen were looking for Jamie and Lori as Alfie said, then they must not present their faces like photographs off a wanted poster.

A uniformed officer walked toward them. He looked at Lori's face, letting his gaze slide down her once and then up again. He looked away, frowned, and then looked back.

"Laugh," Jacob said softly; then he looked at her and guffawed loudly. She mimicked him, her laughter bordering on the hysteria of terror.

Two young people out for a walk, having fun. The officer did not recognize her after all. He brushed past them and they hurried, still laughing, to cross the street.

There stood the car, caked in dust, its windscreen dull gray. The tires looked low. Jacob casually unlocked the door, opening it for Lori. He was keenly aware that it was at this point the trap might be sprung. Had Pastor Ibsen's car been identified? Had it been left here just for such a moment as this?

Lori slid into the passenger side. Her father's glasses lay on the dashboard, his gloves still on the seat. She could not suppress a groan as she reached over and unlocked Jacob's door. He jumped behind the wheel, and the three others crammed into the backseat.

Key! Clutch in! Gearshift in neutral! Turn the starter, and—

"What is wrong with it?" Lori gasped.

The engine groaned and moaned, trying to turn over. Then it died.

Jacob pounded a fist on the steering wheel. This far, and now the battery was dead! Could it be?

He prayed and tried again. *Key. Clutch. Gear. Starter.*

The moan sounded more pitiful than before. Jacob sat staring through the filth of the window. Lights from the neon signs blinked in weird patterns on his ashen face.

"Dead," he said dully. "Dead battery." He bit his lip and instructed, "Stay here!"

They could see him as he struggled to open the awkward latch and lift the hood. It creaked open like a gaping mouth. Jacob pounded on the terminals of the battery in hopes . . . *maybe just corroded?*

Cars whizzed by him. He left the hood open and climbed back behind the wheel. *Key! Clutch! Gear! Oh, God! Starter!*

This time there was a slight groan and a click. Jacob's frightened breathing fogged the window.

"Hey, Max!" Mark asked, calling Jacob by the old nickname. "What do we do now?"

Then the unthinkable happened. A green police car slipped in along the curb in front of them. Nose to nose, the vehicle hemmed them in. An officer got out and walked slowly up to Jacob's window. His finger twirled, indicating that the window should be lowered.

Lori prayed, certain that the car had indeed been left here to trap them. Now there was nothing more they could do. No more running. No place left to hide.

Jacob did not look at the police officer as he rolled his window down.

The officer peered in, and a puzzled look crossed his face. He glanced at them, then looked hard at the raised hood.

Alfie blurted out, "Hey, I know you! You are the . . . the policeman who . . . at the corner when I was lost."

Doubt crossed the face of the officer. He squinted into the backseat at Alfie. Same cap. Same coat. Same face. Were there any left in Berlin like this one?

"Yes, I remember you. Ah! Yes. I see you have gotten use from your clothes, *ja!*" He tipped his hat at Jacob. "Your brother?"

Jacob managed an astonished nod. "Yes . . . my . . . my brother."

"We are old friends." The officer opened Jacob's door. "He is the last honest fellow in Berlin, I think. I have thought of him often. So—" he thumped the car—"what is the problem? Aside from a layer of dirt?"

"Battery." Jacob managed to stutter the word twice.

"I can give you a jump start," said the officer with a wave of his hand. "But you will have to keep the engine running until you get where you are going."

The beads of perspiration on Jacob's forehead reflected the colors of the neon lights. In the backseat, Mark and Jamie sat frozen and silent, not believing that a German policeman was hooking cables to the battery of their stalled automobile and advising them to keep going and not turn off the engine.

Jacob cranked the starter one more time. The engine coughed and rumbled and vibrated to a thundering start.

"Let her run a few minutes," advised the officer. "She has been sitting quite a while."

Was that a smile on his lips?

"Yes."

"I checked the license and registration, since it is on my beat. I was hoping someone might pick her up." He looked past Jacob, directly at Lori. "You are leaving Berlin?"

She nodded. Should she tell him anything? *Anything?* Should he know they were leaving?

He rubbed his hand across his jaw and peered up the street and then down again. "Listen to me." He lowered his voice. "There are roadblocks across the bridges, and on the main autobahns from Berlin in every direction. They are looking for lots of criminals; among them a brother and sister . . . *ja*?"

Lori's mouth went dry as cotton. "*Ja*," she managed. "*Bitte*?" What were they to do?

"*Gut.* You understand me." The officer looked hard at Jacob. "I do not know who you are, but if you do not want to end up in prison, you must take the side streets out of the city."

Jacob could hardly make his mouth work. "Which . . . ?"

"Do you know Landsbergerstrasse?"

"Yes."

"It runs past Friedrichshain. The park."

Jacob knew the place well—a wooded area filled with streams and small lakes. He had gone swimming there with friends. "Yes. I know it."

"Leave the city by that direction. If you are followed, drive into the park. Abandon your car and run into the woods. They will not catch all of you that way at least." He looked at Alfie's innocent face with concern.

Alfie held up his kitten. "You see what I have?"

A moment of pain and pity flashed across the man's broad peasant face. "Yes, boy. And it is a nice kitten. Did you find it in the street also, like your clothes?"

"No. He is Werner. His mama and brothers are back in the Halder grave at New Church with my mama. Please . . . will you take care of them?"

The officer exhaled loudly. This appeal was more than he had bargained for. Danger at every turn, and this poor boy was thinking about his kittens at home with Mama. *The purest heart in Berlin. Maybe the last pure heart?* "Yes, boy. I will see to them."

With a curt nod, he backed up a step and turned from them. Unclamping the cables, he slammed down the hood.

"Now get going before someone arrests you for illegal parking."

"We are certain that they were hiding out in New Church like little mice," Officer Hess explained with a shrug. "Gone now, of course. But they left us an itinerary."

"And this is what you have found of the Ibsen children in all this time?" Minister of Propaganda Joseph Goebbels slapped his hand down hard on the road map that had been found beneath the window at New Church. "A road map! My own press prints these. What is that supposed to mean?"

Officer Alexander Hess was a patient man. Because of his patience he had earned the reputation of achieving his goals. He traced his finger along the blue ink that followed the line of the new autobahn from Berlin to the train crossing at the Polish border.

"You will notice two things, Reichminister Goebbels," he said. "They intend to cross *here*, where the express train to Danzig passes the border."

"Maybe this is nothing! *Mein Gott!* Such a line could have been drawn by Pastor Ibsen years ago and the map discarded by the children."

Hess smiled. Patient and clerklike, he had reasoned it all out. "If one is going to cross into Poland at the train crossing, it would be customary to board the train in Berlin, you see." He waited for that ordinary fact to penetrate the irritation of Goebbels. "However, the children have marked the autobahn. They intend to drive from Berlin to the border and cross into Poland just *there*. They will abandon their car, no doubt."

"What car? What? They have a *car*? Why haven't we heard about an automobile before?"

"After I saw the map, I checked vehicle registrations in Berlin. There have been no thefts; however, there is an automobile registered to Pastor Ibsen. It is missing." He slid his finger along the marked route to indicate that the vehicle should now be heading north and east toward the Polish border. "I have sent out a description of the Ibsen children to all the towns along that route—and a description of the vehicle, of course. Nothing could be simpler. A reward is offered. They will be picked up within hours, and we will transport them to their father's prison, a mile from the border crossing. You will have your statement from Pastor Ibsen. The world will have it." His matter-of-fact attitude reassured Goebbels.

"I will give the Führer *your* word on that." A thinly veiled threat lay behind the comment. If Hess failed to find the children, he would also fail to break Ibsen. And the Führer wanted badly to add the Ibsen name to his roster of faithful churchmen.

Lucy lay staring up at the dark ceiling. Wolf's heavy arm stretched across her as if to hold her there beside him even as he slept. When she tried to turn, the arm tightened, a prison of flesh and desire that kept her chained to him like a slave.

Hours ticked past slowly. When the clock tolled nine-thirty, she imagined Karin Wallich and Marlene on board the train leaving Vienna at that moment. She wanted to pray for them, to remind the Lord of His mother's eyes. She wanted to ask that everything go well. There was no question about the authenticity of the passports. She only hoped the mother and daughter had not been pulled aside for questioning.

The night slipped by and Lucy found herself thinking that at this hour, the train would pass through one city or the other. Perhaps tomorrow she would also be passing those checkpoints. But it was a long way from Wolf's bed to tomorrow.

Lucy was afraid. Alone with him like this, she knew what he would do to her if he suspected. She had told Frau Singer that he would not beat her, would not kill her. In reality, she knew better than that. And if, by some miracle, he only had her locked up in the Lebensborn, he would have her eliminated after the baby was born.

The baby!

A gentle butterfly fluttered briefly in her womb. She felt it every day now. It filled her with the purest love she had ever known, and the deepest grief as well. Mothers like her who had lain in bed and wondered about the mystery of life within them now said good-bye to the children they had borne. Everywhere in the Reich, women like Karin Wallich sent their babies away on trains and hoped that one day they might be together again.

Lucy did not want to send her baby away to be raised by another woman. She wanted to hold him, to feel him turn his face to be nourished by her. She longed to hold his little hands and praise him when he took a step. She wanted his smiles and kisses to belong to her heart, his tears to fall against her shoulder.

She had witnessed the sorrowing eyes of the mother of Christ in the face of Karin Wallich. And in that moment her own fears and sorrows had somehow bonded inextricably with the grief of every woman in the Reich who was forced to say good-bye . . . forever.

Jewish women had their children torn physically from their arms. Christian mothers who had remained steadfast watched as their children were spiritually poisoned, growing finally as dark as the masters of

Germany. This sort of separation was just as real; the grief, though different, just as profound. The end was just as final. *Eternal.*

Lucy wanted to pray, but she did not know how. Like Mary Magdalene at the foot of the cross, she longed to talk to the Son of that sorrowing mother.

Jesus! her heart cried as the clock chimed 1:00 AM. *Lord of hurting mothers . . . hold our babies close. The wolves are at our heels.*

She silently whispered other awkward words. She did not pray for herself, but for her child and the children of other mothers. And then, a small miracle—*Wolf rolled over!*

Lucy rose quickly and dressed in the dark bathroom. She could not take her clothing. No chance to pack. But she rummaged in her drawer and stuffed a change of underclothes into her largest handbag and found her grandmother's crucifix as well.

Wolf groaned softly from the bed. Lucy stood, unmoving, in the blackness. Peter would be at the station now. He would have the tickets stamped. The train would be turning slowly, pointing north toward Berlin, and then to Danzig.

Suddenly the light flashed on. "Where are you going?" Wolf demanded, scowling at her in the bright light.

"I . . . I didn't mean to wake you." She felt like weeping. Now he would never let her go!

"What is that in your hand?" He stared hard at the crucifix.

Lucy held it up for him to see. "My grandmother's—"

"Ah. You are going to Mass again." He switched off the light without looking at the clock and lay down heavily on his pillow. "You and your God of hopeless causes. Pray that I find the Jews, will you? And bring me back a pastry from Demel's."

36

Freedom Ride

The clashing gears of the Ibsen car resisted when Jacob did not push the clutch pedal in far enough. Lori glanced nervously at him. Her father's automobile had never made such terrible noises before. *Maybe from sitting so long without use?*

The missing road map was emblazoned like a neon sign inside Jacob's skull. Streets spun off Alexanderplatz like spokes from a wheel. Some led away to Gestapo roadblocks, spot checks, and certain arrest. Jacob correctly turned onto Landsbergerstrasse. At first it was well lit and broad, later dwindling to two lanes and eventually flanked by fields and farms and thick woods.

This was not as he had planned—no straight highway to set his course and carry them north and east two hundred miles straight to the border at Firchau! The back road they traveled was poorly marked, unlit, and often in need of attention. But some consolation lay in the fact that there was no traffic to contend with.

They passed the Hoppegarten racetrack eleven miles outside of Berlin. *Only eleven miles!* And yet Jacob felt a sense of exhilaration. *I know exactly where we are!* He had driven this complaining car eleven miles closer to the border and had not yet been stopped, had not even seen a police car.

He was driving hunched forward over the wheel.

"Can you see?" Lori asked, noting his uncomfortable position.

"The dirt on the windscreen," he replied.

"Well, you can't drive two hundred miles to Firchau like that," she said. "Your back will be broken."

He had not realized she was commenting on the awkward way he was sitting. He smiled self-consciously. She was right. His back and shoulders ached after only eleven miles. He sat back against the leather. He tried to relax his death grip on the steering wheel and look casual about this, like his father used to look when he drove. Head slightly raised to peer down his nose at the road. Fingers limp as he gently guided the car. Yes. That was better. He could do this. He looked toward her as if to speak, and as he did, the wheels also turned with his head.

The car swerved to the right. He overcorrected, crossing the center and brushing the gravel of the left shoulder like a drunken driver.

Cries of alarm rose from the backseat. Lori sat rigid with her legs braced hard on the floorboard, her mouth open in a noiseless scream.

And then Jacob brought the car back on the road again. "Sorry," he muttered when he could breathe again.

"J-Jacob?" Lori stammered his name. "Have you driven much before this?"

"Some." That had been a long time ago, he wanted to tell her, before the state had confiscated the family car. Their Jewish-owned car had been Aryanized and now belonged to the family of some minor Nazi official. Jacob did not explain all this to her. He had never mentioned it. The humiliation of it was too painful.

"Well, listen," Lori suggested. "*Don't look at me*, but listen. I learned to drive with this car. I passed my driver's test, and . . . maybe I should drive and you navigate?"

He did not speak for a long time. The road was straight. He wanted to ask her if she had guessed he could not really drive. But he did not. He knew she knew. It was easier to pretend that she did not.

"A good idea," he said, braking raggedly and pulling to the side of the road.

She took the wheel and shifted the gears effortlessly; the brakes did not grab or squeal. The three boys in the backseat fell soundly asleep, and for the first time since he had imagined this desperate flight from Berlin, Jacob actually believed they might get out safely.

The great steam locomotive panted and drummed beneath the train shed. The sound was not half so loud as the pounding of Lucy's heart as she hurried into the central terminal!

Peter Wallich stood by the fountain. He leaned against the wall and propped Willie up on his knee to face him.

In a tweed cap, marching knickers, and jacket, Peter no longer

looked ragged. He had replaced his old coat with Otto's camel-hair overcoat, folded on top of his suitcase.

He did not seem to see her at first, although she raised her hand
when he looked her direction. He lifted Willie high above his head and
smiled and talked to him as a gendarme strolled past. The policeman
gave the brothers a warm glance. The officer paused as if to speak to Peter, but Peter did not look at him and continued to make Willie giggle.
No chance to talk. He walked on.

Only then did Peter look at Lucy and then up at the face of the huge
bronze clock on the far end of the station. She was late; it was nearly
three o'clock. He had been fending off the wolves for fifteen minutes
longer than he wanted to! All these things were obvious in the hard look
he gave her as she approached.

"Where have you been, Aunt Lucy?" he muttered under his breath.
"We are the only passengers this morning. Everyone else at the station is
Gestapo."

"Are we boarding yet?"

"We could have been snug inside the train ten minutes ago," he remarked sourly. He seemed to have forgotten who had purchased his
tickets and rescued his passports.

"I told you," Lucy replied, taking his suitcase in hand, "I have a
brother named Peter. He was your age once—a rotten age. I could handle him, too." She shot him a threatening glance. "Manners, *bitte*, and
we will get along nicely." She smiled sweetly. "Is that clear?"

With Jacob as navigator and Lori as pilot, they skirted the tiny walled city
of Custrin and struck out through rolling farms toward Landsberg.

At times Jacob thought he heard the distant shrill of a train whistle
across the land. The tracks, he knew, were not far from the road they now
traveled.

The city of Landsberg cast a soft glow on the predawn horizon. It was
still hours before sunrise, and in the absolute stillness of the sleeping
country, the fact that they were running for their lives seemed unreal.

Just beyond Landsberg, the coughing and sputtering of the engine
jerked them back to reality. Then it clattered loudly and died.

"What's wrong with it?" Jacob slapped the dashboard as though he
could wake up the machine. "Has it ever done this before?"

Lori's face was tense as she steered the dying vehicle to the side of the
road. "Once," she said quietly.

"What is it?"

"Papa said its head broke." Lori winced. "I think that's very bad."

Lucy Strasburg's stern remark served as a warning shot over Peter's bow. It took him by surprise. He liked it, and suddenly decided he liked her, too.

He shrugged his agreement to her peace terms, then stepped back as she proceeded to waltz them through three different passport checks. None of the officials even looked at Peter or Willie. They were too busy looking at Lucy, listening to her talking about her nephews here beside her, and her sister who had sent them to Vienna to keep Lucy company over the holidays.

She talked and talked, spinning such a story that Peter had to shake his head in order to keep himself from believing her as well. The pressure was off, and he suddenly felt very tired.

Everyone on the platform knew all the details of their stay in Vienna within minutes—what parks and museums and concerts they had attended, how long they had stayed, and what they liked to eat best.

Astonished, Peter listened as Lucy named off all the places he had wanted to visit in a lifetime of living in Vienna, but had never had the chance. He heard tales of himself patting the nose of a Lipizzan stallion and being invited to watch the training.

"All this in just two weeks!" Lucy exclaimed.

The passport officer smiled pleasantly as she finished her recital. Only now did he look Peter full in the face. "And how do you feel after such a vacation in Vienna, young man?"

"Tired," Peter answered truthfully.

The officer laughed uproariously. "Indeed! Who would not be? Sleep all the way to Danzig then, eh?"

"No, no!" Lucy linked her arm through Peter's. "He has to keep me company!"

Peter thought she would have stood and chatted another few minutes with this uniformed officer. Did she know that this was a fellow who had people locked up at will? If she was aware, she did not seem to care. He was an excellent audience. And she, perhaps, was the finest actress Peter had ever seen.

The train whistle shrilled the three-minute departure warning. Lucy had become old friends with a man who would cut Peter's throat if he had bothered to take him through the customary physical body search. But the search had not been requested. She had talked until the last possible instant they could board the train.

Peter decided that she was either the dumbest woman he had met or the smartest. She was fearless; he was sure of that.

Four o'clock in the morning. No one was up except perhaps for dairy-men milking their cows. Soon enough, however, there would be farmers driving this road to market. They might notice the abandoned car and ask questions. Maybe someone would even call the police and give the location. Then it would be easy for the officials to check the registration and discover that the car was the property of a certain Pastor Karl Ibsen.

"We'll have to hide it," Jacob said, trying to find a suitable place to stash the vehicle.

Alfie inhaled deeply. "There are lots of big trees over there. And a river too, I think. Let's put it in the water."

Jacob no longer felt like questioning Alfie Halder. As Jamie said, Alfie was smarter than Jacob thought.

With Lori steering and Werner the kitten comfortably on the dash, the boys pushed the useless vehicle toward the sloping banks of the Warthe River. Deep enough for good-sized ships, the Warthe would eas-ily swallow up the car.

After an hour of muscle, they grabbed the kitten, then gave one final heave, sending the derelict car to a watery grave.

They could see the dairyman in the light of his swinging lantern as he walked slowly toward the barn.

Ducking low behind the hedge, Lori brushed the dirt from Jamie's black Hitler Youth uniform and straightened his hair.

"All right, you know what to say to him?" Jacob asked Jamie.

"Yes." Jamie recited. "Heil Hitler." He hated that part especially. "My friends and I are traveling, and we would like to sleep in your barn a little while and then have breakfast. We can pay you well."

"Good," Jacob said, thumping him on the back. It was always impor-tant to know your lines. "If he says no, then walk that way, back toward the river. We will meet you."

They were all exhausted. Days of preparation and anticipation had left them without energy. Now that the car was in the drink, it seemed that they deserved a little sleep in some fresh straw. Lori prayed that this farmer would be a kind man. Papa always said that German farmers were the best people on earth. He had said it even after Hitler had come to power. Plain people, they did not change with the winds of politics . . . they simply grew more seasoned with their land.

This was an older man. His gait was stiff and slow in the early morning cold. Maybe he would not like to hear Jamie give the salute, but it was best to be prepared.

Jamie struck off across the yard and met the farmer at the door to his barn. Up went the arm. Heil!

The farmer did not respond in kind. This was a good sign.

Snatches of conversation drifted to them amidst the crowing of roosters and the impatient bellowing of cows wanting to be milked.

"Why did you want to stay here?" the farmer bellowed also. A no-nonsense man. "There is a Hitler Youth camp just over that hill. Go stay with them, why don't you?"

"Ummm. Not all of my friends are . . . Hitler Youth. And, ummm . . . your barn is a better place for us."

Silence. A big laugh from the farmer. "It's hard to know who to give the stiff arm to; isn't it, Son?"

Moments later, Jamie beckoned them to come at a run. Within fifteen minutes the farmwife had brought them blankets and all five were tucked in the sweet-smelling straw.

They had only four hours' sleep among the belching, cud-chewing milk cows belonging to Herr Schöne and his wife, but it was their best sleep since Kristal Nacht.

They awakened to the voices of the old couple as they argued at the door of the barn.

"They cannot go out. The Hitler Youth will see them, and—"

"Those little black-beetle swastika wavers," growled the farmer in his quietest whisper. "I thought these children were part of that mob. But they can't be. Did you see the big one with the kitten?"

"Shhh!" scolded the farmwife, Frau Schöne. "They will hear you!"

Wide-awake, Jacob rolled over to see if Alfie had heard the comment about him.

Alfie's eyes were open, and he smiled broadly. He held up Werner and whispered to Jacob. "They are talking about my kitten. They like Werner. They like us too, I think."

It was another miracle, Alfie said—thick slices of fresh, warm bread with lots of butter slathered on top, a pitcher of fresh milk, then another, and a third! None of them could remember when they had eaten anything so wonderful! They shouted their thanks to Herr Schöne, who was mostly deaf, as Frau Schöne explained. And the couple would not hear of taking payment!

Little Werner lapped up milk from Alfie's cup until his furry belly bulged. Even the kitten's eyes looked as if they might pop. Alfie told them all he would have to be careful and not squeeze the kitten after such a meal.

A second miracle followed the bread and milk. Herr Schöne smoothed his drooping mustache and peered down at his guests. "It is not safe for you to travel on foot around here in daylight. Not even in the dark. Not with that camp of Blackshirts over there. They'd think nothing of popping that kitten and then going after you."

"Not so harsh," protested the Frau to her husband. "You will frighten them!"

"They need to be frightened. Terrible days, these days. So—" he lifted his chin—"where are you going?"

Lori and Jacob exchanged looks. This was not in the plan. They had vowed to trust no one!

Lori shrugged. Jacob told him. "Northeast to Firchau."

"You hear that, Mama?" shouted the farmer. "North to Firchau!"

Jacob imagined that the Hitler Youth could probably hear it as well.

"*Sehr gut!*" exclaimed the old Frau. "Today Papa is heading just that direction. Cabbages and chickens are going north as far as Schneidemuhl. Would you care to ride?"

The train to Danzig chugged into the enormous new Sudahnhof train terminal in Berlin, a glass-and-steel cathedral of technology and modern engineering. At this latest structure of the Reichsbahn, Nazi Party members in good standing disembarked during the layover for the usual document checks. Murals and sculptures displaying the mythical bodies of strong Aryan workers adorned the place with the perfect ideals for the race.

The steam of the locomotive billowed up and cascaded from the domed roof, and Peter thought they had entered a new version of hell. He did not want to tour the building in spite of the hour layover. Lucy stayed with him as she had done throughout the long trip from Vienna as passengers had gotten on and off all along the way. She had faced them all with her dazzling personality. Those who had been reluctant to talk with her, had, nonetheless, done so.

Not one of the strangers who had entered their lives along the way would even remember what Peter and Willie looked like. When these travelers looked back on their trip, they would remember only that the compartment had been shared with a garrulous blond from Bavaria.

The Berlin terminal was crawling with police and agents. The Biedermeier friendliness of Vienna was nonexistent on the faces of the plainclothes officers who scrutinized everyone from behind their newspapers. Peter had not imagined that the atmosphere of heaviness could be darker anywhere than it was in Vienna, but here in the north every face looked grim and fixed. Perhaps it was the close proximity to Hitler and the policy makers of the Reich; everywhere arms flipped up and lips formed the Heil Hitler. Hello. Good-bye. Heil Hitler. The stuttering blasphemy echoed in the air. In Vienna, Otto had taught Peter how to cross himself like a good Catholic, but here, the religious genuflect was that stiff arm! In Berlin there was no god but Hitler.

A sharp rap sounded on the door of the compartment. "Fräulein?" the porter called. "Everyone is getting off the train."

"Come in." Lucy fixed a smile on her lips, but even that was wearing thin. Perhaps she felt the heaviness, too.

The porter opened the door a crack. "I am ordered to say . . . to tell all passengers . . . the train will be delayed another hour." He gestured toward their windows. "You see?"

A uniformed band filed into the station. Behind them came the black-shirted security forces of the SS. They stood in long rows from the entrance of the Bahnhof to a smaller platform, where a train with only four cars waited.

"The Führer?" Lucy asked.

"He will be coming soon," the porter said. "The Ministry of Propaganda has told us to tell everyone in Bahnhof. The Führer has a political guest—some foreigner. We need to make an impression. If you and your nephews will join the crowd, *bitte*. There are flags provided."

Unconsciously, Peter touched his passport in his coat pocket. The door closed and Lucy made a face to show her distaste of these things. "Cheer loud, Peter," she instructed. "Young men your age consider the Führer their hero."

Peter held Willie in his arms so that he would have a reason not to give the salute. One could not be expected to stand at attention and say those words with a baby in one's arms.

The railway official passed out miniature swastika flags at the turnstile. Hundreds of people came from out of nowhere, then thousands. The band began to play a military march. Peter was given two flags to wave, as though Willie could also hold one of them. Then in the jostling crush and the hum of excitement, they were somehow pushed forward to the front of the mob.

As "Deutschland Über Alles" played, Hitler appeared, surrounded by an entourage of Reich officials. Goebbels and fat Hermann Göring came behind the Führer, and even the brutal schoolmaster Himmler, the man Peter's father called a butcher. All the men who had destroyed their lives.

Peter raised his little flag and screamed "Heil Hitler" along with all the rest. The Führer reached out to touch the hands of his adoring people who had come to worship him. He came nearer down the line until, at last, horribly, he locked eyes on the sweating, frantic face of Peter holding baby Willie.

"Heil Hitler!" Peter managed to snap to attention in spite of the baby in his arms.

"A fine example of young Aryan manhood!" the Führer said. He took Willie into his arms, and the bulbs of a hundred cameras popped to capture the tender moment.

God! Oh, God! Help!

"Heil! Yes. Heil . . . Heil . . ." Peter stammered. The men around the Führer laughed with amusement at the young red-haired Aryan so overcome by the attention of his lord.

"Your name?" the Führer demanded.

"Peter . . . Ruger . . . mein Führer."

More laughter.

"This is your brother?"

"Ja. My brother."

"You must both grow up to serve the Fatherland. *Ja?*"

"*Ja. Ja.* Mein Führer."

All this was caught by the camera's eternal eye. Someone scribbled down Peter's name. The Führer returned the infant prop and passed on to the next target of his attention.

Peter could scarcely breathe as the ceremony ended with echoing chants of *"Sieg Heil!"*

Lucy, ashen with fright, guided him back to their train. They were allowed to keep their flags, and all along the way people patted Peter on the back and rubbed Willie's soft curls for luck as the Führer had done.

Peter could barely answer questions during the document check, and when they were allowed back into their compartment, a fellow in a black SS uniform filled the space across from him. It was still a long way to the border.

From within their hollowed-out nest among crates of chickens and cabbages, Jacob could clearly hear the voices of the young men who manned the roadblock.

"We will have to take a look through your cargo."

Farmer Schöne replied with his usual flair. "Eh? Speak up! Cabbages and chickens; that's what."

The youthful soldier replied with equal volume. "We are looking for fugitives known to be heading this—"

"No! Cabbages and chickens. You can look, but they have been loaded since last night, and you have to put them back."

The soldiers talked among themselves. *"Himmel!* Gottfried, will you look at that pile of crates? Like the Eiffel Tower with feathers. It will take us hours!"

They addressed the old farmer again. "We are looking for two children. A boy and a girl. Traveling in a tan car."

"Eh? Two children? *Nein!* We have eight children. Thirty-three grandchildren."

"The old fellow doesn't even know what we're talking about."

"And on the truck is cabbages and chickens. You can look, but put them back right, and in a hurry. They are for the garrison in Schneidemuhl, and the general doesn't like to be kept waiting!"

After a few seconds more of mumbled conversation, the guards waved the old farmer through the line without the usual *Heil.*

The locomotive whistle howled farewell to the demons of Berlin as Peter leaned back in the corner of his seat and let weakness wash over him. The devil, clad in brown, had touched him and burned the energy out of him. He was exhausted.

Lucy was already talking familiarly to the SS officer.

"I loathe these stiff-collared tunics." The officer unbuttoned the top button. Peter thought this round-faced man looked more like a shop clerk than an SS. "But there are times when duty dictates . . ." He frowned. "I know you! Vienna! You keep company with a certain major . . . Wolfgang von Fritschauer!"

Lucy giggled with pretended delight. "What a memory!" She leaned forward. "I confess . . . I do not remember you."

"I was not in uniform." He snapped his fingers. "Your name is . . . Lucy. Lucy, is it? Who could forget you?"

This was the penalty she paid for talking to everyone from railway porters to street peddlers. "What a mind! I don't have any memory at all."

The officer extended his hand. "No matter. My name is Alexander Hess. Special investigations."

"Lieutenant Hess."

"Alex, please. We are old friends, although you do not know it."

She tilted her head slightly and brushed her hair back from her forehead. "And how far are you traveling?" she asked the lieutenant.

"All the way to the border of Poland," he replied, warming to the look in her eyes. "An unpleasant duty. Dealing with traitors."

"I am so relieved we will be traveling together," she said in almost a whisper. "My nephew . . . I have worn you out; haven't I, Peter?"

Peter nodded. The words sounded as if they were coming from a deep canyon in the Alps, echoes in his head. He was too tired to be frightened of the skull-and-crossbones insignia on the uniform. The lightning bolts appeared harmless enough. Baby Willie had already drifted off to sleep on the padded bench beside Peter.

Lucy laughed and tucked her arm beneath that of the officer. "You see? He can't even keep his eyes open. I need a little company. I am best late at night." Her smile dazzled the officer.

"*Ja?* You are?"

Lucy smiled patronizingly at Peter. "Just close your eyes and go to sleep, Peter. We won't pay any attention to you, and you don't pay any attention to us, eh?"

As Peter closed his eyes and the train lurched forward out of the station, Lucy asked the lieutenant if he had any schnapps in that little silver flask of his.

37

The Angels' Gift

When Peter opened his eyes, the reading lamp was on above the head of the SS officer. Lucy was not in the compartment. Willie was gone.

The SS lieutenant sat across from Peter. His tunic was unbuttoned, his boots off. His face was unshaven and his hair disheveled. He smelled strongly of schnapps. And he was staring.

It was a hard, curious sort of stare, the kind of stare that asked, *"Haven't I seen you someplace before? Someplace besides where you say we met?"*

The look instantly sent a shot of adrenaline through Peter. He sat up, suddenly wide-awake. "Where is my aunt?" he asked in a croaking voice.

"Took your baby brother to the washroom. Change his diapers."

"Ah." Peter focused his gaze out the window. The expression on the face of the officer did not change. Peter prayed that he would look somewhere else, or that Lucy would come back. No one ever looked at him when she was around. Why had she taken Willie out to change him? Why had she left Peter alone with this iron-jawed SS officer? Then Peter remembered. Willie was circumcised. One look at that, and the lieutenant would know everything.

"So, what Hitler Youth unit are you in?" asked the officer, the smell of schnapps sour on his breath.

"You mean Aunt Lucy didn't tell you everything about me?" Peter wished now that he had not slept through her conversation. No doubt she had told this fellow all about Peter—details that Peter did not know.

"No, she didn't. So—"

"Pardon, *bitte*. I have to use the toilet," Peter said. He fumbled with the door, pushing against it instead of pulling.

"Pull." The man's voice held an edge, even in that one word—some doubt he wrestled with when he studied Peter. Had he seen the photographs of the Wallich family? Was he trying even now to put the name and place to the face?

Peter escaped the closeness of the compartment and leaned heavily against the wall of the corridor. Where was Lucy?

The train rattled hollowly over a trestle bridge as Peter walked toward the washrooms. Why had Lucy left him there alone and given the officer time to look at him, time to think?

The door of their compartment swung back and the officer emerged, following Peter. The corridor light glistened on the man's close-cropped blond hair. Shadows emphasized the pocked skin. His blue eyes were bloodshot beneath a jutting brow. The train rocked off the bridge and settled into an even rhythm again just as Peter reached the line to the men's room. It was a single compartment. *Thank God!* More Jews had been discovered and massacred in men's rooms than any other place in the Reich.

The lieutenant stood in line behind Peter without speaking. Peter grew more nervous as each man moved forward into the stall. He imagined the lieutenant breaking down the door after him, shouting to everyone that here was another circumcised Jew! Peter Wallich had been hiding at Otto's so long that he had forgotten the terror of public toilets.

"You want to go ahead of me?" Peter asked the officer.

The strangeness of the question reflected in the man's expression. "Not especially." He smirked.

"Well," Peter bumbled, "it's just that you had so much schnapps to drink, and . . . I thought maybe . . ."

The SS chin went up slightly in response to such stupidity. Peter felt the eyes of the man boring into the back of his head. If this fellow knew Wolf, did it not stand to reason that he had seen the photographs of Karin Wallich and her children? Maybe every SS officer in Vienna had seen them!

Nauseated by the time he entered the stall, Peter threw up, then stared at the door for five minutes, fully expecting the hinges to come crashing in any instant. He left the stall without ever unbuttoning his trousers. He would wait to use the toilet until Lucy came back to occupy the officer. Then Peter would come back. Alone.

There was a thirty-minute layover in Landsberg—time enough to stretch the legs and breathe a bit.

But Peter did not wish to see the Bahnhof when SS Lieutenant Hess asked him. Nor did Lucy wish to accompany him for a quick snack. She would stay, she said, and feed the baby. The layover was just long enough to get the child settled for the long journey ahead to Danzig.

Both Peter and Lucy gave an audible sigh of relief when the officer buttoned his tunic and stepped off the train. Lucy had done a magnificent job of talking and drawing attention away from Peter and Willie, but still she saw that same nagging *something* in the man's eyes.

The fact that he knew Wolf was terrifying to her. Wolf would find out where she had gone. Even without the note on the mirror, he would figure out who had sprung his prey from the trap!

"We will not reach the border for hours yet," Lucy said thoughtfully. "I will try to get him out of here—in the saloon car or the dining car—until then. When we come back, the light must be off. Pretend to sleep. I will hope it does not come to him where he has seen you before."

So there it was. She said it. It was not Peter's imagination. "And if he remembers?"

She looked at Baby Willie, who slurped noisily on his bottle. "He is getting off at the border station. After we cross the border into Poland, the train compartments will be sealed, locked on the outside, until we get to Danzig. We will be safe then."

"That is still a long way."

Lucy smiled knowingly. "I will do what I can to keep his mind off you and Willie. If it comes to it, the doors will not be sealed until we reach Poland. We might jump . . . but then again, it would be better if *we stayed* on the train and *he left*."

They were comrades in arms, indeed. Peter decided once more that he liked Lucy Strasburg very much. She knew exactly what she was saying; every word and gesture was calculated. Some other time, such ability might be despicable. Right now, it was admirable.

"He asked me what unit I am with in the Hitler Youth."

"And?"

"I told him to ask you."

"Good. And I told him . . . to ask you! You are a clever boy. I told him about your visit to Vienna—the same stuff—but you may write whatever autobiography makes you happy. You did well enough with Wolf the other night. All that nonsense about the SS motto. Very good. Be whatever you want to be. I did not tell this jackal anything. But it is better to stay out of his attention and sleep, *ja?*"

For ten hours Peter would be cooped up in a very small cage with a hungry tiger. Yet Lucy seemed to believe they could manage even this, even if they had to boot the SS lieutenant out of a moving train. Peter had misjudged this woman the first night he had seen her at the side of Wolfgang von Fritschauer. Now he grinned at her as she fussed with the baby. Maybe Lucy was really an angel beneath her lipstick and rouge. For the first time in his life, the story about Rahab, the prostitute in ancient Jericho who hid two Hebrew spies, no longer seemed shocking to Peter. He found himself hoping that if and when the walls came down, Lucy Strasburg would be spared just as that harlot had survived long ago.

"What are you looking at?" She colored slightly at his stare. Had she never been admired, one soldier to another?

"You are a righteous woman," Peter said simply. Then he excused himself and hurried to use the toilet before the tiger got back on the train.

When Peter returned, the SS lieutenant was sitting next to Lucy. Her arm was draped over the back of the seat. She touched his face with her finger, and the man did not even look up at Peter as he entered.

Lucy could only pray that the uncertainty she felt about their chances was not transmitted to the sensitive adolescent across from her in the train compartment. They must exude confidence, or this Nazi would smell their fear and know.

Like Wolf, this SS lieutenant might be fooled for a while by sheer bravado, but if the facade of her courage ever slipped, the passage to Danzig would end in leg irons.

Peter had not seen the SS officer enter the phone booth on the Berlin platform. The boy had been busy looking at Lucy, as if she were some sort of saint. *Ah, well, if it makes him feel better'.*

But from her position, she had been able to see the phone booth, watch the SS lieutenant flip through his little black book. She had seen his expression change from confusion and suspicion to a sinister pleasure at whatever news he had heard on the other end of the line.

Had he called Vienna? Had he contacted Wolf and casually mentioned that Lucy Strasburg had not gone to church to pray after all, that the trip to Demel's for a pastry was actually a journey to Danzig?

She brushed her fingertips familiarly against the man's cheek, playing for her life. But perhaps this fellow was also playing a game with her. What did he have to lose, after all? It was a long way between here and the border; she was amusing company. He could simply have her and the children arrested at the crossing. Until then, she touched his cheek and made pleasant conversation to pass the hours.

Inside Jacob's head, the neon road map flashed: a hundred and ninety-seven and one-half miles from Berlin to Firchau. Between farmer Schöne's barn and this deserted spot in the woods outside their destination, the truck had been halted at seven different roadblocks. The Nazis had orders to search for other things besides Lori and Jamie, but not once was the cargo of cabbages and chickens inspected.

"It was a miracle," Alfie said without surprise. They stepped out of their hiding place like five feathered clowns emerging from a giant cake.

It was dark. For once the old farmer was quiet as he spoke, and cautious, even apologetic that he could not get them closer to their goal.

"Over there is the big new prison they are building—" He pointed to a rise. "They don't want anyone to know it is there, but it is. And we do."

Jacob spread out his mental map and tried to take his bearings. Which way was the border? And where was the customshouse where the train would pass through the gates into Poland?

The farmer answered that question without waiting for him to ask. "Fifty yards through the woods is the railroad track. Follow it. Stick close to the wooded side. Straight on to Poland. You can't get lost. Just don't get found. They patrol with dogs, I hear."

With that, the old man passed them a sack of provisions and wished them Godspeed. Patting each head, including Werner's, he left them there to travel ahead on their own.

"What are you trying to do? Get me drunk?" Peter could hear the coarse laughter of Officer Hess outside the compartment. "Oh well. A long way from here to Firchau. Time enough to sober up after a little fun!"

The voices of Lucy and the lieutenant penetrated the door of the compartment. He reached up quickly and switched off the light, then leaned over and pulled his cap down across his eyes. Sleeping. He must be sleeping—just sitting there like a piece of luggage while Lucy and the SS officer talked around him and over him.

Hours would pass before they would be at the border. She could handle the passport and customs officers easily after this.

The door burst open, and light from the corridor flooded the compartment. Lucy and Officer Hess were laughing. He was drunk. Peter could smell it on his breath, hear it in the slurring of his words as he lunged for the seat.

He patted his lap for Lucy to sit. "Come on! *Come on!* My lap is more comfortable than the seat." He pawed her crudely.

"Wolf would have you shot if I did!" Maybe Lucy had been drinking, too. Peter frowned beneath his cap, the movement exposing his eye slightly. He did not like the way the SS lieutenant was touching her. Only a dead man could sleep through this.

"Wolf might have you shot anyway, eh?" he asked, pulling her against him.

Lucy was not drunk. From the corner of his eye, Peter caught an instant of fear in her expression. *Sober fear.* And then it was gone. She struggled as the lieutenant yanked her down.

It was a playful struggle. The officer tried to kiss her. She pushed him back. "Please . . . you will wake my nephews."

"Let them wake up," he slurred, holding her wrist.

"But . . . *please* . . . Herr Lieutenant . . . Wolf will not—"

"So who cares about Wolf? You are not afraid of Wolf. You have left him, eh?" The voice became harsh. Demanding. The hand clamped harder on her arm, and he threw her back on the bench. "Call me Alex, remember? Old friends. *Lucy.* I never forget."

"You are . . . hurting me . . . *bitte*! Alex! Herr Lieutenant!" There was no charade in her appeal. She struggled harder. The man held her down beneath him on the bench.

Peter could not pretend to sleep. He sat up and switched on the light. His cap fell to the floor. He glared hard at the angry officer. "Leave my aunt alone," he said, standing slowly to his feet.

Lucy lay where the scowling officer had her pinned. She shook her head at Peter. He must not interfere!

The officer did not let her go; he simply sneered at Peter as if he were an insect to crush when he was not busy with the woman. "Get out of here!" the lieutenant snapped. "And take the brat out with you."

"Let her go, I said!" Peter threatened. "You are drunk!"

"Yes? Drunk? In a few hours I will be sober, but you will still be a Jew! You should pray I do not remember the way you order me around!" He sat up. Lucy did not move. Her face reflected all the things she had dreaded. *He knew!* Maybe he had known all along.

"I . . . I don't know what you mean," Peter stammered.

"Oh yes?" The officer pulled his pistol from its holster and waved it at Peter's face and then at the still sleeping Willie. "You don't know?"

"*Bitte,* Herr Lieutenant." Lucy tried to pull his attention back to her. She laughed as though this was a drunken fantasy. "Don't play such games. He will leave . . . *won't you Peter?* Leave us alone, Peter! Take Willie."

Peter clenched and unclenched his fists. He would not let Lucy do this for him and Willie. "*I will not leave!*"

"Too bad." The officer pulled back the hammer and put the barrel behind Willie's ear.

"Oh! Please . . . Herr Lieutenant! *Don't*," Lucy begged.

He pushed her back hard. "You see, boy, this woman and I were about to strike a bargain. She was going to give me something in exchange for your life. You see?"

Peter licked his lips. He stared at the gun against the baby's head. "All right!" Peter cried, looking from his brother to Lucy. "Just let me take him and get out!"

"Sure, sure." Lucy tried to sound soothing, but her hands trembled. The usually smooth voice cracked. "Let them go, Herr Lieutenant."

"Too late!" The gun pointed back to Peter's face. "I am out of the mood for love! I prefer to *hunt* now!"

"Don't do this," Lucy whispered. "You will be sorry. My nephews . . ." She tried to recapture the illusion.

"Nephews?" His voice was low, barely audible. "Wouldn't Wolf be surprised that your *nephews* are the Jews he has been looking for?" He laughed explosively. "Ah, you are going to be in a lot of trouble—"

"Please . . . just too much schnapps!" She sat up slowly, trying to reason with him.

"Imagination, is it?" The lips curled down. He jumped up and pressed the gun into Peter's heart. "Drop your trousers, Jew! If you aren't a Jew, prove it!"

Peter looked at Lucy. Such agony on her face! Why had he interrupted this sloppy drunk? Why hadn't he let her take care of him?

"Did you hear what I said, you circumcised swine? Drop them!"

The gun pressed hard into Peter's chest, but he did not move. He would not do it! Let this evil man shoot him through the heart! He would not take down his trousers in front of Lucy . . . or anyone! He lifted his chin in defiance. "You are the swine, not me," Peter said evenly, daring the man to pull the trigger.

Instead, the lieutenant simply reached down and grabbed the baby, who wailed unhappily in sleepy confusion. The gun went to Willie's mouth. The baby waved his arms in pain as the officer jammed the barrel into his throat. "Suck on this, you little *Judenschwein*!"

"*All right!*" Peter cried, fumbling with the buttons of his trousers. "*Don't!* Put him down!"

The drunken lieutenant then pointed the gun at Peter and smiled.

In that moment, Peter glimpsed Lucy's handbag rise behind the SS lieutenant and come down in an arch on top of his head. There was a loud thump, and the officer's eyes rolled back as a trickle of blood dripped down the side of his head. The gun fell from his hand. Willie hit the seat with a thud and gasped for breath before shrieking with rage and indignation. Officer Hess hung in the air for an instant longer before his knees buckled and he fell back on top of Lucy.

They ate in silence as they walked the first miles in the center of the rail-road tracks. The oak ties across the gravel snagged the toes of boots and shoes, causing each of the children to stumble in turn. Mark tripped on a crosstie and fell, bloodying both knees. He did not cry out, but Lori could see the black stain of blood seeping through his trousers. Jamie stepped into a hole and tumbled down, biting through his lip. Even within the narrow borders of the straight track there were small traps on the roadbed.

Only Alfie seemed never to trip. Lori walked behind him and watched as he held the kitten carefully and walked in a high-marching kind of step.

To the right above the treetops shone an eerie white glow. The prison camp, a nameless enclosure where men were caged. Although Lori could not see the guard towers of the electrified fences that stretched for miles, this unnatural light illuminated their path and cast shadows that hid the dangers of uneven places.

Somewhere Lori could hear the steady, distant drone of the generating plant that powered the floodlights and made the fences here and at the border deadly to touch.

It reminded Lori not of the true Light but of the power Darkness had to distort their vision. That ominous hum encircled all of Germany, keeping some people out and others in. The unnatural light pursued them at this moment. She felt it above her and behind her. It sought to close the gate to their freedom, sealing them in this gray, colorless world, where blood was black and flesh was ashen. It distorted what was real, raising small depressions in their way to make them fall and concealing bumps to make them stumble. The light of Darkness made even their straight path treacherous and painful.

As never before, she felt the nearness of personal Evil tonight. It lurked there, in the shadows of the woods, in the iron gray light of the prison, in the small puddles of blackness beneath their feet.

"Is he . . . *dead*?" Lucy shuddered as Peter propped Hess into the corner of the seat.

"Only sleeping like a dead man," Peter replied with grim amusement in his voice. He pulled the peaked cap down over the officer's forehead, then stepped back to study the effect. *Not dead, only sleeping. Yes. Drunk and sleeping.* Peter crossed the officer's legs at the ankles, giving the over-all impression of a man who was very comfortable.

"You were very brave," Lucy said firmly. She did not scold him for being too brave, although that was implied in the tone of her voice. "My knight."

Peter hefted the handbag at her feet; it must have weighed twenty pounds. "What have you got in that thing?"

"My inheritance." She smiled and opened the bag, allowing him a glimpse of a large, solid silver crucifix.

"Ha!" Peter cried. "The only weapon against vampires and demons, I hear! Now all we need is a wooden stake through his heart . . . providing he has a heart."

Lucy cradled Willie, whose bottom lip was split and swollen. He frantically sucked his bottle and looked wildly around the compartment for any sign of other monsters. At last his eyelids drooped. He breathed a ragged sigh; his little body relaxed, started awake, then relaxed again.

It was a dilemma they had not anticipated. Peter sat on the edge of his seat and considered what to do with the unconscious SS lieutenant.

"Very natural looking like this, don't you think? At the passport check we tell them he is drunk and asleep. Give them his papers, then dump him out the window on the Polish side."

"If he wakes up, we are dead."

"Too bad we did not kill him."

"I do not relish the idea of being arrested for murder," Lucy said.

"You think they will punish you less for helping Jews? Why don't we get rid of him?"

"Because if we throw him off and he wakes up and manages to stag-ger to a telephone . . . he will call ahead and—" she frowned—"he is SS! One phone call, and we are arrested."

Peter examined the tall shining boots of the officer. The boy had al-ways wanted a pair of boots like that. "Let me handle it," he instructed Lucy. "Go to the dining car with Willie. I can handle this."

"I am not going anywhere until you tell me what you intend to do." Lucy was adamant.

"You know what makes this fellow an SS?" Peter replied as the officer moaned and stirred slightly. Peter pointed the pistol at him as a precau-tion while they talked.

"He is waking up," Lucy said in a frightened voice.

"Yes. The SS lieutenant is waking up. If we throw him off the train like this, he will crawl to some farm and terrorize the farmer and tele-phone the border guards. Then we will be arrested. A very frightening thing, this skull and crossbones, these lightning bolts. They make a very homely, stupid fellow like this feel man enough to rape women and jam guns into the mouths of babies."

For a second Peter considered shooting the officer.

"What are you getting at?" Lucy's heart was racing. The lieutenant was going to wake up, and they would have to fight him again!

"It is the uniform, you see. What happens when you take those clothes off a man like him?"

"Disgusting."

"A naked, barefoot Nazi," Peter continued. "I, for one, would never let any naked, barefoot stranger come to my door and demand to use the telephone." Peter smiled slyly. "Herr Lieutenant Hess and I have much to talk about between here and the Polish territory. Now take Willie out. I do not want my brother to be frightened again by this monster."

First Peter threw the SS tunic out the window. He counted to sixty and tossed away the cap, the trousers, and then the army-issue underwear and socks. The small hand-carried suitcase followed. Finally, at gunpoint, Peter instructed the naked officer to lay the briefcase on the opposite seat.

Peter dumped out the contents. A small handgun tumbled out. Peter tucked it into one of his new boots and sat back with the Luger pistol pointed squarely into Hess' face.

Peter had donned Otto's overcoat; he was chilled, but not unbearably so. "Now shred your papers," he ordered, "and out the window with them."

Hess obeyed in jerky, uneven movements. "There are more where these came from," he snarled, at last picking up his own identity documents.

"Small pieces." Peter lowered the aim of the pistol toward the man's abdomen. "Very small."

The fragments of passport whipped out of the officer's hand. "Now close the window," he stammered. "I will freeze to death."

"No. I want to make certain you are sober before I kill you," Peter said with a grin.

"You are a smart young man." Hess managed a smile, but it quickly disappeared. It was too cold to maintain this illusion of a man in control. "Smart like your father was smart. You don't . . . need to kill me. We can make a deal, *ja?*"

"What kind of deal?" Peter mocked him. "You expect me to let you go free in exchange for my own life so that you can turn in Wolfgang von Fritschauer?"

For an instant, Alexander Hess looked very sober indeed. "Wolfgang von Fritschauer? No. I swear I would not!"

"You think I will let you go so you can undermine their operation? Exchange my life for Lucy and Wolf? After what they have done for me? For hundreds like me? *My honor is loyalty*, Herr Lieutenant Hess. Wolf has been like a brother to me. No! I would not think of giving a man like you a chance to ruin it all. I am afraid I will have to shoot you and throw you out the window like your clothes, eh?"

"You won't shoot." Hess looked panicked. "You are . . . too young to murder a man . . . like this." He held up his bound wrists. Hands clasped together, he seemed to be begging for mercy.

"You mean in cold blood?" Peter was smiling. The freezing wind held Officer Hess in a much stronger grasp than either the pistol or the belt on his wrists.

"Give me your coat . . . *bitte*. I will pay you . . . I swear I will not have Wolfgang or . . . Lucy arrested. Untie?" His skin took on a definite bluish cast.

Peter pushed him a bit further. "It was you who killed my father, wasn't it?"

"No! I swear it!" Now Hess had something to argue against. "I never met your father!"

"I do not believe you! Justice has delivered you into my hands, Herr Lieutenant Hess! I will not have long before I can avenge the blood of Michael Wallich!"

"No! *Really!* This I am not guilty of! I swear it! Someone else! Not me!" Again the trembling arms rose to beg. Hess was altogether sober.

Peter had created his own story, as Lucy suggested. The result was enjoyable. He was in no great hurry to end the play. "There is still some time before the whistle blows."

"The whistle?" Hess' teeth chattered violently. "So? The whistle?"

"I do not want anyone to hear the gunshot that takes your miserable existence."

"Just listen to me—"

"There is time. Tell me, why should you live, Herr Hess—a cockroach like you?" Peter smiled as Hess proceeded to renounce all his former associations with the Nazi cause. He was doing this, he said, because it was the law of the land, and he must obey. But really, the system was corrupt, he said.

"And what about the Führer?" Peter asked.

"Rotten. Evil and dark! He has brought me to this! The Führer should die."

"Not the Jews?"

"No! Never! The whole Nazi Party! Corrupt. Rotten."

"But not you?"

"No, I tell you . . . please . . . close the window." The voice was pitiful.

"Not yet." Peter said as the wind mussed his red hair. "I have not decided yet whether or not to let you live."

They had been following the tracks for hours when the light of the Danzig train appeared like the giant eye of a cyclops behind them.

A wide field fringed with fir trees bordered the right side of the track. Jacob took Lori's hand as they scrambled down the berm and the others followed.

They stepped into the trees to watch as the train—their train—thundered toward the border checkpoint. The lights several kilometers up the track made a faint, pleasant glow against the night sky. They had fixed their hopes on this point—until now.

"Well, there it is," Jamie said gloomily.

"We will never make it now," Mark added.

"If we hurry—" Lori cried, as the headlight on the train sprayed a circle of track and gravel with illumination.

Locomotive. Coal car. Dining car with candles and waiters and passengers sipping wine. Then the sleeping cars and the first-class compartments, and then . . .

Like a spirit on the wind, something shot out the window and flew up in the air. Then another object—and another, and another—swept out on the updraft. Like bats, they flapped and floated to earth.

Gathered all together, the clothing tossed from the window of the Danzig train made up the uniform of an SS lieutenant. Everything was there except the boots. Jacob tried on the tunic. It fit a big snug across the shoulders. The trousers were too loose around the waist. But in the moonlight, at any rate, the effect was impressive. Beneath the peaked cap visor, Jacob could easily pass for twenty-one. His crooked nose and his fighter's physique completed the deception nicely. Mark found an extra pair of size ten boots inside the suitcase. Perfect!

The train could delay for several hours for an examination on the German side of the border. They were not too late, and now they had a Nazi lieutenant as well as a black-shirted member of the Hitler Youth among them!

Jacob had not yet figured out what use he would make of his marvelous costume, but Lori declared it must be another miracle. Alfie said that the angels had sent them the clothes.

38

The Gate of Liberty

Ten minutes to Firchau! Next stop Firchau! All passengers for Firchau! Customs check for the Polish frontier! Please have all documents ready!"

Peter and Hess could clearly hear the instructions of the porter through the door. In spite of his shivering, spasmodic muscles, Hess managed to look relieved. Hopeful. Maybe he had convinced the young Jew not to shoot him after all.

"Close the window," Hess begged. "Untie my hands. Let me have your coat!"

Occasional lights from isolated houses slid by.

"I don't think so. I still do not trust you. If I let you live and Wolf is arrested, I could not forgive myself. No. It is best if an insect like you does not live."

"Don't shoot me, please. I was just—"

"And I don't like the way you treated my brother, besides. Or Lucy." Peter raised the gun as if to ready it for the shrill of the train whistle.

"Just a . . . a little joke. Too much schnapps."

"But you are sober now."

The head bobbed in wild agreement. "Yes!"

"Good. Now sit on the window ledge."

"*Mein Gott!* Don't shoot me!" He crawled up to crouch on the window ledge.

"I am going to blow your brains out when the whistle blows, Herr Lieutenant Hess. And then I am going to push your faceless body out on the tracks." Peter was smiling. The hammer on the Luger was cocked and ready.

"No! Please, no! *Bitte!* I am begging! I promise!" He no longer noticed the wind or the smoke from the locomotive.

"When the whistle blows . . ." Peter raised his voice as the train rounded a curve and began to slow. "Unless—"

"*Anything!* Please, yes!"

"Unless you prefer to jump."

Hess' eyes grew wide as he stared briefly at the gun in Peter's hand, then out at the passing countryside. He raised his arms as if to dive, then launched himself out of the window like a stark white ghost into the night.

The curtains flapped in the dark compartment where he had been. Peter laughed out loud and stuck his head out to watch the body of Herr Hess tumble like a stone down the gravel embankment into a hayfield.

"*Auf Wiedersehen!*" Peter called and closed the window.

"Herr Hess will have a hike," Peter said to Lucy as the train slipped into the electrified enclosure and up to the platform in front of the customs-house. "The night air will clear his head."

Lucy still looked worried. On the platform two matrons sat inside glassed cubicles flanking separate entrances into the German customs house. One door was marked *Men* and the other *Women.*

Peter followed her eyes and blanched. *The physical search!* Here Gestapo doctors randomly chose passengers for complete physical examinations. Those wishing to cross into Polish territory from the Reich were required to submit to this, if asked, or face arrest. The obvious reason given for these searches was to make certain that nothing of value was smuggled from the Reich. It was impossible, after all, to conceal currency or valuables in such a situation.

The main side benefit for the Gestapo was the apprehension of male Jews masquerading as Aryans with false passports. Like the men's room, these examinations had become the gauntlet through which every circumcised Jew must pass to freedom. Not everyone was selected for this indignity—only those who seemed suspicious to the matrons in the glass booths. Lucy was counting on the possibility that once again she could talk their way out of it, and the trio could pass with a superficial customs clerk.

They were close enough to see the dour expressions on matrons on the customs platform. Voices rang out distinctly in the night air.

"*Schnell! Schnell!* All passengers disembark! Have your documents and all luggage ready for examination!"

It was perfect except for one minor detail. The train had rolled through the massive wire gates without stopping. The gates had been instantly closed and re-electrified. Train and passengers were now imprisoned inside an enclosure that could not be entered or exited until the deadly current was switched off long enough for the train to slip through the gates on the Polish side of the compound.

Customs and passport examinations when leaving the Reich were the last chance the Gestapo had to apprehend those they considered criminals, whatever the charge might be. Every offense, real or imagined, was considered one final time within this massive barbed-wire enclosure. Every passenger was considered guilty until proven innocent. The electrified fence assured that no one could run away.

There was still a chance for Jacob to retreat from their position thirty yards outside the fence. The gate did not keep them in; it kept them *out!* It prevented their passage through the other side.

As Jacob watched the examination of the train, he realized that perhaps it was no accident that they had been locked out. The flashlights of Nazi soldiers probed the huge iron hulk of the Danzig train. Every inch was being explored, from undercarriage to roof, for possible stowaways.

They all watched the procedure with sinking spirits—except perhaps Alfie, who seemed untroubled by the fact that they were on their bellies in the underbrush within shouting distance of those who would most like to throw them all into prison. Outside the fence uniformed guards stood every few feet. There seemed no way that Jacob could causally stroll up in his newly acquired SS uniform and order the gate to be opened so that his friends might enter and board the train.

No one dared ask the question that lay heavy on Jacob's mind. They had come all this way—for what? And now it was only a matter of time before the guard dogs caught their scent and flushed them out.

The platform bristled with soldiers and Gestapo inspectors as Peter and Lucy stepped from the train. She held Willie. With her impeccable Aryan looks, it was less likely that she would be asked to strip or ordered to undress the baby for a search.

Willie was miserable. Lucy had deliberately left his diapers soiled so that the inspector would not be eager to examine the child for circumcision.

"Males here!" barked a matron. "Females in this line! *Schnell!* The train is waiting, please!"

Passengers shuffled onto the cold platform. Some faces were sullen, some fearful. The fearful faces were pulled aside and ordered into the examination rooms.

In the meantime, Nazi officials ransacked luggage; experts who knew every smuggling trick probed the compartments. Up and down the lines officers pulled out suspects and roughly ordered them to comply.

Behind Lucy and Peter a slight commotion arose as a man and a woman resisted feebly and were handcuffed and immediately shoved out of sight into the room marked *Documentation Verification.*

"You! To the examination!" the matron said to a timid-looking man three places in front of Peter in line. She skipped the next fellow, a round-bellied Bavarian in lederhosen and tall woolen socks. She scarcely looked at the man in front of Peter; instead, she blinked in amusement at Peter. "It is you!"

The color drained from Peter's face. He looked behind him, hoping that she meant someone else! But she was staring right at Peter!

She grasped his arm and pulled him out of the line. Then, whirling around, she spotted Lucy and Willie. "And there is the little brother! *Himmel!* Look! It is the two brothers!"

She was shouting at the top of her lungs. Soldiers and plainclothes Gestapo men looked away from their charges. Peter considered running, leaping from the platform and diving into the shadows that flanked the tracks, but he was certain he would be shot full of holes. He prayed they had not captured his mother and sister at this same checkpoint.

Lucy gazed miserably at him. They had tried . . . they had come so close to making it!

"Look, everyone!" The matron's voice rang out in the night. "Here are the two brothers from the evening paper! Look! The boys who know the Führer!"

Peter's mouth dropped open. Another matron rushed toward him, carrying the front page of the Nazi Party newspaper in her hand. There, beneath the banner headline announcing the formal signing of a non-aggression pact with France, a photograph showed the benevolent Adolf Hitler holding a baby. *That very child! Willie Ruger!* The one with the stinking diapers! And there was this fine example of young Aryan manhood! *Peter Ruger!*

"Ach! To think we shake the hand that the Führer has touched!"

Peter glanced down at his own photograph. Could it be? Two adoring brothers within the circle of the Führer's admiration. Their names were given right there in the caption.

Peter noticed how pale and wild-eyed he looked in the picture. Did no one see that the expression on his face was a grinning, hysterical fright?

"Look! Look how much it looks like him!"

His heart pounded frantically.

"You would like to have a copy of this; I am certain," said the uniformed officer in charge of the station. He patted Peter on the back and greeted Lucy, the boy's aunt! He ordered a matron to go fetch two copies off the stack, because the family might have difficulty getting more once they crossed the frontier.

Lucy babbled on about what a delight it was to meet the Führer close up like that, how special that Adolf Hitler had singled out her own nephews for recognition.

Peter moved through it all grinning wildly, like a marionette who had no control over his own trembling legs. No doubt the facial expression he now wore was very much like the photograph in the newspaper.

Alfie pulled his toy general from his pocket as they lay hidden in the underbrush. While the others were too frightened by the nearness of danger to move, he played happily with horse and rider.

Lori watched him, taking a strange sort of comfort from his utter trust that they could not be harmed. He whispered to her, "The angels said it is all right. Don't worry, Lori."

She smiled at him and put a finger to her lips to remind him of the rule of silence. Instead he tugged on Jacob's sleeve. He pointed far down the track. "There they are," he mumbled. "See them?"

"Shhhh," Jacob warned.

"But look—" Alfie's voice sounded too loud. "They are not stars or angels! Here come the dogs and their men!"

Five heads turned in unison to stare in horror at the approach of three German shepherds dragging soldiers behind them as they sniffed the undergrowth outside the compound.

"Headed right for us!" Jacob muttered, banging his fist on the ground. "I will try to distract them. You make a run for it."

"No!" Lori gasped. "We stay . . . together!" They had come too far for it to end like this. Tiny pinpoints of light probed the bushes. Jacob looked back wildly to see if they could make a run for it. Inside the compound, guards and other passengers were crowding around a young man on the platform. They called out his name, smiled, and laughed with him. No one was looking this way. *Maybe now?*

Jacob jumped to his feet. At that instant a dog lunged against his leash, breaking the hold of his master. Barking and snarling, the animal ran full bore toward Jacob and then, twenty-five yards from where Jacob stood, a naked man screamed and dashed out of a shallow ditch.

Whistles trilled a warning! The celebration on the platform silenced. Jacob ran up the track toward the fugitive, shouting, "Stop that man! Stop that man!"

"*Tor auf!*" shouted the commandant from the customs building. "Open the gate. *Tor auf!*"

Someone threw the switch; the red warning light changed to green. Soldiers and guards poured from the compound in pursuit of the shrieking man who now fled to the other side of the tracks in an attempt to escape into the woods.

Dog handlers eager to try their well-trained animals issued the command and pointed toward their target. Guard dogs charged to the capture.

Passengers inside the compound crowded to see, pushing through the open gate to witness what was certainly the end of an escaped convict from the prison camp over the hill!

Alfie stood and slipped the kitten into his pocket. He reached down to help Lori to her feet as Jacob, in his SS uniform, jogged to meet them. Alfie linked his arm with Mark and Jamie as Jacob had taught him in the drill.

"All right," Jacob said in a gruff voice. He herded them through the crush of spectators. "That's enough! Enough sightseeing, now! An escaped criminal, no doubt. Back on the train! Back on the train."

No one noticed as they passed through the gate. "The gate is *open!*" Alfie smiled at Lori. "They told me they would open it for us." He stepped into the train. "Did you hear them calling my name? They were cheering, Lori! *Tor Alf*, they said! *Alf* . . . just like Mama used to say my name!"

"A miracle, Alfie," Lori said softly. "Just like you said."

Epilogue

Captain Samuel Orde had trained his soldiers well.

"Halt, who goes there! Hands up or I'll shoot!" In his excitement, Artur Bader had shouted the words in his native German. But the meaning was clear enough in any language: I am deadly serious.

Bader took no chances, nor did he wait to see what he had caught. He blew three sharp blasts on the signal whistle around his neck without once taking his eyes or the muzzle of his rifle off the lighter shadow on the hillside.

His alarm was answered by three whistles from the guard post on his left and three more from the right. The sound of running footsteps could be heard converging on Bader's position. When other guards were covering his flanks, he ordered loudly in Arabic, "Come in slowly, with your hands high!"

A low chuckle came from the brush, followed by carefully enunciated English, "Don't shoot. I'm coming in."

Bader rocked forward on his feet at the sound of the voice but still did not move or lower his gun. A figure detached itself from the darkness and walked carefully toward the fence surrounding Hanita.

Only when the figure stood beside the barbed wire with both arms raised overhead did Bader advance from his position to a gun barrel's length away.

"Well done, lads," remarked the man. "I would have bet a week's laundry detail that I could still sneak in this way."

"Captain Orde!" exclaimed Artur. "Is it really you?"

"Well, I'm not the Ghost of Christmas Past, if you follow me. Where's Zabinski?"

"Here, Captain," answered a voice from the left.

"Since you've caught me, better march me in proper," suggested Orde.

"Yes, Hayedid . . . Captain. You others, back to your posts."

"But, Captain," called Bader, "we thought you were dead. You've been missing for days! Where have you been?"

"Adding another chapter to the manual," Orde replied. "Now, are you going to keep me standing here all night, or will you hurry up and open the gate?"

Digging Deeper into *Danzig Passage*

No one who was present at the Wall in Berlin on November 9, 1989—nor anyone who saw even a glimpse of the television coverage—could possibly forget the emotion of that moment when the Wall was finally broken down, the gate opened, after twenty-eight years. Holding candles high, innumerable souls circled the Wall in a joyous vigil.

It was a night of loud celebration and shouting . . . and also unfathomable sorrow for so much pain, so many years lost. Tears rained down each face. Once again East was truly meeting West; brothers and sisters, parents and children, were being reunited. And in those candles that ringed the Wall was the symbol of true light once again shining in a dark nation. A nation that had been held captive ever since the horror of Kristal Nacht.

And that takes us to you, dear reader. Have you at times felt as if you are "held captive" by the scars of the past? Do you long for true light to shine once again? We prayed for you as we wrote this book and continue to pray as we receive your letters and hear your soul cries. No doubt you have myriad life questions of your own. Following are some questions designed to take you deeper into the answers to these questions. You may wish to delve into them on your own or share them with a friend or a discussion group.

We hope *Danzig Passage* will encourage you in your search for answers to your daily dilemmas and life situations. But most of all, we pray that you will "discover the Truth through fiction." For we are convinced that if you seek diligently, you will find the One who holds all the answers to the universe (1 Chronicles 28:9).

Bodie & Brock Thoene

SEEK . . .

Prologue

1. Imagine *you* are standing at the Berlin Wall on November 9, 1989. You have been separated from your brother or sister for twenty-eight years. As you wait for that gate to open, what are you thinking? What are you feeling?

   _____

   _____

2. Is there anything in your life that holds you "captive by its very existence" (p. ix)? that is a scar across your soul? If so, what is it?

   _____

   _____

3. How could you "open the gate" (p. xi) of your soul to let true light shine in on that area?

   _____

   _____

Chapters 1–3

4. Kristal Nacht was carefully planned. "No man was allowed to participate in the demonstration in his own neighborhood, lest he come across a Jewish neighbor and take pity" (p. 5). Do you think it's easier to do evil to those you don't know, or to those you know? Why?

   _____

   _____

5. "Although he trembled at the evil these men brought upon others, he no longer feared what they would do to him. . . . *A perfect peace has filled my heart*, [Theo] wrote in that terrible hour. *The mouth of hell has opened wide here, yet I believe in the coming justice of the Holy One. Even now I feel His perfect love, and all fear is cast away from my heart, cast into the fires and burned away*" (p. 11).

   Reflect on your response to 9/11. Was it similar to Theo's when faced with his own possible death? or different? Explain.

   _____

   _____

6. Have you ever realized, as Lucy Strasburg did, that the person you love doesn't really love you? that, in fact, that person is merely using you? How did you respond to that knowledge (see how Lucy responded on p. 21)? Did it change your life or thinking in any way?

_____

_____

Chapters 4–6

7. How do you respond when you see someone like Alfie Halder? or someone who is paralyzed or unable to speak?

_____

_____

8. Captain Samuel Orde said, "We will do what is in our power, and the Lord will do the rest" (p. 48). Do you think he was on the right track? Why or why not?

_____

_____

9. Do you think the Christian church today is "asleep" in any ways (see pp. 64–66)? If so, name one or two. Is there anything you can do, even in a small way, to wake the church up?

_____

_____

Chapters 7–9

10. If you were Pastor Karl, would you have expelled the Jewish members of your church to keep the rest of your church intact and safe (see p. 68)?

_____

_____

11. "Tell them you have witnessed the death of your God and yourself tonight!" (p. 73). What connection do you see between the evil perpetrated against the Jews and the fact that Hitler wanted to spread the message that God is dead? (See also Captain Orde's words on p. 94).

_____

_____

12. *"Remember who you belong to!"* (p. 79). Whom do you belong to, in your soul? How is that ownership shown in your life?

_____

_____

Chapters 10–14

13. Step back in time to the morning after Kristal Nacht. If Berlin were *your* town and you viewed the devastation, what would your response be publicly? behind the closed doors of your own home?

_____

_____

14. Do you agree with Theo's statement, "Unless we fight [evil], we have no right to hope" (p. 115)? Why or why not?

_____

_____

15. Imagine that you are Lori or Jamie or Jacob or Mark—hiding from the Nazis in New Church. Describe what your life was like yesterday (activities, thoughts, plans, dreams). Then describe how your life has changed in just 24 hours.

_____

_____

16. If you were Michael Wallich (see p. 131), would you swallow a pill that guaranteed you an easier death? Why or why not?

_____

_____

17. Have you ever "given up righteousness for the sake of ease" (p. 131), as Otto realizes he has done? When?

_____

_____

Chapters 15–18

18. "In 1933, the year [Hitler] came to power, one million babies were aborted in Germany. Then came permissible euthanasia, mercy killing of the old. That led to *selective* euthanasia, the murder of those who are mentally unworthy, racially unworthy. And then there were the children like Charles—the killing of babies who

were considered imperfect" (p. 151). Do you agree with Theo that these events are connected? Why or why not?

_____

_____

19. Have you ever been "up to [your] neck in hot water" (as Samuel Orde was—see p. 155) for doing what is right? When? What were the results?

_____

_____

20. "*Look out for yourself,* her heart whispered. *You are the only one you can count on*" (p. 162). Lucy's life is shattered by Wolf's betrayal. Have you felt like Lucy? In what situation? Does thinking of Christ's mourning and suffering with you change your perspective in any way? If so, how?

_____

_____

21. If you saw each person you meet daily as "an individual of untold value and unmeasured worth. . . . *A face. A name. A man. A soul . . .* worthy of love" (p. 169), how would your actions change?

_____

_____

Chapters 19–20

22. "Why did He [Jesus] weep?"
"Because He knew what men could do to one another."
"He saw us here. It broke His heart" (p. 193).
   Do you believe Jesus weeps over the world today? over events in your life? Why or why not?

_____

_____

23. Do you think Pastor Karl did the right thing when he refused to sign the commandant's paper (see pp. 205–206)? Why or why not? What would you have done if you had to choose between your family and your faith (see also pp. 314–315)?

_____

_____

Chapters 21–23

24. *"God never promised us that life would be without difficulties, but He did promise that we will overcome them as He has"* (p. 213). Even in difficult times, what little glimpses can you see of this truth in your life? and of Leah's triumphant words: *"We will win! We will make it! Don't worry or be afraid!"* (p.214)?

_____

_____

25. "Could a just God care even for evil men?" (p. 218). What do you think? Explain.

_____

_____

26. "He has seen what he wants to see in God's Word. He believes what makes him feel best about himself" (p. 228). In what ways have you seen people (like Dorfman) misuse the Bible? How has this affected your view of God and the Bible?

_____

_____

27. Why do you think God chose *"Love the Lord your God with all your heart and with all your soul and with all your mind"* (see Matthew 22:37 and p. 230) to be the first and greatest commandment?

_____

_____

Chapters 24–28

28. In what area(s) of your life do you need to heed Churchill's words: *"Never* give in to fear. Never, never, never give in!" (p. 250)?

_____

_____

29. *"Once I was of use to God. Now what good is my life? What testimony do I have in this utter silence and loneliness?"* (p. 277). Have you, like Karl, heard this dark "whisper"? Describe the situation—and how you chose to respond.

_____

_____

30. Would people say of you, "There's a truly righteous person—a person who cannot be compromised" (p. 296)? Why or why not?

_____

_____

Chapters 29–31

31. Think of a friend or family member who is struggling right now. How can you encourage that person to not give in to evil and discouragement (pp. 318–319)?

_____

_____

32. Have you ever been a part of evil without meaning to (much as Lucy was forced to visit Otto's apartment to catch the Jewish family—see pp. 324–328)? Explain what happened.

_____

_____

33. "With prayers and deed together fight, and put the evil hosts to flight" (p. 333). Do you believe this poet is right? Why or why not?

_____

_____

Chapters 32–33

34. When you are told, "Can't be done . . . out of the question" (p. 349), how do you respond?

_____

_____

35. Reflect back to when you've come close to a dangerous situation . . . and at the last minute "a tiny pebble of suspicion dropped into the pool of [your] mind" (p. 351). Who or what do you think forewarned you? What was the result?

_____

_____

36. Can you say, "My strength is in the Lord! In the Spirit of the Almighty! I have no faith in myself!" (p. 361)? Why or why not?

_____

_____

37. "It is Christmas! God has come among us! The miracle is accomplished! . . . The Gate is open!" (p. 362). If you truly believed this, what would change in your present? in your future?

_____

_____

Chapters 34–35

38. What changes do you see in Lucy Strasburg from the beginning to the end of *Danzig Passage*? Would you dare to do what she did at the end? Why or why not?

_____

_____

39. Is there a relative (a sibling, a parent, a child) who has been "the bane of [your] existence" (p. 391), as much as Marlene has been in Peter's life? If you knew that today was the last time you would see that person, what would you say to him or her?

_____

_____

40. "Jewish women had their children torn physically from their arms. Christian mothers who had remained steadfast watched as their children were spiritually poisoned, growing finally as dark as the masters of Germany. This sort of separation was just as real; the grief, though different, just as profound" (pp. 397–398). Do you agree with Lucy's assessment? Are physical and spiritual separations just as profound, or is one worse than the other? Explain.

_____

_____

Chapters 36–Epilogue

41. Peter cannot believe it. Here he is, trying to escape Nazi Germany, and he is held up in a newspaper as an example of Aryan perfection. And yet what he had thought was so horrible actually ended

up for his good (see Romans 8:28 and p. 426)! Has this ever happened to you? When?

_____

_____

42. What miracle—large or small—have you experienced lately?

_____

_____

43. Have you opened the gate of your heart to God? to His miracles? and to His Son, who has suffered on your behalf? Why or why not?

_____

_____

Know, dear reader, that He waits for *you* with deep longing on the other side of the gate. No matter what you've done or what has been done to you. No matter how you've strayed off the path. God's love is eternal . . . yet so is His justice and vengeance against evil. Which side will you choose to be on? *Tor auf!*

Bodie and Brock Thoene (pronounced *Tay-nee*) have written over 45 works of historical fiction. That these best sellers have sold more than 10 million copies and won eight ECPA Gold Medallion Awards affirms what millions of readers have already discovered—the Thoenes are not only master stylists but experts at capturing readers' minds and hearts.

In their timeless classic series about Israel (The Zion Chronicles, The Zion Covenant, and The Zion Legacy), the Thoenes' love for both story and research shines.

With The Shiloh Legacy series and *Shiloh Autumn*—poignant portrayals of the American depression—and The Galway Chronicles, which dramatically tell of the 1840s famine in Ireland, as well as the twelve Legends of the West, the Thoenes have made their mark in modern history.

In the A.D. Chronicles, their most recent series, they step seamlessly into the world of Yerushalyim and Rome, in the days when Yeshua walked the earth and transformed lives with His touch.

Bodie began her writing career as a teen journalist for her local newspaper. Eventually her byline appeared in prestigious periodicals such as *U.S. News and World Report*, *The American West*, and *The Saturday Evening Post*. She also worked for John Wayne's Batjac Productions (she's best known as author of *The Fall Guy*) and ABC Circle Films as a writer and researcher. John Wayne described her as "a writer with talent that captures the people and the times!" She has degrees in journalism and communications.

Brock has often been described by Bodie as "an essential half of this writing team." With degrees in both history and education, Brock has, in his role as researcher and story-line consultant, added the vital dimension of historical accuracy. Due to such careful research, The Zion Covenant and The Zion Chronicles series are recognized by the American Library Association, as well as Zionist libraries around the world, as classic historical novels and are used to teach history in college classrooms.

Bodie and Brock have four grown children—Rachel, Jake, Luke, and Ellie—and five grandchildren. Their sons, Jake and Luke, are carrying on the Thoene family talent as the next generation of writers, and Luke produces the Thoene audiobooks. Bodie and Brock divide their time between London and Nevada.

For more information visit:
www.thoenebooks.com
www.TheOne Audio.com

suspense with a mission

TITLES BY

Jake Thoene

"The Christian Tom Clancy"
Dale Hurd, *CBN Newswatch*

Shaiton's Fire

In this first book in the techno-thriller series by Jake Thoene, the bombing of a subway train is only the beginning of a master plan that Steve Alstead and Chapter 16 have to stop . . . before it's too late.
ISBN 0-8423-5361-5 SOFTCOVER
US $12.99

Firefly Blue

In this action-packed sequel to Shaiton's Fire, Chapter 16 is called in when barrels of cyanide are stolen during a truckjacking. Experience heart-stopping action as you read this gripping story that could have been ripped from today's headlines.
ISBN 0-8423-5362-3 SOFTCOVER
US $12.99

Fuel the Fire

In this third book in the series, Special Agent Steve Alstead and Chapter 16, the FBI's counterterrorism unit, must stop the scheme of an al Qaeda splinter cell . . . while America's future hangs in the balance.
ISBN 0-8423-5363-1 SOFTCOVER
US $12.99

for more information on other great Tyndale fiction
visit www.tyndalefiction.com

THOENE FAMILY CLASSICS™

✪ ✪ ✪

THOENE FAMILY CLASSIC HISTORICALS
by Bodie and Brock Thoene
Gold Medallion Winners

THE ZION COVENANT
*Vienna Prelude**
Prague Counterpoint
Munich Signature
Jerusalem Interlude
Danzig Passage
*Warsaw Requiem**
London Refrain
Paris Encore
Dunkirk Crescendo

THE ZION CHRONICLES
*The Gates of Zion**
A Daughter of Zion
The Return to Zion
A Light in Zion
*The Key to Zion**

THE SHILOH LEGACY
*In My Father s House**
A Thousand Shall Fall
Say to This Mountain

SHILOH AUTUMN

THE GALWAY CHRONICLES
*Only the River Runs Free**
Of Men and of Angels
*Ashes of Remembrance**
All Rivers to the Sea

THE ZION LEGACY
Jerusalem Vigil
Thunder from Jerusalem
Jerusalem s Heart
Jerusalem Scrolls
Stones of Jerusalem
Jerusalem s Hope

A.D. CHRONICLES
First Light
Second Touch
Third Watch
Fourth Dawn
and more to come!

THOENE FAMILY CLASSICS™

✪ ✪ ✪

THOENE FAMILY CLASSIC AMERICAN LEGENDS

LEGENDS OF THE WEST
by Bodie and Brock Thoene

The Man from Shadow Ridge
Riders of the Silver Rim
Gold Rush Prodigal
Sequoia Scout
Cannons of the Comstock
Year of the Grizzly
Shooting Star
Legend of Storey County
Hope Valley War
Delta Passage
Hangtown Lawman
Cumberland Crossing

LEGENDS OF VALOR
by Luke Thoene

Sons of Valor
Brothers of Valor
Fathers of Valor

✪ ✪ ✪

THOENE CLASSIC NONFICTION
by Bodie and Brock Thoene

Writer-to-Writer

THOENE FAMILY CLASSIC SUSPENSE
by Jake Thoene

CHAPTER 16 SERIES

Shaiton s Fire
Firefly Blue
Fuel the Fire

✪ ✪ ✪

THOENE FAMILY CLASSICS FOR KIDS
by Jake and Luke Thoene

BAKER STREET DETECTIVES

The Mystery of the Yellow Hands
The Giant Rat of Sumatra
The Jeweled Peacock of Persia
The Thundering Underground

LAST CHANCE DETECTIVES

Mystery Lights of Navajo Mesa
Legend of the Desert Bigfoot

✪ ✪ ✪

THOENE FAMILY CLASSIC AUDIOBOOKS

Available from
www.thoenebooks.com or
www.TheOneAudio.com